THE NUDE DIANA

The painting had been in the de Boys family for three centuries; *The Nude Diana*—an exquisite Rembrandt— was well known to everyone in the art world though few had been lucky enough to see it. For generations it had hung in the gallery at the Hall, enjoyed only by members of the family in the privacy of their own home. Then, in 1944, the peaceful existence of the *Diana* was rudely shattered. During nearly thirty of the oddest years of its life the painting became the centre first of a love affair and then of a scandal where its very reputation was at stake.

To different people it meant different things. To Delphine de Boys it marked the beginning and the end of her love affair with Franco—and something else, too, a less pleasant memory. Franco himself was a prisoner-of-war detailed for indoor duties at de Boys Hall, where he met the two loves of his life—Delphine and *The Nude Diana*. To Franco, a painter, a brilliant imitator of the old masters, *The Nude Diana* was the most perfect painting he had ever seen and his whole heart went into the masterpiece he created in its likeness. To Timothy, Delphine's younger son, its value lay only in hard cash—a legacy which would enable him to set up his own art gallery. But in his eagerness to build a new life he unwittingly triggered a sequence of events that threatened to destroy it. And to Corinna, Delphine's love-child, *The Nude Diana* became the symbol of her love for Andrew Tait, a young art dealer, until in the end she discovered that Andrew loved Diana's image and all she stood for more than Corinna herself. For him it opened up possibilities which had long been unattainable—providing he had the nerve to carry through a deal way out of his class.

By the same author:

THE POWER BOX

The Nude Diana

Diana

HUNTER ROWE

CASSELL

LONDON

CASSELL & COMPANY LTD
35 RED LION SQUARE, LONDON WC1R 4SJ
Sydney, Auckland
Toronto, Johannesburg

First published 1972

I.S.B.N. 0 304 29037 8

Printed in Great Britain
by Northumberland Press Ltd
Gateshead
F. 572

At a popular singles bar in Manhattan, a young couple sat at a table on the balcony. They were watching the activity on the crowded floor below. A man threaded through the seething mass of bodies, pushing desperately, as if fighting for air. At the bar he spoke to a lone girl. She nodded. Her bored expression did not change. They danced.

At the end of the number, they separated. The girl went back to the bar to wait for the next approach. The man was already looking round for another possible partner. From the balcony, in the flattering light, everyone seemed attractive. Perhaps the girl down there actually had a bad complexion, or legs like tree trunks....

'Isn't this a funny place?' said the girl on the balcony.

'Funny? I'd say it's pretty damn peculiar, if that's what you mean?'

'Oh I think it's great. It's funny.'

'A flesh market, if you call that funny?'

'Oh Andrew, don't be so *English*.' She laughed and reached across to put her hand on his.

'I *am* English, for heaven's sake.'

'Yes. Of course. But most of the time I don't notice. You're —well, you're sort of *New York*...'

'I've lived here three years.'

'... and then suddenly now and then you make these snappy remarks, like Queen Victoria.'

'It's still a flesh market.'

Andrew was tall, his suit discreetly cut in the modern style. But he was a good ten years older than the girl. His hair was thinning. The lines were stacking up at the corners of his eyes.

'Oh Andrew. You are being English. You like to pretend, to play games. Everyone's after the same thing. And I bet you've been here often enough yourself?'

She looked to him for an answer but he met her eye with a defiantly blank expression.

'Have it your own way.' She nodded towards the floor below. 'All the dating, and the dinner parties—this is what they're really all about. This is just more honest. Everyone needs—well, companionship. Someone to be with, someone to screw. I'd rather have this than all that damn polite conversation. There's none of that fancy pretence in this place.'

'A singles bar is a flesh market. It's crude.'

'It's honest.'

'Take your choice. That's why there's chocolate and vanilla.' This was their private joke, and they both laughed.

'You're a hypocrite, Andrew my friend. A damn English hypocrite. Why don't you admit it—you're only after me for my money?'

'That's right.'

'If you didn't know I have a Daddy who is super-rich, you'd be down there yourself, wouldn't you now, in the flesh market?'

'For flesh perhaps. Not for money. For the money I'm up here with you.'

'Well, that's a comfort. I thought maybe you only wanted me for my body.'

They were smiling and looking into one another's eyes, in case one might think there was the slightest seriousness in what the other said.

'And anyway,' the girl went on, 'I really don't have any money at all until Daddy—until Daddy goes away.'

'Dies, you mean?'

She lowered her eyes. 'Yes. Now you're being crude, Andrew.'

'No. Honest, not crude.'

'All right.' She brightened. 'Anyway, he's not going to, to die for ages, so there's no point in talking about it.'

'And meanwhile, you're poor as a church mouse.'

She smiled. 'Practically.'

'And the chinchilla coat, the white Lotus—I suppose you bought those from what you earned delivering newspapers?'

2

'You're not suggesting I'd ever accept expensive gifts from *men*, are you?'

'Well, if that's the kind of relationship you have with your father...'

The smile froze on the girl's lips. 'Let's change the subject, shall we?'

'O.K.' said Andrew easily. 'No offence.'

After a pause the girl asked, 'What happened to that girl you used to go round with—Corinna?'

'Corinna?'

'Oh, Andrew, don't look so guilty, dammit. I'm not jealous. I hardly knew you then. I liked her, that's all. What was it you used to call her? You didn't call her Corinna?'

'No. Fidget. It was...'

'That's right. Fidget. That was it. She was a really nice girl, Andrew. I'd like to see her again.'

'She left. She's gone back to Europe.'

'Oh. That's a shame. She was such a nice girl.'

'Yes.'

'She wasn't like the others on the scene. You know, most of them are in it either for money or for the fun—you know the whole social bit, the openings and the parties at the Modern. But Corinna wasn't like that. You sort of felt, you know, she cared about *painting*—you know what I mean? She didn't care about all the games that went with it.'

'She did care. She didn't care *for* them. She didn't like them.'

'Yes. Sure. That's what I meant. She was on the scene, because that's where the painting was at. But she didn't really care for the rest of it all.'

'That was her trouble. It's a very naïve attitude.'

'O.K. it's naïve. It's also very attractive. Naïve can be right you know. I mean, most of the people on the scene are phoney as hell. They don't give a fig about the paintings. They're there for every other reason, but not because they care about painting. She did, Corinna did. She was a nice girl, Andrew.'

'All right. I know. I know, you don't have to tell me. She was a nice girl. I said that. Her trouble was, she was too nice, that's all. She was too sensitive ... Look, do we have to talk about this?'

'No... No, but...'

'We didn't agree, let's put it that way. We didn't agree.'

The girl shrugged. 'O.K.' She smiled at Andrew. 'So that's why there's chocolate *and* vanilla.'

'You know,' said Andrew seriously, 'I always choose the chocolate. But sometimes I wonder if I don't really prefer vanilla.'

'So?' said the girl. 'What's the problem? You have both. Chocolate *and* vanilla. That's the beauty of it. Chocolate. Vanilla. Chocolate and vanilla. It's a three-way choice.'

'I suppose so,' said Andrew without conviction. He could feel the familiar sensation, the depression gathering like rain clouds at the back of his head. 'She wouldn't have both, not together. She said you couldn't taste one from the other.'

'She? Who?'

'Corinna.'

'Oh. Hey, she really got to you, didn't she? I think I shall begin to be jealous. Why don't you tell me about her? I'd like to know. Really.'

'It's a long story.'

'That's all right. There isn't any hurry. You and me are going to have a lot of time.'

'Yes. Well...'

'Tell me about Vanilla.'

'Corinna.'

'Corinna.' She laughed. 'God! Vanilla! I mean Corinna. Tell me about Corinna. How did she get to New York in the first place?'

'It's a long story.'

'You said that already. Now tell me the rest. From the beginning....'

4

1944

The ancient three-ton lorry, camouflage paint flaking from the bonnet, rattled between the high, overgrown banks of the narrow road. Before they set out the men in the back had rolled forward the canopy and now they stood hanging on to the metal frame, turning their faces to catch the benefit of the breeze. The leaves on the trees were motionless: the grass on the banks ahead of them stood straight and still—but as they careered past it bent and eddied like reeds in a torrent.

One of the older men spat over the side of the lorry and nodded forward to indicate the driver. 'Stupido,' he said. 'E stupido. Pazzo.' Madman.

Some of the younger men laughed. They had unbuttoned their shirts and the rushing wind filled them like sails. 'E fresco,' said one. 'Non te piace?'

The older man spat again. 'No,' he said gruffly. 'No.'

The lorry swept round a corner and, confronted by an old lady leading a white goat on a rope, swerved violently.

In the cab, the man sitting beside the driver gasped. 'Blimey!' he said. 'Mind where you're going, mate.' The driver laughed. 'Never mind,' he said cheerily. 'Get her on the way back.'

'I shouldn't be surprised,' said the first, sardonically. 'There's no bleeding hurry, you know. Anyone'd think you was trying to get down the pub before closing time.'

'No such luck,' the driver said, putting his foot down to make speed again. His shirt was hung over the back of his seat and he leant his elbow casually out of the window of the cab.

The man beside him, in shirtsleeves, wore no insignia or shoulder flash. A rifle was propped against the back of the cab beside him. His battle-dress jacket hung from the handle of the cab door: on the shoulder was sewn very roughly—

7

he had done it himself—the blue-on-red flash, R.E.M.E., the Royal Electrical and Mechanical Engineers. Private Greene fished in the top pocket, took out the green NAAFI packet of Woodbines and shook two into his palm. He lit them both together from a cylindrical metal lighter and held one out to the driver.

'Here you are, mate. Woodbine for you.'

The driver let go the wheel and took it. 'Ta,' he said.

For five minutes they smoked in silence, while the hedges and trees flew past. Occasionally they caught a brief glimpse through a gateway of fields and the distant rolling landscape, but mostly they sped along the narrow green corridor without sight of anything beyond.

Then the truck braked suddenly and slewed into a gateway. The men in the back were thrown forward. They cursed vociferously in Italian, calling on God and the Holy Mother herself to witness the certain fact that the driver, and probably many of his relations, had been born out of wedlock.

The driver himself, who did not hear them—and he wouldn't have understood if he had—leant on the horn with the heel of his hand. A little girl of six or seven, wearing only a pair of brief pants, ran from the lodge to open the gate. The younger men in the back of the truck leaned over the side, whistling and cat-calling.

Private Greene leant out of his window and shouted. 'Shut up. Shut your mouths, you dirty wops, or I'll confine the lot of you. Dirty sods. You're on a cushy detail, and you know it. You'd better behave your bloody selves, or I'll have the lot of you on the fucking latrines.'

The Italians stopped calling, but they did not seem concerned. They could hear from the tone of his voice that Private Greene was threatening, but they did not understand what he was saying. And they didn't have to worry about his threats—he never carried them out.

'Thanks, darling,' said the driver as he passed the little girl. 'I like your bathing suit. Where's your Mum today?'

'She's up the house. She'll be back after dinner. It's her half day.'

'Good. Look after yourself then. See you later.'

As usual the girl waved to the prisoners as they passed.

8

It was the same every morning. They shouted and whistled as the truck drew up. Then Private Greene shouted at them, and they were quiet. Then, as they passed, she waved to them and one of them threw her some chewing gum, or a toffee.

'Dirty sods,' Greene said again, without feeling, as they drew away up the long approach to the back of the house and the stable yard.

'Oh, you know Italians,' said the driver. 'Very fond of children, the Italians.'

The truck bumped over a hump-backed bridge. On the lake below swam dozens of brilliantly coloured ducks.

'A couple of those,' said Private Greene sourly, 'would make a decent supplement to the meat ration.'

The driver grunted. Every morning Greene made practically the exact same remark.

'Beats me,' Greene went on, 'how her ladyship manages to keep them so plump. The rest of us has a job just feeding ourselves.'

'Gives up her bread coupons, I shouldn't be surprised.'

'Well, *I* should, I can tell you. From what I hear, there's not much she's prepared to go without, wartime or no wartime.'

'You don't blame her for that, do you? When the cat's away...'

'Yes I do blame her. I bloody do. Disgusting. How would you like it if your missus was carrying on here, and you was stuck in a bloody P.O.W. camp in bloody Italy?'

'I haven't got a missus.'

'*And* carrying on with a bloody Eyetye, what's more, a bloody Eyetye P.O.W.'

'I got more sense.'

'I think it's disgusting.'

'She never asked you up to see her etchings, that's what niggling you.'

'I shouldn't go if she did, I can tell you. Bloody aristocracy. Talk about setting an example. Like stoats.'

'She's French.'

'What's the difference. She's still aristocracy. They're all the same. Like stoats.'

They relapsed into silence. Beyond the lake and the rich

green lawns the house glowed in the morning sun like a golden wedding cake. The personal standard of the de Boys hung from the flagpole on the west tower, waiting for a breeze to display its device—three oaks, silver and black on a red ground, below a thick zigzag gold line. 'Gules, three oaks, argent and sable, a chief or dancetty,' was how the College of Arms described it.

At either end of the gravel forecourt stood a great stone urn in the style of Robert Adam. Between them was situated a vast Henry Moore bronze. It consisted of several holes, joined by vaguely female shapes of breasts, hips, head and thighs. A peacock was standing on the hip. Thickly encrusted droppings covered the side of the statue. It was evidently a favourite perch.

Proceeding up the back drive, the truck now swung away round the west wing of the house. It made a long sweep that took it past the walled kitchen garden, the old Home Farm dairy, and through a formal stone arch into the stable yard.

As the lorry drew to a sharp halt, Private Greene jumped to the ground, slinging his rifle casually over his shoulder.

'Right, you lot,' he shouted. 'Let's have you. Form up in rear of the truck. Come along now. Look sharp. You're not on the bloody Riviera now.'

The Italians ambled down from the back of the truck. Private Greene always shouted, and they always took their time. He didn't expect anything else. Over six months they had come to this tacit agreement, and nothing could change it now.

*

While the others had stood hanging on to the metal canopy frame, or sat on the side benches and leant out from the truck to catch the breeze, Franco Ruggero had sat silently on the floor with his back to the driver's cab. He didn't feel like joking, or joining in the game of insulting the English with Italian names they did not understand. It was not that he disliked the other prisoners, or that he disapproved of their being high-spirited, while their relatives were engaged in a hopeless battle for their fatherland. A week before, on the 4th of June, the American army had entered

Rome, and Franco's reaction on hearing this news was sheer relief. Soon there would be an end to the fighting and killing. He certainly had been glad to escape from it himself when he was captured in North Africa—even if it had been at the cost of a shrapnel wound in the head. He had almost died from loss of blood. But that had healed now, and his hair had grown over the scar. Perhaps in time the wounds of war would also be covered.

Yet he found himself more and more often overtaken by these fits of depression. At times he was convinced that the headwound had affected his brain. If it did not get better soon he would try to see a doctor. But in truth he did not really believe that his brain was affected. He refused to allow himself to admit it, but subconsciously he knew that his depressions were connected with two things that, for him, were themselves connected: the fact that the war in Europe was evidently in its final stages; and the fact that every morning as the truck turned into the gates of Boys Hall and he caught the first sight of that flag flying on the west tower, Franco's heart filled with mixed emotions, excitement and fear in equal parts.

'Right now. Get fell in,' Private Greene shouted.

The prisoners shuffled roughly into two ranks. Greene had long ago given up any attempt to drill them in any sort of military manner. He watched them with what he imagined to be the correct expression of contempt. Fourteen apathetic men. Decent enough types. It was hard to think of them as soldiers, let alone enemies. The washed-out grey desert uniforms, now with the giant P for Prisoner stencilled on the back, were frayed and stained. Their boots were dirty, the leather scuffed and cracked. They had not bothered to button their shirts. It would be stupid even to try to drill men like that.

The truck jumped forward with a spurt of dust from its tyres and bucketed out of sight through the archway, with its horn sounding. Franco took his usual place on the left of the second rank. In an army squad there would have been competition for this unobtrusive position, but the prisoners did not bother to try to hide their slackness from Private Greene. Franco looked miserable. And he felt it. He hated this moment, the worst ordeal of the day. Every morning,

11

as it approached, he wished he could shrink his tall frame and creep away without being noticed.

'Right,' said Private Greene. 'Ruggero. Interior detail. Fall out. Report to Mrs Boys. Back here sixteen hundred hours. Ruggero—Fall *out*!'

Franco turned quickly to his left and walked away across the yard towards the kitchen entrance.

The other men scarcely took any notice. One or two of them smiled, or put on expressions of mock disapproval. But Franco's 'interior detail' had become part of the daily routine. While they worked in the kitchen garden, under the direction of an old gardener, Franco reported to Delphine de Boys in the house. They did not resent this privilege. Their own work was easy enough. Under the direction of the head gardener—the only one not on active service —they planted potatoes, and cut spinach, weeded the asparagus beds, hoed between the rows of raspberries.... Three-quarters of the produce from the Hall went to the camp, and the rest was kept for the house. In that way the prisoners had a certain amount of fresh vegetables; the camp commandant had a constant supply of unaccustomed luxuries—asparagus, artichokes, white raspberries, alpine strawberries—and the Boys Hall gardens were kept in reasonable order, as well as supplying sufficient for the wants of the wartime household.

For the prisoners it was pleasant work. But even if they had felt some resentment against Ruggero, there was something about his manner that prevented mockery about his privilege. They had the feeling that he would not have noticed if they had tried. He seemed more and more to live in a world of his own. They had seen a difference in him in the last six months. He had always been quiet, a dark, thin, serious Florentine. They knew he was an artist, and artists are 'sensitive'. But he had seemed to enjoy their high spirits, had always smiled at their jokes. Now he was completely silent. He never smiled. They began to wonder if 'interior duties' was actually the sort of activity their ribald jokes had suggested. But Franco said nothing. After a while they began to call him by a nickname—*La Sphinge*. The Sphinx. *La Sphinge Fiorentina*. The Florentine Sphinx.

As Franco reached the door of the kitchen entrance he

heard Private Greene shouting again. 'Right now, the rest of you. Brace yourselves up. Squad. Squad, atten...*shun*. *By* the left...qui-ick *march!*' Chatting cheerfully to one another the prisoners ambled off towards the kitchen garden.

Inside the lobby, with its flagstone floors and white-washed walls, two feet thick, it was suddenly cooler. Franco went through to the kitchen. Marjorie Baxter, at a long table at one side of the great vaulted room, neatly chopped the legs from a rabbit and began to peel the skin from its back. The corpse of a second lay already skinned, pink and shiny, on the wooden table beside her.

'Morning Mr Franco,' she said.

'Good morn*ing*, Mrs Baxter.' Franco smiled shyly.

'Fancy a nice bit of rabbit pie for your dinner, do you? Fresh as a daisy. Old George brought them in this morning.'

'Old George?'

'George the gamekeeper. You know. Lives out in the North Lodge.'

'Oh yes. Yes. Good. Rabbit very good.'

More than I can say for your English, Mrs Baxter thought to herself. But she said, 'See my little Carol, did you, when you came in?'

'Your Carol?'

'Yes. My little Carol. Down the lodge. Didn't she open the gate for you?'

'Oh yes. Yes. Very pretty.' He smiled. 'She have some shooing gum.'

Marjorie Baxter laughed. '*Chew*ing gum,' she said. 'You never learn, do you? I tell you that twice a week, I'm sure. It's *chew*ing gum. You'll have to work a sight harder at your English lessons, Mr Franco.' Then she blushed suddenly, realizing the remark might be misinterpreted. There was an awkward silence.

On the table in the centre of the kitchen stood a tray, elegantly set with breakfast things. It looked somewhat incongruous, too fragile for that practical room, where Marjorie Baxter was chopping up the rabbits. The coffee pot was silver, and the sugar bowl and toast rack: the cup and plate of fine Dresden china with the Boys arms and the Proudfoot motto—*Diligentiae Praemium*. The reward of hard work. The hard work, in fact, more than four hun-

13

dred years ago, of Martin Proudfoot, founder of the family, whose single-minded pursuit of Spanish treasure benefited the coffers of Elizabeth I by many thousands of pounds, and also left sufficient for him to build himself a residence suitably magnificent for the earldom she conferred on him—Boys Hall.

Marjorie Baxter noticed Franco's glance rest momentarily on the tray. 'Madam hasn't rung for her breakfast yet,' she said.... She pronounced it clearly so that he would understand.

'Oh? No?' He seemed embarrassed. 'I go to work,' he said suddenly. 'I go to work.'

'Right oh,' said Mrs Baxter. 'Oh, and Mr Franco—could you leave the shooting-room unlocked when you get your stuff out? Only George, old George, he says he needs to have a look over his lordship's guns in there, give them a bit of an oiling.'

'Guns? What do you say, Mrs Baxter? I do not understand.'

'George,' she said, mouthing the word at him. '*George.* He wants to go in the shooting-room. *Shooting-room....*'

*

At noon Delphine rang down on the house phone from the saloon to the butler's pantry.

'Maitland?'

'Madam?'

'Maitland, Mr Franco and I will have lunch at twelve thirty.'

'In the dining-room, madam?' Maitland asked, with affected obsequiousness.

'Of course in the dining-room,' said Delphine sharply. 'Where would you expect? You can leave everything on the hotplate. We shall serve ourselves.'

'Very well, Madam.'

'And we shall have coffee afterwards in the Red Drawing-Room.'

'The Red Drawing-Room?'

'That's what I said, the Red Drawing-Room. It's cooler there. And quieter.' She sounded displeased. In moments of anger a faint trace of accent revealed itself in her voice. 'I shall be giving Mr Franco his English lesson.'

Talk about the blind leading the blind, Maitland thought. He was leaning back in his chair with stockinged feet on a tapestry stool in front of him.

'We shall not want to be disturbed. You can leave the tray and a flask of coffee.'

I'll bet you won't want to be disturbed, he thought. He smiled to himself. But his voice was heavy with respect. 'Very well, Madam,' he said.

Delphine understood his tone perfectly well. Since her husband had joined his regiment—he had set out, with a formal leavetaking of the entire staff, like a medieval crusader, on the first day of war—and left her in charge of the Hall, and even more since Franco had become a regular visitor, Maitland had perfected a tone of obsequious insult. But he was making rope for his own neck. She would tolerate him for the time being—she did not have any alternative. But there would not be such difficulty with staff after the war. Then she would heave him out of the Hall like a dead rat. She already had someone in mind for the position of butler in his place. She smiled to herself, enjoying the sweet prospect of revenge. And even more the fact that at that very moment Maitland should be polishing the silver and setting a place at the dining-table for the man she intended to take his place.

She knew Franco would have no idea of the time. When he was working he became so absorbed he could have starved to death without noticing a pang of hunger. She glanced at the young boy playing quietly at her feet on the floor, patiently but unsuccessfully attempting to build wooden bricks into a tower. The bricks were painted in bright colours with pictures of strange creatures—owls with triangular beaks, and bulls, and horses with wings, and Minotaurs, the bull-headed men. These bricks had been given to Delphine at the birth of her first child, Giles, by her friend Pablo Picasso.

'Now Timmy,' said Delphine. 'It is time for you to go with Mrs Baxter, to play with Carol.'

Timmy looked up at her and smiled. Sometimes he did not seem to understand what she said. Perhaps at the age of three she should not expect too much. At least he was quiet and unobtrusive. He seemed to take after his father in that as well as his colouring. She wished he had been dark like her. She did not much like these blond English complexions that scorched in the sun. But Timmy would probably grow darker as he got older.

She lifted the phone again and dialled.

Marjorie Baxter answered in the kitchen. 'Yes, madam?'

'Oh Mrs Baxter, I'm sure you'd like to get away. Maitland can cope with lunch now. Just leave everything. You can clear up tomorrow.'

'Very well, madam.'

'Timothy is with me in the saloon. You'd better find a pullover for him in the nursery on your way up.'

Timothy cried when Mrs Baxter carried him off.

'Take him quickly.' Delphine said. 'He'll soon get over it.'

Almost immediately they had gone Delphine herself left the room by the opposite door. It was too hot to hurry. She was feeling wonderfully cool in sandals and the simple cotton caftan she had had made from a Victorian nightdress she had found in one of the attics. It was a beautiful garment, of thick white cotton with inserts of cream lace and layers of lace for the sleeves. The hems and seams were stitched by hand in tiny, even stitches. She wore no conventional jewellery but round her neck on a heavy gold chain hung a 'soft watch' by Salvador Dali, the half-melted shape executed in blue enamel and precious stones. She did not want to get hot now. But she could not suppress a certain excitement as she set out along the West wing. She was soon going to see Franco for the first time that day.

She passed through the library, with its bookcases of priceless, calf-bound volumes, each embossed with the family crest, and the great desk, decorated with gold eagles, that once belonged to Napoleon; then through the Italian Drawing-Room, with its painted panelling, decorated in the eighteenth century at the height of the Pompeian craze, when the ruins of the Roman City had recently been discovered buried under the lava of Vesuvius. It was a temptation, Delphine was thinking to herself, to dramatize oneself in such surroundings, hurrying through these rooms with their priceless paintings, their historic furniture, to a

16

rendezvous with a handsome Italian painter....

Delphine looked out from the window across the park. On the lawn by the upper lake strode the spindly Giacometti Walking Figure, one of her recent acquisitions. She smiled to herself. So many people disliked it, had even seemed to go out of their way to tell her how much they hated it. But if there was one thing she was sure of, it was her taste in art. In many things she was frightened and insecure, however bold a face she put on it. With art, she *knew*. It was almost a physical feeling, that sense of joy, of excitement, and also of fear, a feeling in the gut as well as the mind. When she felt that she had no doubts: she was in the presence of a work of greatness.

And there, setting out now along the drive, his fair hair glittering in the sun, his hand safely in hand with Mrs Baxter, Timothy was happily going off to play with his friend Carol. Delphine had felt guilty at dismissing him so briskly, though she knew it was the best way, and that he would be happier with Mrs Baxter and her daughter than he would have been with his mother. But at the same time she had been impatient for him to leave, and the time to come when she could be with Franco—and that was where the guilt lay.

Even years of familiarity with the treasure of Boys Hall had not yet stilled the gut reaction Delphine felt before a great painting. Stepping out on to the landing at the head of the staircase she saw before her those incomparable paintings—the Rubens, the Van Dyck portrait of the third Lord de Boys, the famous Rembrandt; and down below in the Great Hall, with its tattered battle standards and the historic wooden screen, carved in the high style of the English Renaissance, the other Proudfoot treasure, the Raphael Madonna Dolorosa. The sight of these riches never failed to move her.

Before the Rembrandt, Franco had set up his easel.

'Buon giorno, Franco,' she said quietly. In the public parts of the house they always spoke formally, even though they spoke in Italian. Delphine's Italian was fluent, and Franco's English stumbling. It also made doubly certain that the servants did not understand their conversation.

'Buon giorno, signora,' Franco said.

They stood facing one another, three feet apart, for this formal greeting, but their eyes exchanged looks as intimate as caresses.

Delphine nodded towards the easel. 'How is it coming along?' she asked.

'Oh, it's difficult. It's so difficult.' He walked towards it. 'To get it exactly right, it's impossible, without the right materials, without the same materials *he* used. I'm trying for the flesh only for the time, but that's the most difficult.'

'We'll get whatever you need,' said Delphine. 'Just tell me and I shall get it—whatever it is.'

'I want to learn to make a painting that looks as this looks now. Old paintings are beautiful because they are beautifully painted, but also because they are old.'

Behind Franco's easel the painting hung on the oak-panelled wall. It had been bought by the Proudfoots at the sale of Charles II's paintings after the Revolution of 1688, and ever since had been the jewel of the family treasure. Known world-wide as The Nude Diana, it depicted the goddess reclining on a grass bank after bathing in a woodland stream. There are only three known life-size Rembrandt nudes—this, Bathsheba After the Bath, which is in the Louvre, and a painting of Danae in the Hermitage in Leningrad. And this, the Diana, the only Rembrandt nude in private ownership, was by far the most sumptuous of the three. Diana, plumply female, covered not even with the scant draperies of the other two paintings, reclines in a luxurious pose, exuding an air of sensual satisfaction. No wonder, Delphine had often thought, such a painting should appeal to 'the Merry Monarch', famous for all those mistresses, and all the illegitimate children he fathered on them. Women were more generously proportioned in those days. She guessed the portrait must have reminded him of a particular favourite—Nell Gwyn, perhaps.

'The flesh is so difficult,' Franco was saying in his serious manner.

Here and there on his canvas were odd patches of dark colour, olive greens and khaki browns. And on these he was attempting to reproduce the exact flesh tones of the Rem-

18

brandt masterpiece, the particular pale succulence that conveyed with such subtlety the chastity and the physicality of the Goddess of the Hunt.

'E difficile,' Franco muttered again. 'Molto, molto difficile.'

'Leave it now,' Delphine said tenderly. 'Leave it and come for lunch.'

'It's lunchtime already?' Franco asked, with a slightly startled look.

'Yes. Already,' said Delphine, smiling. She loved to see that expression on his face, when his dark eyes, with their enviable dark lashes, opened in such innocent surprise. 'I knew I should have to remind you of the time.'

Two or three old telephone directories stood on the floor beside the easel. The top one was open. Franco used the pages to work out his brushes, after he had loaded them with paint from the palette, to the exactly perfect texture for the canvas. Beween the feet of the easel he had placed the box of dark polished mahogany that Delphine had given him, beautifully fitted with a palette, china containers for oil and turpentine, the compartments of paints....

Franco laid his brush on the telephone directory, alongside the other he had been using earlier, and began to wipe his hands with an old rag.

'Good,' he said—and, in English. 'Luncheon is served.'

Delphine was smiling. 'No,' she said. 'Lunch will be ten minutes.'

'But you said.... You are telling the time by your funny watch?'

'No. I wanted you to have time to clean your brushes.'

'Oh, that's not necessary. They'll be all right just while I have my lunch.'

'But after lunch I give you your English lesson. Remember?' She was seeking his eyes with hers, but he was avoiding her gaze.

'Oh yes. But that's all right. The brushes will be all right until I get back.'

'You might not come back. You might not be back before the truck comes.'

'Oh no. There will be time....' Franco began. Then he realized what she was implying. A flush spread up in his face, visible clearly even beneath his dark complexion. He

19

appeared confused, but he immediately looked up and met her eye, with a small, dare-devil smile.

'So. Perhaps you had better clean your brushes.'

'Yes. Perhaps. Perhaps I'd better.'

*

The dining-room had been redecorated in the eighteenth century by Robert Adam at the height of his popularity. He had indeed decorated a suite of three rooms, but they did not suit the gothic extravaganza of Victorian taste—of which the Proudfoot family were eager followers—and the ninth Lord de Boys had had the other two rooms completely refurnished in a style of crenellated Camelot fantasy. He had been arrogantly certain of his own good taste. And somewhat eccentric. He had had a dozen portraits of earlier members of the family burned, because he did not like their faces. Mercifully funds had run out before he reached the dining-room, and Adam's original scheme, the cool, pale green and white, and the clean bare lines survived.

Here Delphine hung the cream of her collection of modern paintings. In 1939, as the prospect of war became inevitable, Delphine had set out boldly against the tide of European refugees, determined to save from the advancing armies at least some of the masterpieces of modern art. Had not the great financier, Maynard Keynes, even in 1918, three years into the war, taken £100,000 of British money to Paris to the sale of the Degas family collection and bought paintings by such artists as Corot, Ingrès, Delacroix, Gauguin, Manet, now in the National Gallery in London? And he had bought them at bargain prices. Delphine did not deny to herself that this was also a consideration in her calculations. But she had to travel, not to a single sale, but, in the chaos of a threatened country, to galleries, private owners, the *ateliers* of artists themselves. And they, facing the prospect of actual invasion, the possibility of confiscation, and certainly no sale for their work, took the opportunity for some ready cash. Many indeed also considered that the chances of war might mean that these paintings would be the last examples of their work to survive for posterity, and they parted with their best works to Delphine

20

at a fraction of their usual price. At enormous cost—far more than many of the paintings themselves—she had bought a vast Citroën, and she drove about Paris, and sometimes deep into the country, piling her priceless cargo on the back seat. She scarcely took her eyes off the car and at night insisted on sleeping doubled in the front seat, wrapped in a military greatcoat. War had been officially declared, and the German army was deep into Poland, while Delphine was still in Paris. On the 6th September, alternately bluffing and pleading, in French and English, shamelessly using her husband's title, as well as her own armoury of feminine tears and a persuasive tongue, she got the Citroën with its precious cargo on a boat across the Channel. She never understood what it was that gave her such energy. For ten days she existed on sheer determination, and little else. German planes passed overhead and they had to sail by night without illumination. Delphine was terrified, but also excited. She drove home at a reckless speed, non-stop from the Kent coast and when she reached the lanes near Boys Hall she found herself singing at the top of her voice the old French songs she had learnt as a child. Finally she drove the car into the stable yard—and collapsed over the wheel. She slept for two days.

But it was worth it. In this room she had hung one major work from each of ten great modern painters. Opposite her at the other end of the room hung a masterful Braque bird. Elsewhere, an important Picasso from his early Cubist period, Léger, Cézanne, Van Gogh, Matisse....

Maitland had set places at either end of the long table.

'Come and sit here beside me,' Delphine said to Franco. 'Bring your things and sit here.'

The rabbit pie was on the hotplate, and the vegetables—minted peas and new potatoes from the garden. Franco put the vegetable dishes on the table, and served a portion of pie on to the two crested Sèvres plates that were also keeping warm on the hotplate.

As he put her plate in front of Delphine, he asked, 'I am learning to do it properly?'

She smiled briefly, but said nothing.

Franco had put out only a few mouthfuls on Delphine's plate, knowing her appetite to be so small. But even that she scarcely touched. She refused potatoes, took a small spoonful of peas, manoeuvred them round her plate a little, ate just a few—then she sat back abruptly in her chair, with an expression of disgust.

'Ugh. It's no good. Food is disgusting. Eating is such a disgusting habit.'

Franco had in front of him a good helping of pie, with several potatoes and a mound of shining green peas. He had been looking forward to it. Mrs Baxter cooked this sort of simple food perfectly: the pastry was thick and crisp, the meat beneath in a thick, smooth gravy. And the first mouthful lived up to its appearance—it was delicious.

'Oh, don't let me put you off,' Delphine said quickly. She filled Franco's glass from the decanter of claret. 'I'm sure the food in that camp must be dreadfully unhealthy.'

She put her hand on his thigh in encouragement. But Franco could feel his appetite drain away. He felt Delphine's eyes on him as he struggled through a few mouthfuls. It tasted like sawdust.

Delphine was sipping her wine and looking round the room with a proud expression. 'I shall never tire of them,' she said. 'I know I shall never tire of them. My beautiful, beautiful paintings.'

She pushed back her chair and stood up. She went and stood before a large painting of random shapes, bright colours against a plain ground. 'Oh, this is my favourite,' she said. 'This is such an *important* painting. It is historic.' A strange expression crossed her face. 'If he were not to survive the war, this painting would be the most important painting in the house. It would be priceless.'

Franco watched her. In her soft shoes and simple gown she herself could have been a girl from a Botticelli painting.

Delphine smiled. '*Today* it is my favourite. Today Matisse is my favourite. On other days I have other favourites. I am a *woman*, after all. I ought to change my mind.'

Franco was unobtrusively eating some more of the pie.

'What a shame you don't appreciate my pictures. I wish you liked my lovely pictures.'

'I don't dislike them,' he said. 'They're very pretty.'

'Pretty? They are certainly not pretty! They are magnificent. These ten paintings have a place in the history of art.

Whatever happens, they will remain a part of history.'

But Franco, quiet and stubborn, said, 'I think they're pretty.' He wished Delphine would not make these extravagant claims. Everything she was even slightly connected with had to be in some way extraordinary—the most beautiful, the most important, the most valuable.

'You'll be saying Van Gogh next.'

'What do you mean? I don't understand.'

Delphine laughed. 'It was a joke. Only a joke. In France it is a famous story. Forty years ago—only forty years ago—it was suggested to the director of the Musée du Luxembourg that he should buy a Cézanne for the Collection of Modern Art. And he said, "Cézanne? *Cézanne?* You'll be saying Van Gogh next."'

'I did not say that they were not pretty.'

'Oh Franco, my dear.' She came up behind his chair and held his head affectionately between her hands. 'I know you believe that every painting later than 1750, almost without exception, is decadent art—if it deserves to be called art at all. Art doesn't stand still you know. Those painters of yours are great painters. Of course. They were masters. But there are masters also in our time. Art progresses. Botticelli, Leonardo—they were revolutionary also in their time.'

'I know,' said Franco, with a trace of anger in his voice. 'I know that.'

'Of course. Of course,' said Delphine, running her fingers through his cropped hair. 'You know it better than I.'

As part of his training at art school in Florence, Franco had been sent to copy paintings in the Uffizi Gallery. He found that he had some sort of natural gift for it. He had a sympathy with those old masters that enabled him to reproduce the manner in which they painted. It is the tiny variations in technique that are most difficult to reproduce. Mastering the exact angle at which the brush is held, the pressure and rhythm of the strokes—the secrets of those details is the art of a good copyist.

But Franco also found it depressing work. In the permanent presence of these great paintings, he soon realized that he had no chance of even approaching their standard. And, even if he had, he began to feel that there was nothing left to say in painting—at least that he himself might be able to express—that had not already been said for all time by these men. It was a depressing thought, and it persisted. He could not shake off the depression. It affected his work. The instructors had had high hopes of him. His portfolio for the entrance examination had been so brilliant that they had seriously wondered if he could have done it himself. But his work soon proved his ability—and then, in his second year he came to this sudden halt. He just could not find the inclination to carry on his own work. He would sit for hours in front of a pad, or canvas on the easel, and not have the courage to make a mark on it.

At first his tutor thought it was a temporary block. He urged Franco to force himself, to draw or paint anything, merely to re-establish contact between himself and the canvas. So Franco went back to the Uffizi. He set up his canvas in front of Botticelli's Spring. And he never went back to Art School.

'I tell you though, my darling, this is only the beginning.' Delphine was stalking round the room now, and she indicated the paintings on the wall with a sweeping gesture. 'Already there are new painters who would call these old-fashioned, *decorative*.' She pronounced the word with scorn. 'I don't happen to agree with them. But I understand what they are saying. Art does not stand still. It must not stand still. It must move.'

'I don't see why,' said Franco. 'I don't understand why *movement* should be so important. There is too much to see already. No one looks at pictures properly as it is. No one looks long enough, or deeply enough to understand what they say. More art is less appreciation.'

He was thinking of the people who had bought his copies of Old Masters, of the many times they had come back to tell him how, by having a painting in their house, living with it and looking at it daily, they had begun to learn from it in a way that was never possible in a gallery, where it hung beside hundreds of other pictures. Franco was glad to make that revelation possible. He had accepted the fact that he had not the genius of an original artist. But he had the satisfaction of knowing that his copies were probably more like the original paintings, as the artist had intended

24

them, than even the originals themselves after three, four, five hundred years even. And they were *real* paintings, layers of pigment, brush strokes—living creatures almost, responding to gradations of light, age, atmosphere. Prints are dead things, but these were alive. He loved the paintings and he knew this showed in his copies. In those two years before the war he had finally been happy again. His technique improved. There was a long waiting-list of clients for his copies. He could have spent his life in this practical act of worship. He never thought of politics, or international affairs. The war had started before he had even known that it was a possibility.

But Delphine was not in the mood for this sort of romantic philosophy. She was in an excited state. She could not keep still. Franco suggested she sit down and eat some lunch, but she said, 'No. No. I'm not hungry. I don't want anything. You know I don't like food. But you have some. Help yourself to some cheese.' But she did have another glass of claret. And she continued to circle the table like a hungry jackal. 'Don't you see?' she said. 'For us, for the family, here in this house, there is a *duty*. Here in this house is represented the taste of every century since it was built. Every generation has wanted to add something, or dress up some part of their inheritance in the fashionable style.'

Franco looked up. 'You are going to refurnish the Victorian rooms?'

Delphine had not expected to be interrupted. She looked at him suddenly, and said somewhat sharply, 'No. No, of course not. That's the point. We know better now than they did. They were too arrogant. David's grandfather was actually mad. He burned a lot of family portraits. But they all believed that what they liked was right and what was unfashionable would never be heard of again. We know better than that.'

'Do you think those Victorian rooms will come back?'

Delphine looked at him impatiently. 'Not in a decorator's sense they won't come back. But they're important. They're the real thing. You can't recreate the real thing. Thank God they didn't get to this room. This room should never be touched. We know that, but they didn't.' She lifted the lid from a crystal cigarette box on the table. 'Do you mind if

I smoke?' she asked, and began to light a cigarette without waiting for an answer.

'Of course not,' said Franco. 'So, you will have to build on, you have to make additions. Very expensive.'

'But don't you see? If we don't do this, the house ceases to live. We cease to live. It is a museum. All the great houses are becoming museums. Why, most of them were last altered in the last century. Have you ever seen a 1920's saloon, Art Deco rooms? Art Nouveau even?'

Franco laughed. 'Very few of my friends live in such houses as this,' he said. 'In fact, I'd go so far as to say, none of them at all.'

'No, of course,' Delphine said. 'But I assure you it is so. And it must not be allowed to happen to Boys Hall. I do not intend to allow it to happen.'

'It will be difficult.'

'Of course it will be difficult. But I shall do it. I shall fight for it. You know I'm rather good at getting what I want.'

'Yes,' said Franco quietly, looking down at the table. On his plate a few crumbs remained, sprinkled over those words written in the ancient language of his own country: *Diligentiae Praemium.*

Delphine saw his expression. 'Oh Franco, my love,' she said. 'Am I so terrible? I'm good to you, am I not?'

Franco held the hand that she slid down over his shoulder. 'Yes, Delphine. You are good to me. I am happy with you.'

And it was true, he thought to himself. He was happy with her. Yet to tell the truth, he was also somewhat frightened of her. He had never realized before that that combination was possible.

'You'll see,' said Delphine, tightly grasping his hand. 'I have it all planned. There are people working in America now—painters, sculptors, architects—who will be the masters of the future. We shall build here in their style. We have had Classical, Renaissance, Oriental, Gothic, styles from Italy, France, China—but never yet from America.'

'But how can you build for them? They are so different from—from all this.' He had a sudden terrible vision. 'Rembrandts don't go with skyscrapers.'

'Why not?' Delphine said. 'Well, perhaps not a skyscraper.

26

But surely with those beautiful buildings. They are beautiful. Glass and steel can be so elegant, so sympathetic to every other style.' She took another cigarette and walked to the window, as if she could picture what she planned taking shape there outside. 'You know what we shall do? We shall find a great architect, a great man who understands this new language, and he will build us a bridge, a screen between the East Wing and the West Wing. Out there. We shall enclose the courtyard again, as it used to be—you know they knocked it down in the nineteenth century? They were so cowardly in those days. And there we shall house the *new* masters.'

'It will be expensive,' Franco said.

'Oh Franco, don't be so *practical*. You sound like *them*.' She turned from the window to face him. 'They are always talking about cost. They don't understand what it is to realize a dream. They'll do anything to stop me. They cannot abide new things. They are so *old*,' she added contemptuously.

'Who are "they"?'

'Oh, David's parents. You know. At the Mill House. It's so typical. They give David the house, but they try to make sure he only does what *they* want with it.'

Partly to avoid death duty, and partly because neither of them cared sufficiently about the house—they had always thought of the upkeep as a duty, and were very ready to feel too old to continue—Lord and Lady de Boys had actually and legally made over the Hall to their son David, and themselves moved with Lady de Boys's elder sister and a few personal treasures to the Mill House. There Lady de Boys thought of nothing but her racehorses, glad to forget her duties to the Hall. And Lord de Boys was totally absorbed with his own great interest in life—the preservation of wild life. In his youth he had been an avid collector of specimens to add to the hundreds of stuffed birds and animals that lined the East Gallery. There was a complete collection of every species found in the British Isles, including rare variations and albinos, and several now extinct. In addition, his father had set up a comprehensive display of the birds of India, collected while he was Viceroy. And Richard himself, as a young man in the early years of the

27

century, had made an expedition to South America and brought back many exotic specimens for the collection. But in middle age he had been converted to the doctrine of preservation. Almost overnight he had changed, as if by some divine revelation. He declared that the Proudfoot land should henceforth be designated a sanctuary for all wild life, and no creature should ever again be shot or trapped on it. (Though after a while he did agree that the gamekeeper should keep down the rabbits, hares and pigeons, in order to protect the crops.) And when Lord de Boys moved into the Mill House, his son kept up this tradition. Plump pheasants and partridges wandered confidently about the fields, and even in the grounds themselves. But while her husband was away, Delphine had encouraged the gamekeeper to add pheasants and partridges 'accidentally' shot, to the rabbits and hares he brought to the house. She scarcely ate anything herself, but she liked to impress her guests.

'She has her horses, and he has his memories—and his stuffed birds. That should be enough at their age,' said Delphine scornfully. 'But they watch us like hawks. And David is still frightened of them. It's ridiculous. A grown man. An officer. Fighting for his country.' She noticed Franco's look of embarrassment. 'Well, I'm sorry my love, but it's no good pretending things are other than they are. That's the dreadful irony of war. You're a prisoner here, and he's a prisoner in Italy. It is pointless to let ourselves be embarrassed by it.'

'I hope he is well treated.'

'So do I. Poor David. I do hope so. He's not very good at coping for himself. But anyway, he's still frightened of his parents. He likes to shoot, but you know he won't shoot here. He goes off to friends when he wants to shoot. Isn't that ridiculous? The pheasants walk about here like chickens and he has to go off somewhere else if he wants to shoot one. And I know it was *they* who talked him into thinking we should not build the new wing. Do you know what he suggested? That I should have the stables converted to a gallery, if I wanted somewhere to display my paintings. As if I was a child with a hobby, to be carried on in the stables. That was *their* idea, I'm perfectly sure of that.'

28

'The stables are nice.'

'Yes, Franco. Yes, they are nice. But they are not part of the house. To put my things in the stable—that would be apologizing for them, you know, saying that this is just a little hobby. Have you been in the stables?'

'No. Only from the outside they look nice.'

Delphine smiled triumphantly. 'Oh, you should see what I've done to the stables since David's been away. They look very nice. I *have* converted them actually. And I've had all those things of his father's, all those creepy birds and animals, I've had them taken out there.'

'Does his father mind?'

'I don't see why he should. It's much more sensible. It saves him having to come into the house when he wants to see them. Or not coming because he doesn't like to ask. I gave them the Canalettos too. I loathe Canaletto. They seem to like them. There were twenty-five here when I came. I'm sure half of them were forgeries. David's mother likes them, and his father is potty about stuffed birds. David and I never look at those awful things. In fact, I used to make sure I never went along that corridor. They frightened me, all those dead creatures, fur and feathers and horrible glass eyes. He can look at them out there to his heart's content. And he has a room at the end for his butterflies. You know what he's doing? He's breeding hundreds and hundreds of Swallowtail butterflies. They're extinct in England, or almost, I'm not sure. He's going to re-introduce them.'

'That's nice.'

'You think so? I should have thought he might find something more important to do. There is a war on, after all.'

'Yes, I suppose so.'

'You will see. You will see, Franco. Boys Halls will be famous.'

'It is famous already.'

'Yes. But it will be more famous. It will be famous for its present as well as for its past.'

Franco looked at her admiringly. 'I believe it will. Because I believe you can make it so. But,' he added sadly, 'I doubt if I shall ever see it.'

Delphine came immediately to his side. She looked deep into his eyes. 'Franco! What are you saying? What do you mean? My love, you will be here. You will help me. Do you think I could ever let you go?' She was running her palm over his chest and pressing her body against his arm as he sat in the chair. 'Oh Franco. You must not say such things.' She took his hand and pulled him up from the chair. 'Come. Come. We must give you your English lesson. Otherwise, when the time comes, you will not be ready. Come.'

She led him by the hand along to the Red Drawing-Room. She allowed him to pour her coffee, but she did not touch it. They sat beside one another on the sofa, but neither had the patience to concentrate on the English grammar.

'Knee,' she said, placing her hand on Franco's left knee-cap. '*Ginocchio*. Knee.'

'K-nee,' said Franco, purposely mispronouncing it.

'*Rotula di ginocchio*. Knee-cap.'

'K-nee k-nap.' Franco was laughing.

Delphine, laughing too, silenced him with a kiss. She drew away her lips. '*Bocca*,' she said. 'Mouth.'

'*E labbri?*'

'Lips. *Labbri*, lips.' She slowly approached her mouth to his again. 'And tongue,' she whispered. '*Lingua. Leccare.*' Their tongues touched. Franco felt the urgent response of his body. They kissed deeply.

But Delphine broke away. 'Come,' she said. 'Come.' She led him by the hand. 'Not here. Not here.'

She led him again along the corridors, hung with family portraits, past the cases of priceless porcelain. Franco held back, but she urged him on. 'There's no one in the house,' she said. 'Only Maitland. He has little enough sense, but sufficient not to come up here. No one will see us. At least that's one advantage in having all the staff at the war.'

In Delphine's bedroom, with its incongruous mixture of styles—a large and quite erotic Picasso painting behind the fourposter, with its white silk summer hangings—she and Franco embraced silently. But she sensed some reluctance from him, an almost imperceptible, but still physical restraint.

'What is the matter, Franco? *Caro?* What is the matter?'

'Nothing. Nothing is the matter.'

But she still felt a tension in his body. She pressed herself against him, against his chest, thrusting her hips with gentle pressure against his groin.

'Something is the matter. I know something is the matter. Do I not please you?'

'Oh yes.'

'You are tired of me, is that it?'

'Oh *no*.' Franco sounded shocked. 'Never. Never.' He bent his head to reassure her with a kiss.

'Then why do I not please you?'

'But you do. I love to be with you.'

Delphine drew back from him. 'Oh Franco. A woman can tell when she does not please a man.' With a single movement she dropped her gown to the floor. She stood naked before him. 'There. Do I please you or not?'

'Oh yes. Yes. It's not...'

But Delphine stepped to him and silenced him with a kiss. Then she began to unbutton the faded grey shirt, stroking his nipples, smoothing the hair on his chest with the palm of her hand.

'I am so glad you are dark. English men are so—so *pink*.'

Franco smiled and gripped her shoulders.

Delphine unbuckled his belt. 'It pleases you?' she asked. '*Te piace?*'

'Oh si, si,' said Franco, his voice now thick and hoarse. '*Me piace. Molto. Molto.*'

Afterwards they lay in the bed, with the white hangings like an embroidered tent. Franco could see the rising ground of the parkland, crowned by a clump of oaks round a mock-classical temple. And then the feeling of apprehension returned to him. Afterwards is always a bad time, he told himself. But he knew it was not simple after-love depression. It was deeper, more permanent than that.

As he had lit her cigarette for her, Delphine had said, 'You do it so well. I shall have to give you regular employment.' Then she laughed and briefly touched his groin. 'I don't mean that. I mean the cigarette. You will be such a good butler. I shall be so proud of you—my tall, handsome Italian butler. Everyone will be madly envious.'

Franco had not even smiled.

'What's the matter, my love?' she said. 'Don't you want

31

to stay here? Don't you want to stay with me?'

'Yes. Oh yes—of course I want to stay.... It's just ... well, just that I am not really sure that you want me to stay.'

Delphine had cried, 'Oh Franco! Franco! How can you *say* such a thing.' She had fallen on his body with kisses and caresses, from head to toe, as if she would devour him. 'How *can* you say such things?'

And Franco knew that what he had said was not what he meant to say. At least, not what he wanted to say. But before he could bring himself to think exactly what he had meant, let alone express it, Delphine's caresses, and the reactions of his own body, had driven it out of his mind again.

After they made love Delphine always smoked a cigarette. Those were the best cigarettes of all, she declared. And indeed Franco himself enjoyed the luxury of her Turkish cigarettes. The smoke filled the room with its herbal smell, thick and sweet, while they lay, languorous in the summer heat, and he could discreetly admire the soft contours of Delphine's body against the stark white linen of the bed.

'They tell me I shouldn't use these things,' said Delphine indicating the embroidered curtains with her cigarette. As she drew it down from above her head it left a tiny ring of smoke, and she idly repeated the gesture, leaving two smoke rings, like white halos above them. 'They watch me. In my own house I feel I am watched all the time. The old people out in the Mill House, Maitland—they're watching me all the time. They disapprove of me, of what I do. They hate the Hall to be used. They want it to be *preserved*, like one of those damned birds. They'd have it stuffed if only they knew how.' She angrily blew smoke from her lips and dispersed the thinning halos. 'But that's not right,' she continued. 'They were made to be used. Four hundred years ago they enjoyed them for what they were. They probably even got a little tired of them. Then when they were finished, they threw them out and replaced them.'

Suddenly Franco turned and clung to her, as if in terror. With his mouth at her breast he was murmuring 'Cara. Cara mia ...' over and over like a child.

*

With his back to the driver, Franco squatted on the floor of the truck as it bounced down the Boys Hall drive towards the West Lodge. His fellow prisoners were cheerful, enjoying the cool air of the fading afternoon, quite pleasantly tired after the day's work in the open air. They left Franco alone with his gloomy thoughts. They had some time ago ceased to make pointed remarks about how tired he looked, or, sniffing suspiciously, enquire of one another what was that peculiar smell? Scent, was it? Or—something else? They left him alone now. He seemed so worried all the time, they had actually begun to feel sorry for him.

And Franco was sorry for himself. Crouched on the floor, hugging his knees, he repeatedly told himself that he should be happy. He was young and healthy, and he had the love of a beautiful woman. Could anyone ask more than that? Yes, indeed a man did need something more than that, something even before any of those things—his pride in himself, his self-respect, his dignity if you like. And that Franco had lost. When he was away from Delphine—here, on the floor of the truck—he saw it so clearly. What would he tell any other man to do? What would he tell his best friend if he came to him for advice? There was only one possible answer. If he did as Delphine planned, what would he be? A gigolo, a tame stud, waiting at table and serving on demand in the bedroom. If she really loved him, if she cared about him as a man at all, she would not want to put him in a position like that. There was only one answer, and he should insist that she accept it. If she loved him she should go with him, give up her wealth, and her rank, and her grandiose schemes to make Boys Hall the great monument to twentieth-century art, and go to live with Franco the simple life of an artist's wife. If she wanted a Latin lover, then doubtless she could find a substitute for Franco from among the hundreds of sex-starved young Italians in the P.O.W. camp with him.

The truck slowed at the gates and the children, Timothy and Carol, came out to wave. The men threw them cherries they had picked from the trees that grew against the walls of the kitchen garden. 'Ciao,' they called. The children replied solemnly, 'Chow.'

Franco heard, but did not see from his seat on the floor.

Timothy was a beautiful child, a miniature blond version of Delphine. What beautiful children they could make, he and Delphine, beautiful dark-eyed Latin children! Could she not be happy to be his wife and have the pleasure of bringing up such a family? But he knew it was a hopeless wish. Every time he saw Delphine he planned to say these things, to insist that she make the choice. But in reality he did not have to ask, he knew what choice she would make. And for the time he had not the courage to face it.

1971

1

In the West End of London, and Mayfair in particular, new art galleries open up and close down almost as frequently as restaurants. Every season men and women who love pictures persuade themselves that they have discovered the infallible secret of running a successful gallery. Two seasons later they close. The investment—their own or, if they are lucky, their friends'—has melted away into the absurdly high cost of reliable staff, publicity, decoration, framing and all the remaining expenses, not to mention the overheads of premises at least near enough to give some substance to the title 'Bond Street Gallery'.

Pearl and Dominic Skipton had decided that the secret of success lay in the location. They opened the Skipton Gallery in an old studio in Fulham, persuading themselves that it was easily accessible from the West End, and already smart enough to be considered the northern section of the fabled land of dreams and artistic licence—Chelsea. And at any rate, Pearl's money would not stretch to grander premises.

At 6.30 on Private View day of their opening show, Andrew Tait was standing with a glass of champagne in his hand glancing at the Visitors' Book that lay open on the receptionist's table. The gallery had been open since 11.30 that morning but there was only a handful of names in the book. That signified very little, since Private View people seldom bothered to sign. Only those really at the bottom of the ladder took the trouble to do that. The others knew that the Skiptons would know damn well if they had deigned to turn up: they were watching like hawks, for all they tried to make it seem like a casual private party.

Andrew himself had been greeted effusively by Pearl at the door.

'*An*drew! How *nice!*' she had exclaimed in her low, intimate voice. 'Dominic will be *so* pleased you've come.' She emphasized random words by drawing them out to unnatural length. In a startling dress of floating violet material, she looked as if she was beginning to regret her confident choice when she had dressed that morning.

'How is it going?' Andrew asked.

'Oh marvellous,' she said quickly. '*Mar*vellous. All the crits have been. We're *thri*lled. You *must* have a glass of champagne.'

'Thanks.'

'We're *thri*lled,' she repeated. She seemed at a loss for anything else to say. 'You must ask Dominic. He's over there with our *protégé*.'

'He seems busy,' said Andrew. 'I'll talk to him in a minute.'

'Oh yes, do. You *must.*' She still seemed to be looking for something to say. 'Do you know our *protégé*, our young Philip? Do you know his work?'

'I saw him at the College show.'

'Yes, of *course. Eve*ryone saw his work there. He was quite famous even before he left! We're *so* thrilled to have him. *Eve*ryone knows his work.'

'He's very talented.'

'Oh yes, he is *ta*lented.'

Two years before, Dominic Skipton had been teaching at the Royal College of Art. The young Philip had indeed been a young *protégé* of his. But he had gone off to live with a rather well-known painter who was old enough to be his father. Rumour had it—and in the London art world rumour thrives like maggots in a dung heap—that Dominic was heart-broken. That's the art world, Andrew thought to himself as he glanced across the room to where Dominic was standing. Fifty per cent of them are queer, and a lot of those that aren't are ambidexterous. No wonder Pearl gets to have such a nervous manner. But at least it gives us normals a head start with the women clients.

'I hope you're going to tell your *peo*ple to *buy* him,' Pearl went on. 'He's going to be *very* important. You should buy him while he's still cheap.'

'I'm sure you're right,' Andrew had said, non-committally.

Pearl had thankfully turned to greet another arrival: *'David!* How *nice!*...'

On the desk by the Visitors' Book lay a discreet manilla folder. Andrew opened it, knowing he would find the price list of the paintings. Pearl was right, they *were* cheap. 150 guineas, 200 guineas. And they were large paintings. Even so, none of them had been sold. Quite apart from the mistake of quoting in guineas (it seemed so old fashioned: Andrew would have put straight pounds, and also the dollar equivalent) it was too little. It was a bad mistake to under-value work—bad for you as a gallery, since it gave you the reputation of dealing in small business; bad for the artist because it put him straight away in the second rank, the third rank probably, and it can take twenty years to alter that label.

And that was not their only mistake, Andrew thought, looking round the room. For one thing, it was too obviously a shoestring operation. Despite the champagne—they could hardly dispense with that—there was clearly too little money about. There was rush matting on the floor. The walls were brick, painted white. The curtains were made from hessian. It was attractively simple, but simple of necessity and not, as it should have been, the evidently expensive simplicity of stainless steel, plate glass, slate and marble. The place looked almost as if they had decorated it themselves.

And the people were wrong. Presumably the critics had been earlier in the day, or would drop by later in the week. They would probably not write it up at all. At best they would give it a mention of two or three lines at the end of their article. It was all quite predictable. In the art world stars were not born overnight, as they were in some other branches of show business. They virtually grew up in public. This young Philip was known to everyone, Pearl was right. His friend the painter had talked him up to everyone. And in a way it worked. Across the room, Philip, Dominic and the painter were talking cheerfully—high spirited possibly, but more likely awash with champagne. The group round them included a couple of painters and three or four of the Beautiful People.

Dominic had his hand on Philip's shoulder. On the surface anyway, old differences seemed to have been forgotten.

But although these people filled the room and emptied the champagne bottles, they weren't the *right* people. Friends of the artist, they never bought paintings themselves. They were a specific breed—the hangers-on. They had little money themselves—though many of them came from wealthy families, which enabled them to live well off relatives and friends. They spent all they had on their appearance and a certain expensively casual life style. And in the end that sort of connection devalued the artist too. Critics, perhaps out of envy, refused to take painters seriously if they did not give any sign of doing so themselves. And in the tiny, incestuous world of art there is no hope of distinguishing your private behaviour from your public work.

There were twenty people in the gallery, Andrew guessed. He himself had come at this time because he knew it would be the busiest—a glass of champagne, a chat, a quick assessment of the scene, before moving on to dinner, or a party, or whatever was the 'thing' for that evening. It was, after all, his job to keep up with the people as well as the paintings.

He saw that Timothy Proudfoot, tall and sandy-haired, was among the group round Dominic. He and Andrew had been at Cambridge together, though at different colleges, reading History of Art. They saw one another frequently at this sort of party. Timothy's girl, Sally Marchant, worked in the Old Masters Department at Christie's. Timothy himself was somewhere on the fringe of the art world. For ten years he had been hanging round the Chelsea scene, that organic interaction of film people, rich people, pop people, art people and the younger children of the aristocracy that somehow got London a reputation for 'swinging'. Timothy still had not quite decided, he said, 'what to do'. He led a pleasant enough life, with his flat in Cheyne Walk, and the beat-up old green sports car, supported by a legacy left him by his Aunt Jane. But Andrew guessed he was beginning to think of settling down. He had that look in his eye, especially when he was with Sally—and now that was most of the time. And Sally herself had a really broody look. For her evidently it was nest-making time. Of course 'settling down' for Timothy was only a comparative term; he did not actually envisage routine work in the City, in some 'boring'

Merchant Bank or anything. Something in art would be more 'amusing'. As far as Andrew was concerned there was a simple solution—a gallery, financed with Timothy's money, managed by Andrew. Timothy would not have to work too hard and his connections would be useful....

Dominic had seen him. He detached himself from the group and came across.

'Andrew,' he said, grasping his elbow affectionately. 'How *are* you?' He and Pearl, Andrew had noticed before, caught habits from one another. He supposed it happened often enough in marriage, but it seemed more noticeable with the Skiptons. They over-advertised their unity.

'Fine,' said Andrew, controlling the urge to remove his arm. 'How are you?'

'Tell me,' said Dominic. 'Tell me, honestly, what do you think of Philip's work?'

'I...'

'We have such high hopes for him. He's going to be *very* important,' he echoed Pearl. 'But *tell* me, Andrew. Tell me, *hon*estly, what do *you* think of him?'

Andrew was not in the least affected by this somewhat desperate sincerity. 'I like them,' he said, looking round at the paintings. 'I like them a lot.'

'Oh, I'm so glad. I'm *so* glad.' Dominic's pressure on his elbow just perceptibly increased. 'You know how much we respect your opinion, Pearl and I. I *hope* you know how much we respect you.'

Actually Andrew had been almost shocked when he walked into the gallery. Hung together here, Philip's work looked weak and unoriginal. Two years ago his three or four paintings had dominated the R.C.A. diploma show. Then he seemed years ahead of his fellow students, in maturity and in his sense of what was happening in painting. But in two years he had seemed only to be able to repeat himself. Now every other artist was painting in a similar style. What had seemed so exciting, even so recently, now seemed too easy.

The large canvasses were divided geometrically into regular shapes, mostly at an angle to the edges of the canvas, and painted in clear, paint-box colours. One alone would have been unexceptional—just right for a young

41

middle-class couple to hang in their modern penthouse flat. A dozen together were actually boring. Each had a title that had no apparent connection with the picture: Kings 23, Acronym. No doubt there were private connections.

'Selling, are they?' Andrew asked, though he knew the answer. The pressure on his elbow relaxed.

'Well,' said Dominic, laughing rather falsely. 'Money has not actually changed *hands*. But, you can see, we have several reservations.'

An old trick, Andrew thought. Three of the paintings had half the red sticker that indicates 'sold' pasted on to the card beside them, to show they were 'reserved'.

'I'll bet at least one of those is for Gerry.' Dominic released his arm. He flushed deeply. '*You* know how it is,' he continued, 'with a *new* painter. Everyone waits to see what people are going to do. But we are *absolutely* confident. It's really a very exciting time.'

He sounded as if he was trying to persuade himself. Poor fool, Andrew thought. Couldn't he see that already, on the first day, he had failed? This old crate of a gallery was never going to get off the ground. You had only to look round you to see that. Practically the only man in the room worth having there, in commercial terms, was Timothy Proudfoot. And that made Andrew wonder if he *was* right to be there himself. Of course the London art scene was not the same as New York. In London there was room for a slightly more amateur approach. New York was really tough. But England was pretty damn competitive too, down there under the gentlemanly charm.

Even so, New York was the place for new painting. The Americans were committed to the idea of the new—they had to be, they didn't have anything else. They were ready to believe that a painter could be instantly 'important' and pay the price that went with that status. And they could just as easily forget yesterday's superstar, and stow away in the attic the pictures they bought so eagerly. In the end it reduced itself to the simple fact—the British have the tradition: the Americans have the money.

It was time he left, Andrew decided. But before he went there were a couple of people he wanted to speak to.

42

Dominic went to the door, nuzzled Pearl affectionately, picked up a full bottle of champagne from the ice, and joined a group on the other side of the room. Andrew moved towards the group Dominic had left.

'Poor old Gerry,' the painter was saying. 'He never learns.'

'He can afford it,' said Philip.

'Oh, don't be so *mean*,' said a willowy blonde girl Andrew did not recognize.

'Well, he *can*,' said Philip sulkily.

Andrew knew what they were talking about. Mel German, who was in the group on the other side of the room, was the frequent butt of art world gossip. One of life's natural victims, he seemed to have been born to be laughed at. Not that he needed sympathy. A successful lawyer, immensely fat, and immensely rich, he bought his way into the art scene by patronizing young painters and the fashionable dealers. He was unattractive, deeply shy and socially gauche—but with an evident determination not to be put down by his own faults.

'Well, I like Gerry,' said the blonde defiantly. 'I think he's a darling. Anyone can make mistakes.'

'But no one,' said the painter, 'can make so many mistakes, so often, not as the Gerry.'

'Oh don't call him that,' said the girl. 'It's hateful. It sounds so—so *sneery*.'

Gerry's latest folly had even made the national press. Always eager to do a favour for as many people as possible, Gerry had got into the habit of using various agents to buy pictures for him. Recently he had wanted a painting by Wyndham Lewis that was coming up at Sotheby's as part of the estate of one of the original Bloomsbury Group. He had commissioned one of his agents to get it for him, at any price. He had recently decided to concentrate on pre-World War I English painting: the prices were right for him, and everyone told him that these artists were bound to come into fashion again.

But a couple of days before the sale, he commissioned another agent, forgetting the first—also to get the painting at any price. As a result, they bid against one another, amazed at the sums they were having to offer. Gerry was also amazed. He was actually present at the sale, hoping to keep down the price by buying anonymously. In fact, before one of the agents had the sense to drop out, it reached twenty-five times the previous record for a Wyndham Lewis. It still was not a sensational sum in absolute terms—but it made a good story. In fact, Andrew thought, if Gerry had been looking for publicity, what he got in terms of coverage would have been cheap at the price. And at times you had to believe that publicity was exactly what Gerry was inviting.

Pearl popped the cork from another bottle of champagne and brought it across to them wrapped in a white napkin.

'You *all* must have some more champagne,' she said.

Timothy Proudfoot drew back a step from the group to speak to Andrew. They greeted one another with the easy familiarity of old schoolfellows. Even so, Andrew did not think of Timothy as a friend. They were too obviously far too different for that. But Andrew liked him. He even admitted to himself that Timothy was not actually lazy. He had simply been educated to understand 'work' to mean something altogether different from other people.

'I hoped I'd see you, Andrew,' he said. 'I've been meaning to telephone—but you know how it is. . . .' He smiled indulgently, as if he had learned to tolerate his own ineffectiveness. 'You must come for the weekend.'

'Oh, thanks,' said Andrew coolly. 'That would be nice. I'd love to.'

'I meant to ask you ages ago. You know how it is. Mother keeps saying, "When is that charming young man coming for the weekend again?" You must come again soon. You were a great success with Mother.'

I bet, Andrew thought. So was anything in pants, that didn't look as if it would need helping out of them. Not that he had not gone out of his way to get Delphine interested. She was a sexy old lady, and not even unattractive. Actually she was amazing, with a figure like a girl, stalking about like a panther. It was obvious the Italian butler was not there just to decant the port and keep the keys of the silver cupboard. But even he was not as young as he used to be. Exhausted, probably. But who could blame her? It was common knowledge that her husband got them blown off by a land-mine in the Italian campaign.

Andrew felt suddenly that he had to get out of the gallery.

He had the sensation that he would suffocate if he stayed a minute longer.

'Tim,' he said. 'I have to go. Why don't you call me at the office?'

But Timothy was already fishing in his inside pocket for his diary, insisting that they must arrange something then and there.

Andrew allowed himself quickly to fix to go out to Boys Hall in two weeks' time. But he almost gagged with the sense of physical revulsion as he did so. He had to get away, to get out from among these people, to try to ease the sense of claustrophobia.

The trouble was that he knew what it was. It was not the first time he had had this feeling. And he knew that it was not the people that disgusted him—it was himself, Andrew Tait. These people were not disgusting. At least, they were not any more disgusting than the usual run of his fellow creatures ... but there it was again, that bitterness, that sour view of humanity. The disgust was in his own mind. He saw the world through green-tinted spectacles. Why did his mind produce such acid thoughts? Pearl was a warm and decent woman; her mannerisms no more affected than anyone else. And Dominic, why did Andrew assume that the idle gossip of the art world should be true about him? There was so much smoke over that scene, not all of it could possibly rise from real fires. And anyway, what were Dominic's sexual hang-ups to him? Why did he have to pick on that one thing about him, the one vulnerable fact—and not even a fact at that? And Gerry? And Timothy? And Delphine de Boys... ?

He nodded a greeting to Sally Marchant, to Philip, to the painter, and gravely thanked Pearl for asking him (she seemed genuinely touched by his sincerity) and made for the door.

But Gerry intercepted him. 'Andrew, you're not going?' he said accusingly. 'You haven't even said hello to me yet.'

'Gerry, I'm sorry.' He really could not face Gerry now. The way his eyes were saying all the time, Like me, *please* like me. 'I'm sorry. I feel bad. I really feel ill. I don't know what it is.'

'Champagne, I expect,' said Gerry, 'on an empty stomach.

Can't drink the stuff myself. I am sorry, my dear fellow. I won't keep you. You should get out in the fresh air.'

'Yes.'

'But before you go, I insist you must have dinner with me next week. I have something I particularly want to talk to you about.'

Andrew weakly agreed. Anything to get out of that polluted atmosphere.

'You heard of my latest folly, I suppose?' Gerry asked, wringing his plump, manicured hands.

'Yes, I did,' said Andrew, almost running way. 'Sorry. Bad luck. I wanted to phone you, but...'

'Not at all. Not at all,' Gerry interrupted, almost cheerfully. 'The price of fame.'

2

Gerry's folly was not a mistake Andrew would have made in twenty years. He cared too much for his reputation in Bond Street. But neither, he guessed, would Gerry have let himself be shown for a fool among the lawyers of Chancery Lane.

After two years with Parke-Bernet in New York, Andrew returned to London as exhibitions assistant at the London National Gallery of Modern Art. It was a good job—not too well paid, but it gave him the entrée to every last corner of the British art scene. Wherever he chose to go he was welcome. He was not so stupid as to imagine it was for his own sake. But for the time being it was exactly what he wanted.

'Have you seen Wetherby lately?' Gerry asked from the head of the table. In the basement of his over-designed house, looking over the Regent's Canal in Little Venice, they were waited on by his discreet manservant. Although the question was addressed to him, Andrew left it for someone else to answer.

'Haven't seen him for ages,' said the girl beside him. Her name was Rosemary, and it seemed she had a husband somewhere. This evening, though, she was alone. With the usual signals she had been making it clear that the husband should not be considered a deterrent.

'Oh, he looks so miserable,' said Gerry. '*Miserable.*'

A voice at Andrew's ear whispered, 'More salad, sir?' It made him start. The man wore soft shoes, creeping about the dark, candlelit room in a really sinister manner. Andrew waved him away.

'You know why?' Gerry went on. 'He's waiting for Kroll to die, and he's not sure he can hold out much longer.'

'But I thought Kroll was his artist?' Rosemary said.

She was asking the right questions, Andrew thought. 'He is,' said Gerry.

'Well, surely he doesn't want him to *die*? He can't paint pictures if he's dead.'

'Ah,' said Gerry. 'Exactly, my dear Rosemary. That's exactly the point. While he's alive he's producing paintings. Wetherby doesn't want that at all.'

He really was spinning out this story. Andrew wondered for whose benefit he was making such a production. He could not believe that Andrew did not know what he was driving at. The young couple from Sotheby's must have known the story to the point of boredom, and probably beyond. Presumably it was aimed at the American couple. The evening was evidently for their benefit. The husband was a member of the visiting American Bar Association. Otherwise why should Gerry ask such boring people? Already before dinner they were three parts smashed, and now they were knocking back the wine like Coke. They sat at the table as if poleaxed, occasionally sniping at one another in penetrating undertones. They surely weren't attending to Gerry's conversational set-pieces.

'But Gerry,' said Rosemary, 'Bob Wetherby is Kroll's agent. He makes money out of selling his work.'

'Not the way Wetherby does it, darling.'

Rosemary shrugged, as if it was a guessing game and she was giving up. The Americans had their faces turned to Gerry, but Andrew doubted they could even see him through the alcoholic fog.

47

'The way Wetherby sees it, he might be able to make *money* now, but if he holds off he could make a *fortune* later.'

Under the table Rosemary's knee had connected with Andrew's. He almost laughed aloud. This nostalgia for the thirties was going too far. Was footy-footy coming back? *And is there honey still for tea?*

No one prompted Gerry this time. He went on anyway. 'He's been letting out just enough of Kroll's paintings to build a reputation. If nothing else, after all they have a certain scarcity value. And in the meantime, poor Kroll is starving. After he's actually dead, and there aren't going to be any more paintings, Wetherby will have a limited *oevre*—and then he can really get to work. But Kroll is turning out to be inconveniently tough.' He laughed. 'Wetherby looks so down in the mouth, I begin to wonder if he won't be the first to go. That would be the supreme irony.'

Rosemary leaned her elbows nonchalantly on the table. But underneath her knee pressed urgently against Andrew's. 'I think it's awful,' she said.

'My dear,' said Gerry. 'It's a fact of life. It could be worse.'

Rosemary turned to Andrew. It gave her the chance to look in his eyes, and also to increase the pressure yet again. 'They're bastards those dealers, aren't they? Absolute bastards.'

'Also a fact of life,' said Gerry.

'Not all of them,' said Andrew, shifting his knee, but not breaking the contact.

Gerry laughed again. 'You must be careful what you say. You know Andrew is a dealer *manqué*.'

'*Manqué*? You're a little young to be *manqué*, aren't you?'

'I hope so. Gerry means I'm interested. It's part of my job.'

He guessed Rosemary was twenty-nine, and had been for three or four years. She seemed to be having trouble with her napkin ... her hand was sliding up the inside of his thigh. She'd have to stop that, or he'd never be able to get up from the table.

'Well, I must say, I thought you would defend Wetherby.'

Gerry was somewhat petulant. 'I thought you were a friend of his.'

'Oh no,' Andrew said quickly—too quickly he guessed. 'Not really,' he added, more casually. 'Of course I know him. In fact, we bought one of his artists last year. But I don't think either of us would say we were close friends.' Indeed he guessed it was almost the last word Bob Wetherby would use of him. They had recently had a very icy exchange when they had run into one another at Burke's. Since the Gallery of Modern Art had bought his paintings, Andrew had taken care to cultivate the acquaintance of the young artist. They had become very friendly, and he had quite casually given Andrew a couple of drawings Andrew admired in his studio. Andrew took care to give him the impression that he thought Bob Wetherby was under-estimating the artist's potential. He did honestly think that was so. But making it clear was also in his own interest. Gerry was not accurate: Andrew was not so much a dealer *manqué* as a dealer in training.

That evening at Burke's Bob Wetherby had warned him off. He had stopped behind Andrew at the bar. Without preliminaries he said, 'It's kind of you to help promote my artist, Andrew. But I do hope no one will forget that the sales go through his dealer.'

Andrew had been amused, and quite pleased by this attack. It proved he was using the right tactics, and Wetherby was scared enough of him to show his claws. But Andrew had only used an existing situation. All artists have this ambivalent relationship with their dealers. As soon as their work begins to sell well, they begin to wonder why they need dealers any more. And the dealers have to hang on for their commission, righteously complaining that without them the artist would never have got to the position where he could believe he did not need them. Wetherby charged a commission of 50 per cent on the artists he handled. That was pretty much the going rate. Now, no one likes to watch himself apparently giving away half what his work is worth to a stranger. And Andrew had begun to suggest, in this case, that there were clients he could find, by-passing Wetherby, who would buy the work direct, and

Andrew would take only a token commission—a painting or drawing instead of money, perhaps.

But Bob Wetherby was too sharp to miss those tricks. He had been on the scene too long. And he had had bitter experience. Three or four years previously a long-established artist, with an international reputation, and prices to match, had needed money badly. He'd hit on the idea of selling a painting anonymously—'the property of a gentleman'—in a Sotheby sale of twentieth-century art. Copying his own style of ten years earlier, he had sent in a very impressive painting. But Wetherby proved too sharp. The artist had a prolific output, but Wetherby knew every painting, and where it hung. He knew that this was a new painting. The artist came to heel like a whipped dog. He accepted a large loan from Wetherby in advance of future sales—at the full commission. You didn't get away with tricks like that from Bob Wetherby.

Rosemary left Andrew alone during the dessert. He concentrated on the strawberries and cream, trying to put out of his mind the thought that preoccupied it. He would take Rosemary home. She seemed the sort of girl who would have had the forethought to come in a taxi. They would do what they could to make sure the world kept going round. The first sun of the summer had brought out the freckles on her breasts, as she was obviously aware. His attention wandered repeatedly from the dish in front of him. He tried to concentrate on what the others were saying. But it was only the usual discussion with the Americans about English cream, how thick it was, how they'd asked for this cream for their coffee....

Andrew got upstairs without embarrassment. In the drawing-room Gerry put the latest Stones record—not yet released—on the turntable. Andrew doubted the Americans would be in the pop scene enough to appreciate that.

'Oh,' said Rosemary. 'The new Stones disc. It's not released yet, is it?'

Maybe, Andrew thought, Gerry pays her to stooge for him.

The room had grey silk curtains, two marble fireplaces and thick fur rugs. But it was dominated by the paintings. Spotlights, hung from the ceiling, were masked to throw rectangles of light exactly the size of the frames. There was no other light in the room. Andrew knew the paintings well. His professional eye never missed a worthwhile work of art. He was building a card index of every important twentieth-century painting he had ever seen. Only four of Gerry's were on it—a Robyn Denny (bought very early), a Hockney drawing, a Bakst set design and a beautiful little Picabia (acquired by luck from a client). These, of course, were always on view in the drawing-room. But Gerry made frequent changes among the others. He displayed there only the cream of the hundreds of paintings he had bought. Artists who had not 'come on', or had simply gone out of fashion, were put out of sight in the upstairs rooms.

The creepy manservant had left the coffee on a tray. Rosemary poured. 'I'll be mother,' she said as she lifted the pot.

'My dear,' Gerry said. 'You never told us.'

'Oh no,' she said. 'Not yet.' She looked at Andrew. 'I still haven't decided who's to be the father.'

'Well, I do hope you'll let the lucky man know in good time.' Gerry picked up a silver cigarette box from the tray. 'Now, my friends,' he said, with too obvious emphasis, 'allow me to offer you some marijuana.'

The lawyer and his lady declined—but they wanted it to be perfectly clear to everyone there that they had no objections whatever, either moral, or, for that matter, since they were outside American jurisdiction, legal.

'Oh! They're already rolled!' Rosemary exclaimed, peering into the box as Gerry lifted the lid. 'Oh, that's what I call the perfect host.' She clasped Gerry affectionately round the shoulder with one hand, dangerously waving the coffee pot in the other. 'They don't put that in the books on etiquette. I always hate all that fiddling about—I can never do it properly. The perfect host, who rolls the joints before you come.'

Gerry, squatting like a frog on the edge of the sofa, looked highly pleased with himself. 'Andrew, you light up,' he said. He held out the box.

The five of them smoked, passing the joint solemnly from one to the other. 'Clockwise, clockwise,' Gerry insisted. 'Like port, you pass it clockwise.'

'Oh that's marvellous!' Rosemary echoed. 'I told you you

were the perfect host.' She put on a fearfully cultured voice. ' "Mr Melvin German, our *Vogue* host of the month, *insists* that at fashionable dinner parties this season, it's pot not port that's circulating in the traditional clockwise direction, drawing guests into the modern circle of friendship with the new chic perfume that you don't buy at a department store —Acapulco Gold! " '

She had turned on like a tap, at the first drag it seemed, as if she'd only been waiting for an excuse to drop her inhibitions. What few she possessed.

Andrew was more cautious. Smoking was still a socially self-conscious act. It was not yet as easy as passing round the decanter, or the whisky bottle, or cigars. Perhaps it was because it was a shared activity. It had to be something of a ritual.

In a few moments Rosemary had moved to the other end of the room, dancing by herself, barefoot, to the heavy rock of the Stones. Andrew watched, while he concentrated on holding the smoke deep down in his lungs. He felt calmly detached from Rosemary's movements and the insistent beat of the music—and then he realized that the detachment was the start of his own high. With a great and calm pleasure he felt his body ease, felt himself entering the very fabric of the music. He had the odd sensation that he was floating somewhere in a wide dark space that was actually the area between two grooves of the record.

The joint came back to Andrew from Gerry, on his left. He was just about to take another drag when Rosemary leant over his shoulder and gently took it from between his fingers. '*Excuse* me,' she said, in a slow, deep voice.

Soon Andrew found himself dancing at that end of the room with Rosemary. He tried hard to remember walking there, but could not. Time became detached. The Sotheby's couple also danced at one time. They leant against one another, almost motionless. They seemed very married. After a while they simply disappeared. It could have been that they went upstairs. It could have been that they went home. It hardly seemed to matter.

Gerry sat on the sofa, smiling vacantly to himself. The Americans watched with glazed eyes. 'Are you *sure* you won't join us?' Gerry said suddenly. 'It's *very* good marijuana, you know. The very best, I do assure you.' But they made their excuses and left.

'What a *beautiful* fur,' Rosemary said, stroking the wife's mink cape as they passed. 'It's so sexy. Isn't it?—Andrew, feel it. Isn't it—sexy?'

Andrew stretched out his hand, but it seemed to travel so slowly that they had gone before he reached the fur.

Andrew and Rosemary danced more and more intimately. Gerry was watching them with a strange expression. It seemed like it was time to go. Andrew and Rosemary had no need to say anything. All *that* was understood. With his arm round Rosemary's waist, Andrew faced Gerry. 'Gerry,' he said, 'it was *great*. A great evening.'

'You're not going?' Gerry said sharply.

'Yes. Well ...'

'*You*'re not going,' he repeated, looking directly at Andrew. 'I want to talk to you. I haven't talked to you yet.' He was beginning to sound hysterical. Christ! Andrew thought. A bum trip. 'I have something I particularly want to talk to you about.'

Andrew and Rosemary exchanged a hopeless look. She withdrew from his arm and began to dance again, quietly, with her head lowered, as if concentrating on the music.

'Don't I make myself clear?' Gerry went on. 'I want to talk to you. *Alone*. I have a business proposition I want to discuss with you.'

'But Gerry ... Tonight? ... Neither of us is really in a state ...'

'Speak for yourself. It's up to you. I asked you here to discuss a business proposition. If you don't wish to hear it ...'

Andrew's head cleared instantly. Some time ago Gerry had asked Andrew to buy for him, on commission. But Andrew had refused. He had made it clear then that there was only one business proposition from Gerry he was interested in: Gerry should put up the capital for Andrew to open a gallery. Gerry had hedged, said he had to have time to think about it. Andrew wrote it off as another abortive line of approach. He was not even sure, he had told himself, that it was advisable to go into business with Gerry. In the art world Gerry was not taken quite seriously. Going in with him would be an admission that Andrew could not quite make it at the centre of the scene.

Andrew heard the door of the house slam. He looked round. Rosemary had disappeared.

He heard himself say, 'She's gone.' He wanted to run after her, but his body did not respond. He stood in front of Gerry and repeated feebly, 'She's gone.'

Gerry recovered his composure immediately. '*Now*,' he said in a satisfied tone. 'Now we can talk.'

Andrew still had not moved.

'What's the matter, Andrew? You on a downer?'

'No ... I ...'

'I know what you need. I know exactly what you need.' He moved with surprising speed to the sideboard and fished behind the rows of discs. He held something in his clenched hand as he came back and stood behind Andrew. 'Here. This will clear your head.'

'What is it?'

'Poppers, dear boy. That's all. A popper is what you need. Clear your head.'

'No,' said Andrew. 'I don't want a popper.'

'Why not?'

'I don't like poppers.'

'What's wrong with poppers? I use them all the time.'

'They smell. They smell—like dog farts.'

'Only afterwards. Only afterwards. If the smell bothers you you break another.'

'No, really, Gerry. I'd rather not.'

But Gerry lifted his hand and clasped it over Andrew's nose. The capsule was broken and the sharp smell of amyl nitrate flooded into Andrew's head. 'Come on, Andrew,' Gerry was saying in a soothing voice. 'Let her go. Relax. You don't need her. We don't need her. Stay here and relax with your friend Gerry.'

Andrew struggled out of Gerry's grasp. His mind was crystal clear. That was natural adrenalin, he thought to himself. As long as I have that I don't need poppers.

The depression hit him as he drove across London. The streets were almost deserted. It had been raining. The tyres hissed on the shiny roads. He realized he was driving too fast, tearing at top speed away from that unhealthy, unhappy

54

house and its pathetic owner. The depression was serious. He felt almost suicidal. Could it have been bad grass? Smoking had never done this to him before.

He put his foot down to the floor, screaming the tyres all the way round Hyde Park Corner. Then he smiled wrily to himself. At least there were some lengths to which he was not prepared to go to further his ambition. He had never found himself reluctant to use his physical attractions up to now. Was this real revulsion, or simply the fear that perhaps he might not be able to function? He shuddered.

He needed to be with someone. There were good and bad times in being a loner, and this was one of the bad. He thought of Rosemary. He would go to her. But he realized he had no idea where she lived. London is a big city to start looking for a girl without an address at three in the morning.

It was these times that he began to wonder if he really knew even himself what it was he was aiming at. If this was the art scene—and it was the art scene, exactly, he knew it well enough to know that—did he really have the ambition to make it among these empty people? And if they were empty, what was to distinguish Andrew himself from the same charge?

But underneath this disaffection, Andrew recognized an old enemy—envy. The green dragon lived in his belly, like a rumbling appendix. It gave him no peace. When he saw a man like Mel German, with so much money, so many opportunities, blindly getting it all wrong, he was filled with a blind rage. It spilled over everything, clouded his vision. In these moods he simply hated the world, without exception. Perhaps it was as well that he did not know Rosemary's address. The green dragon made a bad third in a bed.

3

Corinna Proudfoot was a happy, uninhibited girl. There was not a lot of reason she should be, and many good reasons why she should not. Her mother, who had a different kind of vitality, had called her 'Fidget' when she was a girl. The name had stuck. But actually, among the tensions and stormy currents of Boys Hall, Corinna remained an island of calm and serenity.

At the age of twenty-four, Corinna found herself the most stable element in a troubled family. Her mother was an extravagant woman—in both senses of the word. Her father, impotent, sexually and socially. Her brother, Giles (the elder of her two brothers), overwhelmed by the responsibility of his inheritance, agonized over every decision that affected the estates. Tim (the younger brother), was less effectual still—he simply drifted through life, making no decisions at all. And all of them, increasingly, found in Corinna the common sense and confidence they lacked themselves.

Corinna herself knew that, by all the rules of the psychology book, she should have grown up to be a serious case. The fact that she knew it was maybe a good part of the reason why she did not. The rest of the family were troubled at least in part because they refused to give their troubles a name. Financial trouble they understood—only too well. Sexual trouble they thought they knew too—the thing that unmarried girls can get into. But they did not think of the psyche as a place where you could get sick.

Corinna, growing up among them, had watched them all calmly.

Her status gave her a particular sense of detachment. There had never been any secret about her fatherhood. She was born only three months after David Proudfoot came back from the war. And it was common knowledge that he had left his manhood in the Italian peninsula. But he agreed to accept Corinna as his own. The aristocracy can flaunt the rules of society without the usual disadvantages.

Corinna heard from the servants that he had made only one condition: that Delphine dismiss the father, and never see him again. Only the name of the child—Corinna—should acknowledge his nationality. Yet Lord de Boys (as he soon became on the death of his father) could not control her appearance. Her colouring, her black hair and dark eyes, her smooth not-quite-olive skin, were features from a medieval Florentine portrait, not the colouring of the famous English rose.

Corinna never asked her mother if it happened as the servants said. Not that she was indifferent. There were times—particularly as she walked and rode alone through the woods and fields that she loved so much—when she had a desperate need to know her father, to see him and find out what sort of man he was. But she knew that if she asked her mother she would not have told her the truth. Only once, perhaps sensing Corinna's curiosity, had Delphine referred to it. The two of them were dining alone together. Alberto had left them with coffee at the table. Delphine had said suddenly:

'He's not your father.'

'Who?' said Corinna, startled.

'Alberto. He's not your father. I thought you should know.'

'Oh. No. I didn't think he was.'

'Good. That's all right. A lot of people do, you know. Think he's your father.'

'I never did. It's—well, I think my father must have been different—a different sort of person from Alberto.'

'Yes,' said Lady de Boys. 'He was. Very different.'

She never mentioned the subject again.

When she was twenty-one, her parents gave Corinna a cottage about a mile and a half from Boys Hall. She could live there, they said, in freedom and privacy. In the days before machine milking and butter factories, when the dairy herd had required five times the present number of cowmen, it had been the head dairyman's house. The roof was thatched and the walls white-washed. Two white lilacs grew by the front door. To the rear stood an orchard of old apple trees. Among the outhouses were stables where Corinna kept her two hunters, and beyond a ten-acre field where they were turned out to graze.

Corinna had no pretensions to elegance. She had furnished the cottage simply, with a few pieces from the house, and second-hand furniture picked up at local sales. She was happy there. She helped Giles with the estate. She groomed and exercised her horses. She ate at least one meal a day at the Hall. For the remainder of the time she was content in the cottage.

The other members of the family got into the habit of

visiting her there. Even Lord de Boys's dowager mother, Lady Amelia, who never set foot in the Hall, came frequently to see Corinna. It was she who had given Corinna her horses. She came ostensibly to give advice on their care —but as often as not she and Corinna talked for several hours by the fire and she went back to the Mill House without even looking into the stables.

The best furnished room in Corinna's cottage was the kitchen. She had kept the old blue-tiled range, with its open fire and iron hotplates, but she had added a complete range of modern cooking equipment. In the centre of the room stood a long scrubbed wooden table. On this Corinna served her visitors delicious home-made country food—game pâté, jugged hare, pigeon pie ... traditional English dishes.

She had grown to enjoy cooking. She had not always done so. She started almost in self-defence. The food at the Hall was notorious. Neither Lord nor Lady de Boys ever ate for pleasure. When he was blown up in Italy Lord de Boys had suffered severe stomach wounds. He was scarcely able to take solid food at all. He lived on a strict diet of fortified pap. Except on rare occasions his meals were served to him in his rooms. And Lady de Boys, having so little interest in food herself, grudged serving it to others. Visitors were fed Spartan fare. Delphine would sit at the head of the table, watching them eat with unconcealed disgust. As a result, even the little they were given often went back to the kitchen uneaten.

At first, when she realized how meanly they served their guests at the Hall, Corinna had been embarrassed. But since she had had the cottage it had ceased to matter. She made a joke of the notorious food. 'At least,' she told guests when her mother was out of hearing, 'it's kept us children from getting fat.' And she invited them to the cottage for supplementary meals, after the 'official' meal times.

Even Giles's fiancée, Polly, liked to visit Corinna at the cottage. As the future mistress of Boys Hall, she had had a frosty welcome from the current Lady. Delphine objected strongly to the engagement. 'She is quite unsuitable,' she declared categorically, within Polly's hearing. 'Her father is a farmer.' That was perfectly true. But he was a farmer of more acres than the Boys estate had covered for a hundred and fifty years. He ran a highly mechanized system, and it made him vast profits. 'He visits people in a *helicopter,*' scoffed Lady de Boys. 'How extraordinarily vulgar!'

'You musn't mind Mother,' Corinna told Polly.

They were seated at Corinna's kitchen table one Sunday afternoon. 'Tea' on Sunday had become an institution at the cottage. Corinna spread the tea table like a harvest supper.

Timothy had come down from London for the weekend with Sally Marchant. Polly had driven the twenty-five miles from her father's farm on Saturday evening.

'I don't think she does, do you, really, love?' Tim asked.

'No, not really,' Polly said unconvincingly. She always seemed rather on her dignity. It might have been, Corinna thought, that she caught the habit from Giles, but she did seem affected already in advance by the responsibility of her future position.

'It must be such a strain for her, with your father so ill,' said Sally tactfully.

An expression of panic passed over Giles's face. 'Yes,' he said, 'but still ...'

Polly looked gravely round the table. 'Giles thinks,' she announced—then hesitated. 'Giles thinks,' she repeated, 'that it—it won't be long now.'

Sally breathed, 'Oh dear,' but the others were silent.

Timothy looked enquiringly across the table at Giles.

'Yes,' said Giles eventually. 'The specialist was here on Wednesday....'

'How long?' asked Tim.

Giles shrugged. 'You know. They won't say exactly....'

'Months? ... Weeks? ... Days?'

They were all looking towards Giles. The pies and salads and cold meats lay untouched at the centre of the table. After what seemed an interminable pause, Giles said, almost whispering, 'Weeks. Perhaps months, but probably only weeks.'

'I see,' said Timothy.

'Look,' said Corinna. 'It's silly for us all to sit here with long faces. We can't pretend this is a sudden shock. It's sad, unhappy for all of us. I love Father as much as any of you, even if ... He's a dear man. But we've known for years that it was only a matter of time. We've always known it

59

ever since—ever since the war, I suppose.'

'But now we have to face the fact, the practical effects of his ... his ...'

'Death,' Corinna finished for him quietly. 'Yes. But practically it won't really be so different. You've been running things for ages, Giles.'

'Won't death duties make a difference? I mean ...'

'He only had a life interest in the land,' said Polly. She'd made it her business to know all about the problems of her future husband.

'But everything in the house is his absolutely.'

'He should have done something about it before,' said Polly in a slightly complaining tone.

'Of course,' said Corinna. 'We understand how you feel, Polly. It's a terrible worry for Giles. But we're all of us involved. My God—we've discussed it a million times at this very table, before you even knew Giles....'

'I'm sorry. Yes. It's just that Giles...'

'Of course Father should have done something about it. But you can't force a man to part with what's his. Legally he is entitled to sell every stick of furniture in the Hall and give the proceeds to the Mission for Fallen Women. O.K.— the idea that he actually would is absurd. But all the same he refuses to talk about what he *will* do. Whenever Giles tries to talk to him, he gets angry. Or more often just gets ill. Nothing ever gets done. I mean, we all understand why— when you're hanging on to life by the skin of your teeth, psychologically you're bound to refuse to think about death. It's understandable. But he did, he does have a special responsibility. I don't want to criticize him. He's—well, you know he's not my father, but I think of him as a father. Mother should have persuaded him. She could have persuaded him to do something. But she never cared enough about it herself to bother to try. She always says she's done everything she can to persuade him, but I don't believe her. You know what she is. The Hall is merely a good setting for her collection.'

Corinna had never been able to talk to her mother. Delphine could put on an irresistible charm if she wanted, but even with her children she kept up a barrier of formality. Corinna could never penetrate it. There were certain things that were not talked about. And Delphine never left you in any doubt if she thought you were approaching a forbidden subject.

'And it's obviously too late now,' Corinna went on. He would have to live five years after a gift for the death duty on it even to begin to be reduced. But we shall manage somehow, I'm sure we shall. We all want the same things— that's the important point. It sounds embarrassing when you put it into words. But we all want the Hall to go on. You know—it sort of stands for the family. We want to keep it like that.'

'Yes,' said Giles.

'And the fact that we can all sit round this table and talk about it, and we all agree, and know that we'll help one another—that means we shall be able to work it out in the end, somehow.'

'Yes,' said Giles again. He did not sound convinced.

'Good old Fidget,' said Timothy. 'I don't know what we'd do without you, Fidge. You're such a tonic—you always manage to make us feel better.'

'You're so right,' said Polly. 'We do rely on you so, Corinna. It is such a blessing that we're all agreed. None of us, in ourselves, is as important as the family, and everything it represents.'

Polly, Corinna thought to herself, was becoming positively regal at the prospect of the title soon to be hers. But, 'Polly,' she said, 'I wish you'd call me Fidget like everyone else.'

'Well, all right,' said Polly, 'if you like. But I can never really see you as Fidget, you know. You're such a calm person, aren't you?'

'I suppose so,' said Corinna. 'On the surface anyway. . . . Here. Come on all of you. You aren't eating a thing. I didn't cook this lot to give to the pigs.' She began to cut slices of the crusty loaf at her elbow.

'Help yourselves. Polly. Sally. You must be starving after Hall dinner last night, and Hall lunch today.'

She indicated the dishes and encouraged them to help themselves. And gradually, with the good food and the cheerful atmosphere of the room, their spirits rose. They began to think hopefully of the future.

This was Corinna's gift—she gave other people hope and

61

optimism. But she herself, under her surface calm, was deeply worried. She just hoped, when the time came, it would turn out as she said, that they would not find that they were all looking for something different for the future of Boys Hall.

4

With Max Marske Andrew reckoned he had found exactly what he wanted—a really original artist, and a promotable personality. That was what he had been looking for. It was not enough to be a good artist. Not even to be a great artist. London was full of geniuses waiting for the public to beat a path to their door. The art world was a jungle: the public needed the path cut for them, and signs posted to show the way.

Max was perfect. He was a really sharp boy. He had that uncanny instinct for doing the right, *unexpected* thing, at the right time. After a dazzling career at art school, he had given up painting for two years. With paint on canvas, he told everyone there was nothing more to be said. He worked in kinetics, experimented with sound pictures, with environments. Rumour was that he was on to extraordinary work. His reputation grew on air. And the greater his reputation, the more difficult it became for him to put it to the test by actually showing. The block seemed final. He doubted he would ever be able to get back to it.

Meanwhile he had an easy life. He taught in Chelsea a couple of days a week. He went to openings, to the right discothèques, was cheerfully promiscuous with a lot of girls on the London scene. There was always a party at someone's place, a weekend at someone's house, a holiday at someone's *château*....

It was a real coup for Andrew when he persuaded him to have a show.

'We'll have to hire a gallery,' Andrew told him. 'I'm not

just quite ready to branch out on my own—not for a year or so.'

'That's all right, man. That's really O.K. It's really better. I don't want to feel, you know, the pressures. I may never need another show. I mean, this gallery art, it's really full of shit, man.'

'Yeah,' said Andrew. 'Sure.'

Nevertheless, he put a price of five hundred guineas on Max's work. And he guessed Max would not find it too difficult to accept his fifty per cent.

'Sure, man. Screw the pigs.'

There are three or four London galleries that, for anything between five hundred and a thousand pounds, will mount an artist's show. As part of their fee they handle the publicity and advertising, the printing, sending invitations, the opening party and all the necessary organization. It is usually a routine job. The critics ignore these 'vanity' shows. They rarely visit them and almost never give them notices.

Max Marske's show was not going to be like that, Andrew assured him. The gallery was in a good location, and that was worth their fee. But leave the rest to them, and you leave the show to die. Andrew spent three months canvassing support. His position at the Gallery of Modern Art was the best lever they could have. Not only was he known to every painter and every critic on the London scene, but a good many of them could see some possible need of Andrew —a job, a protégé, the loan of a painting for an exhibition— that required them not to offend him now. It all took time. The art world is a fabric of reputations and friendships. Both are incalculables, and both need to be continuously renewed. Andrew was adept at calculating time against worth, and giving the result an appearance of casual friendship.

The night before the opening, Max rang Andrew.

'Andrew. I have to see you, man.'

'What is it? You sound ill.'

'No, man. I'm not sick. I'm O.K. But I have to see you.'

'O.K. Come over. I'm here for another hour.'

'No. I'd rather you came here. Can you do that?'

With some impatience, Andrew took a cab to Max's

studio in Notting Hill. Max opened the door in a thin cotton African robe. He was shivering.

'My God. You look bad,' said Andrew.

Max's girl was on the mattress that was the main furniture of the room, with a pillow behind her back against the wall, smoking. Her legs were under a thin cotton spread. As far as Andrew could see she was naked.

'Hi,' she said to him, without smiling.

Max slid back into the bed beside her and pulled the cover to his chin.

A bottle of wine stood on the floor beside the bed. Andrew went to the kitchen for a glass. The sink was full of dirty dishes, with ash and crushed butts on the plates and in the glasses. He rinsed a glass under the tap.

In the other room, he squatted by the bed and held out the glass. The girl poured him wine. She took care not to cover her breasts. Her eyes were telling him she didn't go in for that bourgeois modesty shit. But she didn't say anything. She knew she had good boobs, firm and full, curving upward. The nipples were red. Were they sore, Andrew wondered, or did she rouge them?

'What's the matter with Max?' he asked her.

She shrugged. Her breasts rose and fell, presenting her nipples to him.

Andrew stood up and turned away. 'Max,' he said going to the window. 'Max, what's the matter?'

Max struggled up. He groped for his cigarettes.

'What's the matter? You on a bad trip?'

'I can't make it, man. I can't make the show. It's all wrong. It's full of shit.'

'What do you mean?'

'I mean, call it off. I can't make it. I don't want it.'

'But, Max . . .'

'Sorry, man.' He lay back, pulling on his cigarette and pushing a jet of smoke towards the ceiling.

'You can't do this.'

'It's my work, man.'

'It's nerves. You're nervous. It's natural.'

'Man, I'm not nervous. I'm not the type.'

'Everyone's the type. It shows different ways. You're nervous, believe me.'

'Cancel it, man. That's what I say.'

'No, Max.' He was beginning to lose his patience—dragged to this joint just for Max to have a fit of first night nerves. If he wanted comfort, he had the girl. She seemed sympathetic. She had beautiful tits. He could see her hand caressing Max under the cover.

'You can't cancel it now. Don't be so damn stupid. You know you can't cancel it. The whole thing's set up. I've worked for three months to set this thing up. I'm not going to stop it now.'

'I said cancel it, man.'

'Oh for Christ's sake, Max. Grow up. If you cancel it now you're finished. It'll take you ten years to make it up. Is that what you want? I don't believe it.'

The girl had pushed the cover back from Max. She hung over him, stroking his legs, moving up under the robe. Her back was to Andrew, bare now as far as the cleavage of her buttocks. Her breasts hung over Max's face. He did not move.

Andrew put down his glass. 'Forget it,' he said. 'Try to forget it till tomorrow. Think of something else. Get pissed. Get stoned. Let the lady help you.'

The girl lowered her head to Max's stomach. His eyes closed.

'Forget it,' said Andrew again, as he went to the door.

Next day Max turned up at the opening. Neither of them mentioned the previous evening.

The show was a success. Andrew talked himself dry. He set up interviews in half a dozen papers. He got Max on TV spots. He provided free prints of Max's work to the Press. He wrote letters, followed up with calls, combining threats with promises, both equally vague. And Max co-operated, as Andrew knew he would. He lectured at the Institute of Contemporary Arts. He modelled some very tight clothes for *Men in Vogue*. On TV spots he came over as sexy, charming and persuasively intelligent on the new directions in modern art.

'The way I see it, there are things you just can't do any more. That's why I didn't paint for three years. It's too late for painting.'

'But surely, plenty of painters do still—paint?'

Max shrugged, and smiled. He was too nice a guy, wasn't he? to knock his fellow artists.

'But you, nevertheless, would call these—er, these works of yours, they are works of art?'

'Works of art? Not creative art. Not any more. There's no place any more for the pretentiousness of "creative art". This is—well, I guess it's demonstrative. You could call it "demonstrative art". Nature. The eighteenth-century idea. What did the man say? "Nature I loved, and next to Nature art." We have to get back to Nature, man. You know, we're killing ourselves with pollution, and we have to get back to Nature before it's too late. That's what I mean—demonstrating Nature, getting into Nature. You know, it's sexual —loving it and getting into it.'

'But your works do specifically make use of mechanical aids, do they not? They employ technology. Indeed, without technology, they would not exist.'

Max's 'demonstrative art'—a phrase that gave journalists and critics a useful peg for their articles—was a simple device. On the wall of the gallery hung rows of blank white shapes. Suspended from the ceiling, one for each canvas, were spotlights, masked to project light in the exact size of the canvasses. They threw coloured patterns, soft-edged blobs, delicately tinted, grouped at random, often crowding to the edges.

'It's beautiful,' said Max. 'Beautiful!' as if astonished at his own creation.

'But would you not call these works of art?' insisted his interviewer, who had himself earlier described them as 'sensuous, coolly erotic'.

'Oh man, you're full of crap.'

Andrew was watching the TV interview on the monitor in the hospitality room. He laughed out loud. Max was really cool. Putting down the interviewer as a phoney, when his own work was no more than an elaborate hoax. Those delicate 'sensuous' patterns were blown-up projections of bacteriological cultures. Andrew laughed again, enjoying the joke. That's the art world, he thought. That's how it is.

But his triumph was short-lived. Ten days after the show closed he had a call from Bob Wetherby. Andrew sensed danger as soon as he heard the cheerful tone of

Wetherby's voice. He seemed to have time to waste. He chatted on about the latest prices, the state of the trade, the rumours of the next gallery to close, the thefts and forgeries.

Then he said—too casually—'Seen Max lately, Andrew?'

'Max?'

'Max Marske. Have you ... ?'

'Not for two or three weeks I suppose. Why?'

'Oh. Oh dear. I thought he would have talked to you.'

Andrew waited in silence to hear what he already guessed.

'He did say he would talk to you himself. I made him promise that. I suppose with Max that doesn't mean too much. Andrew, I find this so embarrassing. I'm sure you will understand that I have been most reluctant to do such a thing. I would never have done it to—a friend, not to a friend such as you. But Max was adamant, that if it was not me it would be someone else. Oh, I do wish he had spoken to you. I'm disappointed in him. He should at least have had the courage to do that. After all, you have done a lot for him. Quite a lot. . . .'

Andrew interrupted. 'O.K., Bob,' he said. 'Don't overdo it.'

He put down the phone. Wetherby was enjoying himself too much. 'Embarrassing!' Like hell it was! He would have gone on carving up Andrew as long as Andrew was willing to let him.

And that's the art world, too, Andrew thought.

He began to feel that familiar sensation at the back of his head—the gathering depression. These moods were becoming more frequent. He panicked now when he felt them coming on. He had tried every way to avoid them. Nothing seemed to work. He never knew how long they would last— an evening, a day, two days. At least he'd learned to understand that, if he hung on long enough, he would come out the other side. The hell was waiting for the mood to clear. Nothing would take his mind off it, but some things helped. Usually he spent the time at the movies, going straight from one to another until he felt he could be sure of sleep. . . . How long would it last this time?

Wetherby was five years older than Andrew. Would Andrew in five years' time be in that position—a gallery in Bond Street, another in Manhattan, a third opening shortly in Paris, and another on the West coast? Everyone knew Wetherby. Even outside the art world he was something of a celebrity. Compared to him, Andrew was just another Bond Street 'runner'—nibbling at the edges of the gallery scene. He was certainly knowledgeable—but that was not enough. There were a thousand other ambitious men around who knew the market, the prices, the clients like the backs of their own hands. Perhaps they, and Andrew, were too keen. Wetherby was cool. That was certainly a point in his favour. The longer you kept your stock, the more valuable it became. That was the great paradox of the art world—the great dealers were always *reluctant* to sell. They said that Wildenstein in New York had a practically priceless stock—two Botticellis, ten Goyas, nine El Grecos, three Velasquezes, seven Watteaus, ten Cézannes, ten Van Goghs, *seventy-nine* Fragonards ... and were quite unwilling to sell. And of course, when they did sell, they made sure if they could that the paintings went to museums or national collections where they were safely off the market. So they made a pile of money and at the same time improved the value of the paintings they retained.

But a new dealer cannot afford to wait, unless he has vast resources. Andrew, in these terms, was penniless. On the other hand, Wetherby had no money of his own either. He'd made the classic move—and made it work. His partner had money and connections, and he had flair. Ten years ago he'd been in the same position as Andrew. It *was* possible, he told himself for the hundredth time. It *was* possible.

But there were times when he wondered, even if it was possible, whether it was worth it. It was fine if you succeeded. Success cancelled out all the mean humiliations on the way. But in these black moods Andrew had so little confidence in the hope of success. His steps up the ladder seemed so small, so amateur, so pathetic.... What had he achieved? He had commissions for a couple of American collectors: for one he had bought $100,000 worth of English sporting paintings—but he worked on the despicably small commission of five per cent. Otherwise the collectors might as well use the regular dealers. There was no future in that if you were looking to stock up with Titians at a hundred or thousand dollars a throw.

Once Andrew had 'borrowed' his parents' life savings. He meant to work up the reputation of an English painter of the twenties, somewhat out of fashion. From his widow, Andrew had bought seven of his paintings—the last that she had. There were few others around. He put one up at Christie's and bought it himself—through two nominees bidding against one another—for three times the previous record for this artist's work. That price got the artist talked about in the art world. Art advisers began to talk about him as a recommendation for investment. Two months later another three paintings were sent in to Sotheby's by an old girl friend of the artist. They were bad examples of his work. When he was with her, evidently his mind was not on his work. The prices sagged. Andrew knew it would be a year, if not two, before they showed much improvement. His parents were nervous for the security of their savings. He sold the remaining six paintings, and only just got his money back. It taught him the same lesson once again— money buys time, and you need to have a stack of both.

Now that he thought about it, all his enterprises seemed ineffectual. What was the extent of his influence? He could arrange a magazine article for an up-and-coming painter (he'd take a painting in exchange). He scoured salerooms and junk shops—one day, he 'knew', he would come across one of the famous lost paintings, Constable's The Glebe Farm, or Stubbs's vast heroic painting of Hercules and Achelous....

Sitting in the darkened cinema, almost deserted at three in the afternoon, Andrew recognized these hopes for what they were, daydreams, as empty as the escapism on the screen in front of him. Again and again in his head he repeated the same phrase: 'I must do something. I must do something.'

5

'Never,' said Lady de Boys vehemently, 'never shall I allow myself to become an ancient monument.'

The party round the pool had been discussing the future of Boys Hall. For weeks Lord de Boys had lain in the East Wing, hanging on to life by a thread. The problem of the future preoccupied them all.

'It seems to me,' Andrew said gallantly, 'extremely unlikely that anyone is ever likely to mistake you for such a thing.'

This was his second visit to Boys Hall. He was fascinated by Delphine. She was so confident, so arrogant. And still sexy. She'd rather obviously taken a lot of care to stay that way. But it worked. Her body was evenly tanned. In June every year she went back to her parent's house in the hills behind Nice and worked on it for three weeks. It was typical of her thoroughness.

In her black bikini, she lay in the deck chair and raised her hands gracefully over her head. Round her neck, on a silver chain of heavy, square links hung a pendant of iron, painted red and black, made for her by Calder. At Andrew's compliment, she smiled briefly. Her eyes flickered over his body. 'The house, of course I meant. Imagine. One becomes an employee of the Ministry of Works. What an appalling prospect. Could anything be less glamorous? I couldn't bear it. Why should I allow all those people to gawp at what I have had to fight for years to achieve? Let them go and make their own collections. They haven't got the guts to do it themselves, that's the trouble. And I don't see why I should be forced to share what I have done with them.'

Andrew rose from his deck chair. The canvas sling seat was decorated—somewhat suggestively, he thought, as he glanced back—with the painted figure of a nude man. Delphine had commissioned seats for her pool chairs from a dozen different artists. Andrew had been lying on the Hockney. He walked now slowly to the diving board, moving slowly, gracefully, aware of Delphine's eyes on him. He felt naked. He wished Corinna would take such obvious interest. Or any interest at all.

'Did you say "gawp", Mother?' Corinna asked.

'Did I? Yes "gawp". Isn't it a marvellous word? I learnt it from Mrs Baxter.'

They all laughed.

Delphine was annoyed. She frowned. 'It is English, isn't

70

it?' Her accent was undetectable. Twenty years ago her English had been almost comic.

'Yes. Yes, but ...'

'But what?'

'Nothing, Mother. It's a perfectly good word.'

'Gawp. That's what they would do. If we were an ancient monument the Ministry of Works would *encourage* them to come and *gawp* at my things.'

Andrew stood at the end of the diving board, and the gesture she made seemed to include him in 'her things'. He dived.

The pool had been built five years ago. That was when Delphine had at last achieved her great ambition and built the 'Bauhaus' wing, joining the East wing and the West wing on the south side of the house. Already it was one of the architectural landmarks of Britain. It was indeed a remarkable achievement—an uncompromising structure of steel and tinted glass erected between towers of red Elizabethan brick. And it was an undoubted success. The materials, instead of clashing, complimented one another. The contrast emphasized the rough 'natural' texture of the bricks, and, equally, the polished elegance of the new building.

On the first floor of this wing were a couple of new bedrooms. But mainly it was taken up with a huge drawing-room. This was furnished in uncompromising modern style, with the 'classics' of modern furniture—Mies van der Rohe's Barcelona chairs, the metal-bound Corbusier armchairs, the Marcel Breuer tables. The walls were painted stark white, and there hung paintings of the New York school—a Jackson Pollock action painting, a monumental Rothko in red and deep purple, an Albers Homage to the Square, a de Kooning Laughing Woman, works by Robert Motherwell, Jim Dine, Nolan, Stella, Olitski, Nevelson. Delphine travelled every year to New York, direct from the South of France. She was well known on the New York scene. All the painters she bought were represented by carefully chosen examples. By buying paintings, Andrew recognized, she bought herself into a certain social scene. But it took at least a certain wit to end up with *good* paintings. 'People think I am playing,' she said to him once. 'But I work. I like doing anything well—collecting well is also hard work.'

As she pointed out so often herself, the paintings she had bought were already worth three times what she had paid for them.

The ground floor of the Bauhaus wing contained the changing-rooms and showers and, along the interior wall, more modern paintings. Opposite the south side was a wall of sliding glass panels that opened on to the terrace of the swimming pool. The pool itself was the last word in luxury. All year it was heated to a temperature of 78 degrees. In cold weather a transparent polythene cover, operated electrically, slid silently into place, covering the pool and the terrace.

'It's a great pool,' said Andrew, standing beside Delphine and towelling himself down.

'Yes,' she said, 'I love it. It was *fearfully* expensive.'

'I'll bet.'

'But it was worth every penny. My father died, you know, and left me some money. It paid for this. I never had any money before, and I haven't any now. I haven't a bean left —not a bean. But I have this. And do you know why I have done it? I have done it for Boys Hall. Boys Hall is alive. You see, that's what I mean. It must never be an ancient monument. Ancient monuments are dead.' There was a strange look in her eyes. The tendons stood out on her neck. 'Nobody knows how much this has cost me,' she said. 'I will defend it with my life.'

'What about the people tomorrow,' Andrew asked. 'Won't they gawp?'

'No. I don't mind them. They are invited. I suppose I should rather that they did not come. But it is our duty to do these things. David taught me that,' she added with grave expression.

You old liar, Andrew thought to himself, almost laughing out loud at her audacity. Over the next two days, the Saturday and Sunday, the annual charity cricket match was due to take place in the grounds. During the tea break on Saturday afternoon the house was traditionally opened to the players, and Delphine showed them the paintings. It was hardly a hardship to Delphine, Andrew guessed, to guide round two dozen sweaty young cricketers.

'I suppose it does me good, really. One is apt to forget

72

what ordinary people think about pictures. It is quite revealing. They've heard of Raphael, and Rembrandt. They snigger a little at the Diana, but they can see that these paintings are important. For one thing, they are old. And for another, they are beautifully painted. With the Impressionists it is rather different. They have heard of Picasso, and Van Gogh. They don't actually like the paintings, but they know they are valuable, and they *try* to like them. But when we get here, to these rooms, they are mystified. Most of the paintings represent nothing. They are immediately out of their depth. I mean, if Picasso paints a girl with two left eyes, at least it is a kind of girl. But these splodges, targets, bands of plain colour.... I can see they think I've been swindled, paying money for these things. I have been taken for a ride.'

'Does that annoy you?'

She smiled. 'No. You see, I know that in time—a long time, perhaps when I am no longer here—in time they will recognize the importance of these paintings. I don't mind if they laugh at me now. I say to them, "You think these paintings are a fraud, don't you?" "Well ..." they say, looking down at their boots. You English—I shall never get used to you. You would rather be polite than tell the truth. "I know," I say. "I know you think they are not serious paintings, they could have been painted by a child. But you are wrong. They *look* easy. Some of them, I know look—well, accidental. But if you think it's so easy, you just try to create that sort of accident yourself. You'll find that it doesn't work." '

On the upper lawn the head gardener, Barnard, was working with a fine rake and a bucket of earth. He was making repairs to Delphine's latest purchase. During a recent visit to New York she had met a young Los Angeles artist and had agreed to pay his expenses to come over and create an 'earthwork' at Boys Hall. He had stayed three months. For two weeks he walked about the grounds and waited for inspiration. For three weeks he measured out a design and laid out complicated guide lines with white tape. And then he decided the ground was too wet to be worked. He mooned about the house, unconcerned. Giles was quite irritated. 'I suppose he was all right,' he told Andrew later. 'Not much

73

to say for himself. You know these young Americans—damn casual. His hair was pretty long.' So was his prick, I bet, Andrew had said acidly to himself. He guessed Delphine was not too concerned that the ground was too wet. But all the same, you had to hand it to her. She never chose her protégés merely for being well hung. This boy evidently had talent too. At the end of six weeks he had tied thick layers of felt round the tyres of a tractor and driven it to the centre of the lawn. Then he had hitched the plough behind it and, very carefully, driving slowly but steadily on his own guidelines, ploughed a clean double spiral, fifty yards across, in the smooth green turf.

Delphine had been delighted. She declared it to be a *great* success. She wanted all the right people to know that she was 'doing interesting things'. She always entertained freely but that spring half the art world came for the weekend—chiefly to admire her earthwork. Barnard was charged as a personal responsibility to keep it free of weeds.

Then Polly's father, thinking he would do least damage where the ground was already dug—he thought it was to be a new flowerbed, he said afterwards—landed his helicopter smack in the middle of it. It didn't do anything to improve his relations with Delphine.

'What did I tell you?' she shouted at Giles. 'The girl is quite unsuitable. Her father is a philistine. An oaf.' She was hysterical with rage. 'I forbid him to bring that damn machine here ever again.'

Delphine's two Siamese cats were sprawled languorously on silver Andy Warhol cushions beside her chair. (Another Warhol cushion, filled with helium, floated up against the ceiling of the gallery. The gas had been escaping and it was somewhat wrinkled.)

Andrew felt that he had allowed Delphine to monopolize him. It was getting a little obvious. He could tell from the expression on Corinna's face that she was miles away. And it did seem almost indecent to be sitting beside that luxurious pool, talking of painting and artists, when Lord de Boys's life was ebbing away somewhere within the house. But that was not Andrew's fault.... Delphine should have been with her husband. But even then—how could Andrew judge? Perhaps Lord de Boys preferred to be alone? Perhaps

74

he had asked her to stay outside in the sun with her guests.

'I'm going to see Father,' Corinna said quietly, not to any-one in particular. They all seemed preoccupied that after-noon. The air was hazy with heat, like a pall lying over the whole countryside. It was somehow sinister, almost frighten-ing, the immense heavy silence.

Tim picked up his towel. 'And I'm going to see how they're getting on down at the ground,' he said.

'I'll come with you,' said Andrew, 'if that's O.K.'

'Sure,' said Tim easily. 'Fine.'

Sally Marchant sank back in her chair. Andrew guessed she had been going to suggest she went with Tim, but de-cided against it when Andrew said he'd go along. It was no news that she did not like him. He had done his best to befriend her, but her dislike was almost a chemical reaction. They talked politely enough, but she was not even able to hide the effort it was costing her.

'If you're going up, Fidget,' said Delphine, 'tell Father I shall come up as usual when Carol goes.' She smiled sweetly at Andrew. 'We are reading Proust together. We read for two hours every afternoon before dinner. I am so enjoying it.'

Andrew felt himself flush with shame.

*

As Corinna walked without hurrying along the corridors to Lord de Boys's room she was thinking of Andrew. All after-noon by the pool she had been watching him surreptitiously while her mother played him like a fish. It was amazing the way Delphine drew men to her. To Corinna her tactics seemed so blatant. And at her age somewhat disgusting. Yet she did not think any less of Andrew for allowing himself to be dazzled. On the contrary, she felt protective to him. ... She understood the insecurities that made him so easy to impress.

Delphine was leading him on quite callously. She saw very little merit in him. At least, that was what she said. The previous evening, after dinner, while the men were sitting over their port in the dining-room, Andrew had been the first topic of conversation among the ladies in the draw-ing-room.

Almost immediately they sat down, Delphine had said, 'I'm not at all sure that I like that young man, Andrew.'

'No,' said Sally. 'I'm sure I don't.' She realized she had spoken too eagerly. 'I mean, I don't really know him, but I don't really...'

'He's a rogue. I'm sure of it.' Delphine was looking hard at Corinna. Corinna herself was thinking how much she wished she could be in the dining-room with the men, where the conversation would not be so bitchy. And they would be making up for the deficiencies of the meal with crackers and creamy Stilton spooned from the cheese on the sideboard. She felt her mouth begin to water.

'I don't trust him. I believe he's on the make,' Delphine went on.

'Yes,' said Polly. 'Yes. I'm sure you're right.'

Corinna said calmly. 'I think he's rather sexy.'

'Oh Fidget. Really.'

'What's the matter? He *is* sexy, surely?'

'He's not my type at all, I can assure you.'

'Oh Mother!' She had vowed never to compete with her mother over men. The idea was faintly disgusting anyway. Her mother's extra thin body seemed too desiccated for sex. But Andrew was not one of Delphine's 'discoveries'. He had been invited as a friend of Tim's—and that made him fair game for all comers.

'Well, I don't find him sexy—in the least,' said Polly. For weeks she had been abjectly agreeing with everything Delphine said, hoping to make up for her father's false landing on the earthwork.

'Well, I certainly do.'

'Fidget, you're disgusting.'

'He's also on the make. I grant you that.'

'Well, good heavens, how *can* you like a person like that?'

'I didn't say I did like him. I said he was sexy.'

'But surely you can't...?' Polly began.

'But actually I do like him,' Corinna went on.

'Oh really!' Delphine snorted and shook her head con-temptuously.

Corinna leaned forward, elbows on knees, holding her

76

coffee cup out in front of her. 'Look, Mother,' she said seriously, her dark eyes looking directly at Delphine. 'You must understand why a man like that is on the make. He doesn't have any alternative. It's all right for us. For us the doors are open. We think we have hard times, but by the standards of most people we do pretty much whatever we like. Well, look at your collection. I know you've worked hard at it. But you could never have done it if it hadn't been for your position here, and the money you inherited from your father. You didn't have...'

'I worked for them.'

'No. They were given you. You worked *with* them.'

'That's a matter of opinion.'

'All right. I don't want to argue with you. All I'm trying to say is that someone like Andrew suffers from pressures we don't understand. He has no security. All the time he's looking for a foothold. It's very difficult to be a decent human being when you're thinking about that all the time. I'm not saying he shouldn't be, that everyone shouldn't be. But I don't think we have the right to criticize him for not being, when we have no real conception of the difficulties. I'm sure there are perfectly good reasons for him being what he is.'

'I'm not criticizing. I'm certainly not criticizing,' Delphine insisted. 'I'm sure there are perfectly good reasons for him being what he is. I simply feel that I don't have to have that sort of person as a guest in my house.'

Corinna had not continued the conversation. She was not, she told herself severely, going to be affected by her mother's bitchy jealousy.

But as she walked slowly along the corridors, musty in spite of the open windows, she tried to define what it was she found sympathetic in Andrew. It was not just his looks. There were plenty of goodlooking studs in the neighbouring country that she hated the sight of. She decided finally that she was able to see, as the others apparently were not, that not far below the surface, Andrew was a vulnerable personality. If only he would allow himself to relax, not to pretend to himself that he was so damn hard-boiled, he might even find a real human being inside there somewhere.

Corinna was smiling as she tapped gently at the door of Lord de Boys's room and went in without waiting for an answer.

'Hello, Father.'

His face brightened as she bent over to kiss his brow. The skin of his face was thin as parchment, etched with deep lines of suffering. His body was fleshless, like two sticks laid in the bed under the blanket.

Corinna dismissed the nurse. 'I will be here until Carol comes,' she said.

When they were alone, she smiled conspiratorially, as if their being alone was a forbidden pleasure. She began to tell him about the simple events of the day—her horse had stumbled in a rabbit hole but seemed unharmed; the preparations for the cricket match (she had spent all yesterday afternoon in the cottage baking cakes).

Lord de Boys specially liked to hear about the cricket match. Now an annual tradition, it had been started by him immediately after the war, twenty-five years before. Before he was ill he used to supervise every detail himself. He would have the gardeners moving covers on and off the pitch for weeks beforehand. And on the day of the match he would be out at 6.oo in the morning to check that the ground was in good condition.

Weakly Lord de Boys reached for Corinna's hand. 'Corinna,' he said huskily.

'Don't talk, Father. It isn't necessary.'

'Yes, I want to talk to you.' He spoke slowly, painfully, with heartbreaking effort. 'I don't want you to say anything to Mother. But I'm soon—I'm going soon.'

Corinna pressed his hand. Tears welled in her eyes.

'Yes. It won't be long now. I knew you would understand that I wished to say this to you. I don't want to say goodbye to anyone else.'

'Father. Please. You don't have to say these things. I understand.'

'No, I want to tell you. I must tell you how happy I have been that you have been my daughter.'

'Yes, Father. Yes.'

'For me, you have truly been my daughter. You have made me happy.'

The words came so slowly Corinna wondered if he would finish the sentences. His voice was rasping in his throat.

'Father. Please. Don't strain yourself.'

'I have made my will. I have made a new will...'

'Father. Please. Don't tell me. I don't want to know. I shall go away if you don't stop. You must rest. I shall go and leave you alone. There will be time enough for all that. I don't want to hear it now.'

*

'If you're going down to the cricket ground,' Delphine said to Tim and Andrew as they came out of the changing-room in shirts and slacks, 'do just have a word with Barnard and ask him to be sure and clean off the Henry Moore.'

'Right oh, Mother,' said Tim, suppressing a smile.

'I do wish peacocks could be housetrained. I'm often tempted to get rid of them. They do make such a mess. But they look so well.'

'They make a damned awful noise in the morning,' commented Tim.

Delphine ignored him.

'She's magnificent,' said Andrew as they crossed the lawn.

'For a weekend, yes, I suppose she is. To live with, she's a pain, I assure you.'

Andrew laughed.

'Oh, don't think I dislike her. I'm very fond of the old girl. But you have to remember that as a person she is three hundred per cent selfish. As long as you keep that in mind, she makes a great mother.'

Tim spoke without rancour. His voice, his movements, his sentiments were all of a piece—the casual English type. But Andrew was beginning to understand that Tim had a tough core underneath that relaxed exterior.

And now he felt a knot of excitement in his stomach. He had been waiting for the right moment. This seemed the perfect opportunity.

'Why don't you do something on your own?'

Tim turned to him. 'What do you mean?'

'Oh I don't know.' It was unbearably hot. Andrew could feel the sweat running down the small of his back. 'You're

79

pretty interested in painting. Why don't you open a gallery?'

Tim looked at him oddly. 'You know, Andrew, that's amazing. That's exactly what I should like to do.'

'Well, why don't you? It's a good time. Everyone's buying art these days. It's even considered a safe investment—you know this as well as I do. But why don't you do it? If'—he hesitated—'I don't know what you're planning, but if you need any help ... you know, I'd be glad to be involved in a thing like this.'

'Thanks. Thanks. I shall take you up on that, you can be sure.'

'I mean it. I hope you do.'

'But where I really need help at the moment is on the financial side. I mean, if you have a bit of money that could set us up, that would be the best help you could give us.'

My god, Andrew thought. This is ridiculous. The man is asking *me* for money. Was it not meant to be the other way round?

He laughed. 'No, Tim. That I can't help you with, I'm afraid. I don't have any money at all.'

'Neither do I. It's a bugger, isn't it?'

'Couldn't your mother ... ?' Andrew began.

'She hasn't got a cent. Spent every penny she ever had—not that she'd part with it if she had any. Of course she liked the idea of having a finger in a gallery. You know what she's like. She tried to persuade Father to put up the money. But he wouldn't. He was sorry and all that. But he says enough Boys's money has been spent on art in the last twenty years. I can't say I blame him.'

'Couldn't he sell something? Is everything entailed?'

'No. The contents of the house are his. He could sell something. But he doesn't want to. That's all there is to it. He wants to preserve the things we have.'

'And you agree with him?'

'It makes no difference what I think, does it? They're his.'

'No. I know. I was just asking how you felt about it.'

'Well—I don't see any reason not to sell something. I don't think one should sell everything. But this mania for preservation—we become the slaves of our inheritance. We're always being told we were born with a silver spoon in our mouths. Sometimes it feels more like a gag.'

They walked in silence across the springy turf, over the neck of the lake on the hump-backed bridge to the lower lawn where the match was to take place.

Andrew could not believe that there was not some way in which Tim, with all the security, and all the connections the family had, could raise the money he needed. That was the trouble with these people. They had never learned to fight. They gave up too easily.

'It's no good,' said Tim, as if it were no more important than missing a TV programme. 'There just isn't the money to be had. Sally's got nothing much of her own either. Her parents are living on capital.'

'Oh,' said Andrew. He was deeply disappointed. He had misjudged the problem with Tim. Somehow he had imagined that the difficulty would be to galvanize him to make some sort of decision. He had not imagined that money would be any real difficulty. Looking round him now at the rich acres of Boys Hall, the well-kept lawns, the gardeners trimming the drive hedges, the fat cattle and the glossy horses grazing in the park beyond the ha-ha ... it seemed ridiculous that anyone connected with such riches could say he had no money.

On the lower lawn the mower had been out over the grass for the last time. At the centre the creases were marked out in perfect white lines, and a great oval boundary line had been drawn round the outside of the pitch. Beside the summerhouse—now changing-room and scoreboard—a refreshment tent had been erected under the elm trees.

As they stood at the edge of the drive looking over at the ground, a girl on a bicycle approached from the direction of the lodge. She was neatly dressed in sandals and a short cotton dress. Her hair was fair, and her pretty face had an open, cheerful look.

'Afternoon, Carol.'

'Afternoon, Mr Timothy.' She smiled cheerfully at him. 'Afternoon, sir,' she added to Andrew.

'Good afternoon,' he answered.

'Pretty girl,' Tim said as she cycled on.

'Who is she?'

'Carol. Carol from the lodge. She's going to do her turn with Father.'

'She live here?'

'Oh yes. Parents been here for years. Mrs Baxter's done the cooking for ages. We used to play with Carol.' He smiled wrily. 'My first fuck, Carol was.'

Andrew smiled. 'You could have done worse.'

'Sure. She's a nice girl. Giles too. I think he was *her* first as a matter of fact. Giles and Carol had a bit of a thing you know at one time. They fixed up one of the rooms in Corinna's cottage—there was no one living there then. They used to sneak out there in the afternoons. But her mother found out.' He laughed at the memories of those good old times. 'She'll be down in the kitchen before dinner. Why don't you try to catch her?' He was evidently delighted by this idea. 'You could do worse. Nice girl. Fantastic tits. Why don't you? Enjoys a good fuck.'

Andrew laughed too. 'Thanks,' he said. 'Maybe I will.' This conversation was quite amazing. The head of the family was up there in the East Wing, at death's door, and the family seemed quite unconcerned. They sat around casually and talked about cricket, and art, and fucking the servants. The British aristocracy were really incredible.

*

And the stiff upper lip, if that's what it was, did not tremble. At dinner that evening conversation was of friends in London—their engagements, their ventures into mobile discothèques and Chelsea boutiques. They spoke of the various dances to be held locally in the summer. Polly's parents gave one every year. 'How brave,' Delphine commented, with scarcely veiled disapproval.

It was not as if they were unaware that Lord de Boys was gravely ill. They discussed his estate at some length. He had made a new will only two weeks ago. Alberto, the Italian butler, had been called to witness it. Alberto was actually at that moment pouring the burgundy for Giles to taste, but they spoke about him as if he was not there. And his own expression gave no sign that he realized they were talking about him.

The meal consisted of thin soup, and then a pike caught by one of the gardeners. Delphine had given him permission to fish in the grounds provided he handed over half of anything edible he caught to the cook. The fish was actually too small to feed them all. But, boiled plainly, without herbs or sauce, its earthy flavour was so unpleasant that Andrew was glad to have such a small portion. They all—except Delphine—made up with enormous helpings of cheese. What they spent on Stilton, Andrew thought, must easily have cancelled what they saved on the rest of the meals.

Later, when the men came into the drawing-room, Corinna was sitting in a corner apart from the others.

Andrew went to her. 'May I sit by you?' he asked.

'I hoped you would.'

'That's a beautiful chess set.'

'Yes, isn't it? It's Chinese, I think. Seventeenth century.'

'And jade.'

'Yes, I believe it is.'

'It's beautiful.'

'Well, yes, I've always liked it. But to tell the truth I wasn't just admiring it. I was hoping *some*one would ask me to play.'

They played for two hours, almost without speaking. The TV set was on at the other side of the room, but they shut it out of their minds. Corinna played coolly, picking up the pieces after long intervals of concentration and moving them gracefully. Andrew realized quite soon that she was going to beat him. But it did not matter. He was playing well enough. It was not important to win. There was not that sort of competition between them. While he was waiting for her to make her moves, Andrew watched Corinna closely. He began to see the details of her appearance—the soft down on her arms, the flat end of her long fingers and the rounded, unpolished nails. She looked so gravely and calmly at the board while she considered her move, scarcely even blinking. The parting in her hair was a deep black shadow. Her hair was so fine and smooth, falling like a black wing over her forehead. He wanted to reach out and touch it.

'Check,' she said finally, without a smile.

'Yes. You have me. You win.'

'Yes. I'm afraid so.' She stood up. 'Thank you,' she said

simply. 'I enjoyed it. And now, if you don't mind, I'm going home.'

'I'll take you,' Andrew said.

'No. Thank you. I have my Rover. I shall be perfectly safe.' Her eyes were telling him not to be offended. 'I'm very tired. I shall see you tomorrow. Thanks for the game.'

Andrew had not realized that the cricket match next day was to be quite such a production. Play started at 11.00 in the morning. At that time there were already two hundred spectators present. The Lord Lieutenant of the County made a speech. He referred to Lord de Boys 'tragically overtaken by ill health in the prime of his life'. Andrew stole a glance at Delphine. She was looking straight ahead into the trees on the far side of the field. She might have been deaf.

In front of the summerhouse a number of seats had been put out inside a rope enclosure—for friends and relations of the teams. And for guests at Boys Hall, of course. Andrew had intended to spend an hour or two looking at the Boys Hall paintings. He had also planned to ask Lady Amelia if he could look at the Canalettos in the Mill House. He wanted to be sure he had them all listed. But Corinna had come to the house before they finished breakfast, and she and Andrew had come down to the cricket match together.

'Are you a cricketer?' she asked.

'I learned to play at school. I wasn't much good at it. I never made the team, or anything like that.'

'You're lucky they didn't ask you to play here. There's usually someone who doesn't turn up.'

'If I'd known it was going to be as grand as this I'd have worn the old school tie.'

Corinna laughed.

At lunchtime the Regimental Band of the local yeomanry played selections from *My Fair Lady* outside the refreshment tent. Inside the two teams sat down to lunch with the Boys family. Every year Lady Amelia insisted that it was her duty to be there—mainly because Delphine insisted that it was quite unnecessary. Lady Amelia's duty, however, was also to her racehorses. She did have to keep an eye on the racing results. She had two runners that afternoon. After some trouble with the aerial her portable TV was set up beside her at the head of the table. She scarcely spoke to

84

the team captain beside her for the entire meal. While her horse was actually running the table was reduced to silence. It finished seventh out of eight.

After lunch cars arrived by the hundred. The cows had been moved from the field behind the lodge and the gardeners organized parking there. People were everywhere. It was like a fairground without the sideshows. Dogs barked at the ducks on the lake. Occasionally one would run on the pitch after the ball. A queue formed at the refreshment tent. The little baskets were filling with plastic cups and ice cream cartons.

Even in the shade of the elms it was unbearably hot. Giles had been batting for two hours. He played a defensive game, content to save his wicket without adding much to the score. It was not very interesting to watch.

'How is your father today?' Andrew asked Corinna.

'About the same,' she said evenly.

'Doesn't it upset you that your father—that Lord de Boys is so ill? You all seem so—well, so calm about it.'

'You can speak of him as my father. Most people do.' She looked at him directly and he could see the anger spark in her eyes. 'Of course we are upset. Because we don't show our emotions for everyone to see, it doesn't mean that we feel nothing.'

'That's a very English attitude.'

'Perhaps. What's wrong with that? You're English too, surely?'

'No. I'm South African. Haven't you noticed my accent?'

'I suppose so. It's very slight.'

Andrew cursed himself for offending Corinna. They had spent the day in one another's company. A sense of intimacy had grown between them. They were both aware of it. Andrew had begun to feel he could be natural with her, he could relax some of that defensive dishonesty that he built round himself.

Corinna stared ahead, with a stony expression on her face. But after a minute she turned to him and said, in an almost tender voice. 'Andrew. Look. He is ill. He is extremely ill. He's not going to recover—there's no point in pretending to myself that he is. Nobody knows better than me how ill he is. But you must understand, surely, that the

85

only possible thing to do is to go on as if it was just a temporary setback. It's the only way to cope with it. It isn't just that it's easier for us. I don't suppose it is, in fact. But it is easier for him. He knows we are pretending. But we know he knows. There's no deception in it really. Do you think Mother wouldn't rather spend every minute of the day with him? Why do you think she's reading Proust with him? There are twenty-four volumes of that book.' There were tears in her eyes. 'They'll never finish it. Father knows it. And Mother knows it. But they both pretend they're looking forward to going right through it together. It would take them two years.'

'I'm sorry,' said Andrew. 'I'm sorry. It was stupid of me.'

'Yes,' said Corinna, with a soft smile, warm but sad. 'It was. But don't worry. I understand.'

Barnard's grandson was in charge of the scoreboard, rearranging the tin figures on the hooks at the end of each over. As Giles eventually reached his fifty, the spectators applauded thinly—most of them not knowing why they were clapping.

Andrew said to Corinna, 'Would you do something for me?'

She looked at him, waiting to hear what it was. Questions like that, her expression said, do not need an answer.

'Would you like to make me a cup of tea?'

She smiled. 'Yes. I'd like to.'

They drove to Corinna's cottage in Andrew's old MG, with the hood down. The roads were dusty, shimmering in the heat. They passed great expanses of ripening wheat. There was not even a breath of wind. The fields stood like golden reservoirs, contained by high green hedges. The only movement came from the larks that hung over the fields, rising and falling as if on threads, pouring their throbbing song into the sky.

Andrew knew the way from his earlier visit. He drove steadily, controlling his first inclination to put his foot down and make for the cottage like a madman. The air poured into the car on them like warm water. They neither of them spoke.

Andrew drew up at the gate of the cottage and turned off the engine. Neither of them moved. The silence was almost unnatural, like a physical presence. It was broken suddenly by the sound of a horse whinnying from the stable.

Corinna turned to Andrew and smiled.

'I know just how he feels,' said Andrew. He took Corinna's arms and drew her to him. He kissed her slowly and gently.

The cottage door was not locked. Inside, by contrast, it seemed cool. The sunlight threw squares of brightness on the walls and carpets, spotlighting random objects—a patch-work cushion, a picture, brass candlesticks.

Corinna went ahead, and Andrew followed, up the narrow stairs to the bedroom, with its low ceiling and chintz curtains. Then she turned and waited for him to come to her.

They kissed again, tenderly, their lips gently drawn together.

But suddenly Corinna was urgent. She pressed herself to him, parted his lips with hers, gripped his tongue with her teeth.

'Oh Andrew. Andrew. Quick. I want to see you. Quick.' She began pulling off her clothes, as if the feel of them on her body would drive her mad. 'Take off your things. God. I want to see you. I want to see you.'

Now Andrew was urgent too. He kicked off his shoes, flung off his clothes.

They stood facing one another, naked. Her eyes were smiling into his. Then she stepped forward and grasped him.

With a sigh she said, 'Oh, I wanted to see that.'

'It's . . .' Andrew began.

'Ever since yesterday. I've been . . . Yesterday. By the pool. Ever since . . .'

'You were watching me? I didn't realize you were interested. I didn't know you were even watching.'

'Of course I was watching.'

She lowered her head and touched him with her lips.

But Andrew raised her head. He put his arm round her and took her to the bed. He threw back the covers roughly. 'Lie down,' he said. 'I want to see you too.'

'We don't have so much to see.'

'Oh yes you do. That's where you're wrong.'

He leaned over her, admiring the smooth skin of her breasts, the nipples like dark buds, the brownish aureole, a shade darker than the olive skin. It's good to take it slowly, he thought, when there's no doubt you're going to get there in the end.

'There's a lot to see,' he said, smiling, 'when you know where to look for it.'

He lowered his mouth gently, touching with his tongue.

But Corinna pulled him down on her. 'No,' she breathed urgently in his ear. 'No, Andrew. Quick. I want you now. Now.'

Andrew felt her come with him, felt the tension drain away from them both. They lay together, without moving. The touch of their bodies smoothed all the misunderstandings of mood and gesture and intonation, the edgy dialogue of the last twenty-four hours.

Corinna sighed under him. In his ear she breathed, 'Oh that was so good.'

'For me too.'

They turned on their sides, still clasped together, still joined.

'I'm sorry about last night,' Corinna said. 'I was afraid you'd think I—I didn't want to.'

'Well, I certainly wondered.'

'I wanted time to think. That's all. I wanted to be by myself for a while, to have a chance to think. That's necessary sometimes, isn't it?'

'Yes. All right.'

'And today, I knew I needed to be with you. I'm so glad you're here. Being alone is fine—most of the time I prefer it. But every now and then you need someone.'

'Well, I'm glad I was here.'

'Oh, don't get me wrong. It's not just anyone that you need. You need someone you like, who understands.... I didn't mean that. Don't be offended.'

Andrew was still hard inside her. He pushed his hips against her. 'Do I seem offended?'

'No. Not that I'm fool enough to judge by *that*.' She gave him an answering pressure. '*That* has no conscience, isn't that what they say?'

Slowly Andrew began to move.

'Does it make any difference, that he's not your real father?'

'No. I've always thought of him as my father. I love him as if he was my father. Except...' Her voice was uncertain. 'I don't know. These last weeks I've begun to realize that it's not quite the same. I've sort of allowed him to take the place of my real father. I never knew my father. And Father —Lord de Boys—was there, so I didn't have to think about it. But now I realize it wasn't really the same thing. I think I do need my real father.'

Andrew stroked her back soothingly, drawing her gently to him, moving his hips.

'I think that's natural. We all need to know our parents. It helps understand what we are ourselves.'

'The funny thing is, I've always felt more like Father's— Lord de Boys's daughter than I have Mother's. I'm not really like her at all, that I can see. I look a bit like her, but...'

'She's one of those people. Exceptional. Exceptions to everything. Even their children are not like them.'

Corinna herself was moving against him now, drawing breath deep into her lungs and letting it out in long sighs.

'The only thing we have in common is fancying you.'

'She doesn't fancy me.'

'Oh Andrew. Don't be silly. You know perfectly well she does.'

'You said she only liked dark men.'

'At night all cats are grey.'

They were moving together now, talking wildly.

'But in the afternoon, I'm glad to say, the difference is obvious.'

Outside the swallows were chattering at their nest under the eaves.

Andrew's mouth found Corinna's. The sheets were cool and smooth to their skin. Andrew let himself float away. It seemed he was rising out of his body, yet he was aware of nothing else but its physical sensations. Moving together, the rhythm grew faster, more urgent.

On the table beside the bed the phone began to ring.

Andrew stopped.

'No. No,' Corinna said desperately. 'Leave it. Don't answer it. Oh Andrew. Andrew.'

89

The shrill ring of the phone continued. Whoever was calling was really persistent. Corinna and Andrew clung together, shutting their ears to the harsh sound, concentrating on their bodies.

Andrew could feel his climax approach, an irresistible, rising tide within him. He felt that Corinna was with him. The sound of the phone was there. Or perhaps it wasn't. All that existed for them were their bodies, the aching, deep private joy of their communion....

For a while they were silent, floating still, slowly descending, ballooning by slow degrees to ground level.

'Who was that on the phone?'

'I don't know. It could have been anyone. It doesn't matter. If I'd been out with the horses I shouldn't have heard it.'

'But you weren't out with the horses.'

'No. But that doesn't mean I have to answer the phone.'

Andrew drew away from her.

'What's the matter?'

'You're so sure of yourself, aren't you. All of you, you're so sure of yourselves.'

'What do you mean, all of you?'

'All you people. Your family. All the people like you.'

'Oh. I see.' Her voice was cold. 'No. I don't think it's us particularly. There's surely nothing wrong with being sure of yourself. It's a matter of knowing yourself for what you are. You don't have to be "people like us" to be sure of yourself in that way.'

Andrew leaned from the bed and found cigarettes and matches from his trousers' pocket on the floor.

'Cigarette?'

'No thanks.'

He lit one for himself and put the packet on the table beside the phone.

He felt Corinna was watching him.

'It bothers you, doesn't it?' she said.

'What?'

'It bothers you that there are people like us. People that have things that you haven't. Without working for them.'

'It doesn't bother me. It's a fact.'

'Oh Andrew.'

'What does bother me is when I see the opportunities just not being used.' He was fighting to control his irritation. It was true, it did bother him. The whole world was wide open to these people, and they couldn't even organize edible food. 'When you are born with opportunities like that, you have a duty to take advantage of them. You *ought* to make some constructive use of them.'

'And do you think I'm making "constructive use"?'

'I don't know. I don't really...'

'Oh Andrew. Don't hedge. You don't, obviously.'

'Oh, I understand. I understand how difficult it is. We have these estates in South Africa. I suppose I shall inherit one day. One day I shall get all that. It isn't easy, I understand that.'

'Oh Andrew. You don't have to lie to me. Really.'

'I'm not lying.' He drew on his cigarette through clenched jaws. 'Why should I lie to you?' He couldn't bring himself to tell the truth. Why was it always like this? Why was the truth never good enough for him? Why did he have to treat Corinna like this? He cared about the girl, yet he couldn't even pay her the compliment of telling her the truth. She wasn't deceived, he knew she wasn't. Yet he had to go on lying. And she was so frank and open with him. Even sexually she was frank, frank about wanting him. 'Oh that was so good,' she had said, frankly acknowledging her own pleasure. But of course it was easy for these people. They could tell the truth. It didn't matter what they said. The rest of us, he thought bitterly, are vulnerable. The rest of us have to be careful, even with the truth.

The silence was broken by the sound of a car approaching the cottage. It stopped outside. Andrew looked at Corinna. She was staring at the ceiling, as if she had not heard it.

A car door slammed.

'Corinna!' The voice was Delphine's. She called urgently, angrily. 'Corinna!'

Corinna did not move. Nor did Andrew. Some force held him down on the bed, some instinct that told him he was not part of the drama that was about to unfold in front of him.

'Corinna!' Delphine beat on the front door with her

fists. 'Corinna! Where are you? You must be here. The car is here. Someone must be here.'

Now Andrew heard her in the room below them. 'Corinna!' A note of anxiety had entered her voice. 'Corinna! I have to see you. Where are you?'

She was coming up the stairs. Still Corinna lay motionless.

'Corinna. You must come. Where are you?'

The bedroom door burst open. Delphine gasped. 'Oh! Oh! Corinna!'

Suddenly her voice was controlled. With deep, cold fury she said, 'Corinna, you must come. Father is dead.'

'I know,' Corinna said quietly. 'Yes. I will come.'

Delphine stood at the door. Her face was flushed. Her eyes ran over the two bodies. Andrew did not move to cover himself. He watched her eyes move down his body again. At least he was not going to give her the satisfaction of getting a rise out of him.

*

Corinna told Delphine they would come straight to the house. But Delphine waited in her car at the door of the cottage until they came down.

They dressed in silence. There was nothing to say. Corinna had wanted her mother to see her in bed with Andrew. She recognized that, and was ashamed—as if Lord de Boys's dying was not painful enough, she had to add this sexual taunt, like a cheap whore. She had known when the phone rang what it was. She had deliberately ignored it. He was not *her* father, she had told herself. He could die with his own family, without the benefit of her attendance. When her real father died, would they gather at his bedside? Perhaps he was already dead. Perhaps he had died alone somewhere, without the comfort of the woman he loved, without the child of their union.

As they stood ready at the door of the bedroom, Corinna kissed Andrew solemnly. 'Thank you,' she said. 'I enjoyed it.'

Andrew held her arms and kissed her lightly. 'That's what you said after our game of chess.'

'Yes,' she said. 'I enjoyed that too.'

When they appeared at the door of the cottage, Delphine drove off. Andrew followed. It was difficult to keep up with her. She was driving flat out, taking corners on the wrong side of the road, not even hesitating at crossroads, recklessly overtaking. Whenever they drew up close behind her, Corinna could see that she was hardly looking at the road, but turning her head from side to side, repeatedly adjusting the rearview mirror. She should not have been allowed to drive. Corinna cursed herself for not thinking of this. Delphine was in a state of shock. She was beside herself—was it grief or anger?

By some miracle they reached the Hall without an accident. As they turned in to the drive Corinna looked across the lake to the house. She almost gasped. The fact that for twenty-four hours she had been refusing to acknowledge, hiding it in her heart like a guilty secret, was there displayed for the world to see : the Boys' standard was at half mast.

6

Lord David de Boys was buried in the family vault in the mausoleum on the estate. Andrew sent a simple wreath.

Corinna called from the cottage and asked him down for the weekend.

'Won't your mother object?'

'I don't see why she should,' said Corinna calmly. 'It's no business of hers who I ask to stay here.'

'Oh, I see,' Andrew said. 'I thought you were inviting me to the house.'

'I'm asking you to stay with me.'

It was a busy time for Andrew at the gallery. They were getting together two separate travelling exhibitions of British artists, ready to tour in the winter. As usual, everyone was behind schedule. The artists did not deliver their work on time. The framers were late. The packing-cases took two weeks longer than planned. The printers failed to keep their date.

Andrew himself had written the catalogue introduction for the show of British Surrealist Art—the first serious study of the British branch of the Surrealist movement ever undertaken. After touring ten cities, the show was planned to end up at the Gallery of Modern Art during the following summer.

His job was going well, but it gave him no satisfaction. He had been doing it so long it was becoming a routine. And the chance of breaking out on his own seemed as remote as ever. He felt hopeless, with a growing desperation. At thirty, there were not many years left of being a bright young man. The moods of bitterness recurred more and more frequently. The green dragon was growing restless. A break, that was all he needed, Andrew told himself. Oh, he knew everyone said that. But in this case it happened to be true.

Andrew had seen Mel German at one or two parties, and several openings. It was inevitable. Andrew's job took him to these places, and Gerry was practically part of the furniture.

They had neither of them referred to the evening at Gerry's house. They met by chance, and they talked of the usual topics of the narrow world of the art scene. They never talked for long. There were no more invitations to dinner.

But one evening, at a candlelit reception given in the Tate Gallery by the Friends of the Tate, Andrew found himself in a corner with Gerry. Gerry had evidently been working at getting his money's worth of champagne. But alcohol did not seem to give him a lift. He looked lonely, and desperately unhappy. Andrew began to feel sorry for him.

Though not as sorry as Gerry was for himself. 'Nobody wants to talk to me,' he said miserably.

'*I'm* talking to you,' said Andrew.

Gerry touched his elbow. 'Yes, dear boy. Of course. I do appreciate it. Thank you.' He seemed perfectly serious. 'But you know what I mean. They don't even seem to want to laugh at me any more.'

'Who do you mean? Why did they laugh at you?'

'Oh, you know. Everybody. I know they were laughing at me. I didn't mind them laughing at me. As long as they don't ignore me. They can laugh at me as much as they like. It's the price I have to pay for them to take any notice of me at all.'

'Oh Gerry. Don't be ridiculous.'

'No. It's true. If there's one thing the law teaches you, it's to see things as they are and not to allow your judgement to be clouded by emotion. These people have tolerated me for two reasons. One was money. But I have only a very limited amount of that, as you know. And anyway, money alone is not enough. There are plenty of successful men about with more money than sense. But as well as a little money, I give them someone to laugh at. They like laughing at other people. I am vulgar, and ugly, and pathetic....'

'Gerry. For God's sake. Don't do this to yourself.' He'd always suspected Gerry enjoyed the humiliation he got from some of those people. He actually looked for it. And now he was desperate that no one despised him any more.

Gerry took Andrew's elbow. 'You're so kind to me, Andrew. You've always been kind to me. I'm very conscious of that.' He drew Andrew further into the corner and turned his back to the crowded, noisy room. 'As a matter of fact,' he said, lowering his voice, 'I was going to telephone you. I have taken the liberty of recommending you to a friend of mine....'

Andrew felt the anger rising in him. What right had this fool of a man to recommend Andrew without asking him first? He could imagine the sort of embarrassing friends that Gerry would try to get him involved with.

'... An acquaintance I should say, perhaps. More of a business acquaintance than a friend. An American. Unlike me, he is *extremely* rich. A *multi*-millionaire. Indeed, according to *Fortune* magazine, he is one of the fifty richest men in in the world. Oil, I believe, was the foundation of his fortune. But his net is now spread very wide. His corporation has interests in canned food, TV, films, timber, property, newspapers.... As I say, he is extremely rich. Fortunately, however,' he said with a sly look at Andrew, 'there are some things that money can't buy.'

95

'I hope so,' Andrew said. 'And you have recommended me to this ... this...?'

'Lennox. His name is Lennox. His name wasn't always Lennox, of course. Lennartowicz. His father, I believe it was, was a Polish immigrant. You know how they are over there. There seems to be no *loyalty* to a family name.'

'But what can I do for—Mr Lennox?'

'My dear boy, can't you guess? You know these multi-millionaires. You've lived in New York—where I understand the streets are paved with them. As soon as they realize they're rich, what's the first thing they want?'

'Good taste—and they need it retrospectively.'

'Well, culture, at least. I'm not sure that even they imagine they can acquire good taste. But culture they believe is attainable. They feel insecure about it, of course. They only understand the judgements of computers. Everything has to be put to them in terms of monetary value, so that the computer can read it. They manage it somehow. Even women are pretty well assessable. But with culture, they need someone to translate it for them into computer terms.'

'Forget the philosophy, Gerry. What are you getting at?'

'Calm yourself, dear boy. I merely recommended to Mr Lennox that you might be prepared to advise him in connection with acquisitions for his museum.'

'His museum?'

'Of course. Don't they all have a museum? Mr Lennox does at any rate. In California somewhere. I suggested that you might be prepared to keep an eye on the Continent for likely pieces....'

Andrew was fully in control of himself again. 'That's nice of you, Gerry.'

'Not at all. Not at all. As I told our friend Lennox, I only wished I could afford to make use of your services myself.'

'Gerry, you old fraud. You know damn well you don't need me....'

Gerry eased his collar with his finger. 'My goodness, it's hot in here, isn't it?' Sweat was running off his forehead. In his black tie and dinner jacket, with his gross stomach bursting the starched white shirt, he looked, Andrew thought, like a penguin trapped in a turkish bath.

96

'Go to see him, dear boy. He's at Claridge's. He's expecting you to get in touch with him.'

*

Ashton Lennox's suite at Claridge's was impressive but colourless. Even the sprays of orchids in the vases were unobtrusive shades of cream and brown.

Ashton Lennox himself was quiet and serious. With so much money he had a lot on his mind.

His assistant, McIntyre—a stocky Scotsman of about forty, with greying hair and frown lines set permanently in his forehead—poured Andrew a drink at the sideboard. Andrew drank 'Scotch, thank you, on the rocks, no water ...'

Without further introduction, they put him through a whole education on the Lennox collection. McIntyre produced a list of paintings, in alphabetical order.

Andrew glanced through it. The entries ran from:

ADAM, Albrecht 1786-1862 Bavarian Battle Scene

all the way to:

ZUCCARO, Frederigo 1543-1609 Italian Portrait of Mary Stuart

Two hundred and thirty-four paintings were listed.

'You have all these?' Andrew asked.

'Yes,' said Lennox. 'Quite a shopping-list, eh?'

'It's very impressive. What are the asterisks?'

McIntyre answered him. 'On those,' he said, with great dignity, 'the authenticity is not wholly satisfactory.'

'In other words,' said Lennox, with a straight face, 'there's some folk say they're fakes.'

Meanwhile McIntyre had set up a portable screen and plugged in a projector. They gave Andrew a tour on slides of the museum at Santa Barbara, of all fifty-two rooms, and close-ups of all the major paintings. McIntyre gave a running commentary, with facts about each of the paintings, which he had obviously repeated many times before. Andrew guessed Lennox was always putting on this show to impress his friends. It was almost as bad as holiday movies.

But apart from the commentary, Andrew *was* impressed. Many of the paintings he recognized. They had been on the market over the last three or four years. Two Gainsboroughs and a Van Dyck came from a sale at Christie's less than a year before. Almost all the big names in painting were represented. They must have added up to a cool fortune of several million dollars.

In some cases Andrew too would have had grave doubts about the authenticity. The Raphael was almost certainly a student copy. The Titian looked like a fake—though it was difficult to tell with Titian. Either way, it was a very impressive show.

'How long have you been collecting, Mr Lennox?' he asked.

'Five years,' said Lennox, allowing a slight hint of pride to enter his voice. 'What do you think?'

'I think it's a remarkable achievement,' said Andrew. 'Remarkable.'

'And you would say the collection was—weak any place?'

'The Italian Renaissance. But that's inevitable. They're in short supply. There are almost no genuine Renaissance pieces that will ever come on the market again.'

'Yes?'

'The moderns. There's very little post-Impressionist. Perhaps that's a matter of taste?'

'It is, as you say, a matter of taste. I don't hold with that abstract junk.'

'If you don't mind my saying so, you may well find you grow to appreciate it in time. Painting is rather like music. Many people think they'll never grow to like the progressive stuff. It seems like a complete contradiction of everything they appreciated in the classical style. And after a while, after they get to know more about the subject, they find they get to like it....'

'Maybe,' said Lennox laconically. 'Anything else?'

'The Dutch,' Andrew said. 'The Van Dyck is beautiful. It's a great painting. But the Rembrandt—that's a very minor Rembrandt. If I had to guess, I'd say it was painted by a student. Rembrandt often signed student work if he liked it. Honestly, I don't think he should have signed this one.'

'Good,' Lennox said simply.

'Good? Why?'

'Because it's a fake. McIntyre here says it's not, but I'm telling you it is.'

McIntyre opened his mouth to object, but thought better of it.

'So you see,' said Lennox, as if it were a simple matter, 'what we need is a genuine Rembrandt. The real McCoy. A few other little things as well of course, but Rembrandt's right there at the top of the list. Think you can do that for us?'

'Well,' said Andrew cautiously, 'as a matter of fact, I think I might.'

Lennox's expression showed nothing. He could have made his millions playing poker. 'Good,' he said. He held out his hand. 'Mr Tait, you are working for us.'

They shook hands.

'You have my word on it. You can work out the details with McIntyre later.'

'O.K.'

'I want the Lennox Museum put right there on the map of the art world. A big red spot. A capital. Not just a hick town.... How much is my Rembrandt going to cost me, Mr Tait?'

'Two million dollars. Two and a half. Maybe three.'

'O.K. Whenever you're ready.'

Andrew did not go straight back to the gallery after his meeting with Lennox. Outside Claridge's the doorman had a row of cabs at his disposal. He made to open the door of the first in line as Andrew walked out. But Andrew waved him away. He walked up through Mayfair to Park Lane, walked along to the subway and crossed into Hyde Park.

And for an hour he walked there, turning over in his mind the implications of the interview with Lennox. Before he left he had arranged with McIntyre to have a duplicate of the 'shopping-list', and he was going back before Lennox left Europe with suggestions for filling in the gaps in the collection. He also had a commission to round up a dozen paintings for Lennox to take home as gifts for his family.

99

'You know,' Lennox said, 'good minor stuff, say a couple of thousand dollars apiece.' Andrew agreed to work for seven and a half per cent. Gerry had warned him he would have to offer himself at bargain rates.

Walking along by the Serpentine, half-watching the boats on the water, shimmering in the sun like a Seurat painting, Andrew decided that he liked Lennox. He was laconic, but he was straight. He did not pretend to knowledge that he didn't have. In fact he put himself over as some kind of red-necked philistine. But he really cared about painting. Maybe he didn't have a lot of aesthetic sense, maybe he cared more for the history of painting: 'This paint was worked on this canvas three hundred years ago in a castle in Florence, while this princess, in this ermine, posed by this window'—that was the idea that really turned him on. But it was a genuine, deeply felt response. He was evidently somewhat embarrassed by it. He kept insisting that the money was all that interested him. But Andrew could see that was not true.

But it was the Rembrandt business that really set Andrew's heart beating. Here at last was the break he had been waiting for. There was only one good Rembrandt in Europe that there was any hope of prying loose. And that was a great Rembrandt. And Lennox would really flip for it. That was important. That was the art of dealing—matching the painting to the buyer. For a good work, that his collection needs, a collector will pay a high price. For something he really falls for, he will ignore his financial advisers, and go mad. The Nude Diana was absolutely Lennox's painting. Andrew knew it was. Now he had to prise it loose from Boys Hall. That would not be so easy. But if it ever was to be gathered, now was the time when it was ripe. If he didn't get it now, it would be stuck there at least for another generation. Andrew did not think that that should be allowed to happen.

7

Corinna had asked Andrew to the cottage for the weekend, in case she needed protection. That was what she said. On the Saturday afternoon Lord de Boys's will was to be read. The family lawyer was coming from London.

'It's the traditional way,' she answered, when Andrew asked why such formality was necessary. 'An awful lot depends on it.'

'I can believe that,' Andrew said.

'Polly and Sally are stalking about up there at the house with terrible expressions, like Shakespearean queens.'

'But they won't be present when the will is read.'

'Good heavens no. Strictly family.'

After breakfast on Saturday morning they had saddled Corinna's horses and ridden for two hours through the woods and fields of the estate. They had not seen a single person. The hay had been carted, and the wheat was dark gold, almost ripe. The countryside was peaceful. It was that waiting period, the lull before the activity of harvest.

When they got back they watered the horses and rubbed them down. Then they went upstairs to bathe. Corinna was due at the Hall for lunch at 12.30.

'When it comes to money, people can turn really nasty,' Corinna said as she sat on the edge of the bed. 'Believe me. I trusted Father. While he was alive, I was one of the family. But now—well, it might just be convenient to remember that I'm not really "family" after all.'

'Your mother will look after you.'

'I wish I could be sure. . . . Give my boot a tug, would you?'

'But surely . . . ?' Andrew gripped the heel and toe of her slender black leather boot and drew it off.

'She has her own problems.'

'Maybe she's doing a bit of a Lady Macbeth herself.'

Corinna laughed. 'Something like that,' she said lightly.

Andrew drew off the other boot.

'Anyway, it isn't really fair to ask you to protect me from my own family.'

'I don't mind.'

'And it's certainly not the only reason I asked you here.'

'Oh?' he said, looking up with a smile. 'And how else, pray, might I be of service?' He had put down her boots and was squatting on his haunches at her feet.

'Take off your clothes, and I'll show you.'

Andrew laughed and stood up. 'Shameless. Quite shameless. I shall need protection. *I* shall ask *your* family for protection.'

'I wanted to when we were in the woods, but you didn't seem ...'

'I was too busy making sure I didn't fall off that horse. She can't have been exercised for weeks.'

'She's used to me, that's all. No one else rides her.' She smiled. 'Perhaps if you had fallen off it might have occurred to you.'

'I don't have your imagination, that's my trouble.'

They made love lightheartedly. Andrew lay on his back. Corinna sat astride him. They made a joke of it. She directed him into her, gripping him with her knees—riding him with the same smooth graceful rhythm she had ridden her horse two hours before.

While she showered and dressed to go off to the Hall, Andrew lay and smoked a cigarette.... He wondered why he had allowed Corinna to take the initiative. She had wanted him to make love to her earlier in the morning, out in the woods—and he had not even thought of it. It was not usually like that. He could not understand it. He really cared about Corinna. Yet he could not resist congratulating himself that she had asked him down to be with her on the very weekend that the future of the Boys inheritance would be settled.

He tried to put the thought out of his mind. But he could feel the depression settling in. He was glad Corinna had to go to the Hall and leave him alone to fight it.

*

Conversation over lunch was stilted. No one dared ask the

questions they all wanted to know. The lawyer did not help. Nothing seemed to interest him. An owlish old man, he seemed embarrassed by the situation. By the end of the meal all of them were convinced that the will contained provisions that would put every one of them out on the street.

Delphine suggested they ask for coffee to be served in the library.

The lawyer, seated at the leather-topped desk, accepted brandy and a cigar. Perhaps at lunch he would have talked about cigars, Corinna thought, if one of them had raised the subject. He seemed quite an expert. He held it under his nose and smelt it carefully. He produced his own silver cigar cutter and delicately trimmed the end. Before he finally lit it he warmed the tip with half a dozen matches.

Lady Amelia sat in a deep leather armchair and watched him with ill-concealed impatience.

Eventually, releasing a cloud of smoke, and a heavy sigh of satisfaction, the lawyer cleared his throat. 'This is a sad occasion for us all,' he began. 'I will be as brief as possible. The document before me on the desk is the last will and testament of the late Lord David de Boys. In a moment I shall acquaint you with its contents.' He cleared his throat and drew deeply at the cigar. 'It is quite short. As I am sure you all of you know, the lands and estates of the mansion of Boys Hall were not within the gift of the late Lord de Boys. Being entailed, they have already passed to the elder extant son and heir, Giles.' He nodded briefly in Giles's direction.

Lady Amelia snorted. 'Why doesn't he get on with it?' she stage-whispered to Corinna.

The lawyer cleared his throat. 'I, David Herbert Richard Suivant Proudfoot, fourteenth Baron de Boys, hereby revoke all former wills and testamentary dispositions made by me and declare this to be my last will....'

Corinna glanced right and left at the semi-circle of expectant faces. Anxiety, tension, even fear showed in every one. You might have thought they were criminals awaiting sentence, not a devoted family expecting a share of paternal benefits. And in a way, she thought, they were awaiting sentence—a sentence to a particular type of life, harsh or easy according to the whim of Lord de Boys. What terrible power money had.

Delphine's hands were clasped in her lap. Her knuckles showed white. Her name did not occur in the first part of the will. There were a number of small bequests, to Lord de Boys's batman, who had worked at the Hall after the war; to Carol Baxter and two or three other of the Hall estate servants.

The next section dealt with Lady Amelia. It was Lord de Boys's earnest wish that she be allowed to remain at the Mill House for the remainder of her life should she so desire. All the paintings by Canaletto at present hanging in the Mill House became her property absolutely.

Delphine's face was like stone.

'To my son Timothy I bequeath any such six paintings that he may select from those I die possessed of, to dispose of as he may wish.'

Giles and Timothy exchanged a quick glance. But Giles turned away almost immediately, as the lawyer read out his name. To him Lord de Boys left all the contents of Boys Hall and the entire residue of his estate, expressing the wish that he preserve it as far as possible without decrease for posterity and successive generations of the Proudfoot family. At the same time he entrusted to Giles the care of Lord de Boys's wife and Giles's mother, Lady de Boys, knowing that he could rely on Giles to make proper provision for her comfort and livelihood from the income of the estates. He further expressed the desire that Delphine, who had done so much to create Boys Hall in its modern form, should be permitted to remain in residence therein for the remainder of her natural life.

'These are all the material clauses. The remainder are concerned only with the formalities of administration and estate duty.'

Then, almost before any of them realized what he was doing, he rose from his chair, quickly shook hands with them each in turn, and left the room.

Delphine was the first to collect herself. Without a word she stood up and walked regally from the room.

*

The whole family filed out of the library in silence, avoiding one another's eyes. Polly and Sally were waiting in the saloon. They were pale and tense, but dignified, both of them. Like the wives of condemned men, Corinna thought. Everyone moved as if in a carefully rehearsed mime, finding their partners and separating to different parts of the house.

Giles and Polly went up to his study in the east wing. Polly went to the window and stood looking out over the park.

'Well?' she said.

Giles briefly ran through the provisions of the will. As he went on Polly's face began to assume a satisfied expression. She frowned momentarily at the bequest of paintings to Timothy. But she did not care much about paintings herself, and half a dozen fewer paintings from the hundreds in the house would hardly leave noticeable spaces on the walls.

When Giles came to the final clause a triumphant smile came to her lips.

'The entire residue? What does that mean?'

'Everything else presumably. All Father possessed when he died.'

'But what about your mother? Does she have money of her own? She says she hasn't a bean. Or did he provide for her while he was alive?'

Giles went to the bookshelves. One section of the shelves opened out, being in fact a door with rows of leather spines glued to it. In the cupboard behind were drinks and glasses.

'Would you like a drink?' he asked.

'No, thank you,' said Polly.

'Well, I think I shall. Are you sure?'

'Yes, quite sure.'

Giles poured himself a generous scotch. He drank the first mouthful with exaggerated pleasure. 'Ah. That's better,' he said.

'You haven't answered my question.' Polly was beginning to suspect that something was wrong.

'What question?'

'You know. What about your mother?'

'Oh yes, well ...'

'You're looking very sheepish, Giles,' Polly said sharply. 'What is it?'

'Well. Father wants—Father *wanted* Mother to go on living here, in the Hall, that is ...'

'No.'

'Well, I'm sorry old girl....'

'Never.'

'Well, I'm afraid that's what the will said.'

'But you said he left everything to you—the entire residue, you said. The house is yours already. How can the will give your mother the right to the house when it's already yours?'

'Well, it doesn't give her the right, that's true. It's Father's wish. He particularly wished that she continue to live in this house, which she has done so much to create.'

'To create? To create? She's practically ruined it. Your mother is the worst thing that's happened to this house for five hundred years.'

'It hasn't been here that long.'

'Oh, you know what I mean. The swimming pool. It's the most vulgar thing I've ever seen. That new wing of hers. It looks like a cheap plastic box. You should hear what people say about the things she's done here.... She's the laughing stock of the county. Of the *country*. She's spent a fortune on rubbish. Absolute rubbish. Imagine paying someone to plough up the lawn. Heaven knows how much she paid him —paid to have the grounds ruined.'

She was beside herself with fury. Her eyes were blazing and angry patches of red had appeared on her cheeks.

Giles sipped at his whisky and watched her with a strangely calm expression.

Polly turned to the window and pointed out into the garden. 'Look at them. *Look* at them.'

On the lawn below the window two of Delphine's sculptures were visible—one rising from the ground like giant sections of plumbing, made of polished shining steel; the other consisted of iron girders, leant against one another, apparently casually, painted raspberry and almond green.

'You know, I am ashamed. When people ask me what they are and I have to tell them they are sculptures, part of your mother's priceless collection of modern art, I am ashamed, I tell you.'

'But why?' said Giles quietly. 'Why should you be ashamed?'

'Well!' she said, as if the answer was too obvious to need expressing.

'Why should you feel ashamed? They're nothing to do with you.'

Polly looked at him incredulously. 'But surely you don't intend—you never intended to keep them? Don't tell me you like them. I know you don't. You told me a hundred times....'

'No. I don't like them. I don't understand them. But I certainly was not intending to remove them. I don't understand French poetry either, but I should not want it destroyed.'

'But ...' Polly looked at him as if she were seeing him for the first time, as if at that moment she had realized that all she knew about him was based on totally false assumptions.

'Polly,' he said. 'I intend to carry out my father's wishes. Mother will remain in this house for the rest of her life.'

'But no one else can ever be mistress of this house while she is here.'

'Perhaps not,' said Giles with a lethal calm. 'Is that all you want, Polly, to be mistress of this house?'

'Of course not. Of course not, Giles.'

'You have a simple choice.'

'I want to be your wife.'

'To live here with me on those terms....'

'I love you, Giles.'

'Or not live here at all.'

'I love you, Giles.'

'And if I ever hear a single word of disrespect from you towards my mother—at any time, either to her face or behind her back, you will go.'

Her tone changed suddenly. Her anger returned. 'You wouldn't dare.'

'I assure you.'

She stepped back and looked him up and down. 'My God! What sort of a mother's boy are you? You don't have to take any notice of the will. It's not legally binding, you said so yourself. You're frightened of her, that's what it is. You're a sissy, Giles, that's what you are. You're frightened of her. It's disgusting. Tied to your mother's apron strings. It's taken this to make me realize it. That's something I suppose. Do you think I'd want to marry a man like that? I always thought there was something peculiar about you. Now I know what it is. A mother's boy, that's what you are. A *pansy.*'

'I don't think you really mean that, Polly.' Giles's voice was icy.

Polly ran to him. 'Oh no. No. I didn't mean it. Oh Giles, I didn't mean it. Forgive me.' She clung to him, sobbing. 'I didn't mean it. I was so upset. Forgive me. It's been so terrible, Giles. It's been such a terrible strain.'

Giles held her in his arms. Polly buried her head in his shoulder. But Giles was looking over her head at the sculpture out in the grounds. As he watched, a peacock, on its favourite perch on the Anthony Caro 'girders', proudly opened the giant fan of its tail. A hundred eyes stared at Giles, unblinking.

*

Alberto rang the first gong for dinner as usual at 7.30.

Corinna and Andrew were alone in the drawing-room. They had arrived ten minutes before. No one else had come down yet.

In the car on the way over Corinna had told Andrew about the will. She would not speak about it earlier. She had come back from the Hall, pale and evidently distressed. 'Let's go to bed,' was all she would say. 'What, again,' Andrew had laughed. 'No,' she had answered. 'I don't want sex. I just want to be with you. To be close.' Even so, as she clung to him, her hand found and grasped him. Andrew had tenderly made love to her. The third time that day already, he thought, and only five in the afternoon.

In the car she had tried to tell him how she felt. That was not easy, since she was not at all sure herself.

'I'm certainly not upset,' she said. But she was not sure if even that was true. 'I don't need money,' she answered Andrew's unspoken question. 'The cottage is mine. I have a small income from Granny—from Amelia. I don't need much. Giles gives me feed for the horses.'

'But the will didn't say anything. He didn't mention you?'

'No. That's it. That's what hurts. He didn't have to give me anything, but at least ...' Her voice broke, and she turned away from Andrew. The road was narrow and the hedges sped by close to her face. 'He could have acknowledged my existence. Left me some little thing—a ring or something. I don't understand. I loved him. I loved him as if he was my father. And now ...'

She left the sentence unfinished. For the rest of the journey she was silent. She found a handkerchief in her bag and now and then pressed it to her eyes.

The second dinner gong sounded at 7.45. Dinner would be ready at 8.00. Corinna and Andrew were still alone.

'Where is everyone?' Andrew asked.

'They're all afraid. They're afraid if they're alone with anyone, the others will think they're cooking something up.'

'Christ,' said Andrew. 'It's worse than politics.'

'Yes.'

They lapsed into silence. Andrew read the morning's *Times*. Corinna held the *Telegraph* in front of her, but her eyes did not focus on it.

On the stroke of the hour the rest of the family appeared. Delphine was at her most impressive. She wore a long, narrowly fitting gown of black velvet. Her hair was drawn back and coiled meticulously on top of her head. It was the first time Andrew had seen her without at least one piece of her famous jewellery. She wore no more than her wedding and engagement rings. Giles and Polly followed down the stairs. Timothy and Sally were at their heels.

Delphine did not even sit down. 'Let us go in to dinner,' she said.

Then at the door of the dining-room, she stopped. 'Giles,' she said. 'I hope you don't mind. I told Alberto to rearrange the table.'

Only at one end of the table was a place laid. 'You are now the head of the family. You shall sit at the top.'

'Oh Mother,' said Giles. 'I don't want it to be like that.'

'I'm sorry, Giles,' Delphine said firmly. 'But I think you should understand the responsibility of your position.'

She took Polly's arm. 'Now, my dear,' she said. 'You come and sit over here.'

Polly followed her direction obediently. She understood the significance of Delphine's placing perfectly well. Delphine herself was to sit on one side of Giles, Corinna on the other. They were family. They belonged there. Polly, at the other end of the table, between Timothy and Andrew, was a *guest*. Well she thought, that's pretty well what she was: like a guest, she was there on suffrance of the host. Even when she and Giles were married, she'd still be a guest, as long as Delphine was on the scene. But she smiled. She'd pasted a noncommittal smile on her face before she stepped out of Giles's study, and she knew she damn well had to keep it there.

Alberto served the soup and poured the first glasses of wine.

As soon as he left the room, Delphine said, 'I think we should talk about the subject that is in all our minds, don't you?' She was addressing Giles. 'I'm quite sure we don't have any secrets from the guests we have asked to be with us at this sad time.'

She gave Andrew a hard, antagonistic glance. But she had more important fish to fry.

Giles mumbled, 'Yes, yes. Of course.'

'I'm sure you are all relieved to know the contents of Father's will. Of course, he had discussed it with me. But it didn't seem right for me to tell you what he intended.'

In fact, Corinna had said, the will had knocked her sideways. That made sense, Andrew thought. She was now totally dependent on her son. She would hate that. But she had made a rapid recovery. She had not wasted the last few hours. She had got it all worked out. She dominated the table. Andrew wondered if it could be generations of inbreeding that rendered the Proudfoot males so ineffectual, so easily dominated by new female blood. Perhaps it was a genetic fault. These tough females, like Delphine and Lady Amelia, married into the family, but they did not pass on their own qualities to their offspring.

'Of course, you must all have known that Father would provide for us, but still, it is a relief to be *sure*.' She smiled at Polly. 'We can all go on living here, just as we always have, which, of course, is exactly what Father wanted.' Her manner was grave, but charming. She looked round the table. No one was eating. 'Giles,' she said. 'Don't you think you should press the bell for Alberto?'

Giles blushed. 'Oh yes,' he said. 'Sorry. I knew I shouldn't have sat here.' He pressed the button under the carpet at his feet.

Alberto took away the soup plates and served roast lamb, carved wafer-thin, and swimming in gravy.

When he had gone, Delphine turned to Timothy. 'Timmy, darling,' she said, 'I don't know how you feel about things...'

Timothy shrugged. Andrew watched him closely. He could see that Sally's knee was pressed against Timothy's under the table.

'... but I must admit that Father and I did not agree about what he wanted to do for you. As you know, I did try to persuade him to finance you in a—a venture of your own while he was still, while he was still with us. I really did think that that would be best.'

Timothy was watching her warily. Andrew felt the excitement begin to knot his stomach. His instinct warned him to watch for a major confrontation.

'To tell you the truth, darling, I think Father misunderstood me. After all, he did expressly ask Giles to preserve our inheritance, "without decrease" I think was the lawyer's expression.'

'Yes,' said Timothy.

'I think he felt so unhappy that he couldn't do what I had asked for you. I honestly don't think he wanted to split things up. He wanted to help you, of course, darling. I'm not saying he didn't want to help you....'

'If you're talking about the paintings....'

'Yes, I am, darling. That's what we're all concerned with surely. We none of us would want to see a single one of the things we all treasure so having to leave the Hall. Once things go out, they never come back, do they? And our things are irreplaceable, that's the point. Once they're gone, they're lost for ever. Of course, if you want to borrow paintings for your flat, or a house, well, I'm sure Giles....'

'Well, actually, Mother'—Timothy's voice was deceptively

111

casual—'we've already decided which paintings we shall have.'

'We?' said Delphine sharply.

'Sally and I. We decided this afternoon.'

Delphine looked at Sally as if it could only be her influence that caused Timothy to defy her so flagrantly.

'Look, I say,' said Giles. 'It would be the most damned awful shame....'

But Delphine came straight to the point. 'And which have you decided to *take*?'

'Well, actually, we haven't decided exactly which ones. What we have decided is to have only one really big painting. We decided that would make less of a hole than half a dozen medium-range things. We don't want to take them either. We don't want to take Proudfoot things.' He was talking to Giles, not his mother. 'Obviously we could take the six biggest of the lot—the Raphael, the Rembrandt and so on. I suppose we could have lived in luxury for the rest of our lives. But we worked it out the other way. We started with how much we thought we'd need, and tried to think how we could get that and do the least damage.'

'How much you would need for what?' said Delphine.

'To open a gallery, Mother,' Timothy said patiently.

Andrew felt his heart jump. It was almost a physical sensation. Maybe a woman feels this, he thought, when she first feels her baby move in her. His eyes were smarting with excitement.

'But these paintings are our *inheritance*,' said Giles. 'I mean, Timmy, Father asked us to do all we can to preserve that. Isn't that what we all want?'

'He gave me the pictures to sell, Giles. He knew I had to have money. The will says "to dispose of", doesn't it?'

'But Timmy, you *can't*.' Giles looked helplessly at his mother. 'You can't just sell our paintings.'

Andrew had been pretending to concentrate on his food. Now he put down his knife and fork and said, 'Giles. How do you intend to pay the duty on what you have inherited?'

'I fail to see what concern that might be of yours, young man.'

'Mother!' said Corinna. 'Really!'

Andrew looked steadily up the table at Giles, waiting for

an answer. His nerve was cooling now. It was always like this. He was only nervous in anticipation. When the engagement finally came, he was cold as steel.

'I ... I,' stammered Giles.

'You'll have to sell paintings, surely? The contents of the house are worth millions. The paintings alone. You'll have to pay duty on that. And Lord de Boys must have known that. He must have expected that you would have to sell quite a number of paintings. Otherwise he would have made them over to you during his lifetime. Or at least made some other provision.'

Delphine was trembling with rage. 'How do you come to know the contents of my husband's will?' she asked.

'Because I told him, Mother,' Corinna said quietly.

'It's not a secret, Delphine,' Andrew said. He could see from the expression of disgust on her face that she regretted insisting he call her by her first name. 'Anyone can get a copy of the will from Somerset House.'

'Exactly,' said Timothy. 'Thank you, Andrew. It's not fair to treat us as some sort of—well, traitors, when you're going to be doing exactly the same yourself.'

'But Giles has no alternative,' Delphine said. 'He will be assessed on the whole of Father's estate.'

'I believe he could refuse the gift,' said Andrew.

'Oh really!' Delphine snorted.

'And the more valuable the paintings we take, the less duty Giles will have to pay.'

'Timothy, be serious. How can you joke about this?'

'I am serious. I've never been more serious. We've given it a great deal of thought.'

'One afternoon!'

'You can do a great deal of thinking in one afternoon, Mother, if you have to.'

'And what did you decide then? Which of our paintings are you going to take from us?'

'Well, it was a matter really between Raphael and the Rembrandt.'

'Oh no!'

'But I don't think we'll need as much as the Raphael.'

'Oh no! No!'

'Is Raphael worth more than Rembrandt?' Polly asked.

She had not spoken during the whole meal and she was beginning to feel she had to say something.

'Yes,' snapped Delphine with a really vicious smile.

'It's quite complicated,' Timothy went on, 'because of course we shall have to pay duty ourselves on whatever the paintings fetch. The Raphael would fetch two million at least. Above £1,000,000, the estate duty is 85 per cent anyway. By the time we've paid the auctioneer's commission we should be out of pocket.'

Andrew was beginning to think he had underestimated Timothy. He was shrewd and clear-headed. And thinking straight in that company needed a really cool nerve. It looked as if their partnership should use Timothy's brain as well as his social connections.

'We! We! We!' Delphine almost shouted at him. 'Who is we? This is your responsibility, Timothy. You can't avoid responsibility by trying to share it. You are responsible. You will bear the responsibility for what you are doing for the rest of your life.'

Something terrible seemed to be happening to Delphine. Andrew watched with horror. The defiance of her maternal authority seemed to be destroying her, almost literally. Her face was collapsing, its structure caving in before his eyes.

'And what,' she said hoarsely, 'what did you decide?'

'We decided that the Rembrandt would be best. The Diana.'

'Oh no! Oh no!' She held her chin high. Her face was a tragic mask. Tears ran from her eyes, streaming down her cheeks. 'Timmy,' she almost whispered. 'Timmy, darling. *Please*. Please, for my sake. Not the Diana. That painting—that painting I love best in the whole house. Anything but that. Please. Take anything but that.'

'But Mother'—Tim spoke evenly, calmly, but his jaw was clenched—'it will be painful whatever we take. What would you rather? The Madonna?'

'Yes. Anything.' She was trembling with emotion. 'Take the Madonna. But not the Rembrandt. Not the Diana.'

'No.' Giles's voice was firm. 'Not the Madonna. That painting must never leave the house. That is the Proudfoot Raphael.'

'Timmy. Please. I beg you. Not the Diana.'

'Giles.' Corinna's voice was quiet but firm. 'We are all upset. Surely this is not the time to decide.' She stood up. 'If you'll excuse me, I think I shall go home.'

*

Corinna and Andrew talked long into the night. But Andrew did not tell her of the things he was hoping for himself. For one thing, he believed in the power of secrecy. Shared plans never succeed. And he wasn't sure she would understand. He had the feeling that it would sound far cruder in words than it did in his head.

But his brain worried continuously at the possibilities. Two great chances had opened before him at once. If only he could pull off the double—persuade Timothy to sell the Rembrandt to Lennox, and then invest the proceeds in a gallery with Andrew as partner. No wonder he was not able to sleep. He lay in the dark and listened to the unfamiliar country noises: an owl hunting, a fox barking in the wood, sparrows fidgeting in the eaves. Corinna slept peacefully beside him. It was an effort to make himself lie still, so he should not wake her.

Soon after breakfast next morning, Timothy phoned. He wanted to come and see Andrew.

'Do you want me to be out?' Corinna asked.

'Well . . . Well, no, it doesn't matter.'

'That's all right. I've loads to do in the stables. Would Sally like to exercise the horses with me?'

'Well, I think she'd like to be there.'

'Oh, all right.'

'It sounds awfully mysterious,' Corinna said to Andrew. 'I hope they're not plotting something. I told you it would be like this.'

'You did. And to tell the truth, I didn't really believe you.'

But his mind was filled with his own plans. And plots, he thought, is only the word for plans you disapprove of. He lit a cigarette. His hand was shaking.

Tim and Sally, on the other hand, were brisk and self-possessed. Andrew had never seen them like this. They really were together. They both wore superbly tailored tweed suits, not quite his and hers. Andrew poured them the coffee Corinna had left, but they did not waste time with polite talk.

'We wanted to thank you for your support last night,' Timothy said.

'Oh. Well. That's all right. I only said what I thought.'

'Nasty business,' said Tim.

'Your mother seemed extremely upset.'

'I shouldn't worry too much about that,' Tim said drily. 'She has a low threshold of emotion. I've seen it too often to be much affected. And usually when she is not getting her own way.'

Sally left the talking to Timothy. She was watching Andrew. Knowing her dislike, he found her scrutiny disconcerting.

'How much should we get for the Rembrandt?'

'One million, eight hundred thousand pounds.'

'You're very precise.'

'That's my job,' Andrew replied. He smiled. 'And I am also accurate.' Two could play at the bright executive game.

'Yes. That's what we thought,' Sally said. 'More or less.'

'Sally's incredible,' Timothy said proudly. 'She always knows exactly what a picture will fetch.'

'She works in the right place. But of course, a lot depends —on what else is about. And who.'

'Yes,' they both said together.

There was an awkward silence. Andrew offered them more coffee. They both refused. So he waited for them to tell him why they had come to see him.

'Well,' said Timothy. 'I expect you're wondering why we came to see you. Well, the fact is, we thought we ought to tell you what we plan to do.'

Andrew felt his throat tighten. 'Oh yes?' he said. He hoped he sounded casual. 'I gathered last night that you *are* going to get into the gallery game. That's marvellous. Can you tell me about it?'

'Yes, well, that's roughly it. We shall go and stay at the castle for a while, while the formalities are sorted out. Sally has some holiday due.'

'The castle?'

'Sally's parents' place. Then we shall put the Diana up at Christie's.'

Timothy put on that tone of voice often adopted by the rich or famous that is meant to indicate that staying at the castle and selling a Rembrandt or two are everyday matters.

'The thing is,' Timothy went on, 'we thought—well, Sally thought'—he glanced in her direction, but she was looking out of the window. Andrew held his breath: this was the moment he had been waiting for, it seemed for as long as he could remember. 'We thought it was only fair ... well, we thought perhaps you were interested in some sort of partnership with us....'

Andrew opened his mouth to speak, but Timothy continued.

'... but, well, it would be super, of course. I'm sure you'd be a terrific help—but, well, we decided in the end we'd rather like to try and make a go of it on our own. I'm sure you'll understand.'

Andrew could taste the disappointment like bile at the back of his throat. 'Yes, of course,' he managed to say. 'Of course I understand. I think I should probably want to do the same myself, if I was in your place.'

He smiled as he said it. But the bitterness was choking him. It was Sally who had set this up. He guessed that. That bitch had never liked him. 'Sally thought it was only fair...'

If she thought it was so damn fair, why was she so busy avoiding his eye and looking out at the apple trees in the orchard. She must have seen them a hundred times before? She was getting a kick out of it. She'd got Timothy to come to the cottage just so she could watch him rub Andrew's nose in it.

He didn't intend to give her the satisfaction of seeing his disappointment. And he hadn't finished yet.

Perhaps it was not the best time to raise the idea of Lennox buying the Diana, but it was the only time he had. He could see they could hardly wait to get the picture off the wall and up to St James's. And it was not going to be easy to persuade them. Now the cards were on the table Sally was watching him as if he had crawled out of a crack in the wall.

Andrew had two arguments in his favour. First, that by selling to Lennox, they avoided the auctioneer's commission.

'But when you get above ten thousand, the commission's only ten per cent,' Timothy said.

'Ten per cent of two million is twenty thousand.'

'And eighty-five per cent of it goes to the Estate Duty Office.'

'So does eighty-five per cent of the rest of whatever you get. You'll need to keep every penny you can.'

'But it's important to Sally. Don't you see, Andrew? Christie's will be pleased she brought it in.'

'But she'll be leaving anyway, surely?'

'Oh no. Not for a year at least. Not until the gallery is on its feet.'

But he could see that his second argument got home to Timothy. Selling to Lennox would be discreet. A sale at Christie's would get maximum press coverage. Famous Rembrandts are not sold every week. The TV cameras would record every detail. The gossip columnists would be up at Boys Hall getting the reactions of the family. Particularly Delphine, the famous collector. And that was a reaction Andrew was sure they would rather avoid.

'Yes. But we could suffer it if necessary. And I somehow think Mother would take care not to make too much of a fool of herself in print.'

'But that's not the real point. A sale to Lennox could be discreet, yes. But much more important—the actual price could be secret. I'm sure Lennox would co-operate. We could fix an "official" price, and arrange some sort of additional payment on the side. There are ways and means. The Estate Duty Office need never know.'

'I see,' said Timothy thoughtfully.

'You're really going to have to think about that estate duty. If you're not careful, you'll find yourself without even enough left to set yourself up. Eighty-five per cent away from anything doesn't leave much to put away in the bank.'

'Well, yes. We had realized that it isn't going to be easy.'

Sally crossed the room and stood by Timothy. She faced Andrew squarely.

'I don't think you understand,' she said. 'I'm sorry

Andrew, but the fact is that Timothy and I would just rather not do business with you.'

'I see.'

'I never liked you, as I think you know.'

'You've made it quite clear.'

'I've always tried to be polite. After all, you were a friend of Timothy's.'

'Oh, you've always been exceedingly polite.'

Sally took hold of Timothy's arm. 'I didn't tell you before, Tim,' she said. 'But do you know what he did on Friday? He insisted on telling me some disgusting story about you and that girl from the lodge—Carol Whatsername?'

'Oh, Sally. That was a joke.'

'I don't know about a joke,' she snapped. 'He even tried to make it seem,' she continued to Timothy, 'that there was some sort of *relationship* between you still.'

'Don't be ridiculous, Sally. Of course it was a joke.'

'He was trying to break us up, Tim. He knows I can't stand him, and he was trying to break us up. He's despicable. I wouldn't sell the Rembrandt through him if he had the last customer on earth. I wouldn't sell a ... a *postcard* through that man.'

Andrew turned on his heel and walked from the room. There was no point in staying. She really hated him. Arguing about it was not going to do any good.

He crossed the yard to the stables. The black mare he had ridden the day before was in her stall. Corinna was out on the bay gelding, her other horse. Why did they have to cut the balls off everything, he thought?

He was almost blind with rage and frustration, but he worked frantically. The mare's tack hung where he had left it. He lifted the saddle from the post and laid it on the mare. She began to shift her feet uneasily. Andrew reached under her belly for the girth. He speedily fastened the buckle, tight enough for him just to be able to slip his hand sideways under it. Then with a sudden sharp movement he tightened it another two holes. The mare lay back her ears, sidling away from him.

'Stand still,' Andrew hissed at her.

He slid the bridle over her muzzle and pressed the bit between her teeth. He handled her roughly. She was kicking

119

back her head to get away from him. He smacked her nose sharply. 'Cut that out. You can cut that out,' he said.

By the time he had mounted her and taken her out into the yard she was nervous and excited, skittering sideways, pulling at the bit. 'Whoa. Whoa,' he said roughly, bringing her round in a tight circle. 'Quiet, damn you. Whoa.'

Sally and Tim appeared at the door of the cottage. They looked at him in amazement. 'Does Fidget know that you . . . ?' Sally began.

But Andrew turned the mare towards the house and dug his heels in her side. She bounded forward, a great leap up from her haunches, her hooves clattering on the stone yard.

Sally and Tim stepped back. 'My God!' Sally turned to Timothy. 'Stop him. Tim. You must stop him.'

Andrew laughed. He would not have cared if he had ridden over her. He loathed that girl. If there was one certain way to make him dislike people, it was their disliking him. He did not understand why she disliked him so heartily. What had he done to annoy her? Of course that story about Carol was meant as a joke. Why did she have to bring that up? How could any girl make a scene about a thing like that these days? But maybe it was what he had not done that annoyed her. Should he have made a pass at her? Maybe that was it. Sexually she did not interest him. So she was insulted. She wasn't his type, that was all. Those thoroughbred aristocratic girls, thin and leggy like racehorses, he probably wouldn't even be able to get it up for her.

He ground his heels into the mare's ribs, urging her on across the fields at full gallop. The sides of her neck were soon showing dark sweat marks. As they entered the woods he tried to reign her in, but she ignored him. He sawed the bit roughly in her mouth, ducking his head under the branches of the trees.

He and Corinna had come this way the day before. The woods were intersected by long grass rides as a fire precaution. Pheasants used them as a feeding-ground. They were quite tame. Lord de Boys's ban on shooting had provided them with an easy life. They flew squawking into the undergrowth as Andrew galloped by.

He was sweating himself now. The mare was strong. He

could feel her under him angry and fighting. She tossed her head against the bit and flecks of white foam flew back in Andrew's face.

Then, in the distance he saw Corinna. She was riding towards him, trotting easily. Andrew began to pull in the mare. She resisted. He jerked at her mouth. 'Come on,' he said through clenched teeth. He was pulling at her now with all his strength. The reins had raised blisters between his fingers, and broken them open. The mare's head was drawn back, the skin of her neck creased. Andrew's fingers stung as he fought with her. 'Whoa there,' he shouted angrily. 'Whoa.'

'What's the matter?' Corinna asked as he drew up to her. Coins of sunlight were dancing on her face through the branches of the trees. She shaded her eyes and looked anxiously at the mare. 'What's the matter?' she repeated anxiously.

'Nothing,' said Andrew shortly. The mare would not stand still. She circled Corinna, shaking her head, picking up her hooves in high, dancing steps.

'What is it?'

'I thought I'd take the hint,' he said.

'What do you mean?'

'Get off. Get off that horse and I'll show you.'

'But ...'

'Get off, I said.' It was a command.

Corinna dismounted. She held her horse by the reins just behind the bit. Andrew threw his leg over the mare and jumped from the stirrup. 'Let go,' he said. 'Let him go.' He had left the mare's reins lying on her neck. She shook her head. As soon as she realized she was free, she galloped away along the ride.

'She's bolted,' Corinna said.

'Let him go,' Andrew said.

Corinna looked at him blankly.

'Did you hear me? Let him go.'

Slowly Corinna took her hand from the reins. The horse stood still beside her.

Andrew shouted. 'Go on then, you stupid creature. What's the matter with you? What are you waiting for, you stupid fucking creature?'

He stepped forward and slapped it as hard as he could with the flat of his hand on the haunch. It jumped and laid back its ears. Then it turned and galloped away after the mare.

Andrew turned to Corinna. 'Right,' he said.

'Andrew. Andrew, what is it? What's the matter?'

'Shut up,' he said viciously. He was pushing her to the ground, pulling at her shirt. 'I'm going to fuck you, Corinna. Corinna *Proudfoot.*' He spat the name at her. 'That's what you wanted, isn't it?' He ripped open his trousers. 'You wanted to see it, didn't you? How's that then? Is that good enough for your ladyship?'

'Andrew. Please. Please . . .'

But her mouth was crushed under his. His weight was on her. His hands tearing at her clothes.

'Oh God!' he gasped. 'Oh God.' He forced himself into her, thrusting at her like an animal. 'You can cut the balls off your horses, you people. You can cut the balls off your bloody horses. But you don't ever cut the balls off me.'

Then he collapsed. He buried his face in Corinna's breasts. His shoulders heaved. He was sobbing, deep dry sobs gagging at the back of his throat. 'Oh God!' he said. 'Oh my God!'

Corinna held his head in her arms. 'What is it, Andrew?' she said tenderly. 'What happened? Tell me what happened.'

But only when they were walking back along the ride to find the horses did he answer her. He told her everything then—his hopes, his schemes, the elaborate structures he had built up in anticipation of the partnership with Timothy. And the sale of the Rembrandt.

'It's a beautiful painting,' he said. 'It's such a beautiful painting.'

The weekend of the cricket match he hadn't had time to look at all the Proudfoot paintings, but he did manage to spend half an hour with The Nude Diana. Standing in front of that painting he knew he was in the presence of greatness. It was so simple, and yet so subtly complicated. The goddess lay back on the grass bank. A greenish light fell on her from above, filtered through the trees round the pool. She wore pearl earrings, and a gold bracelet on her upper arm. Other-

122

wise she was quite naked. By modern standards she was a somewhat lumpy figure. She was certainly not depicted as an unattainable spiritual being. She had lived, and her body showed the consequence of it. Her skin was yellowish— Rembrandt put that deep golden varnish over all his paintings. Her thighs and her stomach, swelling in deep folds even as she lay on her back, were soft with fat. The pubic hair was dark and wiry. She did not conform to the modern ideal of an antiseptic beanpole. Obviously Rembrandt did not want his women to be plastic dolls. He saw them as they are, and appreciated them like that. Diana was a real woman. But for all that, there was an air of authority about her. She was human, but also definitely superhuman, a goddess whose deity lay in the celebration of her human body, not in the ascetic rituals of self-denial.

'It's such a beautiful painting,' Andrew said.

'But you wanted to sell it?'

'Yes, of course.' Andrew looked at her with innocent eyes. 'It's good it should be sold. Different people get to see a painting when it's sold. It circulates a little. The same people look at it all the time, and after a while they forget to look at it any more.' He gave her an odd smile. 'And there is another point, of course. I am a dealer, you see. Whatever else I might do to make a living, that's what I am, a dealer. And the point of being a dealer is, everything that goes through your hands, in a sort of a way, you own it. That's why you're a dealer. Thousands of things, thousands of paintings, say, go through your hands. You can't afford to keep any of them. But they're yours. And they stay yours. If I'd been in on the sale of the Diana, it would have been mine. Do you see? Whenever I saw it, or talked about it, I'd have thought about it as "my" Rembrandt. That's what being a dealer is about.' Suddenly his expression changed. 'And she screwed it.' His voice was filled with hatred. 'That supercilious bloody bitch ...'

'Perhaps it's for the best.'

'For the best? Christ! What do you mean? God moves in a mysterious way his wonders to perform?'

'No. Of course not. I just mean that it's better to find out now than have it all go wrong when you're really involved.'

'Yeah. I suppose I shall have to get back in the queue again.'

'And anyway, it's more satisfying in the long run to build up something yourself surely?'

'Oh, don't give me that!'

'What's the matter?'

'Christ. You people, you have it so easy. You can afford to take up these beautiful moral positions. It's "more satisfying" to do it by yourself. That's just a lot of propaganda put round by you people to keep the natives happy. O.K. So I have to get back in line and wait my turn until *my* old man gets round to calling it a day.'

'Andrew. Please. You don't have to.'

'At least, I'm the eldest. And everything the Taits have isn't sunk in some pile of old bricks that no one would ever want to buy anyway.'

'Andrew ...'

'My inheritance will be mine to do what I like with.'

'Andrew. Please. Don't lie to me. I understand why you do it. I do understand.'

'Understand? God help us! I don't want to be understood. Don't you ever dare to understand me. My God, you people are so damn patronizing. You don't even begin to know what it's all about.'

Corinna did not answer.

Ahead of them the ride opened into a hayfield. The second crop of the summer was already a rich, pale green. A shimmering haze hung over it. They could see the horses were out there, quietly grazing.

But in his mind Andrew saw a different version of the scene. At the edge of the blue sky, black clouds were gathering, threatening the whole sunlit landscape with gloom and bitter despair. And in the meadow, the green dragon was lurking. He shuddered.

'What's the matter?'

'Nothing,' he said sharply.

8

That weekend at Boys Hall snapped something in Andrew's head. He could not wait around any longer. He had to take action.

He gave notice at the gallery. He had come into money, he told them, from relatives in South Africa. In time he would be opening his own gallery. But right now he planned to tour Europe and accumulate some stock. Maybe some artists as well. He'd show old stuff and new together. He did not intend to specialize.

He borrowed his parents' savings again. He told them he had been tipped off where he could buy, for a few thousand, a painting that was worth at least a million. It couldn't fail. He had a buyer waiting for it.

He cabled Lennox: EXPECT GOOD NEWS STOP ON TRAIL OF UNICORN. He guessed Lennox would probably not even remember his name. He would certainly be mystified by the cable itself. But faithful McIntyre would put him right.

He changed his car for a shooting-brake. In future he would need something to carry pictures in. At the end of September he took it on the ferry from Harwich to the Hook of Holland.

For three weeks he worked his way south, from Amsterdam, through Belgium, then east into Germany, then west to Strasbourg, then east again to Austria. In every town he visited galleries and antique shops. Most often he found what he wanted in small towns. He preferred to buy from the old-fashioned dealers, the old men that hung on in a crowded shop, in a backstreet, scarcely making a living. But there weren't many of this type left any more.

And he bought very little. By the time he drove into Venice and parked in one of the two great garages at the Piazzale Roma, he had six large seventeenth-century paintings in the back of the brake. He had not given much for them. The artists were unknown. The canvasses were badly executed, and on most the surface was damaged. They were practically worthless. And they were exactly what he needed.

*

Not all of Venice has succumbed to the mercenary embrace of international tourism. Well away from St Mark's Square and the Doge's Palace, a different Venice exists, a warren of narrow alleys and dark courtyards that the sun never reaches, where the canals are only wide enough for a single gondola. Occasionally tourists penetrated this hinterland, but never intentionally. They might have lost their way, or hopefully followed a gondolier or waiter, and found he was on his way to his family. And when they smelt the water, and saw the floating rubbish, and a rat maybe run across in front of them, or they slipped on the slimy steps as they tried to avoid it, they did not stay.

In October in Venice there are days of rain and mist and sudden cold, that drive the tourists to take shelter in the cafés, and the pigeons to huddle under the porticos of the hundred churches that are the pride of the city.

On one of these mornings, in that hidden quarter of the city, in his cluttered and filthy room, an old man was preparing to go out. Over his threadbare jacket he put on a dark, shapeless coat. Once it had been the grey uniform of the Italian Army. Now it was almost unrecognizable. The hem was frayed. There were dark, shiny patches of grease on the cuffs and round the pockets. He put a broad-brimmed black hat on his head, and left the room.

The old man double-locked the door with keys heavy enough for a dungeon. He glanced quickly to left and right. The courtyard was empty. Furtively he hurried across and disappeared into the dark alley on the other side.

The *vaporetto* was packed with clerks and office workers and shop assistants on their way to work. The heat of their crowded bodies raised steam from their clothes. The old man closed his eyes with an expression of distaste.

The boat puttered up the Grand Canal, under the sharp

126

angle of the Ponte di Rialto. At each stop passengers jostled off and on, folding and unfolding umbrellas with lethal urgency. At the Ca' d'Oro, the House of Gold, the old man stepped ashore. The richly carved stone façade had once been heavily gilded, and lavishly painted with red and ultramarine, but it stands now somewhat forlorn, a grey uneaten wedding cake.

But the old man did not even raise his head to glance at it. He hurried down the Calle del Ca' d'Oro, into the market in the Strada Nuova. Ignoring the stalls of brightly coloured fruit and vegetables, and the multitudinous varieties of fish from the Adriatic, he turned left, then right into the Calle delle Rachetta, crossing two bridges, without pausing, until he stood overlooking the water on the Fondamente Nuova. He seemed relieved to have left the crowds and to be alone again. As he looked out over the Lagoon, a gondola, intricately carved, painted black and heavily gilded, hung with black velvet, slid silently out from under the bridge. The old man took off his hat and held it against his breast. The rain plastered the grey hair to his head. Behind the hearse followed a full funeral procession, slowly making its way over to the cemetery of San Michele.

The old man watched the funeral until it disappeared into the rain out on the water. He put his hat back on his dripping head and walked to his right along the waterfront. He turned to the right along another *calle,* the pedestrian street of Venice. Ahead stood the church of Santa Maria Assunta. The old man went in.

Inside, in the gloom, it seems at first that the walls are draped with green and white silk, hung with thick tassels. But it turns out that the drapery is executed entirely in coloured marble. The elaborately painted ceiling is framed in gold and white. On the altar stands a tabernacle of brilliant *lapis lazuli.* Marble statues of saints and angels look down from every corner of the church.

But the old man did not look at them. Instead he turned to one side, knocked on a heavy wooden door, and opened it without waiting for an answer.

The verger looked up. He had his breakfast spread on a sheet of newspaper in front of him—coffee and a thick slice of *pollenta,* the yellow corn cake that is the basic food for poor Venetians. 'Ah,' he said. 'Buon giorno, Professore.'

'Buon giorno,' mumbled the old man gruffly.

Against the wall under the window stood an old, paint-spotted easel, a very old mahogany box, and a large canvas wrapped in an old sheet. One at a time the old man took them out of the verger's room. The verger did not offer to help.

The old man left the canvas until last. He took it across to the small chapel off to the left of the aisle and placed it on the easel. He took off the sheet. The painting was partially completed: a marble temple, lit by a flickering fire and by a beam of light that shone down from the dark night sky: soldiers with torches: their helmets also catching the light.

The old man studied it carefully. Then he looked up to where, above the altar hung the complete painting—Titian's Martyrdom of St Lawrence.

On the old man's painting the figure of the saint was still only sketched in. He opened the wooden box and lifted out his palette. He took one of the jars he used for paint, unscrewed the top, and dipped in a brush.

For the first time that day, his face took on a contented expression.

*

At noon the old man reversed the morning's operation exactly. He packed away his equipment in the verger's room. He retraced his steps to the jetty at the Ca' d'Oro. He took the slow *vaporetto* along the Grand Canal, under the Ponte di Rialto. The *vaporetto* was almost as crowded as it had been in the morning. The siesta is the unwritten law of Italy—and one that every Italian obeys.

Andrew had been waiting half an hour outside the old man's door. A woman had come out from next door, when he had knocked earlier that morning.

'Non e qui, il Professore. He is not here,' she said.

'He will be back?' Andrew asked.

She had shrugged and opened her palms. 'Perhaps. Sometimes he goes away. For weeks sometimes he is not here.'

'He was here this morning?'

'Si. If he has not gone away he will be home at midday.

For *la colazione* you know. Though I don't know what he can eat. Sometimes I ask myself if he eats at all. He is so thin. I tried to give him food, many times, long ago. But he never would take it. He allows no one into his room. He has the oven in there, but ...' She threw up her hands, as if she did not have to explain what a man was like with a stove. Andrew guessed he had let himself be caught by the local gossip. In her black dress, with the scarf over her head, she was a typical old Italian lady. But she was also just like every curious neighbour everywhere.

She came close and bent her head to talk into his ear. 'They say in there it is filthy.' She was pressing against him. 'Sometimes there is such a smell—pphoui!' She held her nose dramatically. 'When he is *making* something.' She rolled her eyes to heaven and crossed herself. 'The Lord knows what he is using. It's not paint that would smell like that. It can't be food either. Not food for *humans* at any rate. Signor, you know, they say ...' she had begun, but whatever it was she could not bring herself to tell Andrew what it was that people said.

So Andrew had come back at noon, and stood in the rain for half an hour. He had even bought himself an umbrella. It was ridiculous—in London he refused to carry one. And in Venice, the first thing he did was to go out and buy one— the real thing, *Made in England*!

The old man hurried through the rain to his door, digging in the pockets of his coat for his keys.

'Scusi,' Andrew said. 'Professore?'

The old man looked at him. A heavy beard hid the lower half of his face. His dark eyes were bleary and bloodshot. He did not answer.

Andrew stepped forward. 'Professore Ruggero?' he said.

'No,' said the old man. 'You made a mistake.' He began to unlock the door. But his neighbour must have been watching from behind her lace curtains. She came bustling out, with her scarf over her head. 'Ah. Professore. The gentleman has found you.' Then to Andrew, 'You have found Professore Ruggero then?'

'Yes, thanks,' Andrew said. He wondered, did she expect him to give her something. Surely not. He had not even asked for her help.

'You'd better come in,' said the old man, in an irritated voice.

He led Andrew down a dark passage to another locked door. Behind it was a room large enough to be a warehouse. And it looked like a warehouse. Dozens of canvasses were stacked round the walls. There were heaps of canvasses on the floor. Others leaned against the two vast tables, covered with pots and jars and jumbled rubbish, that stood in the middle of the room. Another stood on an easel in front of the high window. At the far end of the room was a gallery, that looked as if it might be some sort of bedroom, reached by a ladder from the ground floor.

The old man shook his hat and went to the end of the room to take off his coat. Andrew walked to the window. He found he was looking straight out on to a canal just above water level.

'It's a fine studio,' Andrew said.

'What do you want?' asked Franco.

'What do you do here?'

'What do you mean?'

'What do you do? What kind of painting?'

'I make copies. Sometimes for an order. Someone wants a "real" painting, but they can't afford to buy an actual Botticelli. I can paint them a new copy. Americans usually. Sometimes I make a copy myself, hoping to sell it later.'

He looked tired Andrew thought. And old—unshaven, and bent, in his shabby clothes. Yet it was evident he was no more than fifty or so.

'Yes?'

'Also I do restoration work.'

'Ah.'

'After the floods in Florence. And here too in Venice. There is a lot of restoration work.... But you did not really come here not knowing what work I do.'

'No. I had heard about you, of course.' Andrew was beginning to look through the paintings. 'And it pays well —the copying and the restoration?'

'Do I look rich.'

'No. But appearances can be deceptive.' He was only giving Franco part of his attention. He seemed to be looking for something.

'What do you want?' Franco asked. There was fear in his voice now.

Andrew looked up. He held the painting he had been looking at steady with the palm of his hand. 'Why did you let me in, Ruggero? Why didn't you send me away?'

'I... I... Sometimes people come whom I have to see. I can't send them away. I thought you were one of these people.'

Andrew was going through the canvasses again. 'I think you were right,' he said. 'They tell me.... Ah!' he exclaimed suddenly. 'Ah. Now these, these are *very* interesting.'

There was a hunted look in Franco's eyes. 'I knew it,' he whispered half to himself. 'I knew it. What is it you want?'

'They told me no one could "copy" a Rembrandt like you. You know what you are called? They call you the Rembrandt master.'

'I won't do it,' Franco burst out. 'I won't do it.'

Andrew ignored him. 'But what is this? What are these sketches? These details—these are details of The Nude Diana?'

Franco looked away and did not answer.

'When did you see it? They're perfect. This is the Proudfoot Rembrandt. When did you see it?'

'I never saw it,' Franco stammered. 'I never saw it. I made these sketches from a reproduction.'

Andrew was studying the canvas closely. 'It's incredible,' he said.

'But I will not do what you want.'

'How do you know what I want?'

'Because you all want the same. All the people like you, you want the same.'

'Are there many people like me who come here?'

'No. Not many. But every few years someone comes. And you all want the same. But I will not do it, I tell you. This time I will not do it.'

'I don't see that you have very much alternative, Signor,' Andrew said. 'You no longer have the choice.'

'I will not do it. I *will* not do it any more.'

The old man was near to tears. But Andrew himself was trembling. His heart was beating like a drum in his chest. He forced himself to speak calmly.

'I don't know when you first did it, Signor. But the first time was the last time you ever had the choice. I myself know definitely of three paintings that fetched a great deal of money, and were hung as genuine old masters—two of them in museums. Two Titians and a Velasquez. And they started here, in this room, as blank canvasses—or at least, as different paintings. I congratulate you, Signor. They are magnificent paintings. They are masterpieces. But they were not painted by old masters.'

Franco sank on to the stool at the table and buried his head in his hands. 'No,' he said.

'You'll be well paid.'

Franco looked up. 'Of course,' he said in a bitterly resigned voice. 'You have to pay me well to make me a criminal. But I won't do it.'

'Signor,' Andrew replied through clenched teeth. 'You are wasting the time of both of us. You will do it. I'm afraid you have to.'

After Andrew had gone, Franco remained at the table, staring into space. He knew Andrew was right. He would have to do it. He did not have the choice.

His eyes filled with tears as he recalled how happily it had all started. Even in England in those days it seemed that the sun was always shining. A prisoner, in a foreign country, and he was so happy! And now, in 'sunny Italy', his own country, there was nothing but gloom...

When he knew Delphine was pregnant, he begged her to let him stay at the Hall. He wanted to marry her, of course. He would have done anything—servant, gardener, anything just to be near her. But she would not hear of it. She insisted he must go back to Italy with the rest of the prisoners. He pleaded with her. He had not realized she could be so unreasonable.

In the end she had agreed he could stay, hidden away in a cottage, miles from the Hall. And only on condition that he paint for her a replica of the Proudfoot Diana.

He did it willingly, to be near her, and to see his child. But he wished he had not agreed. She scarcely came near him, except to see how the work was progressing. She let him see the child twice only. And as soon as the painting was done, she packed him off to Venice with scarcely a word of regret. Even the old dog that had come to keep him company, she had had shot by the gamekeeper.

And here he was now, living a lonely, furtive life, hating the work that should be giving him so much pleasure, old before his time. She had sworn so often that she loved him, but all her actions had been cruel and selfish. She loved her paintings. She loved herself. But she never loved him. He had long ago realized that.

*

Andrew had given Franco three months to make him a new 'Rembrandt'. He knew exactly what he wanted. It had to be a nude. Lord Duveen, the great Edwardian dealer, had made the point long ago: take two old masters, he had said, one of an ugly old man and the other of a beautiful girl. They are both old masters—but the second is also a painting of an attractive woman. In the saleroom the second will always outprice the first.

An unknown Rembrandt nude would be a rare but possible discovery. There were three known nudes of his already, and several women bathing, wearing loose shifts or raising their skirts and showing their legs. Even so, Rembrandt had only ever once flaunted convention to the extent of painting a woman without a few tactful draperies. That was the Proudfoot Rembrandt, the famous Nude Diana. A total nude would command the highest price. It would also provide a convincing reason why the painting had never been seen. Rembrandt had probably painted it secretly, at that time in the mid-1650s when he made other nude studies of Hendrickje, his common-law wife. Always desperate for money, he had perhaps sold the painting on the understanding that it was not publicly displayed.... The story of the 'discovery' was already forming in Andrew's mind. And the picture was not even painted!

Before Andrew left Venice he and Franco paid a visit to the car park on the Piazzale Roma. At dusk one evening they took a *sandalo*, the Venetian rowing-boat, to the nearest jetty, and told the boatman to wait. They took the paintings from the back of the brake and leaned them all round it. Franco studied them closely. He took out a magnifying glass and peered at the surface. He clicked his tongue. 'Impossible,' he said. 'In this light it is impossible.'

He made a dozen circuits of the car, at snail's pace. Andrew was losing patience. The fee for the *sandalo* was mounting all this time....

Eventually Franco selected two of the paintings. He and Andrew replaced the others in the back of the brake. Andrew told Franco to meet him on the jetty, and not to come near until he had loaded the pictures on to the boat. He was too noticeable, with his wild appearance, in his ragged coat and high black hat.

When he joined Andrew in the boat, Franco could not keep his hands off the paintings. He touched their surface, stroking them gently with his fingertips, as if he could read some message from them in Braille.

As soon as they were safely in his room he said to Andrew, 'Now you must go. I have work to do. You must go.'

Despite his reluctance to undertake it, he was excited at the prospect of the work. Andrew was glad to leave him to get on with it. 'All right,' he said. 'I'll go. But remember, Franco. It has to be perfect. You understand? *Perfect.*'

'Go away,' Franco growled at him.

Andrew left.

The chaos in Franco's room was deceptive. Under the dust and litter, the sketches and scraps of paper and jars and broken brushes and stained rags, Franco knew where everything was. One table was set up like an alchemist's laboratory, with crucibles, pestles and mortars, jars containing lumps of resin and substances like coloured clay. One corner of the room, by the sink, was arranged as a photographic bench. On the shelf above, micro-photographs of brushwork, or of the granular pattern of paint, lay in jumbled confusion. Near by, the door of a great pizza oven stood open. It appeared that Franco used the inside for storing his canvas.

Franco knew where everything was. And in that room was everything he needed. He set to work to make his Rembrandt.

Both the paintings he had taken from Andrew were genuine seventeenth-century Dutch works, in their original frames. They were of no artistic merit whatever. That had the advantage that no one had ever bothered to improve their condition. As fashions change, original frames are often replaced. The 'stretchers'—the struts that keep the canvas in shape—suffer shrinkage, or attacks of woodworm, and are replaced too. And modern nails would probably then be used to fasten the canvas to the new stretcher, in place of the old handmade variety. In extreme cases a painting may be 'backed': the picture, taken from its stretcher, is pasted face downward on heavy paper; the old canvas is softened and picked away, strand by strand: a new canvas is then glued to the back of the thin sheet of paint, temporarily held together by paper and paste. It is a delicate operation, but quite often necessary to give an important painting hope of longer life.

The two paintings were very similar. They were both very dark—almost black. Both were landscapes—one of farm buildings, the other of cows in a country lane. They were both almost the same size. And most important, nothing had been done to either of them since they left the artists' studios. Only time and neglect had altered their materials. And that was exactly what Franco needed.

He examined the surfaces with his fingers. He looked at them through a strong magnifying glass. He had to decide which to use. And his decision would rest on the quality of the crackle—the crazing of the paint that takes place in all oil paintings as the paint dries. It is this, and the hardness of the old paint, that are so difficult to reproduce artificially. Compared to these, a convincing style is easy. There is no scientific test for the character of a painting.

Oil paint takes years to dry thoroughly. It may cease to be tacky after a few days, but the complete drying can take fifty years. As it dries it cracks, not just on the surface, but through all the layers of paint from the varnish down to the first coat of ground colour. The pattern of the crackle is set where the paint has least freedom of movement—at the canvas. Artificially aged paint, dried in an oven, will crack *back* from the surface. An expert will spot this in ten minutes.

Franco made his choice. He set the other painting aside safely, in case of disasters. He prayed God he would not need it.

First of all he removed the canvas from the frame. No need for particular care over that. Anyone seeking to authenticate it would have been sure to take it out to see if the back held any clues.

But taking the canvas from the stretcher had to be very carefully handled. The nails would have to be used again. They had to go back in the exact same holes. Behind them were squares of leather, to save the canvas from tears. These were dry and brittle with age. It was a delicate task to lift them away. The edges of the canvas, naturally worn and discoloured with age, must be left intact. The canvas shrinks in from the edge, and is held in place by the nails, so that over the years the edges develop a scalloped effect. A straight edge to the canvas would immediately make an expert wary. Was it a 'fishy' painting?

Franco put the nails carefully aside. Then, using the same holes, he nailed the canvas to a sheet of ply. Now he was faced with a task of almost surgical delicacy—to remove the top layers of paint, but leave the last intact, with its pattern of crackle unspoiled. And an operation of such delicacy had to be carried out on paint so old, and so dry, that it was virtually insoluble. That's another test for a 'fishy' painting: if the paint is soluble, it has been recently applied.

For years Franco had experimented, but he had never found a solvent that was strong enough to move old paint, but could be limited to save the ground—and even the canvas—from damage. There seemed to be only one method that worked. It was slow and laborious, but it worked.

Franco laid the board, with the canvas attached, on the table. Then, with soft soap and a smooth pumice stone, he began to rub gently at the surface of the paint. It had to be done with infinite care. He caressed the surface with his fingers, feeling every gradation of the paint. Continually he had to clean off the surface and inspect it, to make sure there was no part of it coming away too quickly. Laying open the last precious layer to danger. He worked at it slowly, as if caressing it, with gentle, circular motions, for fear of tearing scabs of paint and taking too much away. The concentration brought sweat to his brow....

Every day of three weeks he spent bent patiently over the

136

table. His shoulders, his arms, his fingers ached from the continuous motion. But finally he had what he needed—the original grey ground, now clean and even. And if you looked at it closely you could see the irregular hair-line web of crackle, safely preserved.

*

Sally Marchant stood at the door of her room at Christie's waiting for her mother. She hoped she was not going to be late. There was half an hour yet before the sale started, but the rooms were already packed. The desk had run out of catalogues a quarter of an hour ago. Taxis were queuing at the King Street entrance, with its imposing classical doorway, and the doorman could not keep up with the number of arrivals. Inside, the stairs were crowded with gossiping dealers, art critics, socialites and tourists, speaking half a dozen languages—Spanish, French, German, English, Italian —as if it were some crowded international cocktail party.

Every Friday in the season there is a sale of paintings at Christie's. But on this day the air of excitement rose from something more than the usual anticipation. Today was the big one. Today was the day when records were to be broken. The TV cameras were installed. In the actual sale room all the seats were reserved for dealers and buyers and friends of the house. An amazing collection of paintings had been assembled, from various owners. But the star of the show was undoubtedly the Velasquez, Portrait of a Nobleman. Probably the last important Velasquez to come on the market for many years, it stood a chance of surpassing the amazing price of £2,310,000 paid for the Velasquez portrait of Juan de Pareja in 1970. The media had built up the sale into a great event. Everyone in London was quoting the odds like a horse race.

Sally's mother was not travelling up from the castle for the sale. She detested London, and very rarely visited it. But she had told Sally that she wanted to sell 'a little picture that no one ever looked at', and she wanted Sally to arrange it. Sally knew the painting—a beach scene by Bonnington that would certainly bring several thousand pounds.

And she knew why her mother wanted to sell it. Tim

had stayed at the castle for a month. Sally's parents had entertained him royally. They had taken on extra servants from the village. They had had the most expensive food sent from Fortnums. They had given large dinner parties for the local gentry. On the 1st of October, when the pheasant shooting began, they had arranged a shoot over their ground to which they seemed to have invited half the county. Tim and Sally were touched, but also slightly embarrassed. It was perfectly evident from their manner that this was not the way in which Sally's parents were accustomed to live. Nor, though they did not know it, was Tim. Yet Sally was not able to say this to her parents. They were not that sort of people. They did not believe that one spoke about such things. She knew exactly what they would have said if she had tried to speak to them. 'I don't know what you're talking about, my dear.'

At the castle, Tim had tactfully been given a room next to hers. And now her mother, Sally knew, was thinking of 'the wedding'. It would be a matter of pride that they 'do things properly' for her. And so the Bonnington would have to pay for it. It certainly was not a picture that 'no one looked at'. She knew it was one of her mother's favourites. She and Tim would be quite happy to marry in a registry office. But she knew her parents would never understand that. Her mother thought a girl only married in a registry office if she could no longer hide the fact that she was pregnant.

All Sally could do was to make sure that they got the best possible price for the picture. She had spoken to Quentin Gold, the art director she worked with. He had promised to give her mother his advice. He had stayed as long as he could, to meet her mother and see the painting, but he had to go for a final briefing, before taking his place on the rostrum in one of the overflow rooms.

Before he left their office Sally had told him about the Proudfoot Rembrandt. She decided this was the opportune moment. At first he'd seemed politely interested, no more. And she understood why. He had heard it a thousand times, as they all had—the vague mention of sending this or that painting to auction. As often as not it was a way of getting attention, of making sure he accepted an invitation to dinner, or sent a free catalogue, and nothing came of it.

But Sally had anticipated that. She had already had Tim sign the letter of authority for Christie's to handle it. When he saw that, Quentin became very excited.

'My dear girl,' he said, putting his arm round her shoulder. 'That's fantastic. How *clever* of you.'

'Well, Quentin, it wasn't exactly clever. It does belong to my fiancé.'

'Cleverer yet,' he exclaimed, chuckling excitedly. Sally could see he was impatient to get away and tell the other directors. She could hardly blame him. The sale of that one painting would bring Christie's about £200,000.

When her mother arrived Sally took her straight to their seats in the main sale room. They had to fight their way through the crowds that blocked the doorway, and stood, jammed solid, at the back of the room.

'My goodness. Is it always like this?' her mother asked in amazement.

'Oh no. This is because of the Velasquez—there.' She pointed to where the portrait, in a carved gilt frame, hung behind the auctioneer's rostrum.

'Oh,' said Lady Marchant in her down-to-earth manner. 'It doesn't look to me to be very different from any other picture.'

Round the room hung the other paintings. They didn't look much either, hung at random against the red hessian walls.

In front of the rostrum the heads of a dozen microphones were poised like snakes at the edge of the desk. The arclights already made the room unbearably hot. Two sets of TV cameras were mounted at the rear of the room, one for the closed circuit to the other rooms, the other for news film of the sale.

The auctioneer took his place at two minutes to the hour. At 11.00 precisely he struck the desk with the ivory hammer. He was brisk, almost impatient. 'Let us begin the sale, ladies and gentlemen,' he said firmly, when the conversation did not stop.

And when he did start he raced through the lots at an amazing pace.

'Number one. Anyone to start it? Fifteen? Fifteen thousand guineas. Twenty. Thirty. Thirty thousand guineas. Two places.... Thirty-five.... Forty.... The bid is in the front. Forty thousand guineas....'

Lady Marchant whispered to Sally, 'I don't see anyone bidding at all.'

'No. He knows them all. He just looks at them. If they want to drop out they just shake their heads.'

'... Fifty-five thousand guineas.' An assistant with a phone in his hand nodded to him. 'Sixty thousand. In the other room sixty-two thousand. Sixty-four thousand. Sixty-four thousand. The bid's in the middle. Any more? Sixty-four thousand guineas. Any more. Sixty-four thousand guineas.' *Crack* with the hammer. 'Agnew.'

There was a buzz of conversation. But the auctioneer hurried on. 'Number Two,' he said. An assistant indicated the painting on the wall. The TV camera transmitted its image to the screens in the other rooms. It was brisk and business-like. Great paintings were disposed of like cattle. And fortunes that could have supported thousands for life were spent in seconds on a few square feet of canvas and paint.

The sale held plenty of surprises. And not all for the vastness of the prices. Sometimes the buzz as a painting was knocked down had a different sound.

'That was bought in,' Sally said to her mother. 'It didn't reach its price.'

'But someone bought it—Frost didn't he say?'

'Oh, that's only us buying it back. It's a false name. It looks better than withdrawing lots because they don't reach the reserve.'

'Bad luck for the owner,' said her mother.

'Yes. It's all right for us, though,' Sally whispered. 'We still charge a commission. On the last real bid. Not so much, only two and a half per cent. But we don't lose.'

'Would you please mind not continuing your conversations?' The auctioneer rebuked them like a schoolmaster. 'We must get on with the sale.'

The Velasquez was the last lot of the morning. The auctioneer went into it without preamble. 'Number twenty-seven. Three hundred thousand guineas offered. Twenty.

140

Fifty. Eighty. Four hundred thousand guineas. Where are you? I can't see you.'

Now the excitement was intense. The bidding rose at breakneck speed. There were murmurs as it reached one million guineas. But at that price there was not even a pause. The bids still rocketed upwards.

'... One million five hundred thousand guineas. Against you, sir.... One million six hundred thousand guineas. One million six hundred thousand guineas. For you, sir.'

For a few tricky moments bidding slowed. But the auctioneer skilfully led it on. His face showed no emotion. He kept up his schoolmasterly manner. At the price of two million guineas, there was a gasp, and a scattering of applause. He silenced it with a frown.

'Two million one hundred thousand guineas. Any more? Against you, sir. Two million one hundred thousand guineas. Two million one hundred thousand guineas.'

The room was silent. Everyone held their breath. It had now reached the previous record price of any painting anywhere in the world.

The auctioneer seemed unimpressed. 'Against you, sir,' he said calmly. He was looking round the room for further bids. He glanced at the assistants on the phone to the other rooms. No one moved.

Then with a glance at the back of the room, he said, 'Two million, two hundred thousand guineas.'

There was a gasp from the spectators. Many of them turned to see if they could identify the bidder.

'Two million two hundred and fifty thousand guineas. Two million three hundred thousand guineas.'

Once over the hump of the previous record, bidding quickened again. After a brief battle between an American and Colnaghi, the Bond Street gallery, the American secured the picture at a price of two million four hundred and fifty thousand guineas.

The whole audience broke into applause and excited conversation. The auctioneer looked at them disapprovingly, but made no attempt to quieten the din. The time was 12.20. He had averaged four minutes for the sale of each picture.

The room began to clear immediately. Andrew had been

watching on TV in one of the outer rooms. He had not had time to see the Velasquez before the sale. He decided to go in now and look at it. He waited for the crowd to thin a little, and then fought his way against the tide into the main auction room.

He would not have expected Sally to be pleased to see him. And she wasn't. But since she was directly in his path, she could hardly avoid him. She introduced him briefly to her mother. 'A friend of Tim's. They were at Cambridge at the same time.'

'Fantastic price,' said Andrew, 'I hope they give you all a bonus.'

'Yes,' said Sally, as if she had not heard him.

Andrew glanced towards the Velasquez. A TV commentator, microphone in hand, stood before it, talking to the cameras.

'So another record has been broken,' he was saying. 'Another of the few last great paintings that remain in private hands suffers the indignity of public auction. Two million six hundred and ninety-five thousand pounds—the highest figure paid for a painting ever, anywhere in the world. A king's ransom. But how long will such a record stand? Not for long, I would venture to suggest. We may see even this phenomenal price overtaken in the very near future, in fact. And in this very room. But five minutes ago I was informed by the director of paintings here at Christie's that they have been entrusted with the sale of another world-famous painting—The Nude Diana, by Rembrandt, which has been the property of the Proudfoot family for generations. The painting comes on the market following the recent death of Lord de Boys. And though they would never be so rash as to commit themselves to a figure, I believe the people at Christie's here think they stand a good chance of breaking the record once again with that picture. We shall see. And you can be sure we shall be here with our cameras once again to witness the event....'

Sally's face was ashen.

'What's the matter?' said Andrew.

'Nothing,' Sally said abruptly. 'Excuse me. We must go, Mother. Excuse me.' She pushed past Andrew.

Andrew changed his mind about having a look at the

Velasquez. Looking at it was not going to make any difference. He knew he was not going to like it.

He waited until Sally and her mother were lost in the crowd. Then he made for the door himself.

On the stairs young men from rival galleries greeted one another with a sort of languid friendship. They talked as if they might have been buying for their own collections.

'David. Hello.'

'Hello.'

'Did you buy the Canaletto?'

'No. The Greuze.'

'Your father here?'

'No.'

Andrew tried to push his way down the stairs. In front of him another similar exchange was taking place.

'Did you buy anything?'

'No. On the Van Dyck we were also rans.'

'Nice picture.'

'Yes.'

These casually superior young men made Andrew see red. Their laconic conversation assumed a whole world of privilege. And the privilege, even still in these days, was inherited privilege. These younger sons of the aristocracy used to be able to play about with pictures, because there was so much money from land that they didn't have to earn a living. Now, money was tight, but pictures were big business—and these people had the connections to take advantage of both.

It was the same with Sally Marchant. He had felt quite sorry for her. Her mother was so dowdy in her country tweeds. He thought Sally seemed embarrassed. He should have remembered that nothing embarrassed these people. It was simply that she could not stand the sight of Andrew.

When he finally fought his way out into the street, he drew deep breaths of air, as if he had been suffocating in there. He decided to walk back to the gallery. His mind was teeming with his plans. They would see. Those people, they would see what he could do.

*

Andrew banged at Franco's door for ten minutes before he would come out.

'It's not ready,' he said as soon as he saw Andrew. 'Another week. Come in another week and it will be ready.'

But Andrew pushed past him. 'I'll stay,' he said. 'Maybe I can help you with the finishing touches.'

Franco shrugged. 'Help? How can you help? You would only hinder.'

'Then I'll stay and hinder,' Andrew said.

Inside the room he saw no sign of the painting he expected. 'Where is it?' he asked. Had the old man taken him for a ride? Perhaps there never would be a picture. He'd been reluctant enough to agree to do it.

Franco could see what Andrew was thinking. A flicker of amusement appeared in his eyes. 'It's in there,' he said, nodding to the closed door of the pizza oven.

'In the oven?'

'Yes.'

Andrew crossed the room.

'Don't touch. Leave it. It must stay another two hours.'

'It's warm. You're cooking it? This is for the *craquelure*?'

'Ah. You know, of course. So you see, you will not see it until tomorrow.'

'Is this the last time in the oven?'

'No. There's one more—the varnish.'

'Has it worked? Has the crackle come through? How many layers have you put on?'

Franco raised his hand to silence him. 'You will see. You must be patient. It's a slow process. Slow. One mistake, just one tiny mistake, and the whole painting is ruined.'

'Of course I am impatient to see it. But tell me anyway— does it work? Has the crackle come through?'

'Yes. It's coming. This is the best way. The first time, I remember ...' His mind was wandering off into a reverie. 'Then I thought I should do it with a new canvas. And I made the glue myself, you know, as it used to be made, with skins, rabbit skins and bones boiled together.' His nose wrinkled in disgust. 'Ugh! The smell!'

'What's the smell in here?'

'... But it was not good. It looks all right, the painting looks all right. But you could see the canvas is not old. It

144

was out in the sun for a long time—what sun there was—but you can see it was not old. It's not so good.'

'What is that smell in here? Not the paint. A sweet smell. Scent?'

'What?' Franco seemed startled by Andrew's question. 'What do you say?'

'The smell. What is the smell in here? Lavender—that's it.'

'Ah.' Again a flicker of amusement appeared in his eyes. 'You like the smell of lavender?'

'Come on, Franco. I know it isn't after-shave.'

Franco's face crackled into a wry smile. 'No. It is—what shall I say? A trade secret.' He was torn between pride in his craftsmanship and the habit of secrecy that had become ingrained in his character after years of these clandestine activities. He hesitated. Then, with a gesture of resignation, he went to one of the tables. 'I will show you. Look.'

Andrew stood beside him. Franco picked up one of the dozens of jars that lay half buried in the clutter. 'I will give you a lecture, eh?'

'All right.'

'You know what is our chief problem—we paint a canvas today, and it must seem tomorrow that it has been drying for three, four hundred years. Those old paints you cannot dissolve, not with alcohol, not with anything at all practically. They are like rock. So we have to find something that will harden the paint like that for us. It must also dry very quickly. And it must not reveal itself when the painting is—what shall I say, tested. It's not easy to find something like that.'

'Others have done it?'

'How do you know?' Franco said sharply. 'Those that have not been discovered you do not know about. And those that have been discovered—have been discovered.'

'You have not been discovered.'

'That is because I have found the technique. But it was not easy.'

Andrew was beginning to suspect that Franco was in a sense disappointed by his success. He seemed to have some sort of death wish, a desire to be found out. Andrew supposed he could see the attraction. Franco was an artist, and he was starved of recognition. In secret he painted master-pieces—they could hardly be called anything less—and no one acknowledged him. The more successful he was, the less the chance of acknowledgement. There must have been a temptation, even if it were only subconscious, to make just one small error that might betray him. A chill ran up Andrew's spine. 'Go on,' he said.

'But I thought of plastic. Plastic is a liquid. And when it is cooked, it changes. It is hard. Nothing will dissolve it, People are complaining that they can't get rid of plastic. Pollution.' He held up the jar. 'Phenolformaldehyde. Phenol is carbolic acid—that is from carbon, which is the base of plastic, as you know.... You see, I am quite a chemist. It hardens so quickly, I add it only just before I apply the paint.'

'But that's not the smell of lavender.'

'No. Of course. But I cannot apply the paint without some oil. What is the colour—dust, most of it. And this'—he touched the jar again—'this is like water. You can't paint with that. But the oil of lavender is an essential oil—you know what that means?'

'Yes, of course.'

'You don't need me to go on. You know what I am telling you?'

'No. But I do know what essential oil is.'

'All right. It dries quicker, yes? And it *evaporates*. And with a little heating it evaporates even quicker. So we are left with a solid compound, which analysis will show contains pigment, and perhaps a little natural oil ... nothing suspicious. And it is hard—hard as rock.'

'I hope it's as good as it sounds.'

'Why not? It has taken me years to make this solution.'

'Sure,' said Andrew. He was beginning to move round the table. He was satisfied by Franco's explanation. But not as impressed as Franco evidently expected. It was well known in the trade that the process of successful forgery had to be very much as he had described.

Andrew picked up a paint brush. The hairs were crudely bound to the shaft with twine. 'You make your own brushes?'

'Of course. The brushes Rembrandt used were made from

badger hair. They don't make such paint brushes now. But there are shaving brushes. It is necessary to get these things correct.'

Andrew was relieved that the old man was taking such care.

'Perhaps we leave a hair "by mistake" in the paint. Maybe an expert will pick it out. "Ah," he will say—so clever—"A *badger* hair. That is correct."'

'And the colours you make yourself?'

'You are checking on me? You will not find I make mistakes.'

'No. I'm not checking. I am not expecting you to have made mistakes.'

'Yes. I make them myself, of course.' He moved along the table, touching the jars and bowls of strange mixtures. 'This is cinnabar, for the red.' A jar containing rocky lumps of reddish ore. 'White lead—not zinc, because we did not have that until eighteen hundred and so. Also it's good for covering the old work. The X-rays don't like it. It's good you wanted a nude. A lot of white. . . . But one must take care. Rembrandt did not use so much.' He moved to an old marble pestle and mortar. 'And not too much blue for the nude either. That's lucky. The blue must be *lapis lazuli*. There is no alternative. Cobalt, ultra-marine, Prussian blue —they all come later than Rembrandt's time. And *lapis lazuli* is very expensive. Even for so little I spent a fortune.'

'And you grind it by hand?'

'Rembrandt ground it by hand . . . !'

'Yes, but . . .'

'. . . and if it is ground by machine, the grains are even, you understand? In the pestle they are not even. With a powerful microscope these differences can be seen.'

'O.K., Franco. O.K.'

'You are satisfied?'

'Yes, I am satisfied. Technically I am quite satisfied. But I still want to see the painting.'

'But you know what that is like. We decided before you left how it should be. I made a sketch for it.'

But Andrew could tell from Franco's manner that he was keen to show him the painting. Obviously he was proud of it. That was a good sign. Unless he was playing some elaborate joke, and he couldn't wait to get to the punch line....

'Come tomorrow. I shall varnish her tomorrow. Come tomorrow and you shall see her.'

Andrew knew he would not sleep that night. He ate dinner alone in his hotel. The dining-room was almost deserted. Afterwards he took a gondola to Harry's Bar on the Calle Valaresso. But, out of season, it was patronized by regulars. They looked at him as if he was intruding. He ordered a 'Bellini'. It was the speciality of the house, they said. He watched the barman shake cognac, peach juice and champagne. He poured it into a glass with sugar round the rim. It tasted rich and sweet. A woman's drink. Andrew drank it down quickly, and left.

Outside, at the San Marco boat station, a gondolier leered at him. 'You like a nice time, signor? My sister. Beautiful lady. Fantastic.'

'How much?'

'Fifteen thousand. Twenty-five dollars.' He help up his hands, with fingers extended, then again, then one alone. 'Twenty-five,' he said.

'Fifteen,' said Andrew.

'Twenty-five, signor. Very special. Fantastic.'

'Fifteen.'

'O.K. For you, twenty.'

Andrew climbed into the gondola. He didn't know why he was doing this. He didn't really need a woman. Certainly not like this. It was years since he had been with a prostitute. He really did not want to go along. Yet he did not see any reason why he shouldn't. He had the money. He had nothing to do. He knew he would not sleep.... He sank back on to the cushions.

He couldn't help smiling at the thought of himself, here in the most romantic city in the world, lying back in a Venetian gondola, the boat that is made for lovers—on his way to a prostitute.

The gondolier took him through a maze of narrow canals. And he charged an exorbitant fare for doing so. Andrew had not the energy to argue. The girl worked at the top of an old house. The gondolier rang the bell twice. She looked down. In dumb show he indicated Andrew and she beckoned him up.

'Hello lover,' she said when he had climbed the stairs. There were ninety steps. He counted them on the way up.

'You speak English?'

She was quite young—eighteen or nineteen he guessed: it was hard to tell. Her hair was black, teased into an elaborate pile on top of her head. Her skin was pasty and she was considerably overweight.

'Oh yes.'

'Well, I speak Italian.'

The room was dimly lit. She had draped a red scarf over the single lamp beside the bed.

'Oh.'

'And I don't want to talk.'

She shrugged. 'O.K. You pay the money. You put it on the table. How much did he say?'

'Eight thousand—fifteen dollars.'

'Liar!' she said without malice. 'The price is thirty!'

'We agreed twenty.'

'O.K. Twenty. I'll take twenty. Off-season rate.'

'But I have lire. That's ten thousand.'

'Oh no you don't. It's twelve thousand. You can put it on the table.' She did not seem concerned that he had tried to trick her.

'Wash yourself there,' she said. She took off her sweater and skirt, kicked off her shoes, and lay naked on the bed.

Andrew pulled off his clothes. He washed himself at the basin. He didn't need to, but he didn't want an argument. When he came to the bed, she raised herself on her elbow and inspected him. She squeezed the head and peered into the eye. *A medical inspection,* Andrew thought. *Twelve thousand lire for a medical inspection. It was ludicrous. In a minute she would tell him to cough.*

But she lay back and looked at the ceiling. In the rosy light her flesh was like a rolling pink landscape. Seeing her there, apparently defenceless, still young, and without hope, condemned for the rest of her life to these joyless encounters, he felt sorry for her. She did not have a chance.

He took her gently. For some reason, he wanted to give her pleasure. He worked at her with long steady strokes. And as he approached the climax, raising himself from his hips, he saw she was biting her lip. But she kept silent. Hadn't he told her that he didn't want to talk?

Next morning Andrew was early at Franco's studio. He had stopped at a bakery by the hotel and bought fresh sugared rolls.

'I've come for breakfast, Franco,' he said. 'I hope the coffee's brewing.'

Franco led him silently along the passage. He had put the painting on the easel in the window.

Andrew had intended to react coolly. But when he saw it he exclaimed without thinking, 'She's beautiful, Franco. Beautiful.'

As they had agreed, she was the twin of the Proudfoot Diana. Evidently painted at the same time, here was Hendrickje again, with her plump, cheerful features and her soft, pneumatic body. The background was the same: the same trees, filtering the same green light; the pool throwing up the same dark reflections. But in this picture Hendrickje's pose was more sensuous. One hand was between her legs. Her head was thrown back on the grass. Her hair was dishevelled. There was an expression of sublime satisfaction on her face.

Franco came and stood beside Andrew. 'She is too pale, of course. But you know his varnish—like black treacle.'

In fact Rembrandt's final varnish contained asphalt. He liked, he had said, 'friendly colours'—brown, yellow ochre, red-brown. The varnish was made up of two thirds resin, one third oil.

That morning Andrew watched Franco at work. The varnish was so thick he had to warm it in his hands before he could apply it. He put it on the canvas with his fingers and the heel of his hand, working it across the picture until the whole surface was covered in a filter of honey brown.

Then he baked it again in the oven for two hours. When it was cool he took out from one corner of the room a great cylinder he had constructed from six oars and the centre of a cable drum. He wrapped the painting round this, face outwards. The edges failed to meet by two or three inches.

'Now,' he said, taking up a jar of black fluid from the table. 'What would you suppose this to be?'

'I don't know.'

'Dirt.'

'Dirt?'

'Yes. That's what I said. Did you ever see a *clean* old painting?'

'No. But they can be cleaned. It . . .'

'Not in the crackle. The crackle holds the dirt of centuries. This is where you have to be so careful. Not just any dirt will do. Modern dirt can be *recognized*. They can take dirt from a crevice with the point of a needle and *analyse* it. Modern dirt has diesel fumes in it. Did you know that? Pollution. But here is what is beautiful—in Venice we have not had diesel fumes so much.' He smiled slightly. 'It seems funny, but in a way, here the dirt is clean. And this is my special *old* dirt. I have a special place. It is an old church. In a poor district. The canals are too narrow round there for motor boats. The people are too poor for central heating. The dirt has lain there, in the roof, for hundreds of years.' He held up the jar. 'And this is it.'

He shook the jar. Then with a thick brush he covered the entire surface of the painting on the cylinder with the thick black slime. Andrew held his breath. He was beginning to understand the nerve it required at every stage of an operation like this.

Franco wiped the canvas clean with a cloth. Then he unfastened it and laid it on the floor on the ply to which he had originally attached it.

'See,' he said. 'Now the cracks close. The excess dirt is squeezed out. There. Now it is almost finished.'

His voice was calm, but Andrew could see that his hand was trembling.

'Now it must dry. I shall not put it in the oven again. The crackle is sufficient. It must dry by itself. You can come back in two days and it will be dry enough to take away.'

*

Two days later Andrew went back to the studio. The painting was on the easel, in the frame. It was perfect. He would have sworn it was the work of Rembrandt's own hand. Franco had captured it exactly—the brush strokes, the texture of the paint, the sense of light, the confidence. . . .

'What about fly specks?' he asked.

'I think they would have been removed if the surface had been thoroughly cleaned with alcohol. At least, one could say that, and no one could prove otherwise.'

'Good,' said Andrew simply. He went over to the table and rummaged among the debris.

'What are you looking for?' Franco asked.

'This,' said Andrew. He held up the stump of a paint-brush, a handle and the empty metal holder from which Franco had pulled the hairs. 'This will do.'

He walked to the window. He stood in front of the canvas. For several moments he gazed at it. Then, with a sudden fierce movement, he thrust the rough metal edge of the broken brush through the canvas, just at the point where Diana's foot entered the water.

Franco cried out. 'No! My God, No! What are you doing?'

Andrew looked at him over the top of the painting. He smiled. 'You will restore it,' he said. 'I will come back for it in a week.'

'But why? Why do you do this to my painting?'

'It was too perfect, Franco. That's all. You did it too well.'

'But ...'

'It didn't look right. It was too perfect. In three hundred years, nothing has happened to it? Now it has had an accident. It will have been restored. Then it will be really perfect.'

1972

1

Corinna and Andrew went to New York on a French ship, the *Josephine*. Corinna went from London on the boat train and joined the ship at Southampton. Andrew was coming aboard at Cherbourg. From there the *Josephine* sailed direct to New York—as the brochure said, 'five days of *haute cuisine* on the high seas'.

Corinna had been surprised to get Andrew's letter. He had told her, as he told everyone, of his South African inheritance. She had not believed him. And she told him so. But he insisted it was the truth. It saddened her that he should have to lie to her. He had sent her postcards—of a lacemaker, from Bruges: from Brussels, the Manneken-Pis, dressed as John Bull in honour of some visiting English dignitary. He wrote a few words on them that told her nothing. She guessed he was working out some scheme. She wondered what it could be. Perhaps it was simply that at last he had found financial backing, and his backer wished to remain anonymous.

At Boys Hall everything seemed exactly as it had been before Lord de Boys died. But in some way Corinna could not understand, it was not. She found she spent most of her time alone in the cottage, or exercising the horses. Her mother was kind to her, but preoccupied with her paintings and her artists. Yet that was not unusual. Delphine had always been like that. Perhaps it was Polly that made things different. Now that she and Giles were definitely to be married, as soon as a 'decent interval' had lapsed after Lord de Boys's death, Polly had become impossible to talk to. She just made polite remarks, innocuous and perfectly boring.

Whatever it was, Corinna no longer felt part of a united family, as she once had. She no longer prepared her Sunday teas to supplement the meagre provisions at the Hall. Tim and Sally were too busy in London to come down often. And Polly had now decided that she found the food at the house perfectly adequate.

Corinna told her mother she was going to stay with a girl friend in New York.

'Oh, how nice,' Delphine said. 'Have you got enough money?'

'Yes, thank you,' said Corinna. She doubted Delphine would have noticed if she had said she was going to the moon.

She almost might as well have been. She could not think why she had agreed to go. Andrew's letter had not been very pressing. He had written to say he was going to New York, to take some paintings for Lennox (so that was what he had been doing); he knew she had friends there; he felt sure she needed a holiday—so why didn't she get herself a reservation and travel over on the same boat? She noticed he carefully did not offer to make a reservation for her—in case she might think he was going to pay her fare.

But after all, she thought, why not? She had the money. She did have friends in New York. She was always saying she would visit them, and she never had. It was time she went to America. She was feeling restless. No one seemed to need her in England. She *did* need a holiday, Andrew was perfectly right....

As the *Josephine* slid alongside the quay at Cherbourg, Corinna was leaning over the rails, searching for Andrew's tall, spare figure in the crowds below. What if he wasn't there? A hundred things could have held him up. Would she have to sail to New York alone? She smiled to herself. Even if she did, she doubted if she would be lonely. Between Southampton and Cherbourg already—four or five hours' sailing—the assistant purser had made it clear he was prepared to be very attentive.

A stiff breeze was blowing across the docks, carrying the smell of tar and diesel and the unhealthy aroma of the sea. Down by the galley portholes, the gulls flocked and fought for scraps.

There was music on the quay below. A very rough version of 'Colonel Bogey', on drums and trumpets, echoed between the terminal sheds and the side of the ship, drowning the noise of the gulls and the shouts of the porters. A team of drum majorettes was marching and countermarching between the feet of two giant cranes. They wore the briefest tunics, grey trimmed with scarlet, and white boots tied with ribbons. Their leader was a monumental blonde. She threw her staff in the air, but she did not seem quite confident she would catch it. As Corinna watched she realized all the girls were like that—they weren't sure what to do, and they didn't seem to think it mattered. They looked round to check that they had made the right move. They chatted with their neighbours. They looked as if they'd only just got on parade in time. Their boots were scuffed. They didn't wear make-up. Their complexions were bad. Many of them were overweight.

Corinna did not see Andrew anywhere. But he had plenty of time. The ship did not sail for another hour. She thought she might go down and have a drink. That was the trouble with sea travel—there were so many times when the only thing to do was to go and have a drink. She had already spent several hours in The Pub. The bar on B Deck had been fashionably re-decorated in the style of an English pub. The only other occupants were an English couple. They insisted she call them Stan and Doris. That was another thing about sea-travel—the instant friendship. Stan and Doris complained all the time that it wasn't *their* idea of a pub. There wasn't even a barmaid, Stan said. But they stayed. They seemed to think it would be wrong not to take advantage of the cheap liquor. Where the other passengers were, Corinna could not think. It couldn't have taken them five hours to unpack. Perhaps there was some way of passing the time other than drinking. If there was, she could not see anyone doing it. The stewardess had told her that most passengers would come aboard at Cherbourg. And even so, she said, the ship would not be more than half full 'at this time of year'.

Just as she was about to turn from the rail and go down to the bar, Corinna caught sight of Andrew. Her attention was drawn by a porter pushing a trolley loaded with a strange package—tall and flat, wrapped in green canvas. She

157

guessed it must be a painting. Behind the porter was Andrew.

*

'Well come, monsieur,' the stewardess said to Andrew. 'Well come aboard. A good voyage.'

Mme Morin was proud of her English. And of course it was necessary to speak it. The British and the Americans liked to try out their High School French on her. But if they really needed anything they had to ask for it in English. And Mme Morin always made out she understood, even when she didn't.

'If you like,' she said, 'this you leave to me, to *defaire* the *valises*. You can get to the deck to see the last of the passengers come on the *Josephine*.'

Andrew found Mme. Morin irritating. She had a permanently resigned expression, as if life owed her something better than this. And her accent was like one of those professionally foreign actresses, 'vairy French'. 'I'll unpack myself thanks. I can manage that all right.'

She looked annoyed. She probably enjoyed going through other people's cases, hoping for dirty pictures, or rubber-wear.

'Who else shall we have on the trip?' Andrew asked, to humour her. With Corinna on board, it occurred to him, he might need Mme Morin's co-operation.

'Oh—nobody. Not anyone—you know. It will be very dull, this crossing.'

'That's a shame. I thought these ships were meant to be so glamorous.'

'Not any more. People these days—they are all in such a hurry. In the old days they believed one should travel in style. Speed. Nowadays all they think about is speed. There is no romance any more. Those—how do you say? Jumbo Jets, they get you to New York two hours before you have left Paris. Where's the romance? It's not natural.'

Ah, the old days! The famous crossings! Papa Hemingway's great romance with the Kraut. Scott Fitzgerald. Those were the days!

Mme Morin sighed. She looked round the cabin as if

remembering all the glamorous ghosts. Her eyes rested on the package of paintings. 'You are a painter?' she asked hopefully.

'No, Madame. I am taking them to New York for a friend.'

'I see,' she said. She was one of those people who give you the impression that they don't believe you. Andrew wished she would go.

'Monsieur will permit me to show him the appointments of the cabin?'

'Please.'

Swiftly she toured the room, opening drawers, indicating light switches, radio, air conditioning, telephone, curtain pulls: then, in the bathroom, shaving point, alarm bell, shower mixer. 'Remember,' she said, 'this is a French machine. The C is for *chaud*, and that is *hot*. Not C for *cold*.' She had said this piece so many times that even in English it ran glibly off her tongue.

She seemed reluctant to go. Surely she was not waiting for a tip?

There was a knock at the door. Mme Morin looked startled. 'Who can it be?' she said.

'A friend, I expect,' said Andrew. 'Une amie.'

'Oh.'

Andrew guessed it must have seemed fast work, even by the standards of shipboard romances. He opened the door for Corinna. They embraced on the threshold.

After Mme Morin had gone they bolted the door.

'Oh, it's good to see you,' said Corinna. 'It's been such a long time. What have you been doing?' She looked round the room. 'I saw you come on board with the painting. I'm dying to see it.'

'There are three of them,' said Andrew. 'But there's nothing to see. They're not very exciting. Not worth undoing all the packing.'

Corinna drew away from him. 'But Andrew,' she said, looking into his face, 'I want to see them.'

'They're not worth unwrapping. I tell you.'

'But Andrew. You're taking them all the way to America. You're not just sending them. You're taking them yourself. If they weren't important, you could just send them over.

You must think they're important if you're taking them to Lennox yourself.... Don't you want me to see them yet? You wanted to give me a surprise in New York?'

'That's it,' Andrew said, with a smile. 'I want to keep you in suspense.'

Corinna released herself from his arms. 'And I'm going to keep *you* in suspense,' she said. 'Let's go up on deck and watch the ship leave. It'll be five days before we see land again.'

'But,' Andrew protested weakly. 'It's been five months ...'

'No,' said Corinna firmly. 'I want to go up on deck.'

She wondered why Andrew would not show her the paintings. There was some secret about them he would not tell her. She had given him a feeble reason, and he had gratefully taken it up. It was almost insulting that he should lie so casually to her.

As sailing time approached the passengers lined the rails. Corinna and Andrew found a space next to a small man in a grey Homburg. He touched the top of his hat in acknowledgement as they took their places.

The majorettes were playing again. They were formed up opposite the gangplank, listlessly prancing on the spot.

'My God,' said Andrew. 'They're coming aboard.'

'They are indeed,' said their neighbour. He seemed to find it amusing.

'Who are they?' Andrew asked.

'The New Royal Netherlands Girl Majorettes. They are going to New York, I understand, to take part in a competition.' He smiled wrily. 'I suspect they are wasting their time.'

'I'm damn sure of it,' Andrew said.

The *Josephine* was singled up, held now only by one hawser forward and one astern. Two tugs were in position under the bows.

On the rail to their right a dozen short-haired American boys were hanging over the rail, avidly watching the majorettes. They laughed in sudden unnatural gusts, and then looked round self-consciously.

'Oh dear,' said their neighbour. 'I wish my boys did not have to be quite so crude.'

'Your boys?'

'Yes,' he said, delighted at Andrew's mystified expression. 'In a manner of speaking mine.... The name is Jonas Field, incidentally.'

'Andrew Tait.'

They shook hands. Corinna, on the other side of Andrew, had not been listening to the conversation.

'Oh, not like that. They're my choir. You don't believe it now, do you? It's really true. Well, not *absolutely* true. I do succumb to parental pressure here and there. But all but two are in my choir. I am their chaperone. I bring them every year. Not the same boys of course—but every year I bring boys from the choir. It's really all a joke, of course. I take them to Chartres, the King's College at Cambridge. Actually, the boys don't give a damn about all that stuff. The parents really know it, but they don't let themselves think too much about it. It gets the kids out of their hair for the summer. For the kids it's a free trip. So ... it's really all a joke.'

'A very expensive joke.'

'Oh dear. Don't you think it's fair? They're all *very* rich, you know. Oh *my* they're rich.'

The hooter of the *Josephine* blew two deep long blasts to announce the departure of the ship. The Dutch girls were at the foot of the gangway. It was already hooked to a crane, ready to be lifted away when they were aboard.

The blonde major raised her staff. Along the rail the movie-cameras began to whir. The boys began to call out from the rail. Andrew hoped the girls could not understand what they were telling them to do.

'Your boys seem very—high-spirited,' said Andrew.

'I know,' said Jonas, 'I'm not responsible for their behaviour. I wasn't going to get caught like that. I set out with twelve, and I take twelve back. In between they can do what they like.'

The majorettes started in on their final number. They played everything at the same breakneck speed. But Andrew thought there was something familiar about this last tune. Then he realized—it was the National Anthem. The girls didn't understand the rhythm at all. The trumpeters swayed their bodies, hips and shoulders in time with their own eccentric beat. Half the drummers drummed, while the others mechanically whirled their sticks from thongs on their wrists.

'I think I've had enough of this,' Andrew said to Corinna. 'Let's go and have a drink.' He nodded to Jonas.

Jonas indicated the band. 'Isn't that "Rule Britannia"?' he asked. 'No,' said Andrew. 'I think it's meant to be "God Save the Queen".'

'They probably think this is England,' said Jonas, chuckling.

*

Half an hour before dinner Andrew knocked at the door of Corinna's cabin.

'Am I forgiven?' he asked when she let him in.

'Do you need forgiving?' she asked. She had changed into a dress of deep dusty pink that he had not seen before. He wasn't sure if it was this colour on her but she looked vulnerable, and her dark eyes seemed deep and sad.

'You've certainly been acting as if I did. You've hardly spoken to me.'

'I didn't mean to give that impression.'

'Kiss and make up?'

'Make up, but no kiss.'

'What's the matter, Corinna? You're getting to be a real tease.'

She looked at him seriously. 'It's such a long time since I saw you, Andrew. It's almost like having to get to know you all over again.'

'I don't feel that about you.'

'Don't you? Well, I don't know. Something's different. One of us has changed. Perhaps it's me.'

'Are you trying to tell me you've gone off me?'

Corinna laughed. She took hold of his arm tenderly. 'No, Andrew. No. I'm sorry. It must be me. I'm so confused. I've been so confused in the last few months. Since Father ... Lord de Boys ... Oh, I don't know.' She broke off and turned away from him.

He took her chin in his hand and turned her head to face him.

162

'You're crying, Corinna,' he said. 'What's the matter?'

'It's nothing. I'm sorry. I'm feeling rather emotional, that's all. It's nothing. Let's go and have a drink.'

Once again, having a drink seemed the only thing to do. At least liquor on the ship was duty-free.

Corinna had thought that when she saw Andrew again she would find her bearings. She realized now that that was probably the reason she had decided to come. Her relationship with Andrew had been something separate from the Proudfoot family, and she had expected, if she took it up again she would find that sense of herself that she seemed to have lost at Boys Hall. But of course, the fact that Andrew was quite separate from the family, and indeed was pretty much disliked by some of them, could actually have been the reason she was attracted to him in the first place ... oh, she really was confused. There was no doubt about *that*.

They went to The Pub. Stan and Doris were still there. They had changed since Corinna saw them earlier. Otherwise she would have believed they had been there all afternoon.

Stan was trying to get the barman to sell him a warming-pan that hung on the wall.

'Come on,' he said. 'I'll give you fifty quid for it.'

'But, monsieur. It is not for sale.'

'Come on. Seventy-five.'

'I'm sorry, monsieur. It is not for me ...'

'Hello, dear,' Stan said when he saw Corinna. 'We're still here, you see.'

Corinna introduced Andrew. She had the feeling she was dreaming. These people did not seem real at all. Perhaps it was that effect of being on a ship, being thrown together with total strangers, meeting people you would otherwise never have come across, just because you chanced to be on the same boat at the same time. She was coming to the conclusion that she had led a very sheltered life.

'You'd think they'd have a proper barmaid in an English pub, wouldn't you?' Stan said to Andrew. 'This one doesn't even understand the lingo. See that bedpan on the wall over there? Well, Doris has always had an inkling for one of those. So, I thought to myself, that's it. I'll buy it for her. But do you think I could get any sense out of him? Not likely. They ought to have a proper barmaid. After all, it's meant to be a blooming pub.'

Doris did not want Stan to make a fuss about the warming-pan. She primped her hair and set her glasses straight and said, 'Don't worry, Stanley. Don't worry, dear.'

But Stan said cheerfully. 'Not to worry. Not to worry. You want it, my dear. You shall have it. A word with the Captain ... I might even have to buy the boat.' He laughed heartily at the prospect.

'Oh Stanley, I don't mind. I don't, really.' She turned to Andrew. 'You see, the trouble with my Stanley is, if he decides he wants something, he doesn't stop until he gets it.' She was proud of him as a mother hen. 'Just to look at him, you wouldn't think butter would melt in his mouth, would you? But if there's something he wants, he'll never rest until he's got it. You wouldn't think it to look at him. A real jackal and hide, my Stanley is. A real jackal and hide.'

'I don't see why you shouldn't have it,' Andrew said. 'They'd hardly notice it was missing.'

There were rows of horse brasses on the plastic beams. Hung on the walls were cases of stuffed birds, needlework pictures, hunting horns, jelly moulds and various shiny brass household equipment. Among the bottles behind the bar stood traditional Staffordshire china figures of Bonnie Prince Charlie, Prince Albert, and several sporting dogs.

'Oh well ...' Doris said. 'I don't want to make a fuss.'

'They'll give it to *me*,' said Stan. 'They wouldn't want to offend a regular customer.'

'Ooh,' said Doris. 'We've never been to America before, actually,' she explained to Andrew. 'Stanley's going to look at a machine. There's only three of them in the whole world, and Stanley's thinking of buying one.'

'I'm in scrap,' Stan said. 'Scrap metal. Some people call it salvage, but I call it scrap. You have to keep ahead.'

'So I said to him, "Stanley," I said. "You're not going to America without me," I said. "All my life I've been waiting to see America." '

'It has the most powerful crusher in the world, this machine.'

' "And while you're at it," I said, "you can have a few

days' holiday and go over on one of those boats." You know he's never had a holiday as long as I can remember. He's a real tartan for work, Stanley.'

'A whole car smaller than a brick before you can say knife.'

'My God.'

'So here we are.' Doris looked proudly at Stan. They might have been honeymooners. Andrew almost felt he should leave them alone.

Corinna was looking down into her glass. There was a slight smile on her lips. But Andrew could see her mind was miles away.

Doris was flushed, and her eyes were bright with excitement. She looked at Andrew. 'Here,' she said. 'You think I'm tiddly, don't you?'

'No. Why ever should...?'

'Well, I'm not.'

'I didn't think you were.'

'Well, I'm not. I just want to make that clear.'

Andrew raised his hand to summon the waiter. 'I never thought you were. But just to prove it, I'll buy you another drink.'

'Oh no. You think I've had too much already.'

'Go on,' said Stan. 'Go on. Have a drink. You haven't got dinner to cook.'

'Oh all right then. Brandy and soda. I think I'd better stick to that. I'm not sure if I'm going to be a very good sailor.'

'We're not out of the harbour yet,' said Stan. 'The bar's not moving.'

'Don't you be too sure,' said Doris, suddenly cheering up. 'I could have sworn it was.'

The dining-room was half empty. And it was shabby. They clearly had not got round to redecorating it since the fifties. There were pillars covered with beechwood veneer, and light flowed from the top of them up on to the curved sections of the ceiling.

Corinna and Andrew were seated together at the First Officer's table. When they went in, the seat next to Andrew was empty. But in the seat beside Corinna's she was surprised to see the purser who had been so attentive earlier in the day.

He had evidently been looking out for her. He leapt to his feet and held her chair. And he smiled at her knowingly, as if this was something they had arranged between them.

Andrew did not know what to do. He was taken by surprise. The guy was wearing a uniform. Perhaps it was merely excessive politeness—all part of the service.

Corinna was pleased to see the purser, she realized. She was beginning to feel better. She had not thought that she would eat any dinner, but now she decided she might even enjoy it. The look of amazement on Andrew's face had been a real pleasure. A little rivalry would do him no harm at all.

'Allow me to introduce myself, mademoiselle. My name is François Lapierre. I am delighted to find that we are neighbours at table.'

'You didn't know?'

He gave her a Gallic shrug, and a sleepy smile. 'Sometimes one is able to use a leetle influence ...'

Corinna thought that perhaps after all she did not care about dinner. But the flirtation was going to be quite enjoyable.

With Corinna ignoring him on one side, and an empty seat on the other, Andrew turned to the menu. He had intended not to be impressed. But he was. Every conceivable luxury was there—salmon, venison, quail, wild duck, swordfish, sturgeon, plovers, *écrévisses*, sucking pig, peach-fed ham.... And none of them served plain: fish was smothered with shrimps, grapes, caviar, cream. The meat with truffles, wine, cranberries, horseradish. The pheasants *en plumage*. The fruit with liqueur, cream cheese, port. The brochure had promised 'the perfection of gourmet experience'. He wondered if they had any tricks left to pull for a special occasion.

His thoughts were interrupted by a voice beside him. 'Oh Mr Tait. You must forgive me.'

Andrew turned, 'Good heavens!' he said. 'Mrs Roscoe!' He stood up and held her chair for her as she sat down.

'Oh, I'm so glad,' she said. 'I hoped you wouldn't know I was on board. I wanted to give you a surprise. Was that awfully silly?'

'Of course not. And you certainly did, Mrs Roscoe.'

'Now look here,' she said, laying her hand on Andrew's arm. 'You simply can't be so formal on board ship. There really is not the time. You must call me Enid.... And I shall call you Andrew.'

'Please.'

Andrew was amused. He had met Mrs Roscoe three or four times in London. Her husband had been American, but she was English. She lived in New York but travelled every year to London, to see the plays before they came to Broadway, and to buy some paintings. She bought carefully, real middle-of-the-road stuff. She was not an art nut, like Delphine de Boys. She liked painting, she liked the life that went with collecting, but she was not going to lose five minutes' sleep if her little Bonnard got lifted. She'd get something else she liked with the insurance money.

'I wondered if it might be you when I saw the passenger list. And then I saw you come on board, with a package that couldn't be anything but a painting. I had a word with the purser. I arranged for us to sit together. I hope you don't mind. I knew we should find a lot to talk about. It is the most marvellous coincidence.' She looked round the dining-room as if happy coincidences were always turning up for her, and there might be another waiting out there somewhere.

Now Mrs Roscoe, Andrew thought, was a lady. In some indefinable way that was obvious. It was the first thing you noticed about her. Also—but equally indefinable—she was *nice*. She was direct, but she was not vulgar. She was warm and friendly. She concentrated on you and did not look around, but she wasn't overpowering. Her hair was loosely waved and there was a hint of fervour in her prominent, clear blue eyes. She was certainly nice, but you did not forget she was a woman.

'And who is that beautiful girl on your other side? Do you know her?'

'Yes,' said Andrew. 'I know her quite well. It's Corinna—Corinna Proudfoot.'

'Oh? Is she connected with the de Boys I wonder?'

'Yes,' said Andrew. 'She's the daughter of the late Lord de Boys—he died just a little while ago.'

167

Andrew felt a shadow of irritation cross his mind. Why was it these people, whenever they came across anyone new, always asked, first thing, whether they might be connected with this or that well-known family. That damned English social snobbery!

'Yes, I had heard. Poor girl. She is such a beautiful creature. I really must not monopolize you. I'm sure you want to talk to your friend.'

'She seems to be quite busy practising her French,' Andrew said.

Enid Roscoe smiled. 'In that case,' she said, 'you will have to witness my shameful ritual.'

She was already lifting a huge purse of black braid on to the table. 'My husband used to hate it,' she said, 'when I started to take my pills.'

She took out a small tube and stood it on the table. Then another. Then a small white packet. 'Oh dear,' she kept saying. 'I'm so sorry.' But she was enjoying it.

Before she found what she was looking for, she had a dozen or more phials and packets lined up on the cloth in front of her. The rest of the table were openly watching her.

'Ah!' she said at last. '*Here* it is. Felamine. I always take a couple when I think I might eat more than usual.' She smiled disarmingly. 'Just in case.'

'I'm so sorry,' said Andrew. She did look extremely healthy. But that could have come out of other bottles.

'Oh no,' she said. 'I'm not ill. Oh no.' She seemed amused at the idea. 'That is why I have these. To *prevent* me becoming ill. You see,' she held up her drugs one at a time before replacing them in her purse, 'cold pills: Copyronil and Redoxon. You haven't a cold about you, have you now?'

'Not as far as I know.'

'Avolium. Vitamin A.'

'Mmmm.'

'Valium. Well I have to admit that *is* a little bit of a tranquillizer.'

Andrew admired her confidence, and her ability to laugh at herself. If Corinna was going to refuse to talk to him, Enid made an amusing companion.

She repacked her medicine bag. She picked up the menu. But before she settled down to make her choice, she looked round the dining-room again. In the corner opposite them Jonas Field sat at the head of a table of his boys. They were shouting and throwing bread at one another. 'I do hope they don't redecorate this room,' Enid Roscoe said. 'It's so genuine. They ruin these ships trying to bring them up to date. Look at the QE2.... That style,' she added mischievously, 'is known as stockbroker's swinging.'

*

Andrew scarcely spoke to Corinna during the entire meal.

But afterwards, when he suggested they went to the discothèque, she politely wished the purser goodnight and went with him.

In the old days the discothèque had been the ship's night club. Then it had been called The Blue Angel. Now to keep up with the times, it had been renamed Le Cave Napoléon.

It was a small, crowded, noisy box. They did not try to talk. The pulsing strobe lights made Andrew dizzy. Corinna danced dreamily, her eyes closed.

In a pause between numbers, Andrew asked if she would like a drink.

'No, thanks,' she said. 'I think I want to go to bed. I'm tired.'

They went together through the warm, humming corridors of the ship to Corinna's cabin. Andrew did not know what to expect. Corinna was so distant. Yet they knew one another too well for him to make a pass at her.

At the door of her cabin, as she searched for the key, she said, 'Would you like a drink? I've got some scotch.'

Andrew sat on the bed. Corinna fetched two glasses from the bathroom. She picked up the bottle of scotch and came and sat beside him.

'Let's talk,' she said. 'Talking helps.'

'I don't talk too well to order,' Andrew said.

But having said that, they didn't need so much to talk. They sat together on the bed and kissed, only touching with their mouths.

'If you don't talk,' Corinna said, 'you might as well go away and do it by yourself.'

Andrew took a deep gulp of scotch. He put his glass on

the floor. When he kissed her again, Corinna's mouth was warm and slippery inside, tangy with the taste of scotch.

'You must talk,' she said again, as if it were vitally important.

'You are beautiful,' Andrew said.

Corinna smiled wistfully. 'You have on too many clothes,' she said.

'This isn't turning out to be such a brilliant conversation.'

They kicked off their shoes and lay close together on the bed.

'But talking is important.'

'We are talking, love. It's another language, but we are talking.'

'Yes,' she said. 'All right, I think we are.'

Andrew ran the zip down the back of her dress. She raised her hip for him to slide it off. Against her bra—a strip of white lace—and her cream tights, her skin was brown and smooth as an Indian.

'That's better,' he said, unhooking her bra.

She fumbled with the buckle of his belt. He unfastened it for her.

Their mouths were frantic now. Andrew's hand ran over her back. His tongue probed her mouth, her ears, under her arms. Her hand was on him, stroking, tenderly grasping ...

Afterwards they lay together. 'I'm not going to talk for a minute,' said Andrew, 'because there's nothing to say. I'm with you. I'm not going away. It was marvellous.'

'All right,' she said tenderly. 'All right.'

For five minutes the lay together, making small movements to savour the fading sensation. Then Corinna kissed him deeply on the mouth, and turned on her back.

'Cigarette?' Andrew asked.

'Yes, thanks.'

He lit two together and passed one to her. She drew deeply.

Then she said calmly. 'I'm sorry I was such a bitch....'

'You weren't a bitch.'

'Well. It was a good imitation.'

He stroked her breast lightly with his palm. 'It didn't fool me.' He took her nipple tenderly between thumb and forefinger. 'I knew something must be the matter. Can you tell what it was?'

'I don't know. That's the trouble. I really don't know what it is. I just know I feel—well, I feel I don't really know who I am any more. I suppose that's what it is. I used to be so sure. I used to be sorry for people who didn't know absolutely what they were.'

Andrew's hand moved down her stomach, brushing her hair, now stroking her thighs.

'I used to be sorry for you, you know. I used to think you really didn't know what you wanted, where you were going.'

'I guess you were right.'

'No I wasn't. You might not be sure where you are going. But you know where you come from. You know your family, your parents. . . . I don't have a family like that. My mother —well, you know my mother. And my father—I don't even know if my father is alive or dead.'

Andrew withdrew his hand suddenly. He drew sharply on his cigarette.

'Having a family doesn't make the slightest difference,' he said. 'You can have mine any day you like. I don't want them. They're no good to me. I wish I didn't have them at all.'

'That's easy enough to say when you *have* got them. It's only because you have had them that you have the strength to say you could do without.'

'You don't know what you're talking about,' Andrew said stiffly.

Corinna turned and put her arm across him. 'Oh Andrew. I don't want to argue. I just know how it feels to be me. And I feel lost. Maybe it's this ship. It's unreal. Like a dream. It's like being nowhere. It's not like real life at all.'

Andrew slid out from under her arm. 'I don't know,' he said. 'I think we both need some rest. You'll feel better when you've had a good night's sleep.' He had pulled on his under-pants and was getting together the rest of his clothes.

But after he had gone Corinna lay awake. She had never felt so lonely in her life. Andrew must have known she wanted him to stay. She was too proud to ask him. After a while she felt her chest begin to tighten. Sobs were swelling in her throat. She curled on her side and held the pillow

171

against her, and sobbed herself to sleep.

And next morning she felt no better. She waited for Andrew to call her, but he didn't. She had always said she understood why he was so evasive about his family. Now she wasn't so sure. It was unforgivable to be ashamed of your mother and father.

The ship was an unnatural environment. Those five days on the Atlantic seemed to be out of your life. So none of the usual rules of life apply. But if you do want to break them, you have to be quick. This other life is only five days' long. So there gets to be a frantic air of licence. Virtual strangers proposition one another—there's no time to waste on the preliminaries. You'll never see them again anyway. The bars are open from breakfast to early the next morning. Liquor is so cheap you can persuade yourself you are saving money as you spend it. Corinna had the feeling that some sort of orgy was on the point of breaking out, from stem to stern of the ship. But she still felt an outsider. She certainly was not in the mood for that.

Françoise Lapierre came after her as if they were on a desert island together. He was sexy and attractive, but she just did not want to get into all that with him. At meals his dark eyes kept looking into hers with a pleading expression, like a faithful dog. On the second night she agreed to go to the discothèque with him. She had to admit to herself it might be partly to annoy Andrew. She had had a furious argument with him that afternoon, when she finally called him on the phone. She asked if she could come and see the paintings he was taking to Lennox. She really wanted to see them very much, she said. But he refused to show them to her. He was so adamant she was convinced there was something fishy going on. She had stormed out and gone to the Winter Garden—for a drink. At dinner she had found François's attentions enjoyable. So she went to Le Cave Napoléon with him.

But François assumed that going with him was a straight invitation to screw. Corinna practically had to fight him off at the door of her cabin.

'But why do you come with me?' he kept saying. 'If you do not like me?'

He actually made her feel guilty for wasting his time. One

whole night out of five, when he could certainly have been screwing someone else....

Every morning the majorettes practised on deck. They got no better, but they grew more confident. The passengers never tired of filming them. The girls began to think they really must be good. They stamped across the deck, swinging their hips and trying to make some sort of musical sense of 'The Star-Spangled Banner'.

Corinna did not spend much time there. Nor at the deck quoits. Or the game of guessing the mileage of the ship's run. She found herself more and more frequently gravitating to the bar. The Winter Garden was quieter than The Pub. It hadn't been redecorated for years. Corinna could go and sit quietly there among the potted palms, and look out across the sea, and sip her scotch. She felt at ease there. Perhaps, she thought, she was becoming an alcoholic. Perhaps that was why she had this feeling of detachment, of dislocation.

François had found her hideaway quite soon. He came often and bought her drinks. He looked into her eyes and occasionally ran a beseeching glance over her body. He certainly did not seem to have been put off by her rejection.

But Andrew did not come. Corinna had breakfast in her cabin, and never ate lunch in the dining-room, so she only saw him there at dinner. And then he was falling about over Enid Roscoe all the time. It was horrible to see him, making amusing conversation and handing her things like a gigolo. It was partly Corinna's own fault, she supposed. She had been difficult and not very friendly to him, but could he not understand that there were reasons for that, and they were nothing to do with him? The trouble was, she understood him too well. She knew it wasn't just to make Corinna jealous that he was making up to this rich old art-loving woman.

They went about together all the time, Andrew and Enid Roscoe. If Corinna ran into them, Andrew behaved with perfect manners. They would stop, and the three of them would chat, about the ritual shipboard subjects—the weather or the Dutch majorettes. But Andrew took care not to stay too long. Once he and Enid looked into the Winter Garden while Corinna and François were there together.

But Andrew smiled and looked round as if he was looking for someone. He went away immediately.

'Your companion is—er, very friendly with the English widow.'

'How did you know he was my companion?'

François shrugged. 'I am the purser,' was all he said.

'And how do you know he is so friendly with her?'

He smiled. 'This is a ship, remember.' Sometimes his smile was infuriating. 'On the transatlantic run, even the gossip is in a hurry.'

On the fourth night Corinna went to bed with François. It was absurd, but she had got to feel she owed it to him.

François was triumphant. In her cabin, on the narrow bed, he came at her again and again, smothering her under his hairy body. He was insatiable. In a sort of passive way she enjoyed it. She just lay back and let him make the running. He hardly seemed to need any encouragement. And somehow, like that, she did not feel so involved. If she hadn't actually done anything, she couldn't take any blame. God, she thought, I don't have to feel guilty now, do I?

The final straw for Corinna was Enid Roscoe's party. Mrs Roscoe gave a party every year on her way back from Europe to the States. The paintings she had bought on her trip were displayed round the walls of her cabin. She was one of those people who was on friendly terms with half the ship before they had been on board twenty-four hours.

She asked everyone who sat at her table at dinner, including Corinna and François.

After what François had told her, Corinna certainly did not intend to go. Andrew had been helping hang the pictures. It had apparently been difficult to decide on the best arrangement. According to François, he had been working on it in Mrs Roscoe's cabin until the early hours of the morning.

'If you will allow me to be with you,' François said gallantly, 'I too shall not go.'

'Oh François,' Corinna said. 'You don't have to.' She blinked away the tears that had come to her eyes. She had never known herself in such an emotional state.

'No. But I should like to.'

'I should like it too,' she said. And she meant it. She felt

174

a sympathy with this passionate Frenchman, a kinship with his Latin blood and swarthy colouring that made her feel at home with him. 'And there is something I think I might want you to help me with.'

François's eyes were sparkling. 'Yes?' he said eagerly. 'At any time ... '

'Not that,' she said.

'Ah,' he said. He made a face like a disappointed child. 'Perhaps after I help we shall have that? As a reward?'

'I should have thought you had had enough of it.'

'But that was yesterday. Today is another day, to start again.'

Corinna laughed. She told herself that she must not take François too seriously. He had one of these romances, she was sure, every trip he made. It was probably the way it had to be for him—he was highly sexed, and easily bored.

Enid Roscoe's party was an after-dinner affair, starting at 9.00 p.m. François and Corinna did not go into the dining-room that evening. Instead they drank for another hour at the bar and then had a hamburger and a milk shake at Le Drugstore. François kept asking what it was Corinna needed help with, but she would not say.

But when they came out she stopped at the head of the stairs and said, 'Now. Here is the key of my cabin. I want you to go there and stay until I phone you.'

François looked at her doubtfully. 'This is very mysterious,' he said.

'You have to trust me,' she said.

'Of course,' he said. 'Of course.'

Corinna herself went down to Andrew's cabin. At the end of the corridor was the stewardess's room. She knocked boldly at the door. Mme Morin came out, with a suspicious expression on her face.

'Ah, Mme Morin,' said Corinna brightly. 'Would you like to open the door for me now?'

Mme Morin frowned. 'Mademoiselle?' she said.

'Mr Tait's door. Would you open it now for me please?'

'But mademoiselle ... ?' Mme Morin was mystified. She recognized the girl. She had seen her with Monsieur Tait the first day. His *amie* he had said she was. ... But ...

'But, madame. Don't you remember? Mr Tait arranged

with you to let me in to his cabin.' She lowered her eyes. 'Really, madame, this is rather embarrassing. I know he spoke to you. He told me himself this morning that he had arranged it.'

She could see the panic in Mme Morin's eyes. Had she forgotten? Had she misunderstood something Monsieur Tait had said to her? She did not remember him saying anything about the key. But she did not always catch what they said. . . .

Once in Andrew's cabin, Corinna gave Mme Morin time to get back to her room. Then she called her own cabin on the phone and told François to come down. 'But be sure to come from the front end of the ship—yes, the bows—so you don't have to pass the stewardess's room. And bring the nail scissors from my dressing-table.'

While she waited for him, she looked round. The room was exactly the same, yet it seemed quite different. It smelt of Andrew—she had not noticed that before, when he was there.

François shut the door silently behind him and turned the catch on the lock. 'Now,' he said, as he came into the room. 'What wicked schemes have you planned? We've to make an apple-pie bed, is that it?'

'No,' said Corinna. She pointed across the room. 'There,' she said. 'We are going to investigate that package.'

'Only investigate?' François was smiling. 'This is not to be a robbery.'

Corinna could not help laughing. She was not at all certain why she was there at all, but it certainly was not with any idea of carrying off Andrew's secret paintings. Though, come to think of it, that might serve him right. She did have some idea of getting her own back on Andrew. It was his idea that she came on this trip, and now he was ignoring her. In a way she was ashamed of what she was doing. But she had learned that lesson long ago, not to be ashamed of the fact that you sometimes do things you are ashamed of.

'No. We won't take anything. I just want to see what's inside. Andrew made such a *secret* of it. I want to know what it is.'

She was glad François was there. She decided she must have drunk a little too much.

François inspected the package carefully. 'It's sewn in,' he said. 'We shan't be able to do it up again. And there are Customs seals. Italian. French.'

'That doesn't matter,' she said. 'I want him to know what I've done.' She stood by him and grasped his shoulder. 'I'm glad you are here.'

She sat on the bed while François carefully cut the thread on two sides of the package with her scissors. 'There's three frames in here,' he said.

'Right. We'll look at them all.'

François slid them out of the bag. He took off the individual packing that was taped to the frames. There were these paintings lined up against the wall of the cabin. That was all. Nothing happened. Corinna was not sure what she had expected, but she had expected something. She shook her head. The paintings were still there, still the same. Three old Flemish landscapes, dirty and in bad condition. She knew enough about painting to know that these were third rate. The only thing in their favour was that they were genuinely old. That alone would make them worth a few hundred pounds. But as far as she could see there was nothing else about them to make them worth any more.

'Well?' François said.

'I don't know. I really don't know what to think.'

She stood up and stepped across to the pictures. She peered at them closely. They were exactly as they appeared —three old but bad paintings. She touched the surface of one. They had not even been cleaned.

'What's this?' said François. With his fingernail he was picking at one corner of the canvas. 'The frame is too big. The canvas doesn't reach the edge.'

'That's impossible. The canvas is folded behind . . .'

But François was right. In that one corner a straight edge of canvas was clearly visible. Corinna touched it with her fingernail. She could just lift the corner. But all round the rest of the painting the edge was hidden under the frame.

'It looks as if it's stuck on. I don't understand. What's the point?'

'Perhaps to hide the painting underneath?'

177

'Yes,' she said reflectively. 'That's it. There's another painting. Hidden underneath.'

'Shall we pull it off?'

'No,' she said sharply. 'No. We mustn't damage it ... It doesn't matter. It's not so important.'

'Good,' said François, brightening. 'So, we put them back. And then it's time for our little reward, eh? You want to put them back first?'

'Oh yes. I think we should put them back.'

At that moment the screaming began.

At first there was one thin, high scream, somewhere outside in the corridor. Then the sound changed. There were sharp stabbing cries. Then the scream again.

François and Corinna looked at one another. 'What's that?' they both said together.

They opened the door of the cabin and looked out. They could see a crowd gathered at the end of the corridor. Shouts mingled with the screams—men's shouts. And different screams, at a different pitch.

They put up the catch on Andrew's lock and left the door open, as they went towards the crowd. When they drew near they heard women's voices shouting 'No! No! No!' One or two were hysterical. Doors were banging. Men shouted. 'Get them! Get them!' one cried. 'Help!' from another. Doors were flung open and slammed shut. The cries and shouts came and went, pleading, screaming ...

They came up in time to see the Dutch bandleader seize one of Jonas Field's boys by the wrist and drag him towards her cabin. Her shortie nightie was transparent.

'Help! Help! Help!' the boy was shouting.

The girl called her roommates to assist. Laughing, they came out to drag him in.

'Retreat! Retreat!' came the cry from the next cabin. Two boys came out, waving handfuls of girl's underwear over their heads. 'Success! Success!' they shouted.

But evidently things were not going so well in other cabins. The Dutch girls were tough and uninhibited. And strong. They didn't hesitate to use their fists. As well as their natural weapons—tooth and claw. The American boys had been taught that was dirty fighting. Their faces were gouged. There were teeth marks on their wrists.

The girls were screaming from sheer excitement. From one cabin a boy flew out on to the floor of the corridor. A girl was still fastened to him. She bit a piece out of his ear. Another sailed from the doorway and pinned the boy to the ground. Deliberately she ground her knee into his groin. Her mother had given her practical advice before she let her on this trip.

The boy was moaning under the two girls. Another boy stood over them, crying, 'You can't do that. My God, you can't do that.' But all the same they did.

'Retreat! Retreat!' the boy called desperately. He could see who the next victim would be.

Stewards and stewardesses pushed their way through the spectators. 'Mesdames! Messieurs!' they cried. But they hesitated to intervene. They stood at a safe distance and tried to sound like scolding parents. 'Boys! Girls! Mesdemoiselles!' But it made no difference.

'For Christ's sake get these bitches off me!' The boy was recovering. The girl bounced viciously on him again, nightie above her waist, screaming rhythmically.

Jonas Field pushed his way through the crowd. He was wearing a dinner jacket. He had evidently been summoned from Mrs Roscoe's party.

'Boys! Boys!' he shouted vainly, nervously rubbing his hand over his bald head. 'Boys! Get back to your cabins at once. *At once!*' But he shouted in vain. They would probably have been glad to obey him if they could, but they couldn't.

Meanwhile the bandleader and her friends had stripped their victim naked and thrown his clothes out of the porthole. They dragged him out into the corridor. One sat on his head, the other at his feet. They pointed derisively at his genitals, shrivelled with fear.

'Leetle boy,' they shouted. 'Wot a leetle boy.' One was beating his balls lightly with a drumstick. The boy's scream was muffled under the girl on his head.

'Go back. Go back to your cabins at once,' Jonas Field was vainly crying. His voice was rising. '*Do* something, for God's sake,' he shouted at the stewards. But all they did was shout louder, '*Mes*demoiselles! *Messieurs!*' Nobody took any notice.

Then the bandleader and her friends spied Jonas Field. He was obviously responsible. They got up from the naked boy. 'Le smoking,' they cried. 'Le smoking.'

The boy they left was weeping. He crumpled at the side of the corridor and buried his head in his hands. But another of the girls came up to him, took hold of his hands and pulled them away. She spat in his face and threw him back his hands.

Now all the girls advanced on Jonas Field. He tried to back away, but the crowd was thick behind him. 'Boys! Boys!' he cried. But the boys slipped through the crowd and made their getaway.

'Oh no! Oh no! God! Please!'

The girls were still shrieking. They were determined on vengeance. Perhaps they had understood all the things the boys had said as they watched their daily rehearsals.

'Mesdemoiselles, Mesdemoiselles. *S'il vous plait. Als tu bleift.*'

'Those boys are nothing to do with me. Stop! Leave me alone! I'll tell the Captain. Where is the Captain? Fetch the Captain someone.'

But the girls surrounded him and began to take him away towards their cabin.

François began to push forward through the crowd. He was laughing. 'I'm going to stop them,' he said. 'This is going too far.'

'I'm going back to my cabin,' Corinna said. 'I'll see you later.'

As she turned to leave, she found herself face to face with Andrew.

'Oh!' he said, as if he had just realized something. 'It was you?'

'Yes. It was me. Don't worry, you won't find any damage. ... Now, if you'll excuse me, I think I'm going to bed. Good night.'

2

Reaction set in as soon as François left her, that night. Alone at three in the morning, Corinna was desperate. She decided to phone Andrew. 'I am sorry, mademoiselle,' said the duty operator. 'Number 217 is not answering.'

It couldn't be true. She had to speak to him.

'Are you sure?' she said. 'I expected an answer. I had arranged to phone ...'

'I am sorry, mademoiselle. There is no reply. *Il n'y a pas de réponse.*'

It didn't take a genius to guess where he was. For the second night she lay alone and sobbed into her pillow. Tomorrow they arrived in New York. She wished she had never come. She had felt unsettled at Boys Hall, but nothing like as bad as this. Now she was frightened. She couldn't face New York alone.

She tossed and turned on the bed. It was so hot in the cabin. She had never taken sleeping pills in her life, but she would have given a fortune to have just one right now.

After breakfast she got the operator to try Andrew's cabin again. This time he was there.

'Andrew,' she said. 'I'm sorry. I'm sorry. It was such a stupid thing to do.'

'I'm sorry you had to do it.' His voice was cheerful. At least he didn't seem angry. 'You should have believed me. I told you those paintings weren't worth unpacking.'

'But ...' she began. She checked herself. 'No,' she said. 'It wasn't worth it.'

'Cheer up,' he said. 'You sound miserable.'

'Well ...'

'How's the boyfriend? Are you staying with him in New York?'

'Oh Andrew. You don't understand. He has—well, he has family in New York, he tells me.'

'Oh, I see. The proverbial shipboard romance. But fun while it lasts, at least?'

'I suppose so.' François had been so eager to get away. He had to be on duty first thing, he said. Obviously he had no family. He was bored with Corinna and already looking for the next affair. 'Was yours?'

'My what?'

'Your romance. Was it fun?'

'I shouldn't have called it a romance.'

'Oh. Maybe Enid Roscoe would.' She was glad he could not see her. The tears were running down her cheeks. But she kept up the lighthearted tone.

'Oh no she wouldn't. Don't get the lady wrong, Corinna. She might not be serious, but she certainly isn't stupid. She took it for what it was. We both did. We should never have been together at all if it hadn't been for you in the first place.'

'Andrew, do you mean ... ?'

'I mean, if you hadn't been so damn frigid with me, and then started making eyes at that French gigolo ...'

'Oh Andrew.' She so wanted to believe him. 'Andrew. I want to talk to you. Can I see you?'

'Well ... Right now I'm getting my stuff together. I haven't packed a single thing yet, and we dock in an hour. Why don't we have some lunch one day? You're staying at the Foxleys', is that right?'

'Well ... yes.' She thought she would break down. Her hand was gripping the sheet. 'Yes. Did I give you the number?'

'No. But I know the Foxleys. Everyone in New York knows the Foxleys. I'll give you a call there. O.K.?'

'Yes,' she said. She forced her voice to sound cheerful. 'Fine. I'll see you later then.'

Corinna found a quiet space at the rail to watch as they came into New York. A cloud of gulls had come out to greet them, scavenging for scraps at the side of their wake. The sky was bright, but a stiff breeze blew down the Hudson from the north.

The Dutch girls were warming up. This morning they were nervous. They kept adjusting their braided caps, pulling down on their tunics, shifting from one foot to the other.

The Statue of Liberty rode on their left, her hand flung high in welcome. Corinna felt more threatened by the gesture. Liberty looked as if she had got up on that pedestal to attract their attention, and she meant to be heard.

But the other passengers were excited as children at Christmas. They knew the approach to New York was one of the great sights of the world, and they weren't going to miss a minute. They thronged on the rail at the front of the ship, pointing out to one another every new thing that came into sight, and photographing it at the same time.

The *Josephine* slid by the Lower East Side piers. Corinna read their names above the docks—United Fruit Co.: Venezuelan Line. Cranes were dipping slowly into the holds of docked ships, emerging with slings of bales. Ahead, the tugs were waiting to turn the ship's bows across the river into her berth.

Above Corinna the *Josephine*'s hooter released a long, deep boom. The New Royal Netherlands Girl Majorettes started into 'The Star-Spangled Banner'.

And, as if on cue, Enid Roscoe and Andrew came up on deck. Enid, in an ensemble of soft heather purple, looked healthily feminine. Her cheeks were smooth and pink, her eyes bright, her colourless hair simply waved. Andrew too was looking spruce in his blazer from Blades. Any woman would be glad to be seen with him, Corinna thought. Especially a woman of Enid's age. She probably had not yet reached the stage of having to pay for it. Not directly, at any rate.

Corinna turned back to the rail. She was disgusted by her own thoughts. She could tell New York was going to be a dirty city.

*

Andrew lay back in the bath. He noticed that his balls looked pink against his tanned thighs. Perhaps next year he should go to St Tropez, to one of the nudist beaches, and get brown all over. Didn't he know someone with a private villa? But maybe balls don't get brown. It might turn out to be awfully painful—even damaging. Who would know about a thing like that? Perhaps a letter to *Playboy* Forum? *Dear Editor—For some time now I have been concerned* ... He chuckled to himself. No more absurd than some of the questions that already did get printed.

'May we share the joke?' Enid spoke from the dressing-table in her bedroom next door.

'Oh,' Andrew was startled. 'Oh—well, actually I was thinking of writing a letter to *Playboy* Forum.'

'Oh really, my dear, I hadn't noticed you were having difficulties. I'm sorry to hear it if you are.'

'No. Well, it's just a little—masculine problem, shall we say?'

'In that case, I don't think I should ask any more.'

'No. Better not.'

'At any rate, I think you should hurry. We shouldn't be late you know.'

Andrew had not realized Enid Roscoe was quite so rich. Her brownstone was up in the East 70s, right near the Rothschild's New York pad. And she didn't have to feel like a poor relation. On Thursday afternoon the chauffeur brought the Rolls along from the garage and they went out for the weekend to friends in the country, purring out of New York with a low swishing sound, like waves breaking on shingle.

Even in the bathroom you'd know you were not in an ordinary household. It had recently been 'refurbished' by David Hicks, with marble and stainless steel and his usual geometric carpet. But the rather masculine tendency was offset by feminine colours, rose and dove grey, specially to match a set of charming Boucher water colours that hung on the walls. In the sitting-room pride of place was given to a superb Matisse collage. 'It was my husband's acquisition,' Enid always hastened to say to its admirers. 'I don't buy things like that any more.' Nevertheless, Andrew thought to himself when he heard her say this, if you own them you don't need to buy them.

'You have to be early—and bright,' Enid said in a joking tone, that nevertheless carried a hint of warning. 'This party is being given for you, remember.'

Andrew had forgotten that ruthless New York hospitality. 'I begin to feel like a performing dog.'

'I wanted to show you the art world in New York, I'm

going to teach you all about it, my dear. You must let me help you.'

'I know all about it. I lived here two years, didn't I?' He took a thick Turkish towel from the warm rail and began to dry himself.

'In two years there have been a lot of changes.'

'But I know *that*. London is not exactly a monastery. We do hear what's going on.'

Enid appeared at the door of the bathroom with an eye-brow pencil in her hand. 'My dear, don't sound so *fractious*,' she said. 'You must realize I am only trying to help.'

Andrew grinned sheepishly. 'Sorry,' he said.

Enid went back to work at the mirror.

'But I only came over,' Andrew went on, 'to deliver a painting to Lennox. I didn't come to catch up on the scene.'

'Oh Lennox can wait. There's no hurry for that, surely?'

'He's waiting for it. And it's important for me. I need the commission. I can't live on nothing.'

'You can stay here, you know, as long as you like. So that's no problem is it? But I must say, I think that painting is *very* suspicious. Why don't you show it to me?'

'It's not my secret. I would show it to you, but he asked me to keep it to myself. I told you.'

'You ask to put it in my safe, and you won't even let me see it. I tell you, I know you're smuggling it. It's another Raphael. You're going to sell it to Boston to replace the one they had to give back. The Italian police are hot on your trail. You know what they do, don't you? They hold up your luggage at the airport and search it secretly. That's why it was so long coming through. Then they follow you and arrest you in the act of handing it over.'

She appeared again at the door of the bathroom, smiling.

Andrew had finished drying. He put the towel back on the rail.

'I must say,' said Enid, 'You don't look very frightened.' She stepped forward and cupped his balls in her palm. It always took Andrew by surprise when she made gestures like that. She seemed such a *lady*—and then she stepped right forward and touched him up like any other woman.

'I think you should stay,' she said in a low, intimate voice. 'New York is really the centre of the art world.

Englishmen are rather fashionable. Your friend Wetherby
is having an enormous success.' She squeezed him playfully.
'I could be a great help, you know. I know a lot of people.
I'd like to help you, Andrew. I do hope you understand
that.' She looked down and smiled. 'Unfortunately, I think
we should go.'

The party was on the west side. In the car on the
way over, Enid gave Andrew a rundown on who would be
there.

'Well, Horace, of course. He's the host. You know him.'

'Yes.'

'He's still drinking rather a lot, I'm afraid.'

Horace ran the quite successful New York branch of an
international gallery. On the surface he was an amusing
talker, waspish and gossipy. But underneath he was deadly
serious and extremely knowledgeable. He had once offered
Andrew a job. But Andrew guessed he would find himself,
whatever Horace promised, not much more than a cultured
tea boy. He reckoned he would break into the New York
scene a litle higher up the scale than Horace's gofor.

'Rosalyn Brandt. I expect you know her.'

'Is there anyone who doesn't?'

Enid laughed. 'She's collected a few more paintings since
you knew her, I expect, but she's still the same Rosalyn she
always was.'

Rosalyn's collection was well known. In a certain way it
was restricted, but it was quite valuable. She only had the
paintings of contemporary, not-too-old, heterosexual male
artists. She got their paintings by having affairs with them.
Not that she went at it quite so crudely. She was herself a
half-good painter, and nobody's fool. She certainly wasn't
any sort of dizzy art groupie. But with her great gift for
sympathy, and her ability to share the kinds of problems that
artists get into, she drifted into affairs and broke up the
marriages of an amazing number of well-known artists. She
always picked the best. She must have had some sort of
physical aversion to second-rate painters. And it was not all
one-sided. She was a beautiful girl, intelligent and understanding. But she always came out at the other end of the
encounter with at least one really good example of her
lover's work. They hung round the walls of the studios like

186

trophies. After a while it had become a matter of pride to get a painting on Rosalyn's wall—and there was only one way to do that.

It began to look as if the scene really was going to be there. 'Who else?' he asked.

'Oh, I don't know my dear. A lot of people. The usual people. You'll see them all soon enough.'

Enid was right. Not all the usual people were there when they arrived, but most of them turned up in the course of the evening. And Andrew soon realized what Enid meant about the party being in his honour. Everyone in turn, it seemed like, came up to him, either to remind him when they had met, or to say, 'Ah, so *you're* the famous Englishman Enid met in London.' Then they waited for him to prove he was worth throwing a party for.

The clothes were uptown straight, or international kooky, and either way quite evidently expensive. The girls dressed in extremes—revealing all they had, in see-through minis, or practically nothing, in granny dresses.

Some of the men were. Some evidently were not. Some were probably not even sure which way to go themselves.

Frank Williams, for instance. He came over to Andrew quite soon after they arrived. 'Hello,' he said, holding out his hand. He was dark, handsome and dapper in a dark suit. 'I'm Frank Williams. We met, remember? When you were in New York before. At the opening of Louise's show at Pace.'

'Yeah. Sure,' said Andrew. 'How are you?' He'd never met him, he was certain, but he knew perfectly well who he was. 'How's business?' he said.

'Business? The whoring, you mean?'

'Whoring?'

'Oh Andrew. Let's not be squeamish. An art whore is what I am. I'm not ashamed of it. I'm thinking of having it printed on my cards.'

Frank Williams was an 'art adviser'. He had no money of his own, but he came from the right sort of family, and was known to, or connected with, practically any family worth knowing in the western world. And they liked to have him around. He advised them what paintings to buy. He was a great talker and he kept their dinner tables and their yacht decks amused. He wasn't particular who he screwed, male or female.

'Well, how's it going, anyway?'

'Oh fine.' He shrugged and smiled. 'You know—we don't have any money but we do see life.... Say,' he asked suddenly, 'isn't it a friend of yours who's staying with the Foxleys?'

'Who? Oh, Corinna—yes. Why? How did you know?'

'Oh, you know New York. There really are only five hundred people in New York. Not *the* Five Hundred, but five hundred. I know the Foxleys of course. Great friends. I was on their yacht in the summer. She's a nice girl. Isn't she some kind of a lord's daughter?'

'Yes, she's ...'

'On the wrong side of the blanket, that sort of thing?'

'Well ...'

'Such a nice kid. Really nice. Sincere....' He gave Andrew an odd, knowing look. 'And you're—er, staying with Enid?'

'Yes. You know her of course?'

'We did a little business, Enid and I, a long time ago. But you know how it is—fresh fields and pastures new?' He didn't say any more, but Andrew had the distinct impression that Frank didn't think it was a very smart thing to do to hang around Enid too long. 'She's such a *nice* person,' he said enthusiastically.

In fact, Andrew felt quite at home at that party. It was just the same backbiting, bitchy round it always had been. He might never have been away at all.

But according to Horace, things were very different. 'It may seem the same superficially,' he said. 'But it's really awfully different. In the last two years we've had the whole loft scene here, you know. Everyone has moved to SoHo now.'

'But they did that years ago. Louise Nevelson bought that sanitarium on Spring Street. Ken Noland had that storage building. Bob Rauschenberg had that flophouse on Lafayette. Roy Lichtenstein, Barney Newman—they were all there.'

Enid was with them. 'SoHo always makes me laugh,' she said. 'At least, when Americans in London call Soho, So*Ho*, that makes me laugh.'

188

'It actually stands for South Houston Industrial District —it's a light industrial area.'

'Does it really? I didn't know that.'

'But the point is, Andrew,' Horace went on. 'It isn't just the artists who have their lofts there. All the galleries are opening downtown branches. Castelli, André Emmerich, Sonnabend, everyone. You see, there's a certain sort of art that just does not fit in the uptown scene.'

He went on to explain to Andrew how it was. Andrew knew perfectly well, but he did not want to offend Enid. She was watching to see if he was attending.

There was a whole generation of new painters, Horace said, who were out of sympathy with the uptown scene. They rejected capitalist art, and private collectors, and the whole society that that entailed. Since that also included the dealers who took fifty per cent of whatever the private collectors paid, their objection was not just idealistic. They were in a real dilemma. They put together all sorts of funky work, they did the anti-gallery thing, with earthworks, and self-destructive art and all that. Yet they still appreciated the things that, for the time being anyway, only money could buy. The downtown galleries were a compromise. The dealers deliberately set out to make them less intimidating than their main premises. It all seemed very casual. The girls and guys who worked there were young and informal. There wasn't much in the way of décor.... But it all boiled down to the same thing. It was only a matter of time before all that became smart as well, and the artists either accepted it or moved on. Already the chauffeurs and the wild mink coats were down there picking their way through the lines of trucks and the garbage cans.

'Yes,' said Andrew. 'We're getting something like that in London. Just beginning. There's a movement to the warehouses on the river—St Catherine's Docks, Southwark. There aren't any dealers there yet, but some artists show in their own studios.'

'Yeah. Bob Wetherby was telling me about that. Boy, is that man an operator. You know he's thinking of opening up in SoHo himself?'

'No.'

'Yes, I did,' said Enid. 'But, quite honestly, Horace, I know

I'm terribly old-fashioned, but I really don't feel at all at home in that sort of setting. I'm not a snob, I don't think even my worst enemy would accuse me of that. But, well, I think what I'm looking for in art is a sort of beauty. There are hundreds of different sorts of beauty, of course. But I don't find any of them in those places. You certainly don't see my chauffeur down there, I can assure you, unless he goes on his day off.'

'Well, to tell the truth, Enid, I quite agree with you. Not about the beauty so much. But about the SoHo thing. And I think there's a reaction setting in already. To tell the truth, I think Bob Wetherby is finding it difficult to raise the wind. Of course, he's overextended himself.... He's running too fast. He's very short of capital. But he's a great guy. It does us good to have him around. There should be a fund set up to keep him in business—it does the whole trade good to have him.'

Andrew had found that Wetherby was almost a legend in New York. Everyone had stories about him. Half of them must have been apocryphal. But even if only half were true, it was quite impressive to get so much attention. It was something to remember—a prophet gets a lot more attention away from his own country.

Bob Wetherby, they said, had daily reports from all his galleries—London and Paris, as well as New York—on exactly who came in, how long they stayed, and what they looked at. His assistant, another story went, had to impersonate important clients, and Wetherby would rehearse a sale with him.

A rich client showed him two Italian Primitive paintings. 'One is a fake,' the man said. 'It was sold me as genuine.' 'Not by me,' said Wetherby quickly. 'No. But if you're such an expert, you can tell me which is which.' He had taken them both from their frames and stood them side by side on a pair of easels in his library. Wetherby examined them carefully, but not for very long. Then he took one from the easel, put it on the floor, and put his foot through it.

'The other day,' Horace said, 'a woman he didn't know came into the gallery. She looked rich, and vaguely familiar, but he didn't know her name. He spoke to her himself. She started buying wholesale. And not the cheap stuff—Léger,

Van Gogh, Monet, Utrillo. He recommended things to her as if he knew her. "Now, I know you'd like this..." He had to find out who she was. He scribbled a note to his secretary to go and find out from the chauffeur. Just in time, the girl came back and put a piece of paper in his hand. "Now..." said the lady with a triumphant smile. But Bob interrupted her, "Mrs Patrakis, I must congratulate you on your choice. Your new apartment will be superb. If you need any advice on the hanging of these pictures, of course..." I tell you, the man's a genius.'

'One day, he will go too far,' said Enid darkly.

'Perhaps. Perhaps. But for the time being he is practically by appointment dealer to the *nouveaux riches*. He delivers. If they want a Picasso, or a Monet, he delivers. It's not a *good* Picasso, but it's *genuine*. Those people wouldn't know a good from a bad anyway.'

'Exactly,' said Enid. 'Exactly.'

Yes, thought Andrew, it's just the same as it used to be. He felt quite at home. Yet he was wondering more and more whether this was the home he wanted to spend the rest of his life in....

Before Andrew left, Horace insisted that he must visit him in the gallery.

'Come for tea one afternoon,' he said.

'He's going to California,' Enid said. 'He says he has to go soon.'

'Come before you go. Come tomorrow. We have tea almost every afternoon. If someone is coming, it makes a nice excuse.'

'O.K. Yes. Thanks.'

'What are you doing in California?'

Enid answered for him. 'He's taking out a secret painting. I'm sure it was stolen from Italy, or France.' She laughed.

'There are more secret collections in Texas than California,' Horace said. 'There are twenty-five that I know of, and there must be others.'

'Oh, there are several in California,' Enid said. 'After all, they've only got to sit on them for ten years—at least the Italian ones. After ten years Italian law can't touch them.'

'But no one's going to put a whole raft of pictures on display suddenly and defy anyone to try and get them back.'

'Of course not. They really only buy them as investments —except for the few real monomaniacs. After ten years they start *selling* them. Discreetly. They trickle into museums, and collections, after twenty-five years or so. Somehow it doesn't seem so bad then.'

'Well, I'm sorry to disappoint you, but the painting I have has not been stolen. I can assure you of that. I wouldn't risk my neck. It's simply a recent acquisition for a private collector. And I've sworn not to divulge what it is. I don't want to lose my commission. That's all.'

At the party, Enid seemed satisfied with this explanation. But later she came back to the subject.

'Are you sure that painting is all right, Andrew?'

'Yes, of course,' he said somewhat irritably. 'I wish you wouldn't keep on about it. You have to take my word for it.'

'I do, my dear. Of course I do. It's just'—she placed her fingers briefly, absentmindedly almost, on his thigh— 'it's just that I'd hate you to get into any trouble. I'm very fond of you, you know, Andrew. I do wish you'd think about settling in New York. We could have a marvellous life, I'm sure we could.'

She used that 'we' rather often. It was beginning to frighten Andrew. And those friendly creases round her eyes —he couldn't help looking at them, they were really scary.

'I think it's time I settled down and invested in a little enterprise here in New York. I have some money, you know.'

'Why don't you put it on Wetherby? According to Horace, he's looking for a backer. And he's quite good looking,' he added viciously.

'Yes, he did ask me,' she said smoothly. 'But I told him I'm not really interested in the downtown galleries. I feel more at home up here. Sometimes I'm not even sure that I can face some of those young mainstream American painters. Their work is so—so aggressive. It's very *masculine,* of course. But you feel they would rather like to be able to attack you with the paint if they could think of a way how. I don't mind being disturbed, but I don't always feel able to withstand attacks. And besides...' Her hand was firmly on his thigh now. A breath of scent reached him—the thick, sweet smell of gardenia, rich and feminine, with its hints of oily secretions. 'Besides, I don't feel I could have the same sort of relationship with Bob as I could with you.'

'You mean, he doesn't screw?'

'Andrew, do you have to be so crude? Bob Wetherby is a happily married man.'

'I don't believe that.'

'Well, don't you think I should be more likely to know than you, perhaps?'

'Perhaps.'

'Would you like a drink?' she said suddenly. 'How very remiss of me. I never offered you a drink.'

'No thanks. I drank enough.'

'Kiss me.'

'Of course.'

'Again. You're a nice lover. Why do you have to go away?'

'I'm not going quite yet.'

'I'm going to the bathroom,' she said, almost in a whisper. 'I shan't be a minute. Why don't you just slip into bed?'

'All right.'

Andrew lay in the bed and laughed to himself. He wondered how many vitamin pills she took on these occasions.

After a few minutes she came to the bedroom in a blue negligée, frogged with bands of lace. She turned out the light and slipped into the bed.

Andrew took her in the dark. She talked all the time. She was a very articulate lover. 'Oh,' she cried. 'It's never been like this before.' And 'Oh, this is the most wonderful moment in my life.' Already, Andrew thought, in the middle of the action, she was turning it into a memory. People like that preferred memories—they were easier to control.

＊

Corinna very soon came to the conclusion that she hated New York. She had known the Foxleys in England—their parents were cousins of Lord de Boys. They were a generation older, but she liked them. And she liked them still. They did not seem changed. But she was amazed by their friends. She understood that 'Uncle' Peter was involved in some sort of antique business. She knew a little about English antiques. But she found it impossible to talk to these people. She had particular trouble with a man called Frank Williams. He obviously thought he had been called in to squire her round. (She couldn't believe that the Foxleys would actually have intended that when they invited him.) He was so charming it was frightening. The trouble was they all talked art the whole time, but as far as she could see they didn't care a fig about it. They were on the art circuit, so they talked about art. They only cared about the scandals and the prices and the reputations and successes—it might as well have been show business, or the stock market.

About her only pleasure was to go to the museums. Without her mother looking over her shoulder all the time and telling her what she should like and what not, she could look at modern art without any inhibitions. She preferred to look at pictures alone. With other people it was difficult to know what she really felt. At the Guggenheim and the Museum of Modern Art she at last felt relaxed and unselfconscious. She began to understand what it was that excited her mother about this revolutionary American art.

She was nervous again when she met Andrew for lunch. But he himself seemed so miserable she was immediately concerned. Over the first martini they talked about nothing very much. It was nice to be with him, she thought. She had wondered that morning if she was going to be able to control her emotions. But it was not like she expected. There was no strain. It was just that something that had been there before between them was not there any more.

Andrew ordered them a second martini—gin for him, vodka for her. He didn't look any more cheerful. She just had to ask him what was the matter.

He looked at her. 'I made a mistake, Fidget. I'm sorry. I was wrong.'

'What do you mean—wrong?'

'Well ... because ... I mean, Enid Roscoe. I made a mistake going to stay with her. Of course there's nothing like *that*. And it's a great house. She knows a lot of people. It's really fine ... except ...'

Corinna waited.

'She's so *nice*. She's so damned nice. She's such a nice, helpless lady, with all her pills, and those "pretty" paintings. But underneath she's as hard as nails. And selfish as a

194

cuckoo. You realize all of a sudden that she's taken you over, you're doing what she wants you to do. All that money she has, it means power. It means she can afford to be nice, because she knows in the end her money will buy what she wants for her. She doesn't have to fight for it.'

'Leave,' Corinna said simply.

'She doesn't even know I'm having lunch with you. I didn't like to tell her.'

'Leave,' Corinna repeated. 'Surely, Andrew, she doesn't actually lock you in? Move out. The Foxleys have masses of room if you want a free bed.'

Andrew avoided her eyes as he answered. 'Yes. I will. You're right. I should. But I don't want to offend Enid. She doesn't mean to be so possessive, I'm sure.'

'But Andrew ...'

'I've decided what I shall do. I'll wait until I go down to Lennox. I shall have to go soon. I'll stay until then.'

'Andrew.' Corinna tried to hide the desperation in her voice. 'I suppose I shall sound like a jealous woman ...'

'I don't see why you should,' he interrupted sharply.

'... but I honestly don't think you should stay with Enid. She's one of those people. She's awfully nice, but she's lethal.'

'You're not jealous, are you, Fidget?' he said suddenly.

She smiled. 'In a way, yes, I suppose I am. I mean, I did think we were going on this trip together, and I haven't seen all that much of you.'

'But you were coming to New York anyway. I just thought it would be fun for us to travel over together.'

He looked at her with such innocent, open eyes, she could almost believe he saw it like that.

'Will you be able to see me tomorrow?' he asked.

For a week they met every day for lunch. She didn't know what he told Enid, but obviously not the truth. It was like a clandestine affair, without the glamour, and not much of the excitement. But she liked to be with him. She couldn't explain that to herself. She decided the only thing to do was not to question it.

They sat until after three over their lunch, and in the afternoons they visited the galleries on 57th street. Andrew seemed to know everyone. Sometimes he introduced her. Sometimes she just hung round and looked at the paintings

195

while he talked. Once or twice they spent the afternoon at a movie. Corinna felt almost sinful.

But by an unspoken agreement they kept off awkward subjects. It had to be time out of any sort of reality. On the first day she had made the mistake of asking about the paintings he was taking to Lennox.

'I don't understand. There aren't any regulations about bringing antiques into the States, are there?'

Andrew was reluctant to talk about it. 'No. But there are about taking old stuff out of France and Italy and those places. They put a customs seal on those paintings in France. I wanted to go in and out of Italy with them and not have any trouble. I didn't want the seals opened.'

'But by the time you were on the boat there was nothing to worry about. The American customs weren't going to bother you.' She wished he would at least pay her the compliment of lying carefully.

'I just don't like my private things being interfered with, that's all.'

'And what was the point of the one with the canvas pasted over it. What was underneath?'

Andrew was startled. 'What do you mean?' he started to bluff it out. But he could see Corinna knew what she was talking about. 'Lennox wanted it kept secret,' he said shortly. 'It's an important acquisition. I wanted to keep it from prying eyes. So I covered it. Good job I did.'

He refused to talk about it any more.

*

Andrew went to Horace's gallery the day after the party. It was on the twelfth floor of an office block, but once inside, with its flagstone floors and shades on the windows, it had a solid feel, as if you had walked in off the street.

Horace was bowing out a young couple. He saw them off with exaggerated courtesy. He'd been drinking, but he was not helpless. He took Andrew's hand eagerly.

'Thank God they've gone. Those people are such a goddam bore. He's a stockbroker, of course. They all come in here—on Saturday morning it's ridiculous: it's just a teeny bit smarter to take time off from the office—they come

196

in here and the guy says, "Well, my er wife is er very deep into graphics." My wife is very deep into graphics! Decorator art! The only thing that girl has ever been deep in, I tell you, is a swimming pool. They can't afford paintings, and now prints are very *chic* in the young married set. He stands about and says these things he's heard, like, "signed on the stone" and "the size of the edition". Well, I'm glad to say the price of prints is getting quite *serious*. So one is polite to the awful people. And one day when Daddy dies, they'll come to celebrate by buying their first *real* picture.'

They passed into the interior of the gallery. Lying on the floor and hanging from the walls were limp, stuffed canvas shapes. They did not seem to represent anything, but some were obscurely familiar, and a few vaguely sexual.

'You know David's work?'

'Yes. But I haven't seen these. I'd like to look round.'

'Do. Do.' He turned to the girl sitting at the table at the entrance to the gallery. 'Monica, we need some tea, don't you think?'

She smiled and stood up, as if it was a joke.

'Isn't she beautiful?' Horace asked. 'She's such a beautiful girl.'

Andrew looked quickly round the show. With Horace floating about it was impossible to concentrate. 'Going well?' he asked.

'Oh yes,' said Horace. 'It's a great show. Selling well. And everyone in New York has been to see it. Everyone. Jackie Curtis was in just ten minutes before you came, in the most beautiful thirties' dress.'

'Who's she?'

'You *have* been away a long time. *Jack* Curtis is—well Jackie Curtis, I guess.'

'Tea' was served in the inner office. It turned out that 'tea' was a euphemism—for champagne. It was Horace's little joke. He had got into the habit of cracking a bottle at about this time to help get him through the afternoon. Andrew had forgotten how much New Yorkers drank. It must be the air conditioning, he thought. The atmosphere was so dry. And competition so hot. No wonder you get to feel so often you could use a drink.

Between them Horace and Andrew emptied two bottles of

French champagne, except a couple of glasses they gave to the girls in the office. They were interrupted by two young men who came to collect a painting the gallery was lending for a feature in *Vogue*. Andrew took the opportunity to leave.

He travelled down in the elevator with the visitors. They knew he had come from the gallery, but they talked openly about Horace, darting defiant glances at Andrew.

'Tsk. Tsk. Our friend Horace was overtired again.'

'Overtired? Horace? You think so?'

'Didn't you notice anything?'

'Well not—I mean, how can you tell? Horace acts pretty damn peculiar all of the time.'

'Well, if you want to know what I think, I think he's near as makes no difference in an alcoholic stupor.'

'Alcoholic? I thought alcoholic was out of date.'

'That's where you're wrong. It's coming back. It's the whole thirties thing. I mean, Scott Fitzgerald and all that It's awfully chic to drink. I tell you—grass, acid, poppers, they're on the way out. Getting smashed is *in*.'

3

Andrew did not have an assistant. But he rehearsed the sale of the Rembrandt to Lennox by himself. He'd been through it so often, his only fear was that Lennox might not have rehearsed his own part so well.

He guessed McIntyre would be hovering round. He was right about that.

Andrew and Lennox played it like a game. For two days Andrew was treated as a house guest on Lennox's fantastic estate. The main building was a vast, genuine Norman castle, complete with moat and drawbridge. It had once stood in England, on the Welsh border. Lennox had had it transferred stone by stone and re-erected in the hills behind Santa Barbara.

Andrew flew into Los Angeles, and was met by McIntyre. It had been too late to drive to Lennox's estate, so they stayed the night in the Beverly Wilshire. Next day, in the chauffeur-driven Rolls-Royce Silver Cloud they sailed along the freeway at a terrifying speed. Andrew had been surprised by the Spanish charm and the sunny streets of Santa Barbara. It was such a contrast to the east coast. Andrew's idea of the States was based on New York visits, and short trips from there.

But he was not half as surprised by Santa Barbara as he was when he caught his first sight of the castle towers, as they approached Lennox's estate. In the lush landscape of spreading avocadoes, of orange groves and gum trees, the gaunt grey stone battlements seemed doubly severe.

In the grounds, guest bungalows were disguised as ancient thatched cottages. Inside they were luxuriously furnished with priceless European antiques—the walls hung with French tapestries, the floors laid with Italian marble.

McIntyre gave Andrew a key. 'I can assure you that no one would touch your things, but we thought you might prefer to lock your room. There's no danger of intruders. The grounds are guarded. The walls are fitted with double alarms. You know we have had some rather unpleasant occurrences in this part of the world. You never know where they might strike next.'

Lennox worked morning and afternoon in his 'library'. Andrew had visited him there to say hello the morning he arrived. Three interconnecting rooms made one unit. There were few books to be seen. But there was an impressive array of teleprinters, radiotelephones, computers and other business equipment. Lennox himself sat in a bare room at a vast desk, with three grey telephones.

At lunchtime he made a brief appearance in the diningroom. This was the old hall of the castle. The walls were thick stone and the ceiling was lofty—a cool and relaxing room, perfectly suited to the Californian climate.

But Lennox scarcely spoke at lunch. He ate frugally, drank only iced water and in ten minutes excused himself to get back to his desk.

Andrew spent the mornings at Lennox's museum. The north tower had been converted, and additional buildings added, to house the Lennox collection. There was a separate entrance for the public from outside the estate. This was open every afternoon. Andrew spent these at the pool, or walking in the grounds. But wherever he was, whatever he was doing, there was only one thought in his mind. Over and over he rehearsed his part—the story of the discovery of the painting, the provenance, all the arguments that would bolster the sale. But he was determined not to appear over-eager. He made great play of staying close to his painting, locking himself in the bungalow to inspect its condition. But he never mentioned it.

In the end it was McIntyre who raised the subject. After the first evening, Lennox's wife had not been seen. Andrew guessed she must have gone on a trip, but no one explained her absence. Dinner became an extended repeat of lunch, with the three men at the table, most of the time in silence.

The butler served fresh Scotch salmon, with cucumber sauce.

'You know the Rembrandt that comes up at Christie's next month? Sent in by a Mr Timothy Proudfoot, our information is.'

'Yes, I know it very well. I know the family. It was left to Tim Proudfoot by his father. It's the most important Rembrandt still in private hands.'

'The Nude Diana—is that it?'

'Yes.'

Lennox looked up. 'Is that like it sounds?'

'That's right. It's a great painting. One of the great paintings of the world. Without exaggeration.'

Lennox's eyes flickered in his impassive face. 'Why didn't we buy it, Mr Tait?'

'It's not available.'

'But,' McIntyre said, 'it's up for sale.' Lennox left him to ask the obvious questions. It saved his own breath.

'Sure,' said Andrew. 'But it happens to be one of the world's great pictures. It's the last great Rembrandt we shall see on the British market for twenty-five years, maybe ever at all. They're not going to let it out of the country. People can get very patriotic about things like that.'

'It's not an English painting. Rembrandt was Dutch. It was painted in Holland.'

'Titian was Italian. So was Leonardo. They didn't get an export licence. After two or three hundred years the paintings get honorary citizenship. They'd never allow the Diana out. It's one of those paintings the public knows. They remember the name. It's all right for a painting only the art world cares about. But it doesn't make political sense for any government to let the Diana out of the country.'

Lennox nodded slowly. 'That's what I figured,' he said.

'So,' said McIntyre, determined not to let the subject die. 'May we now ask how you yourself were able to bring a Rembrandt out of Europe—a comparable Rembrandt you say. Presumably other countries have the same regulations. Or is that a trade secret?'

'It is a trade secret,' Andrew smiled. 'But in the circumstances I think I should let you in on it.' He turned to Lennox. 'I want to be quite frank with you Mr Lennox, all along the line.'

Lennox grunted.

'The reason I could take out this painting, to put it simply, was that no one knew of its existence.'

Lennox and McIntyre were watching him closely. He felt a surge of excitement. He was on stage at last. The curtain had gone up.

'I'm sure,' he said casually, 'if they had known about it they'd have slapped a restriction on it right away.'

'Why didn't they know?' said McIntyre. His slight Scottish intonation betrayed his suspicion.

'Because no one knows about this painting. No one has ever known about it. Rembrandt sold it secretly. It was— well, for those days it was somewhat scandalous. You'll see. Neither you nor I would find it the least scandalous I'm sure. But she is a totally undraped nude. And in those days that was considered rather gamey. But Rembrandt needed the money. He always needed money. The bailiffs were always taking off the furniture. He painted this picture as a private commission, at the same time he was painting the Nude Diana.'

Andrew felt rather than saw a stir of interest behind Lennox's impassive expression.

'It was never exhibited. My guess is that Rembrandt sold it on condition that it was not shown in public. After all, he and the girl were living together as man and wife. They were bringing up his children.'

'How did you get to learn about it?'

'Ah,' said Andrew. 'Well, the picture's been in the family since then. They knew what it was, but they weren't particularly interested in art, and they didn't need the money. They passed it on as a family heirloom.'

'But how did *you* get to hear about it?'

'Well—how do you get to hear about these things? Luck in a way, I suppose. A friend of mine gave me the tip. He'd married a Dutch girl. Her parents knew this family. She knew he was in the art world . . .'

'Why didn't your friend want to handle the sale himself?'

Andrew shrugged. He allowed a hint of annoyance to enter his voice. 'He didn't know how to cope with it. He didn't have the contacts.'

'It must have been a temptation to try to find them. A financial temptation.'

'Well, naturally,' Andrew said shortly. 'He's not going to *give* away a tip like that. I have to cut him in.'

'But why,' McIntyre went on, 'didn't the owners sell in Holland if they couldn't sell it abroad?'

'Mr McIntyre, I think you know the answer to that question yourself. They wouldn't get anything like the price in Holland they could get on the open market.'

'What you're proposing, Mr Tait,' Lennox said, 'is not my idea of an open market.'

'How do we know what you say is true? How do we know —excuse me, but how do we know that this is not a stolen painting?'

'It would be a clever thief who found a painting that no one knew existed.'

'And how do we know it is not a forgery.'

'You don't—not yet.'

'The beauty of your story is that there is no provenance —the painting is unknown, the owners anonymous.'

'My "story" Mr McIntyre, is not a story. It's fact. I realize you have to raise these questions. But I'm sure you realize I'm somewhat sensitive on the subject. O.K. There is no provenance. No certification of ownership. But you have to realize that this is the only way you're ever going to get your Rembrandt. The doors are closing all over Europe. There aren't many great paintings left and it won't be long before every damn country in the world clamps down on exports. Coming across this painting is a fantastic piece of luck. *I* know it's a genuine work. You can take my word for it.' He smiled. 'But you don't have to. If you want it, if we can agree on everything else—then you call in your own experts to authenticate it. It's on offer to you until you're satisfied one way or another. You can't ask fairer than that.'

'No,' said Lennox.

'There are three or four Rembrandt people. I guess you've found that out.'

McIntyre nodded.

'There's a guy in Boston. There's the director of the Rembrandthuis in Amsterdam. He'd come over if you asked him. They don't come across a new Rembrandt every week. *You* can go to these people. I couldn't. You can say you've been offered it by a dealer, on behalf of an anonymous owner, and you need their opinion. You can produce the painting, because by now it's untraceable to its country of origin. It could have come from anywhere. What government can claim a painting they didn't know existed?'

'Right,' said Lennox. 'Mr Tait, when are you going to show us your painting?'

'Tomorrow,' Andrew said. 'Tomorrow at lunch time.'

'Good,' Lennox said. He turned to McIntyre. 'I think Mr Tait and I will go to the museum after dinner. I want to know his opinion of my paintings. Will you have the lights turned on?'

'Right,' said McIntyre.

Andrew and Lennox took their brandy with them to the museum. The floors of the castle corridors were thickly carpeted, but the walls were bare stone, hung with tapestries and an impressive collection of antique arms and armour.

In the museum Lennox was a different person. He relaxed his tough, laconic exterior, and his face took on a warm, concerned expression. He moved from one painting to another, as if visiting old friends in hospital. He stood before each in turn, regarding them with undisguised affection.

He and Andrew stood before a magnificent Tiepolo. He grasped Andrew's arm.

'Are you a gambling man, Mr Tait?' he said.

'Not at all,' said Andrew firmly.

'Oh,' Lennox sounded disappointed. 'I should have thought you might have been.' He walked away from Andrew and stood looking at a marble Venus. He did not move for thirty seconds. Then he gave the sculpture an affectionate pat, and came back to Andrew. 'I thought you might be interested in a—a proposition. Not a gamble at all really.'

Andrew waited. He was calm. So far he had not made a mistake. After a long silence he said, 'A proposition has to be proposed.'

'Yes,' said Lennox. 'What I had in mind was to offer, here and now, for your Rembrandt, the sale price of the one that's coming up at Christie's, less two hundred and fifty thousand dollars. No provenances, no authentication. We settle it here and now.'

'But you haven't even seen the painting yet, Mr Lennox.'

'I don't need to see it to know what it's worth.'

'It's worth more than you're offering, Mr Lennox. It's certainly worth more than the sale price of the Proudfoot Rembrandt. I told you that I consider that that painting is offered on a closed market. It will have to stay in England.'

'But no one is going to question its authenticity. Now *your* Rembrandt . . .'

'*I* have no doubt that it is authentic.'

'How do you know that you weren't cheated, Mr Tait? Sold a forgery? The whole story could have been a put-up job.'

'I have made it my business to be an expert, Mr Lennox. So would you if so much depended on it. *You* need the director of the Rembrandthuis to tell you if a painting is genuine or not. I don't. I can tell as surely as him. Probably more so. He has only a reputation to lose.'

Lennox took his arm again. 'I can see you *are* a gambler, Mr Tait.'

'There are two views on gambling. Some would say it's no gamble to bet on a certainty.'

Lennox chuckled. 'Come, Mr Tait. I have something to show you.'

As Lennox steered him by his arm through the galleries,

Andrew was thinking. He knew he had done the right thing, but he wondered why Lennox had made him that offer. Andrew obviously could not accept it. It was not just a matter of convincing Lennox that it was a genuine painting. It would enter the artist's listed works. It would be scrutinized by every art expert in the world. If it did not stand up to that he would have to repay Lennox, whatever the bargain they struck. Andrew had no intention of skulking in some remote village for the rest of his life, not daring to show his face in London or New York. He stood or fell on the authenticity of the painting. Therefore, it was either worth nothing at all, or it was worth the very top price. Maybe Lennox was testing him. If so, he had done the right thing.

Andrew liked Lennox. He liked him more and more as he got to know him. Lennox was rich. But he had made it all himself. Every penny he had was earned by his own sweat. Or his cunning. Andrew did not find that sort of wealth offensive. Lennox had a right to it. And he didn't give himself airs. He knew what he wanted and he used his wealth to get it. He did not boast. He did not patronize. Andrew liked that quiet style. He did not want to cheat him. And he did not intend to. The Rembrandt would be authenticated. When that had happened, it would be a Rembrandt. If the greatest experts the world could produce would say so, to the world's thinking it must be a Rembrandt. And that was what Lennox was getting. The fact that this genuine old Rembrandt had been created by Andrew was his secret. And his triumph.

Lennox stopped in front of a large Monet study of the water-lilies. He released Andrew's arm, and felt along the bottom of the picture frame. He must have pressed a button —the painting moved to one side on a sliding panel. Behind it there was an opening in the wall.

'In here is our storeroom,' Lennox said. He motioned Andrew to go ahead of him.

The door closed automatically behind them. Andrew looked round. Dozens of paintings hung at the side of the room, in close racks, just clearing the floor. They were fixed on tracks at the ceiling, so that they could be run out individually to the centre of the room for inspection. Against the far wall was a bench and a couple of easels. On one of them was a painting, half-cleaned.

Lennox was making some adjustment to the racks at the far end of the room. He stood back. Four of the racks slid automatically to the centre of the room. Lennox was hidden in the corner.

'Come, Mr Tait,' he said. 'I said I have something to show you.'

Andrew found him standing in the corner, facing the blank wall. All the walls of the room were covered with strip panelling of natural wood. At a touch from Lennox part of the wall opened in a doorway.

'Come,' said Lennox.

They walked into a large room, almost the size of the storeroom. But this room was carpeted, and the walls were covered with dark red silk. Two Jacobean armchairs, covered in matching velvet, were placed in the centre of the room facing in opposite directions.

Without a word Lennox went and sat down.

Andrew followed the direction he was facing. He almost gasped. Before him was the Vermeer Woman at the Virginals. It had been stolen from the Rijksmuseum twelve months before.

Lennox turned and smiled at him, almost shyly. 'She's beautiful, isn't she?'

'Yes, but ...'

'I come here often, you know. I can sit here for hours, just looking at her. No one knows she is here, of course. Except McIntyre. He knows. But no one else. Not even my wife. She would not understand. And you. I feel I can trust you, Mr Tait.'

Andrew did not know what to say. 'Yes, but ...' he stammered.

'Like I can trust my paintings.' Andrew realized Lennox was not really talking to him—merely talking his thoughts aloud because Andrew was there. 'My paintings don't ask for anything from me. They are beautiful, and ageless. They never change. They give me pleasure. They give me peace. Sitting here with her, these are the best times of my life. My kids—I give them everything, and they spit on me. They take what I give, and they spit on me. They marry the

wrong men, they kill themselves in automobiles, they take drugs, they get themselves blackmailed by go-go dancers....
But the paintings, they are faithful. I can rely on them. They don't run off. If only my children were like this—people admire my pictures. They are mine, and they stay with me....' He seemed suddenly to remember Andrew's presence. 'I'm sorry,' he said. 'Forgive me. A rambling old man, I am becoming.'

'Not at all,' said Andrew. 'What you say makes good sense. I agree. That's the thing that paintings have. In some peculiar way, they can become friends. But this Vermeer ... She *is* beautiful. But ...'

But Lennox changed the conversation. 'Tomorrow, before lunch,' he said cheerfully, 'we shall have a glass of champagne, and you will unveil your Rembrandt for us, Mr Tait?'

'Yes,' said Andrew.

'I shall look forward to it.'

At least the sight of that secret gallery quietened the doubts in Andrew's mind. He had been shocked. His own deceptions were comparatively mild.

*

Corinna was surprised to get a call from Enid Roscoe. And more surprised still at her friendly tone.

'Have you heard from Andrew?' she asked.

'No,' said Corinna. 'Have you?'

'Oh yes,' said Enid.

But Corinna was sure she was not telling the truth.

'To tell the truth, my dear, I'm worried about him.'

Enid Roscoe really did sound concerned. Corinna's suspicions were fading. She had been half expecting herself to find Andrew was in trouble with the customs, or the police. There was something very suspicious about the disguised painting, and the lies he told her. And he had seemed so tense and desperate. Perhaps Enid Roscoe knew what it was all about. Perhaps that was the reason Andrew had had to keep so close to her.

'I wonder if you'd like to come over. Pick up a cab and come over and we can have a talk.'

In Enid's elegant living-room Corinna discovered she knew a great deal more about Andrew's movements than he suspected. She knew he had been seeing Corinna every day.

'Didn't you mind?' Corinna asked.

'Oh no, my dear. Why should I? You young people like to be together. It's natural.'

'How did you know. Did Andrew tell you?'

Enid laughed, a warm kindly laugh. 'Oh no, my dear. Of course not. Men like to have their secrets, don't they? I wouldn't want to deprive them of that. It seems to be necessary for them. But other people are always very ready to tell you things like that. I don't know why. I'm sure neither you nor I want to spend our time running round making trouble between our friends. But there you are. And in this case, there was no trouble to make, was there? It didn't matter in the least. Why ever should anyone think it would?'

She gave Corinna china tea and buttered toast. In New York, she played on her Englishness. In the apartment the paintings and sculpture were expertly displayed, carefully spotlighted so that only flattering, reflected light fell on the people in the room.

'I won't beat about the bush, my dear. You know he is taking a painting to that man in California, whoever he is?'

'Yes.'

'Have you seen it?'

'Well ...'

Enid lifted her head suspiciously.

'Well, no, I haven't. Andrew wouldn't show it to me. But, I don't know if he told you, but, well, I did do something rather awful on the ship ...'

'No. He didn't tell me. What did you do?'

Corinna told her about bluffing her way into Andrew's cabin with François on the last night of the voyage.

Enid laughed merrily. 'He didn't breathe a word to me,' she said. 'Isn't that typical? He wouldn't risk telling his right hand what the left was doing.'

Corinna was beginning to feel uncomfortable with this powder-room gossip. Enid must have had something else in mind. She kept leaning across and patting her affectionately on the knee. Surely she wasn't going to make a pass at her?

Corinna knew some of these middle-aged ladies started to get some strange ideas.

But when she told her about the pasted-over picture, Enid's mood changed.

'Ah,' she said gravely. 'Now that ties up. That's very interesting. I think perhaps I can tell you what was underneath. You see, we have a safe in this house. My husband had it installed. It's quite large. Of course, everything we have is insured. But sometimes we used to have a painting on approval. Or new things not yet covered. Insurance companies are funny, you know. You can't just get on the phone and arrange cover for a Van Gogh, like you can for a car. At any rate, I have this safe here in the house. And Andrew asked me if he could put a painting in it. Only one painting, mind you. He wouldn't tell me what it was. He had brought it for this man in California, he said. He had sworn not to tell anyone what it was until the man wanted it made public. Andrew said he would lose his commission if he betrayed that trust.'

'That's what he told me.'

'At least he told us the same story. He brought it here sewn into a green canvas bag. It was terribly suspicious. And to tell the truth, I didn't think it was fair to me. One ought to know what's in one's own safe. What if it turned out to be—well, say, a consignment of heroin? Who would believe that I didn't know anything about it?'

'Good God. He isn't mixed up in that, is he?'

'No, my dear. Don't worry. But for all one knew, he might have been, mightn't he?'

'I suppose so.'

'So I decided to investigate,' Enid said firmly, 'I had Horace ask Andrew to go round to the gallery for drinks. And I investigated. Oh, I was very clever. I had already had my maid buy some twine that matched what Andrew had used. Fortunately he's not very neat at stitching. That made it easy ... Anyhow, to come to the point. The painting that Andrew has taken down to California is a Rembrandt.'

'What?'

'Yes, my dear, I know. At first I couldn't believe my eyes. But I do know enough about painting to recognize a Rembrandt when I see one. I don't know where this came from.

I don't think I've ever seen it before.'

'What is it?'

'What do you mean?'

'What's the subject?'

'Oh. It's a nude. One of those women by a pool. A woman bathing. I'm sure I've seen several, haven't I?'

'I don't know,' Corinna answered. 'But there is one in my father's family. It's a Diana. It's very odd.'

'Well, it couldn't be your father's.'

'No. What is the woman doing?'

'Bathing. Didn't I say? At least, she *has* bathed, I suppose. She's lying on the grass by the pool.'

'On the right of the picture?'

'Yes. I'd have thought she'd be awfully cold. But those women never seem to be, do they? When there's a painter watching.'

'I don't understand.'

'I didn't want to worry you, my dear. To tell the truth, I felt I had to tell someone. And I thought perhaps you might know something about it.'

'Where can it have come from?'

'That's what I wonder. I suppose it could have come from a private collection. Perhaps it was smuggled out to be sold privately, to avoid tax, or to get round export regulations. But the tax people are going to want to know what's happened to a painting like that. It must be catalogued. The whole world knows if you own a Rembrandt.'

'It must have come from the Continent somewhere. I'm sure Andrew didn't take it out of England.'

'At the very least he must be in trouble with the customs.'

'I wondered what he was up to.'

'And the only alternative—I hate to think about it even, but the only alternative seems to be that it has been stolen.'

'Oh no.'

'Well my dear, there must be some reason for all this secrecy, this subterfuge. One has heard so much about the secret collectors.'

'Are you sure it is a Rembrandt?'

'Well—yes, I am. If it isn't a Rembrandt, it's a copy of a Rembrandt. It wasn't a new painting. It was old. And if it was only a copy, why all the secrecy?'

'It could have been a forgery.'

'Yes, I'd thought of that. But if it was, there wouldn't have been the need either for all this secrecy. It's the secrecy that makes me wonder if it really is a stolen painting. Do you know if a Rembrandt has been stolen?'

'No. But that doesn't mean anything.'

'My dear, I'm so sorry to trouble you like this. But you can imagine how worried I've been.'

'Did Andrew know you'd looked at it?'

'Oh no, I don't think so. I was very careful. I sewed it up again very carefully.'

Corinna left Enid's house with a hundred unanswered questions churning in her head. She knew she wasn't going to solve the riddle of Andrew's behaviour by worrying at it. All the possible answers filled her with apprehension. One of them had to be the fact. She was scared of what was going to happen.

And that was another question: why had Enid taken such trouble to scare her? She did it with finesse, with real class, but all the same the only reason she had had Corinna over for their little heart-to-heart was to scare the shit out of her. Which could only mean that Enid was scared of Corinna. A little while ago, Corinna might have been glad. But now she faced it she realized she did not care any more.

Next day the problems were driven out of her mind by the Western Union messenger. He delivered a cable at the Foxley's house addressed to Corinna. It was from her mother: ARRIVING KENNEDY FRIDAY AM BOAC 74 PLEASE MEET MOTHER.

*

From the moment he lifted the cover Andrew could see that Lennox fell for the painting. For a long time he contemplated it in silence, sipping at his champagne. But his eyes burned with a deep light, and Andrew knew that he was hooked.

Eventually Lennox stirred. 'It's got class,' he said. 'I'll say that. It's got real class.'

From him that was a high compliment. Lennox did not have the vocabulary of aesthetic superlatives. But his appreciation was no less keen. Under his cool exterior, Andrew was exultant. It had worked. At first sight Lennox had fallen in love with Franco's Diana.

During the afternoon, Andrew was summoned to the phone to take a call from New York. It was Corinna.

'Hello,' he said. 'It's good to hear you. How did you get the number?'

'Well, Andrew,' she said. 'Men like Lennox are quite well known. Even if you don't have the street number.'

Andrew laughed. 'O.K. You're elected secretary of the week. What time is it with you?'

'Evening,' she said. 'Seven o'clock.'

'Good Lord. Yes. What's the weather like?'

'Cold.

'In a city you don't like, it's always cold. Who said that? Hemingway? Raymond Chandler?'

'I don't know. But it's true. I'm freezing. And I hate this city.'

'I'm sorry.'

'Listen, Andrew. I didn't call you to talk about the weather. My mother arrived here yesterday.'

'You called to tell me that?'

'Yes. At least, partly that. I mean, yes, but the important thing is the reason she came. She came to get away from Boys Hall, from England.'

She hesitated. 'Why?' Andrew prompted.

'Well ... Andrew, I wish you were here.'

'Why?'

'Well. You know Tim and Sally were putting the Rembrandt up at Christie's?'

'Yes.'

'Christie's won't accept it. They say it is a forgery. A recent forgery. Not more than twenty or thirty years old.'

There was silence at the other end of the line.

'Andrew? Are you still there?'

'Why did your mother leave?'

'She wanted to get away from all the fuss at home. No one else knows. You mustn't tell anyone. Christie's are being very decent, they're keeping it quiet. They can easily say it's been withdrawn to sort out some tax problem. But you can imagine how she feels.... She loved that picture. It was

212

her favourite in the whole house. You know, when I was born, she wanted to call me Diana. But apparently my father—my real father—wanted me to be called Corinna ... if I was a girl. He wasn't there when I was born.'

'Corinna.' Andrew's voice was strained. Corinna knew there must be some connection somewhere between the Proudfoot Diana and the painting Andrew had taken to Lennox in California, but she still could not figure it out. And she guessed Andrew was not going to tell her. Was it possible that the Proudfoot Diana had been stolen many years ago?—That would have been during the war, when Lord de Boys was away and no one really knew what was going on. And maybe Andrew had traced it. Maybe it had been smuggled to the Continent and hidden. Anything was possible in those days. Or maybe a copy had been made as a safety precaution, and the original had never been replaced. According to her mother, Tim was challenging the opinion of Christie's experts. But they didn't make mistakes about things like that.... There were a thousand possibilities. The only thing she knew was that there must be a connection somewhere. 'Corinna. I'm coming back to New York.'

'When?'

'As soon as I can. Tomorrow. The day after. Will you be at the Foxleys'?'

'No, Andrew.'

'Where will you be?'

'I won't be in New York, Andrew. That's really what I wanted to tell you. I'm going home. I'm going back to England.'

'Didn't your mother come to see you? Doesn't she want you to stay?'

'No. She's with the Foxleys. She hasn't told anyone but me about the Rembrandt. She has a lot of good friends in New York. She's at home here. She doesn't need me. I'm sure she'd rather I went. And I don't want to stay.'

'But when shall I see you?'

'I don't know, Andrew.'

'But ...'

'What I mean, Andrew, is that I'm not sure. I'm not sure what I'm going to do. And I'm not sure that I want to see you. I think it might be better if we didn't meet. I shouldn't have come on this trip. It's too late to worry about it now, but I'm going back. I don't know what I'm going to do. I doubt if I shall stay at the cottage, but I'll go there for the time being. There isn't anywhere else.'

'I shall come and see you.'

'Andrew. Please don't do that. Don't you understand, Andrew? I'm saying that I don't want to see you again.'

She put down the phone. She was not crying. A faint glimmer of light had appeared to her, at the end of the long dark unhappy tunnel of the last months. She began to understand what she was going to do.

4

Quentin Gold had woken with a start at five in the morning. His heart was racing. What had woken him, he wondered. Then he remembered—today the Proudfoot Rembrandt came in to Christie's.

He forced himself to take his breakfast slowly. He had found himself, when he was dressing, carefully selecting a tie, as if he had an important lunch appointment. He was at the office before the commissionaire had put on his cap for the day.

Sally was late. She had driven up from Boys Hall that morning, starting soon after dawn. Quentin was not the only one who was nervous, she told him. Although it was insured for a vast sum, Timothy was reluctant to let the picture out of his sight. He wanted to travel up with it in the van, but the transport men would not allow him.

And the night before Delphine had made an eleventh-hour appeal to Timothy not to take the picture away. She had summoned the family to the top of the stairway in the Great Hall. She stood in front of the Diana and pleaded with Timothy. The way she told it, The Nude Diana was the chief claim to fame for the Proudfoot family. Without it, they would be nothing. Anyone who knew anything about anything knew that this was the family's most important possession. With tears streaming down her cheeks, she told them how much she herself loved this painting, how she had wanted to name her only daughter after it, how it would break her heart to see it torn down from its place of honour and put up for public auction, like a common prostitute.

'It sounds very dramatic,' Quentin said.

'It was. But Delphine thrives on drama. She needs it. She lives her whole life as if she were a dramatic heroine.'

'But she didn't make Timothy change his mind?'

'Well, we were all terribly upset, of course. But Timothy isn't the sort of man who changes his mind at the last moment. He made up his mind long ago, and that was that. And I think Giles was on his side, if in anything, after his mother's performance.'

He was sorry Sally had had such trouble. Unfortunately, in their business, family disagreements were all too common. He'd learned never to take sides, and to insist on the proper authority for every step he took himself. That way he avoided difficulty, if not unpleasantness.

At noon they had a message that the painting had arrived. Sally hurried out to find Timothy. He had followed the van up to London in his car.

A porter was bringing the picture to the storeroom. Quentin hurried downstairs to get his first sight of the painting.

As soon as he saw it, he felt a sudden panic. Something was wrong. He was sure of it. For twenty years he had been training his eyes to judge paintings. He had learnt to trust their opinion. And they told him immediately that there was something fishy about this picture. He could not say right away what it was—simply that the picture was not 'right'. But he did not have any doubt of that. It was more than a suspicion. Those twenty years had given him that confidence. He was absolutely certain it was wrong.

Sally came into the storeroom. She was flushed with excitement. 'Tim didn't come,' she said. 'His car broke down on the M1.' She laughed. 'The painting got here anyway.'

'When did you last look at it, Sally?'

'I don't know. Last night I suppose. I look at it every time I go up the main stairs at Tim's house.'

'I mean really look at it. Look at it closely.'

'Oh, I don't know really. It's just there all the time, you know ...' She caught a hint from the gravity of his voice. 'Why? What's the matter? Is it damaged?'

'No,' Quentin said carefully. 'I don't think it's damaged.'

'Quentin.' Her voice was filled with apprehension. 'Something is the matter. What are you saying?'

'I'm not happy about it, Sally. It doesn't smell right.'

'How can it possibly ...?' Her voice trailed away.

Quentin peered closely at the surface of the canvas. He picked up his magnifying glass and inspected the flesh of Diana's leg. 'It's very good, I must say,' he murmured.

'What do you mean, very good?' Sally was frantic, only just in control of herself. She wanted to run away. But she forced herself to say calmly. 'What is good, Quentin?'

'The brushwork,' he answered automatically. 'Rembrandt's brushwork was bold—almost Impressionist if you look at it. He must have painted quickly. There's nothing finicky about it. Look at that white shift or whatever it is she's put on the grass. The paint's really slapped on. That's just how Rembrandt did it. The paint's not built up with smooth layers. You can't get that effect by painting meticulously. You can't keep stopping to see how you're getting on, to check if Rembrandt's brush went slightly to the left or right ...'

'But Quentin, you're talking as if this was painted by someone else, a copy ...'

Quentin turned slowly and looked at her. 'Yes, Sally. I'm afraid that's exactly what I am saying.'

'But it can't be,' she burst out. She turned on him. 'How do you *know*?' she demanded angrily. 'How can *you* say? It can't possibly be by anyone else. Anyone can see it's Rembrandt. *You* can't just sit here and say it isn't. You don't *know* it isn't.'

'I do know, Sally. For myself I'm quite satisfied.' His own face was ashen. Up to now he had simply been concentrating on the identification of the painting. Now the implications of what he had said were beginning to dawn on him. 'It doesn't quite hang together. It isn't quite confident enough. But that doesn't prove it, of course.'

'What are you going to do?'

'I shall talk to other people. The other people here. We shall have to decide. We could refuse to handle it. We could try to persuade your fiancé not to offer it for sale. That's usually the most tactful way out of these situations. We can make some tests on it.'

'Quentin, how can you sit there and calmly tell me that this painting is a—a forgery? The whole world knows this painting. Hundreds of people come and look at it. They don't think it's a forgery.'

'They don't look at it as closely as me.'

'That painting means a whole life for Tim and me,' Sally said. There were tears in her eyes. 'How *can* you just sit there and tell me it's worth—worth *nothing*? You just look at it and tell me it's worth nothing.'

'Unfortunately, it's my job to tell people these things—if it happens to be the case. Look, Sally. I don't enjoy it. It's a terrible disappointment for me too. I wish I didn't think this painting was wrong. But if I do, I have to say so ...'

Sally ran from the room.

Quentin called the other art directors. At first he said nothing of his suspicions.

'What do you think of her?' he asked.

'Beautiful. Magnificent,' said one.

'It's a fake,' said the other.

'Yes,' said Quentin. 'That's what I thought. What do you think we should do?'

Christie's told Timothy that, in their opinion, it was a suspect painting. He was indignant. How could it be a forgery? It had hung in Boys Hall for three hundred years. He wanted to take it away from them and give it to Sotheby's to auction instead. But they persuaded him it was wiser not to say anything until they had made some tests. While it was still at Christie's they assured him, the matter would be handled with complete discretion.

Finally he agreed.

First they took the canvas out of the frame. They agreed that the frame was genuine. The stretchers on which it was fastened were also genuine—they were certainly of old wood. But here was the first evidence to support their opinion:

217

the edges of the canvas were almost straight and had not shrunk from the nails at all.

They took threads from the edges of the canvas. They sent them to the workshops of the National Gallery and asked for a dating. They were returned with a report that the threads were from canvas of nineteenth-century manufacture, or later. There were traces of bleaching chemicals—not used on old canvas—which caused brown stains when treated with sodium hydrate. Furthermore, the thread and weave of the canvas was of nineteenth-century or later machine-made type.

X-ray photographs showed no evidence of another painting under the Diana. But they did show clearly that the canvas was fixed to the stretcher with machine-made nails. The heads of the nails were covered with paint. Further, a radiograph showed that there was considerably less crackle down at the canvas than a direct photograph, or even visual inspection, showed at the surface—an indication that the crackle had been induced artificially from the surface and not by the natural movement of the canvas as the paint dried.

From three separate places on the canvas a tiny core of paint was taken off with a hypodermic needle. These, under microscopic inspection, showed four or five distinguishable layers—two grounds, two or three layers of paint, and one of varnish. This was perfectly in line with Rembrandt's known techniques. Chemical analysis of the paints revealed a different story. Some of the blue pigment, instead of ground *lapis lazuli*, turned out to be artificial ultramarine. This is obtained by heating together kaolin, sodium carbonate and sulphur. Chemically the components are those of *lapis lazuli*. But under the microscope the particles are not crystalline, as are those of *lapis lazuli*: they are smaller and they are all blue, whereas in *lapis lazuli* there are uneven and colourless crystals. Artificial ultramarine was first available in the nineteenth century. Further, under test with the microspectroscope, some of the blue pigment revealed traces of cobalt, showing absorption bands in the red and yellow, and a bright red band.

Dirt lifted from the surface cracks was shown on analysis to be almost unadulterated charcoal dust.

The Louvre kindly supplied microphotographs of the brushwork of the flesh and the eyes of their Bathsheba After the Bath for comparison with the Diana. A painter's treatment of the eye and the mouth are almost inimitable when looked at in this detail. Although to the naked eye the effect of the flesh tones of Bathsheba and the Diana were identical, in the photographs it was possible to see they had been built up differently. Bathsheba was much more boldly, irregularly worked, with tiny jabbing strokes of the brush.

'That should be enough for anyone,' Quentin said when they had the final report. 'I wish to God I had been proved wrong. Proudfoot won't like it. But he'll have to accept it.'

*

Andrew took the local connection from Santa Barbara for the New York plane from L.A. It was damp and cold when he left. As the plane came in from the sea the rising sun was shining on the yellowish pall of the smog that hung over Los Angeles. For half an hour they circled, until it was clear enough to land—round and round over the same drab landscape, grey houses, grey yards, and chlorine-blue pools.

In New York Andrew put the painting back in Enid's safe. She seemed glad to see him. But it wasn't easy to tell with Enid how much of it was politeness.

'You friend Corinna's mother is here,' she said. 'She is the toast of New York.'

'Really?'

'She's a friend of yours too, is she?'

'I know her. I wouldn't say she was a friend. She doesn't like me at all.'

'She sees a lot of Bob Wetherby. They are inseparable.'

'That's clever of her.'

'Clever of him. I've no doubt she's immensely rich.'

'Yes,' said Andrew. 'I suppose so.'

When Corinna had called him at Lennox's estate, it had taken him ten seconds to piece together the whole story. He intended to get Delphine to confirm that he'd got it right. It meant he would have to put his Rembrandt away for the time being, and see what developed.

Andrew soon discovered that Delphine and Bob Wetherby

really did make the New York scene. They went to all the openings, of course. But so did Enid and Andrew. Even at the party for Henry Geldzahler's important show of Twenty Years' Decorative Art at the Metropolitan, and Alan Solomon's dinner at the Jewish Museum before the Barney Newman retrospective, Enid and Andrew also made the grade.

But it was Delphine Henry took arm in arm for a personal tour of the show. At the Jewish Museum it was Delphine who spent an hour talking to Clement Greenberg—the most important critic in New York, and centre of the circle nicknamed by their rivals, who thought of it as some sinister and powerful cabal, the Kosher Nostra. And Bob and Delphine socialized outside the art world. They were into the whole scene. When Nureyev danced at the Lincoln, they were there in the stalls, naturally. And they went to the party afterwards given by the Leonard Bernsteins for Rudolf and Margot. They were at David Merrick's party for Richard Burton. When Truman Capote gave his second ball, of course he and Delphine were invited. Enid was not. She arranged to spend a few days in the country.

Bob sold paintings to David Whitney, to Mr and Mrs Robert Scull, Norton Simon and a whole raft of the super-rich with their private tax-avoidance foundations. He was a good friend of Barbara Rose, Marion Javits, Leo Castelli. He was everywhere. And he took Delphine with him.

'We shall have to do something about this,' said Enid. And she was not entirely joking.

But Bob Wetherby did not like rivals.

He asked Andrew to have lunch with him. 'Just man to man, eh? Make it the Oyster Bar at the Plaza. One o'clock.'

Bob Wetherby sucked down a dozen oysters and drank Black Velvet.

Andrew did not like that style. He ordered a Bloody Mary and clams. 'How's Delphine?' he asked.

Bob Wetherby ignored the question. 'Been to see Lennox, I hear, Andrew?'

'That's right.'

'You're working for him?'

'I wouldn't say that. He's in the market for some things.

There's nothing exclusive, I'm sure you know quite well what he wants.'

'A Rembrandt more than anything. He says you have one. He thinks he can get it from you cheap. I hope you're not going to give it away.'

'We didn't even discuss a price. I'm not even sure I'm going to let him have it.'

'Quite right. I'm not sure he should be allowed to have a Rembrandt at all. There aren't so many good ones about. Yours is a good one, is it?'

'Yes,' said Andrew. 'The best. The last best Rembrandt there will ever be. It's worth a great deal of money. I don't know where Lennox got the idea it would be cheap. It certainly won't.'

'I see,' said Wetherby. 'How exciting. You know, I'm not altogether sure I trust our friend Lennox. Tsk. Tsk. He doesn't always quite tell the truth.' He shook his head sadly.

*

'But Mr Tait gave us to understand that a Rembrandt would not be allowed out of England. Or any other country, for that matter.'

Ashton Lennox, his eyes shaded by tinted glasses, accepted a glass of iced Coke from McIntyre.

'That's not necessarily true.'

Bob Wetherby, immaculately dressed in a grey lightweight suit, knocked the ash from his Havana cigar into the pool. McIntyre blanched. Wetherby knew he was angry. He had deliberately provoked him. He had flown out to California to teach Lennox a lesson—that doing deals behind Wetherby's back is asking for trouble.

McIntyre had a second glass of Coke in his other hand. He gave it to a girl in a tiny red bikini who was standing by Lennox's chair. She had been introduced to Wetherby as Lennox's niece, who was studying at Berkeley. Lennox's wife, apparently, was in Europe and Linda was staying at the castle. She looked as if her principal study was physical education. She took her Coke and stretched out on her stomach on a towel by the side of the pool. She slid her arms out of the straps of the bikini and settled down to freshen the tan on her back. Lennox's face was expressionless as stone.

'You mean, Tait's a liar?' he said.

'No. I wouldn't say that about a professional colleague. Perhaps he is not so experienced. I have been practising this trade longer than Andrew Tait. All I will say is, that in my experience there are ways and means of moving paintings—perfectly legitimate ways and means of moving paintings from one country to another.'

'Your Rembrandt is in Europe?'

'Yes.'

'We know that one. The Proudfoot Rembrandt.'

'The Nude Diana,' McIntyre added. 'They'd never allow that out.'

'No. I did not mean the Nude Diana. The Proudfoot picture will never be sold.'

'What do you mean? It's coming up at Christie's. It's been announced.'

'Could you give me the date?'

'No. Well, I don't think the date's been fixed,' McIntyre faltered.

'I say it will never be sold.'

'Why do you say that, Mr Wetherby?' Lennox asked in his deliberate voice.

'Because the Proudfoot picture is a forgery, Mr Lennox.'

'What?' McIntyre burst out. 'What did you say?'

'It's a forgery. A fake, Mr McIntyre.'

Lennox took a sip of his Coke. 'And how do you know that, Mr Wetherby?' he asked.

'Because I've seen it, Mr Lennox. I know the family quite well. I've stayed quite frequently in their house. They have some magnificent paintings. But this is not one of them. It is a forgery. I knew it the first time I saw it, and I've never changed my opinion.'

'Is that so?' Lennox said. 'That's amazing. Tell me, how can you be so sure?'

'One has a certain instinct, Mr Lennox. One trains it. One takes notice of it. Our whole system of education, our whole society, tries to persuade us not to trust in instinct, to rely only on such things as proof and logic. In fact instinct is a very accurate instrument. It takes into account all those almost imperceptible clues, perhaps too fine to measure. My instinct is what I rely on, Mr Lennox. I would back it against a whole lot of documentation, and not a little science. So far, I'm glad to say, there has been no conflict between me and the evidence.'

'Do the family know this?' McIntyre asked.

'I doubt it. It's a very good copy. I doubt if there are more than half-a-dozen men in the world who would even suspect the painting without the chance of testing it.' He smiled. 'The other five have probably not seen it. Scientific tests, of course, would prove it. If the family did know, they would be running a very great risk, surely, in sending it for auction.'

'Lady Delphine is in New York, isn't she?' McIntyre made it sound as if he was scoring a point.

'Yes. I haven't spoken to her about it. She hasn't mentioned it to me. As you say, it is commonly assumed that the painting will be sold.'

'Does she know it's a fake?'

'I really couldn't tell you, Mr McIntyre. I haven't asked her. Perhaps you would like to do so yourself?'

Lennox said, 'Have you seen Mr Tait's Rembrandt, Mr Wetherby?'

'No. Why?'

'It was painted, Mr Tait says, about the same time as the Proudfoot painting.'

'You must draw your own conclusions from that.'

'Yes,' Lennox said. 'May I ask you if your instinct formed an opinion as to how recently the Proudfoot painting had been made? It had been known for some hundreds of years. It came direct from the sale of Charles II's collection. He bought it from the artist. Did the artist sell him a fake?'

'Without inspecting it, I couldn't say for sure. I would guess that it was a recent forgery. Not more than a hundred years old. Does it make a difference?'

'Yes. You see, Mr Tait's painting is very similar indeed to the Proudfoot Diana. It's not similar enough, however, to be the same picture in an altered state. Mr McIntyre has checked on this. If the Proudfoot Diana is a recent forgery, an original must have existed. Mr Tait's twin painting therefore seems at least a possibility.'

'Did he offer no provenance? No certification? No evidence of ownership?'

'No.'

'This really does begin to sound suspicious.'

With a deliberate gesture Wetherby threw the butt of his cigar into the centre of the pool. 'Now, listen, Mr Lennox. I'm offering you a Rembrandt. Its provenance is indisputable. It's a portrait of his son Titus. Not dissimilar to the one Mr Norton Simon has in his collection here in California.'

'Did he buy that from you?' McIntyre asked.

A shadow of annoyance crossed Wetherby's face. 'No,' he said. 'He chose to buy it himself at Christie's. I offered to obtain it for him. He wouldn't have had to pay so much. But he chose to buy it himself.'

'And they let him take it out of England?'

'Exactly.'

'How much?' Lennox asked.

'What?'

'How much is yours?'

'It will not be cheap,' Wetherby answered. 'If you want a Rembrandt, a good Rembrandt, a *genuine* Rembrandt, you must be prepared to pay for it. But consider, Mr Lennox, what you are buying. What Tait says has some truth in it. It becomes more and more difficult to get great paintings out of Europe. There are very few left. If you have to think about the price, Mr Lennox, you shouldn't think about collecting this sort of painting.' He appeared to be fascinated by Linda's back, as she raised her head to take a sip of her Coke, holding her other arm across her breasts. 'You know what the great Duveen, the great dealer, used to say? When you pay high for the priceless, you are still getting it cheap. He was right. There's one thing you can be sure of—if you try to buy masterpieces in the bargain basement, you will run into trouble. If they're in the basement, it's because there's some reason they dare not show themselves upstairs in the drawing-room. You, Mr Lennox, have a magnificent collection of drawing-room paintings. Many of them, I'm glad to say, purchased on my advice. If there are any of those paintings, if there is even one, that you now regret, I beg you to return it to me immediately. I should, of course, credit you with the full purchase price.'

'I'm perfectly satisfied, Mr Wetherby. In fact, as I hope you know, I'm proud of every single picture that you've found me. I'm proud to possess them.'

'And I wonder Mr Lennox, if there are any paintings that I have advised you against that you now wish you had bought nevertheless?'

Lennox was about to speak, but Wetherby continued, 'If there are, I will undertake to go to the present owner and, if at all humanly possible, obtain them for you—at whatever the price. And I should be glad to present them to your museum as a gift.'

Lennox lowered his head. There was a slight smile at the corners of his mouth. 'There are none,' he said. 'Mr Wetherby, I'm entirely satisfied with—with your help. Without your good advice, my museum would be nothing like it is.'

Wetherby stood up. 'Thank you,' he said. 'I'm glad to hear it. I wanted to be sure. I thought it worth coming to see you.'

'I am glad you did.'

After he had gone, McIntyre said to Lennox, 'He didn't arrange to show us his Rembrandt.'

Lennox chuckled. 'No,' he said. 'I don't suppose he could. I doubt the owner has even agreed to sell. Wetherby has some work to do on that.'

'Then what was he doing here?'

'He came to warn me off Tait, you fool. It's as plain as the nose on your fat face.'

'What will you do? Will you deal with Tait?'

'I don't know. What we shall do, McIntyre, is wait and see. Remember, *this* is where the money is. We call the tune. The worst mistake we could make is let ourselves be rushed. I've learnt that lesson in the last forty years. Act swift if you have to. Never act hasty.'

'It seems to me, for all the activity, we don't seem any nearer having a Rembrandt hang in the museum over there.'

'You think not? McIntyre, you're too gloomy. Go away. Linda and me, we're going to take a dip in the pool.'

Linda jumped up. She left her bikini bra on the towel. 'Oh yes,' she said. 'Let's go in the pool!' She giggled. 'I'll give you an underwater massage.'

225

'Oh, McIntyre, before you go, get that cigar butt out of the water, will you?'

McIntyre dragged his eyes from Linda's bouncing breasts, and picked up the net that lay by the pool to take out insects and fallen leaves.

Lennox was getting out of his clothes. 'Hurry up, McIntyre,' he said. 'Hurry up. Go on—clear off. Thinking about a new picture gets me horny.'

Linda pushed off her pants and jumped into the pool, shrieking. 'Uncle Ashton. Uncle Ashton. Come and get it.'

*

Delphine tried to avoid Andrew in New York. If they were at the same party, she avoided his eyes and stayed in another part of the room. If he called at the Foxleys' house, the maid always reported that she was out, and they didn't know when she would be back.

But Andrew was determined to see her. The difficulty was to get to her without Enid knowing. He did not want to have to explain to Enid what he wanted with Delphine.

His chance came one afternoon in Sonnabend's SoHo gallery at the Gilbert and George show. Gilbert and George, two precise Englishmen, very properly dressed, gilded their faces and sat in the gallery with impassive expressions. They sat there all day, scarcely moving. Now and then they sang an old popular song.... This was their art. They pulled it off by sheer conviction. They took it so seriously, you yourself felt it must be worth thinking about. It wasn't what anyone else had ever called 'art'. There was nothing to buy and take away and put on the wall of your room. But when you thought about it, it was in some way serious, and convincing. Even if you came to laugh, you went away impressed.

And when word got around, New York came in hundreds to see what it was all about. But at the beginning of the show the gallery was almost empty. Enid did not want to go. She had said so often that she did not care for the downtown scene, she had almost talked herself out of ever going there. She sent Andrew—her ambassador to underdeveloped areas.

When he walked into the gallery, the only other person there, apart from Gilbert and George themselves, and a boy at the desk with shoulder-length hair and green shoes, was Delphine.

Andrew went straight up to her. 'Hello, Delphine,' he said.

She did not hide her displeasure. She adopted her most superior expression. 'Hello, Andrew,' she said, as if he were a servant she had had to dismiss some time ago.

'I'm glad to see you, Delphine. I've been trying to catch you. You're very elusive.'

'I seem to have been frightfully busy.'

If possible, she was thinner than ever, her cheekbones even more prominent. She was dramatically dressed in long boots and a richly embroidered calf-length dress. But she looked ill.

'I wanted to talk to you. It's rather important.'

'Oh?' she said, as if she could scarcely imagine anything Andrew said could be important.

'Yes. I wanted to talk about the Rembrandt at the Hall —the Diana.'

'Why? What do you know about that?'

He was glad she was so insulting. Otherwise he might have felt sorry for her. Those people got away with being rude for so long, they never bothered to learn to be polite. Someone had to teach them the hard way.

'I hear that Christie's are refusing to handle it? They think it's doubtful?'

'Corinna told you?'

'Yes.'

'How dare she?'

'She told me nothing I couldn't have guessed myself. I knew, in a way I knew already. But I'd like to hear the details from you.'

'What did you know already?' Her eyes were beginning to shift with fear. 'What details? You seem to think you know everything already.'

Gilbert or George, whichever it was, began to sing in a thin small voice. 'Underneath the arches . . .'

'Wouldn't it be better if we talked about it somewhere else?'

'If you insist.'

'Would you have lunch with me? The Lutèce is nice at this time of year. All those flowers in the garden room are quite cheering.'

Delphine was half an hour late for lunch. It was just too cool to sit out on the patio, but there was plenty of foliage inside. Andrew waited calmly. He knew she would come. She was scared, and she wanted to find out how much Andrew knew.

And she had evidently decided that her best plan was to be co-operative.

'I'm going to tell you everything,' she said, almost as soon as she sat down. 'I don't know how much you know. But I have to tell someone. And it's probably better to tell a stranger. It's been such a terrible strain. All these years. It's ruined my health. Look at me. I never sleep. I can't eat. Look at me. I look terrible, don't I?'

'No, of course ...'

'Oh, don't be polite. Please don't be polite. I've had this bottled-up inside me for twenty-five years. It's been eating at me all this time. Like a—like a cancer it has been eating at me. How many people look at me and say, "Delphine certainly knows how to get what she wants"? But what's the cost? Is what Delphine gets always what Delphine wants?'

'I'm sorry.'

'Who else knows?' she asked, looking up suddenly. 'Does Corinna know?'

'Nobody else knows,' said Andrew. 'Different people know different parts, but no one but you and I know the whole story.'

'And ... and ...' She could not bring herself to say the name.

'And Franco? Yes—at any rate up to the death of your husband.'

She watched her own nail marking lines in the table cloth. Then she said quietly. 'It was his fault. It was Franco's fault. You know that?' She glanced up quickly at Andrew. There were tears in her eyes. 'He was so proud. So stubborn. After the war I wanted him to stay at the Hall. It would have been quite easy. I was willing to pay for him to be trained. We needed someone to look after the pictures. Some of them were badly neglected. He was very stubborn. He insisted that, if I really loved him, I should run away with him. We should get married and live on his painting. It was all very romantic. But neither of us would have been happy. You know, Italians are obsessed with their masculinity. That Latin *machismo*. Franco would have sacrificed anything to bolster his male pride. And I wouldn't let him.'

'Had he painted the Diana then?'

Delphine's answer was almost inaudible. 'No. He had started. He had made sketches, but he hadn't finished.' She looked directly at Andrew. 'I didn't know what he was doing. I knew he had been copying pictures in the Uffizi. I thought he should keep his hand in. I encouraged him. I was ... very fond of him. I wanted to help him. He begged me to let him stay until the birth of the child. I hadn't the heart to refuse him. I didn't want him to go away. Oh, if only I hadn't been so soft-hearted. If only I had known what he was doing.'

'Did he stay at the Hall?'

'No. Oh no. He went to live in an old cottage on the estate. The cottage that we gave Corinna later. It was quite isolated —you remember?'

'Yes.'

'It had been empty for years. Franco patched it up. Word got about that one of the Italian prisoners had stayed in England rather than go home. The cottage was miles away. Franco never came to the house, so no one ever knew who he was.'

Franco had found work at the houses round about, gardening and odd-jobbing. In those days Delphine had horses of her own. She would take them out every day for exercise, and find her way to the cottage. She took Franco food, money and the materials he needed to continue with his painting.

He had fitted up the stables beside the cottage as his studio. In the woods to the rear he found an old charcoal burner's camp. He renovated the oven in preparation for the final stages of his work.

'Did he use an old canvas?'

'No.'

'Why not?'

'It was a mistake, I know. He should have done. There were some quite unimportant old paintings in the Hall

229

that no one would have missed. Or if they had, they might have been stolen while everyone was away. Things did disappear during the war. But I tell you, I didn't know what he was doing. As far as I knew, as long as it *looked* genuine, that was all he wanted. I bought him new canvas, and he treated it somehow. But of course the Christie's people knew at once that it was new.'

Franco had boiled the canvas for hours and then laid it out in the sun to bleach and fade. But the summer of '45 was cold and wet, and when it did shine the English sun was too weak to be effective.

'I couldn't understand,' Delphine said, 'why he was so keen to get every detail right. Even the back of it. He took old wood out of the rafters of the cottage to make the stretchers. Of course I know why now, but at the time I thought it was just that he was a sort of perfectionist. You know how some people are funny about getting things exactly right.'

For priming the canvas after he had bleached it, Franco made a glue from rabbit skins. The land round about was infested with rabbits, and he soon grew skilful at snaring them. With the meat he fed himself and the old mongrel dog that came to live with him. The skins he cut up and boiled in an evil-smelling mess that eventually he was able to strain and use as glue.

'But there were some things I couldn't get for him. I couldn't get the blue he wanted. *Lapis lazuli.* In the war you couldn't get it. It was practically unobtainable. It was fearfully expensive, anyway.'

After the painting was completed, Franco baked it very slowly in the charcoal oven. Later, in his studio in the stables, he wet the canvas thoroughly and, with a compass point, marked on the back the lines of the main pattern of crackle he wanted. Then he rolled the canvas, paint outwards, repeatedly and carefully. A convincing pattern of crackle appeared on the surface.

'Why did he do it?'

'I didn't know he *was* doing it. All I knew was that he was becoming very strange. I thought he was obsessed with what he was doing, with the creation of a duplicate masterpiece. It was only when he had finished that I realized why he was in such a state. You see, he thought that, if he could put it in the place of the real Rembrandt, and sell the original, he would have so much money I couldn't possibly refuse to go with him. He knew about the secret market. He had come across it occasionally when he was copying in Florence. He was quite sure that this was the answer to all his problems. In so many ways he was quite innocent, you know.'

'Where is it now, the painting?'

'I don't know. I honestly don't know. I didn't want to know. Where do these paintings go? You probably know better than I. I always used to think they were all in South America, but one hears all sorts of stories. I was even told there is one secret collector in England. I refused to have anything to do with it. I didn't know what to do. I knew I shouldn't have anything to do with it. I shouldn't have helped him. But—well, I *loved* him, Andrew. And I was beginning to be *frightened* of him. He was like a man possessed. And then—well, it didn't seem such an awful thing. No one would ever know. I couldn't tell the difference between the paintings myself, from close to, and I do look at a lot of paintings, you know. I know what to look for in a painting. I knew that no one would ever suspect anything while it stayed there on the wall. And why should it ever be taken down? Certainly not in my lifetime. I think I let Franco persuade me that there was no *real* difference in the value of the two paintings. Only for people who didn't matter—investing collectors, and money men. For everyone else, after all, the experience of looking at his copy was the same as looking at the real thing.'

She put her hand on his and shot him a pleading glance. 'He persuaded me. I know it was wrong of me. But you must understand how it was for me. All the things I had wanted to do, all these years, they all suddenly seemed possible. Not for myself. I didn't care about myself. There was so much I could do for the family, for the Hall and ... well, I have to say it, for Art.'

Andrew shifted. That hand on his had been a mistake. Overdoing it. The story didn't ring true. If it was like she said, why didn't she get Franco to forge modern paintings for her and save everyone a lot of trouble?

'But you didn't go with him?'

'I told you, he was becoming so strange. I was frightened

of him. I thought he would become violent. He threatened me—literally threatened me. It was a terrible time. When you see someone you have loved becoming ... becoming so strange. I couldn't talk to him any more. He was a different person. My Franco had been so gentle, so sensitive. This wasn't the same person. I couldn't imagine spending the rest of my life with this man, the man he had become.'

'What happened in the end?'

'He went. I thought he needed help. I wanted him to go to a doctor. And he refused. He was furious. He shouted at me, swore and shouted. It was a terrible time.'

'And he went?'

'Yes. He said that was what he wanted. It was all he wanted, he said, to get back to his own country. I gave him the fare. He went back to Italy.'

'You gave him the fare? The picture wasn't sold?'

'No. I had found a man who said he thought he knew someone.... It all takes time, you know. He had to make some enquiries. It was a terrible time. We had already taken the Diana out of the Hall. It was at the cottage in the stable, in a crate. It wasn't difficult, getting it there. It was quite common for crates of paintings and things to arrive for me at the Hall. I had Franco bring the copy in a crate in a van on the afternoon of the annual cricket match. The house was empty. I said earlier he never came to the house, but it wasn't quite true. He came that day. It didn't take long to change the paintings. It's not a large picture. Getting it out of the frame was worst, but Franco knew how to do that sort of thing.' Her voice took on a dreamy, reminiscent tone. 'It was like the old times, with Franco in the house. It was a beautiful summer day. He stayed as long as we dared. ...'

'So when Franco left the painting was not sold?'

'No,' she said sadly.

'And you never saw him again?'

'No. Never. It was cruel of him. I never heard a word from him. Not even an address.' She was crying discreetly, with her face averted.

Andrew stretched out and grasped her hand. 'I'm so sorry,' he said. 'Don't cry.'

But that was not what he was thinking.

5

The breeze had cleared the blossom from the apple trees in Corinna's garden and it lay on the grass like pink snow. It was beautiful there at the cottage. In the spring it was always beautiful there, but this year it seemed specially so. When she rode through the woods the leaves were such a beautiful green, soft yet vivid. In the fields the wheat was growing strong. On sunny afternoons she heard the sinister cry of the cuckoo. They said the cuckoo throws his voice like a ventriloquist, and she never caught sight of the bird.

That year the English spring was as good as the poets describe it. The season was warm and the countryside smiled under the sun.

Corinna was not blind to this beauty. But it did not cheer her. In the sunshine she was still melancholy. The truth was, she no longer thought of Boys Hall as home. She had left New York, not with the sense of going home, but of getting away from a situation there. And now she was back in England it was the same—she didn't feel that she had come home, but that she had escaped from New York.

She did not like the city. It was not the simple fact that she was used to living in the country. She often stayed with friends in London and she never felt there that she had to get away from the crowds and the traffic and get back to the quiet of the cottage. But somehow in New York, the quality of those elements was different, more desperate, more extreme. The buildings crowded in on her. The traffic came at her, on the wrong side of the road. The whole atmosphere of the city was tense and pressing. But, if she thought about it, at other times such things would have been tolerable. The Foxleys' house was a refuge from the storms of New York. They lived a privileged, easy life, and Corinna could have joined it with them.

She had drifted into a casual relationship with Andrew.

A chance encounter, because he was there when she needed someone. A casual encounter for both of them. And then she found herself taking it seriously. And taking it seriously, she guessed, not because her feeling for Andrew was so instinctively one of love, but because she still needed someone, and she needed someone she had to take seriously. At that time she was adrift, unsure of herself, and a serious relationship would give her an anchor, a sense of purpose. It was the realization that she was trying to tailor a casual affair to suit her own needs that made her leave New York.

When she thought about it, it was a hopeless relationship. Andrew was no more sure of himself than she was. For all his ambition, he lacked direction. She did not even mind that he did not tell the truth. But she did need a man with authority. Perhaps it was a father figure she needed, after so many years of unknowns and substitutes, a man she was sure of, who could fill all the male roles in her life. And Andrew was not that man. He tried to give the impression of initiative, but in fact he was simply quicker than most at following leads. She needed a strong man. She could almost believe she would be content with some sort of brute. There was no point in refusing to face these tendencies in herself. That afternoon in the woods when Andrew was so angry, when he had forced her from her horse and almost raped her—she had to face the fact that she found that episode deeply exciting.

Now, at the cottage, she was still unsettled. She began to think she knew what she wanted, but she needed time to sort herself out, to be quite sure before she took irrevocable steps. The cottage was the best place for thinking. There were no social duties, no demands. To all appearances she took up her old life. She helped Giles on the home farm. She groomed her horses and took them for exercise. She joined the family at the Hall for meals. But she knew it would not be for long.

*

One hot afternoon, as she came back from a long gallop on the black mare, she saw a familiar car at the door of the cottage—a green MG. For the moment she could not remember whose it was.

Andrew was waiting for her. He lay stretched out on the sofa in her sitting-room, asleep.

The sound of the latch on the door woke him. He struggled up, rubbing his eyes.

'Andrew!' Corinna's voice reproved him. She stood at the doorway, as if frightened to come into the same room as him. 'Why did you come? I asked you not to come.'

He rose from the sofa and came towards her. 'Fidget,' he said.

She turned her head. 'Please don't call me that. I'm no longer a child.'

'I'm sorry. Corinna.' He stood in front of her. Her tense attitude warned him not to touch her. 'I had to come.'

'I asked you not to.'

'But I couldn't—I couldn't just accept that I shouldn't see you again. I had to see you. I came over on the night plane. I drove straight here. I haven't slept.'

Corinna sighed deeply. Her body relaxed. 'All right,' she said. 'I'd say you'd better come in, but you haven't even left me that. I've just been out, and I'm hot. I'm going to have a shower, then I'll make you some tea.'

Evidently Corinna had not given up cooking. She brought out seed cake and rich fruit cake for Andrew. But he was too tired to eat.

'I just wanted to see you,' he said.

Corinna stiffened. 'Andrew, please. Let's talk about something else.'

'What?'

'Now you're here you can tell me something. I was going to write to you.'

'You were?'

'Yes. I want to know where I can find my father.'

'What do you ... ?'

'Andrew, please don't pretend. My father. You know where he is. You've been to see him, haven't you?'

'I don't know what ...'

'Andrew.' Her voice was taking on a hurt tone. 'Please try to tell me the truth for once.'

'How do you know?'

'It's the only thing that makes sense. Andrew, please. I want to see him.'

'What do you mean, it's the only thing that makes sense? Makes sense of what?'

'Oh, it's obvious, surely. The Diana. Someone forged that so well that no one noticed for twenty-five years. There has to be a connection between that and the Rembrandt you took to New York.'

Andrew's mouth fell open. 'What are you talking about?'

'Andrew, please. I told you not to come here. But you came, and forced your way into my house. At least now don't waste my time by not telling me the truth.'

Andrew sipped slowly at his tea. It was cool inside the cottage, but his forehead was glistening with sweat. Eventually he said, 'But how did you know? I don't see how you knew.'

'Enid,' she said simply. 'She told me.'

'She looked at it? She opened the wrapping?'

'Of course. You know, you underestimate her, Andrew. You told me yourself she was dangerous, she wasn't the silly old dear she pretended to be, by a long chalk. And you expect her not to do a simple thing like that? Of course she looked at it.'

'Oh God!'

'But she didn't guess what it was. She saw it was a Rembrandt, that's all. She thought it might be stolen, but she didn't guess it was a forgery. Though that was before the Diana was thrown out by Christie's. She may have heard of that by now, and put two and two together. She's very well informed. And she's not stupid.'

Andrew buried his head in his hands. 'Oh God,' he said again. 'Oh God.'

'You don't have to worry. Neither Enid nor I are going to broadcast the news. Nothing has changed as far as you are concerned. We might use what we know to get things out of you, but we shouldn't harm you. I don't know what Enid might want. What I want to know is where I can find my father. That's all. I don't really care about the forgery. I don't really care if every great painting in the world is a forgery. People see what they are looking for when they look at pictures. All I want is to see my father.'

236

'All right,' Andrew said in a low voice. He did not raise his head. 'I'll tell you. Of course I'll tell you where he is.'

Crossing to Andrew Corinna laid her hand gently on his hair. 'Thank you,' she said simply.

Later in the afternoon they walked in the garden. Corinna took carrots to the horses. Andrew stood by the stall and watched her as she spoke quietly to them.

'I think you should stay here,' he said. 'I think you belong here. There's one thing I haven't told you. Did you know that it was here that your father painted the Diana?'

She looked at him. 'Do you mean at the house, or at the cottage?'

'I mean here. Where we are standing. He used these stables as his studio.'

She placed another piece of carrot on her palm and held it out. The black mare fumbled it off her hand with her lips. 'There wasn't a sign when I came here. No paints or anything.'

'I guess your mother took good care to get everything cleared away. She told me he used an old charcoal oven in the woods behind here. To harden the paint. Did you ever come across that?'

She looked up. 'Yes,' she said. 'It's still there.'

'Well, that tallies. Your father stayed here after the war. Your mother used to come over on her horse to see him. This was his house. Why don't you stay here? In a way it belongs to you.'

'Why did he leave here? Because she sent him away, I'll bet.'

'Something like that, I expect. She told me a story. But she did not quite tell the truth. It's funny, isn't it, how no one can ever quite bring themselves to tell the exact truth?'

'Poor Mother.' She looked round the stables, as if trying to imagine how they were in those days. Then she walked to the door and the sunshine outside. Andrew followed. 'Poor Mother,' she repeated sadly. 'She sacrificed so much to get the things she wanted. In the end it hasn't really been worth the trouble.'

'I'd say she's had a pretty good life.'

'Would you? I wouldn't. She's always been in trouble with money. She always spent too much. She had such grand ideas, and she couldn't ever pay for them. I bet she's spent far more than she ever got for the Rembrandt. I suppose she did sell it, did she?'

'Yes.'

'I wouldn't want to go through life with the debts she's accumulated hanging around my neck.'

'It worries some people more than others. You wouldn't ever borrow a lot of money. The sort that do are the sort that can enjoy it like that. They can savour the last glass of champagne while the bailiffs are halfway up the drive. You don't have to worry about them. A lot of us just wish we could get that much credit.'

'Mother isn't like that. She does worry. She worries like hell. She's sick with worry all the time. Why do you think she never eats? Her stomach is raw with ulcers. She's in pain the whole time.'

'She didn't have to do it.'

Corinna shook her head impatiently. 'No. Nobody has to do anything. Kleptomaniacs don't have to steal. Liars don't have to lie. Schoolboys don't have to play with themselves. It's known as free will. All you have to do is stop yourself.'

'O.K. I'm sorry.'

'You know,' Corinna went on, 'when she was a girl in France, Mother was fat. Not plump—*fat*. Her parents loathed her. They were such a beautiful, elegant couple. They didn't have any money, but they were beautiful. They got by on that. They went everywhere. In those days there was a terrific social life in Nice, you know, and Monte Carlo, summer and winter. All sorts of people had villas there. They liked to have her mother and father about. They were so charming. So decorative. That was all they had to pass on to their children. Beauty. "My face is my fortune, sir," she said. For the girls especially it would be the passport to a wealthy marriage and a comfortable life. But little Delphine was fat as a pig. They hated her for spoiling their plans. For ten years her father did not speak to her. Can you imagine? She told me. For ten years he didn't address a word to her. Even when they sat at the same table he would say to her brother, "Tell the fat girl to pass the sugar." Mother was so unhappy, she only thought of two things— eating and killing herself. As she was Catholic, the only thing she did was eat. She got fatter and fatter, and more and more miserable.'

They were walking now side by side in the orchard on the soft new grass. They turned at the fence and began to retrace their steps.

'On the morning of her sixteenth birthday she got out of bed, took off her nightdress and stood in front of the mirror. She looked into her own eyes. She suddenly realized that those eyes did not belong to the fat girl at all. Those eyes belonged to another person, trapped inside that mountain of blubber she had thought was herself. And the other person was pleading to be let out. From that moment, for the rest of her life, she hated food. She ate to keep alive, for no other reason, and not an ounce more than was necessary.'

'God. I'm sorry. Did she tell you that?'

'No,' she said, with a brusque change of tone. 'Of course not. I made it up. What does it matter? It might as well be true.'

She broke away and ran into the house.

Andrew found her lying across her bed, sobbing into the pillow. He sat on the side of the bed and put his hand on her shoulder.

'Can't we talk?' he said.

She turned on her side. 'I'm sorry,' she said. 'I'm sorry to be such a bitch. I shouldn't have done that. But what can we talk about? There's nothing to say.'

'We must talk.' His voice was plaintive. 'You can't expect me to just get in my car and drive off, without a word, and not see you again.'

Corinna turned on her back. She put her arm across her eyes. 'You might as well, Andrew,' she said quietly. 'We both know that's what you're going to do in the end. It might be better if you did it now.'

'But why do I have to go at all? I came to see you. I wanted to be with you. I hoped we could—we could understand one another.'

'Oh Andrew. I do understand you. That's the trouble. I've come to understand you so well in the last month. I've thought about you a lot since I came back.'

'And . . . ?' He took his hand from her shoulder and laid it on the coverlet between them.

'Andrew, you wanted to be with me because I had gone away. That's your trouble—I realize it now. You only want what you haven't got. As soon as you have anything, you're bored with it. You're always envious of other people but you're never satisfied enough to settle down with anything you've achieved yourself. I think perhaps you're frightened to put yourself to the test of actually doing anything. You wanted me to come on the ship with you. But as soon as I was there you were bored with me.'

'My God. You don't think much of me, do you?'

'That's not true. I like you a lot, Andrew. More than that, probably. I don't want to analyse it. There's nothing terrible in what I've been saying. Most people are like that, more or less. It's just that, in a lover, I think I need to look for the exception, the one person in the whole world who that isn't going to happen with. For me, that's not you. And for *you*, it isn't me.'

Andrew flung himself across the bed. He lay on his back, staring at the ceiling.

Corinna caressed his brow. 'Don't agonize, Andrew,' she said. 'It's true isn't it?'

She was praying that he would deny it. But he didn't.

＊

They agreed Andrew should stay the night in the guest room. Corinna made a ceremony of their last dinner together. The table was candlelit. She roasted a pheasant and served it handsomely, as if for a special occasion.

Andrew sat at the kitchen table with a bottle of wine at his elbow while she prepared the meal.

They talked of the Diana. After Christie's rejected it, Corinna told him, Timothy refused to accept their judgement. He threatened to sue them for professional negligence. He had the painting brought back to the Hall and hung in its old place on the stairs. He invited the director of the Rembrandthuis to come over from Holland and give his opinion. He didn't tell him about Christie's report.

The man arrived late one afternoon. After half an hour's preliminary inspection, he declared that—he was not prepared to give an opinion without having the painting taken from the wall for a close look the next day.

After dinner Giles insisted he be shown Christie's report. The director was visibly impressed. He went off to bed without a word. And next day, after half an hour with his magnifying glass, he pronounced the painting an undoubted forgery.

After he left Giles and Timothy had a bitter argument. If Giles had not shown the director Christie's report, Timothy said, he would have judged the painting genuine.

Timothy should never have tried to take the Diana from the Hall in the first place, Giles argued. He should have listened to the rest of the family and left the painting where it belonged.

'And what are you going to do now?' Giles had asked. 'Pull yourself together, man. What are you going to do?'

Timothy had broken down. He was weeping openly, 'I don't know. What can I do?'

'There is only one thing to do. We put the Diana back on the wall, and we say nothing. No one but the family and a couple of people at Christie's know that it's not the real thing. No one's noticed before. I don't see why they should notice now.'

'But who painted it?' Polly burst out. 'How long ago was it put there? Can't we find the real Diana? Who did it?'

Giles glared at her. 'The old Diana is not recoverable. This is the Diana. We've thought of it as that for—for long enough. We can go on thinking it.'

'But what are Tim and Sally going to do?' Andrew asked when he heard this. 'Can they take another painting in its place?'

'Oh no,' Corinna said. 'Giles wouldn't let them. Nor would the lawyer. They've still got the other pictures, of course, but they won't fetch an awful lot.'

'Not enough to finance a gallery.'

'No. They've found someone to put up the rest. A funny man. You probably know him. Mel German he's called.'

Andrew laughed out loud. 'Gerry! Oh yes. I know him very well.'

'And what about death duties? He'll have to pay duty on everything in the house. The rates will be staggering. Giles could save himself half a million pounds—more, if the

Revenue agreed the Diana was worthless.'

'No. No one must ever know. Giles has said, we must never tell anyone. You must never tell anyone, you must promise.'

'Your brother has a very expensive pride.'

'I don't think so, Andrew. It wouldn't make any difference. He could never find the duty anyway, even without the Rembrandt. What about the Raphael, and all the other paintings? The only thing he can do is try to come to some arrangement with the government.'

Andrew laughed shortly. 'So your mother will have to be an ancient monument after all.'

Corinna did not even smile. 'Father must have wanted it like this,' she said solemnly. 'We've all of us always assumed we must do everything we can to keep things in the family. Perhaps he didn't agree with that. Perhaps he *intended* it all to go to the nation. He had a lot of time to think when he was ill. He must have known that's what would happen. And,' she added quietly, 'perhaps he was right. We have been very selfish. Perhaps he was right.'

But what was going on in Andrew's mind was some reckoning of his own. If the Proudfoot Rembrandt was back on the wall at Boys Hall, and the fact of its forgery a closely kept secret, his own 'Rembrandt' once more became negotiable. When he got back to New York he would contact Lennox again. That was beginning to sound like something. The famous Proudfoot family had to put their Rembrandt back on the wall: and he, ordinary Andrew Tait, was able to sell his for a fortune. Hadn't Lennox played into his hands by showing him the stolen Vermeer?

But he had to deal with Enid. If she still thought his painting was genuine, he would be all right. But he had to deal carefully with her. He had had to 'borrow' the fare to England from her.

'You'll be back?' she said. 'You are coming back?'

'Perhaps. It depends.'

'Oh Andrew,' she said. 'Don't be so cruel. You must come back. I shall keep your painting as a security. There, you see the things you make us do. But you must come back. I shall expect you.'

She bought him a return ticket, and made him promise to

242

use it. But he found her attention somewhat cloying.

*

Corinna slept with her curtains drawn back. Outside the features of the garden were quite clear in the moonlight.

At two thirty in the morning she woke with a start. She fumbled for the light.

'Don't put on the light,' Andrew said. 'It's me.'

Corinna rubbed her eyes. As they grew accustomed to the dark room, dimly lit by the moonlight from outside, she could see Andrew was standing by her bed, naked.

'Andrew. What's the matter? What do you want?'

'I've come to say goodbye,' he said.

'Oh Andrew, you must be freezing.'

'Can I come in the bed? I just want to say goodbye.'

Corinna could see him clearly now. 'Oh Andrew. Why do you do things like this?' He was standing, pathetic and limp beside her bed. Her first instinct was to send him away. She hated to see men when they were down. That's why she doubted she'd ever make much of a wife. She understood people's troubles as well as anyone. She sympathized. But she did not want to be there. She did not want to know about Andrew's bad times. She had far rather he had forced his way into her bed and ... and ...

'All right,' she said.

She moved over to make room beside her. Andrew slid between the sheets and she held him to her. He was shivering with cold. She stroked the length of his back, like a mother her child.

His head was buried in her shoulder. He clung to her. He was shaking. Corinna wondered if he had a fever. Then he began to cry. 'Oh my love,' he sobbed into her shoulder. 'Oh my love.'

Corrina held him close. Her first reaction was to push him away, but she held him close. 'Andrew,' she said soothingly. 'Andrew,' waiting for him to gain control of himself.

Even as he sobbed, Andrew's body was pressing to her, working against her. His hands began to move over her. His mouth was at her neck, her ears. 'Oh my love, oh my love,' he was saying.

243

He pushed his leg between hers. She could feel him growing hard against her.

She rolled on her back and pulled him on top of her.

She could taste the salt of his tears on her lips. He raised himself. His mouth was on her breasts.

Corinna threw her head from one side to the other. There were tears in her eyes also. 'Oh God!' she cried. 'Oh God! Hurt me. *Hurt* me! HURT ME!'

6

Andrew flew back to New York with the sense of a new beginning, of being purged of the past. He left England from Heathrow airport, in a Jumbo Jet, with in-flight movies and French cuisine, which was very different from the *Mayflower*, setting sail from Plymouth with the expectation of hymn-singing and ship's biscuits. But he had the same feeling of emigrating, of taking leave of this country and transferring his allegiance to another soil. England, with its old class snobberies still alive and well and living in comfort in the country.... In New York they had that too, but it was less pervasive and there they had an alternative that could afford to ignore American aristocracy.

He took a cab from Kennedy to Enid's house. He had not told her he was coming. With luck he might catch her in bed with another art whore, and he could work some advantage from that. 'Another art whore!' God forbid he, Andrew, should ever get to be like that social butterfly.

Enid was at home.

'How nice,' she said warmly. 'You're just in time to change and have a drink before dinner.'

'Dinner? You know what time it is according to London, and my stomach? Eleven-thirty at night. I'm about ready to go to bed.'

Enid scarcely blinked. 'I expect you'll feel better when you've had a shower,' she said.

And for the next few days it was as if he had not been

away. In the bedroom Enid was volubly passionate. And discreetly demanding. Everywhere else, even when they were alone together, she was propriety itself. With her pink, powdered face, and her friendly manner, she gave the impression that the last thing she thought of was crude physical encounters. She did not expect sex on the living-room rug, or, from the rear, standing up at the kitchen sink—none of the usual variations. Outside the bedroom it did not exist.

Andrew knew it would not last. It couldn't. And if it could, he would not have allowed it. But he decided to play it along for a little. He did not want to make an enemy of Enid too soon. Or even at all. Corinna had said that he was frightened of putting himself to the test. He knew that wasn't true. He didn't have to rush in, just to prove himself, when it was wiser to wait a while.

For the time he went about with Enid—to the same openings, dinners, shows, parties, cocktails, weekends, theatres ...

Delphine was still in town. These days she spoke to him. She was even friendly. Bob Wetherby brought over Max Marske for his first New York show. Max was into sculpture now. He exhibited what looked like groups of ball bearings, different sizes, highly polished. Andrew guessed that was probably exactly what they were. Enid had insisted they go along to the opening. And Andrew knew enough to know that in the art world you hold your grudges behind a smile. At the gallery Delphine had come on so friendly that Enid left after half an hour—taking Andrew with her.

Andrew and Delphine had another lunch. She had heard that the Proudfoot Rembrandt was back on the wall.

'I'm so relieved,' she said. 'You can't imagine how relieved I am.'

'Corinna wants to go and see her father,' Andrew said.

'She can't do that.'

'Why not? Anyway, she's determined to.'

'She doesn't know where he is. Nobody knows where he is. I told you, I never heard from him.'

'*I* know,' said Andrew.

'You know where F ... where he is?'

'Yes. Do you want the address?'

'No,' she snapped. 'I don't ever want to see him again.'

245

'He was so cruel,' Andrew said sarcastically.

'How did you find out?'

'That has to be a trade secret, I'm afraid.'

'I see,' she said coldly. 'And you gave the address to Corinna?'

'Why not? I didn't see why she shouldn't see her father.'

'No reason for her not to see her father. But plenty of reason why I should not want her to. I should have thought you might have realized that.' She drew herself up in her seat and the old haughty expression came to her face. 'Andrew, I took you into my confidence about ... about certain things.'

'Delphine, you didn't take me into your confidence. You told me things that you knew I would find out sooner or later. That's not a confidence. That's an admission.'

'Oh really,' she snorted.

'And don't you try that old haughty snorty with me. I've gotten immune in the last year. Like birds get used to the scarecrow—after a while they sit on its shoulder and shit all down his coat.'

She began to rise from her seat. 'Are you calling me ... ?'

Andrew took her arm and pushed her back on the bench. 'Don't go,' he said. 'There's something I want to say to you.'

She looked at him. 'I hope it won't take long,' she said.

'No. It's just this. It's time you got to realize that the world was not made for your personal pleasure. *You* don't want Corinna to go to her father. What about her? Did it occur to you that it might be important for her? Did it occur to you in all those years Corinna might have needs as well? You never thought. You never looked at her. You only looked at art. You never saw any further than the end of your own Giacometti. Every now and then she passed by and she seemed pretty well together, so you put her out of your head. You weren't a mother for her. No mother and no father. That's not the best start. She made Lord de Boys her father, and she clung to that, though she knew it was only a pretence. It kept her sane. She loved him, because he was the only one in the whole damn family who let himself really love her. Since he died, she's been yawing about like a yacht in a gale. She doesn't know where she is. So she wants to go to her father. I reckon she needs to go to her father. I reckon it's urgent. And just because there's a chance it

246

might cause a little inconvenience to you, you get up on your high horse and look round as if the servants are getting above themselves again. Well, it won't work any more, Delphine. Not with me, it won't.'

'You cheap little ...' Her voice was icy with rage. 'You cheap, flashy little ... gigolo.'

'That's all right, Delphine. You call me what you like. I told you, I'm immune. I said what I wanted to say. I didn't expect you to like it. It happens to be the truth.'

'Well, let me tell you something about the truth,' she said, 'before I go. If you think I'm impressed by that outburst, you're wrong. I know perfectly well what you are doing, even if you don't. Do you think you've treated Corinna fairly yourself? Of course not. You've treated her badly. You feel badly about it. So you come here and try to transfer some of your guilt to me.' She stood up, 'I shan't accept it, Mr Tait.' she said. 'You will have to deal with your own conscience. I'm not going to salve it for you.'

*

For just a moment Andrew felt uneasy under Delphine's attack. Did he really feel guilty about Corinna? Hell no! It was she who sent *him* away. He'd flown all the way to England to see her, and he'd begged to stay with her. That's not walking out, in any language.

The uneasiness was fleeting. On the contrary, he felt good. He'd done something he'd wanted to do for a long time. He ordered himself brandy and a cigar and sat alone at the table for twenty minutes, enjoying the feeling of well-being.

Back at the house, Enid was waiting for him.

'You've been lunching with Delphine,' she said lightly. But there was an undercurrent of criticism.

'Yes. Does it matter?'

'You didn't tell me.'

'Do I have to tell you everything?'

'Of course not.' She sounded so reasonable it was maddening. 'But you know I'm always interested in what you're doing. I like to hear all about your plans.'

'You evidently know, without my having to tell you.'

'In this case, yes. Please don't sound so fractious, my dear.'

'Fractious! Fractious! You make me sound like a child.'

'Oh dear, I can see you are not in the mood to talk. I rather wanted to have a little talk.'

'What about?'

'No, really, Andrew. I'm not going to talk while you're in such a bad temper. It's no pleasure for either of us.'

'All right. I'm sorry. I don't like being cross-questioned, that's all.'

'That's better.' She pressed his thigh affectionately. 'I expect you ate too much. Why don't you have one of my pills?'

'No thanks. What was it you wanted to talk about?'

'Do you think you could pass my handbag? I suppose I should say "purse" since we are in New York.'

Andrew passed it over. 'Here you are. But what is it you want to talk about, Enid?'

'Well.' She opened the bag and was feeling inside for something. Her pill bottles clinked as she rummaged. 'It was your plans I wanted to talk about. I thought it was time we talked about your plans.'

'Oh.'

Enid held up two gold keys. 'These are the keys to the safe.' She held them out to him. 'Here. Don't you think it would be nice if you showed me your painting? I do so hate secrets. Apart from anything else, it means you don't trust the person you have secrets from.'

'But I told you. It's not my secret.'

'Oh Andrew. You know, my dear, it is rather insulting for a woman to be taken for an absolute fool. If I were a follower of Women's Lib—which you know I'm not—I should call you a male chauvinist.'

'A male chauvinist *pig*—why leave that out?' Andrew was frightened. He couldn't figure what Enid was driving at, but the whole set-up scared him.

'I don't like the word. It's really not a very nice thing to say. And I don't think of you as a—pig, Andrew.... Now, please, do go and fetch your painting. I want to look at it.'

'You've seen it already. I know. Corinna told me.'

'In that case, my dear, why on earth are you making such a fuss? Why didn't you say?'

The safe was in the bedroom upstairs. Enid instructed

him how to open it without setting off the alarms. He carried down the painting in its canvas bag.

Enid was holding up a pair of nail scissors. 'Here you are,' she said. 'Use these.'

Andrew swiftly slit the threads and pushed the bag down from the frame.

'Bring it over here. Close to me. I'll take the scissors. Closer. That's it. It's beautiful. Tell me about it. Tell me all about it.'

'It's Rembrandt. An unknown Rembrandt. I found it in Holland. It had been in a private collection, one family, for three hundred years. It's incredible. I got it out without anyone knowing. Now I'm going to sell it.'

'I don't think so, Andrew.' Her blue eyes were looking up at him as he held the painting in front of her.

'What do you mean?'

'I mean I don't think you ought to sell it.' She leaned back. 'You see, Andrew, I've been making enquiries. I had a Rembrandt expert come and look at it while you were in England. He was very impressed. I think I could say he was excited. It was not listed. But obviously it was a genuine Rembrandt. An unknown painting. That would have been very exciting.'

'It's fantastic.'

'But Corinna phoned me the day after you left her. And then everything fell into place.'

'She *phoned* you?'

'Yes, Andrew. It's quite easy now, with the satellites. You can dial direct. Out of office hours you can always get through ...'

'I didn't mean that,' he snapped. 'But, God, why should *Corinna* phone *you*?'

'It does sound rather Women's Lib now you mention it ... but seriously, she phoned to tell me—well, there's no other way of putting it: the painting is a forgery. She told me the whole story. Poor girl. I'm so sorry for her.'

'My God. Why did she have to do that? The lousy bitch. What a vicious bloody thing to do.'

'Andrew. Please. She was terribly upset about it. She didn't do it out of spite to you or anything like that. She did it from a sense of duty.'

'Pah.'

'No. You mustn't scoff, Andrew, if other people don't have the same commercial attitude as you. She did it because she cares about what is right. It may sound terribly old-fashioned to you. She's going to her father for the same reason. She wants him to give up all his—other work, and concentrate on restoration. She wants to learn to help him, to look after him so he can devote more time to this work ...'

'But she told me ...'

'Andrew, I'm telling you what she told *me*.'

Holding the painting in front of Enid, Andrew was forced to stand still. He wanted to move. He lifted the painting back to lean it against a chair.

'No,' said Enid, 'Don't move it, I want to look at it closely.'

'Look, Enid. O.K. It's a forgery. But it's perfect. Your expert thought it was genuine. It's a far better job than the Diana. He's learned a lot. He's got the technique absolutely perfect. Everyone will say it's genuine. The Proudfoot Diana's back on the wall. There won't be any talk of forgery. It will be a new Rembrandt. A great event. It's worth a fortune.'

'Andrew, you know I don't like dishonesty. I'm really shocked to hear you talk like this. I refuse to be involved in anything like this.'

'You don't have to be involved.'

'But I am involved already. The picture's been here, in my safe, in my house.'

'But you didn't know what it was. You didn't even see it.'

'But that's not the truth. I'm sorry, Andrew, my dear. Even if I could suppress my scruples, it's a risk I'm just not willing to run. Try to see it my way, Andrew. I'm very fond of you. Well, even in crude financial terms, I've put money into you. Almost literally.'

Andrew saw red. 'What are you up to?' he shouted. 'My God. You're not the only one. I've been putting all I've got into you. Literally. Which is more than Wetherby could find the stomach for. Happily married! Happily married my ass!'

Enid stood up swiftly and slapped her hand across his face. 'There,' she said, almost calmly. 'Now look what you made me do. You really should not provoke me like this, Andrew. It's all very unpleasant. '

'What are you doing? What are you at?'

Enid was standing in front of the painting. 'Oh dear. I'm so upset. My heart. I must take a Valium.'

'You can tell me first what this is all about. What do you want, Enid?'

'Andrew.' There were tears in her eyes. 'All I want is for you to stay with me. I told you. I think we could have fun together. You would make an excellent manager of a gallery. I have money.'

'But this picture could get me a fortune—as much as everything you have, more.'

'No, Andrew. I don't want you to.'

'Why not?'

'I don't like it. I want you to be with me.'

She drew back her arm. Something in her hand caught the light. Then very slowly she brought forward the scissors.

Horrified, Andrew watched.

With the pointed end Enid made a small hole in the canvas. She inserted one of the blades, and began to cut.

Andrew could not move. He stood, holding the painting while she mutilated it.

She cut out a jagged square at the centre. Then from the corners of this hole she cut deep lines into the remaining canvas. With the ends of the blades she deliberately scratched deep lines in the paint.

Then she sat on the sofa. 'There,' she said. She sighed heavily. 'Now, we shall never speak of that again.'